Generation Compound
Darkness Falls

D M Hersey

Copyright © 2013 Dianca Hersey

All rights reserved. Publisher: Dianca Hersey

Cover Design: Dianca Hersey

www.facebook.com/DMHersey

Dianca.Hersey@gmail.com

This book is entirely a work of fiction. The localities, names, characters and incidents portrayed are the work of the author's imagination or are used fictitiously. Any resemblance to actual persons, living or dead, events or localities is entirely coincidental.

First Edition: 2013

All rights reserved. No part of this publication may be reproduced, stored in or introduced into a retrieval system, or transmitted in any form or by any means (electronic, mechanical, by photocopying, recording or otherwise) without the prior written permission of the publisher.

The scanning, uploading, and distribution of this book via the Internet or by any other means without the permission of the author is illegal and punishable by law. Please purchase only authorized printed or electronic editions and do not participate in or encourage electronic piracy of copyrighted materials. We appreciate your support of the author's rights.

ISBN-13: 978-1493688173
ISBN-10: 1493688170

DEDICATION

To my husband Wesley,
For repeatedly pestering me to read every new chapter aloud at the end of the day, no matter how tired you are. You keep me on my toes and your enthusiasm for my work never fails to remind me why I do this. You are truly my biggest fan.

And to my oldest daughter Sammie,
For sneaking onto my computer behind my back to secretly read every chapter as I went. Yes, I knew all along. For never allowing my coffee cup to sit empty, and for aliens with tuna sandwiches.

ACKNOWLEDGMENTS

Thank you to my parents Donalda and Anthony, for the love and support, and for teaching me to follow my dreams no matter how difficult the journey. Thank you to my sister in law Melissa for being an amazing photographer and lending a hand when I needed it most. To my brother James for being an amazing photo editor. I love you. Special thanks to my fans for the daily messages of encouragement as I faced multiple life events and struggles while writing this book. This book is for all of you.

BOOK ONE

Shelly, I hope you love the story.

CHAPTER ONE
THURSDAY, MARCH 19, 2020
12:45PM

"This movie is probably the most boring thing I have ever watched...," Jacob Dunn whispered from three desks away. I smiled back and playfully stuck my tongue out at him while he looked on in mocked horror. Why someone would create an educational film on the benefits of math, and force us to watch it in class was beyond me. If we could just manage to make it through this period, we only had Biology to suffer through before heading back home to Compound.

The Compound, it was what my family called it for as long as I could remember. Sometimes I like to imagine that I am just a normal sixteen year old girl, with normal worries and problems. What to wear to prom? Does so-and-so like me? To walk through my day like the rest of these brain dead teenagers oblivious to the world outside of school, seems so comforting at times. I am far from a normal teenager, which I guess is alright. If it wasn't for the fact that my family is about as abnormal as they come, Jacob and I might actually gain some acceptance in this town. Outcasts. That is what we seem to be, though we have grown up here our whole lives. The Weird Ones. The Doomsday Kids. Although we somehow managed to gain some friendships, most of the kids our age just ignored us. If they were looking for an argument, they would come at us with all sorts of theories and accusations ranging from cults, to my father having multiple wives. Not that it bothered us as much as I would like it to. I had bigger worries on my mind today.

I ran my fingers through my long auburn curls and turned to watch out the window, which seemed more interesting and beneficial to my education then the math film being forced down my throat. At our morning meeting before school, the adults were gathered around both the television and the radio, seemingly concerned about something they didn't want to let on about. Yesterday was the same. I watched my mother sip her coffee with that same determination I had seen in her face a million times over in my life. Yet this time there was something else there, something that reminded me of fear though subtle enough for most to miss it in her eyes. For the first time in months, she wanted Jacob and me to run through our gear and emergency plans with her before we headed out for the day. Jacob of course, didn't seem to notice the tension at Compound this morning. His concerns were best centered on the head cheerleader's sister. Boys. I will never understand a single one of them. Ever.

The murmurs in class pulled my attention back to see Jacob doing a fist pump in excitement. I rolled my eyes at him before noticing the source of his pleasure. The horrible math film had ended its reign of terror. "What happened? Mrs. Jenkins? The film shut off!" the panic ridden voice came from the front of the classroom, the honor roll student looking around the room with worry in his eyes. I watched our heavyset math teacher waddle to the front of the class to fuss with the controls, murmuring to her students that she would fix it shortly and for all of us to stay calm. We had turned off the lights to better watch the film, now with the television down, the only light filling the room came from the windows.

I slumped deeper into my chair and turned back to the window. It wasn't like I was interested in the film anyway. I would much rather watch birds, or teenagers who ditched school try to sneak back onto campus at the end of the day without getting caught. It was then that I noticed another student in the parking lot storm out of his truck and kick his front tire in frustration before lifting the hood. Obviously, he was one of the lucky kids who didn't have a sixth period class to worry about. His car troubles seem to annoy him to no end as I watched him beat his truck like

Darkness Falls

an abusive pet owner to a sad puppy. I actually found it painful to watch. Such anger in that kid! I watched as he pulled out his cell phone, and frantically tried to get it to work. He walked around with his phone held high as if looking for signal, then try to dial again only to fail and throw his phone like a football across the parking lot. What was with this guy anyway?

It was as if a fog in my mind slowly started to lift in that moment. Everything began to become instantly clearer and a deep fear inside me boiled up. My mind began piecing it together like a puzzle I didn't want to build. The television going out. A car that won't start. Cell phone that doesn't work. This can't be what it looks like... can it? I turned slowly to look at Jacob as he fussed with his phone hidden in his lap. His eyes met mine and he pointed in the direction of the clock on the wall and then back at his phone. I glanced at the clock and then immediately noticed it wasn't changing and took a longer look. The second hand isn't moving? Am I seeing things? I watched for a couple of seconds to be sure, never seeing it move. Jacob moved his phone in his lap, sliding it down the outside of his thigh in my direction to give me the best view possible. His phone wasn't working. Our eyes met again, but this time I motioned toward the window at the angry teenager in the parking lot. He looked passed me, watched and then returned his gaze to me. I glanced around the room at my fellow classmates chatting to each other, unaware that their lives would be completely changed from this point on. My eyes moved from student to student, as I thought about what would happen to them now. The most beautiful sight I've ever seen was in that precious moment. Just then. Right there. In that glorious moment of normality. These were the last normal moments of the world as we knew it. The last laughs, the last smiles. I found this beautiful sight to be almost haunting. Oblivious for now as they were, no one would be the same.

I slowly began to pack up my backpack. I could leave my books in my locker right? I wouldn't need them any longer. I packed up my things as quietly as possible, noticing that Jacob was doing the very same thing. How do we get the hell out of class? What excuse could we possibly use that would explain why both of us were leaving... and with our bags? I made eye contact with Jacob again and he seemed to have a thought that hadn't crossed my mind. He stopped, staring back at his bag in confusion and then begin to empty it. No, not empty it. He was pulling out what he needed and leaving the rest behind, cramming what he could into the pockets of his pants and hoodie. He looked back at me and motioned for me to do the same. I understood what his plan was in that moment. We wouldn't be using our bags after all. We had bug out gear in both of our lockers and in the truck. These bags were no longer needed. I worked quickly, stuffing my pockets with only that which I knew I would need or desperately want to keep. We weren't coming back to school. Maybe ever. What we leave here, we would never see again. Not that it mattered anyway. We had just entered survival mode.

Our exchange went largely unnoticed by everyone in class. The soundless conversation and understanding between us may have only taken a minute. I instantly had a twinge of jealousy as I watched my classmates in deep conversations. All but one of them. Emily Perez. By the look on her face, she had been watching Jacob and me for some time now. Her large brown eyes showed more than just a little panic. She too, was slowly filling her pockets with things from her backpack. I slowly put my finger to my lips and looked around the room, hoping she would understand that not saying anything will keep the panic at bay. At this moment, it would seem just a normal power outage. She nodded and showed me she was done with her task, obviously ready for some excuse to leave class and talk to me about what was going on. I looked at Jacob and nodded.

"Mrs. Jenkins? If you are having problems with the television, I could go down to the art room and grab the spare. It is a newer one anyway. That one may have finally died." he spoke up, motioning to the dead television at the front of the classroom.

"Oh thank you Jacob, how thoughtful. Take someone with you though in case you need help with it." She thanked as she turned to her broken television.

"Can I take two? I mean, it is a larger unit and I may need someone to hold the door open for us?" He asked without hesitation. He must have noticed the brief exchange between me and Emily.

"Sure, sure. Take two. Just hurry back. I want this film over before the end of class today. We are testing on it tomorrow." She waved in his direction as she distracted herself with the task of unhooking the television from the wall.

Darkness Falls

Jacob motioned for the two of us to follow him, and within seconds we were in the dark hallway and headed for our lockers. A couple of teachers were standing in the hall way speaking about a power outage and debating when the power would come back on. Power outages were a normal occurrence in this town, and it wasn't like they would stop classes for it. It would take them about an hour to notice this was more than a normal outage. That is, if no one tries to use their phone, drive or check the time. I hadn't thought of that before. We would have to get off campus as soon as possible. I was suddenly thankful that Emily was paying attention to the soundless conversation I'd had with Jacob in class.

"Fallon, what the hell is going on? It isn't like you to act this way when the power goes out." Emily whispered from the side of her mouth at me as we passed an open classroom door. Her brown eyes flashed at me as the concern washed across her face. "This isn't what it is, right? I mean... I was watching you look out the window and then saw you look at Jacob...," She trailed off deep in thought. "Something isn't right with this is it?"

"Emily, you still have that seventy-two hour bag I had you make up?" I whispered back at her.

She stopped suddenly, eyes wide in horror as she looked right through my soul. "Yes... it is hiding in my trunk. I have that smaller emergency kit in my locker too." She turned and looked down the hallway in the direction we had come as a single tear rolled down her round cheek. "Is this it then?"

"Emily, listen. Now is not the time to lose it. Get to your locker and grab your kit. Head to the southern door, no one will see you leave through that one. Then meet us at the truck. Do you understand?" Jacob now had his hands on her shoulders, forcing her to look at him. "Say nothing to anyone. Just keep going. Don't run and don't stall. We need to be out of here right now without panic. Got it?"

She nodded and took off down the hall with quickness in her steps, her blond hair bouncing off her shoulders as she moved as quickly as she could without bringing attention to herself. When she rounded the corner and left my line of sight, I wondered if she had what it took to get through this. Although she wasn't a child of Compound, she was still my best friend and Compound neighbor. When her parents died two years ago in a car accident, she moved in with her grandfather on her family's land. Her grandfather lived only a half of a mile from Compound's north gate, and my family had taken to bringing them meals and tending their farm temporarily, after hearing the sad news. My mother had kept a lasting friendship with Papa Perez since then, and occasionally offered him help in raising Emily by being a strong female role model and being there when he didn't understand the teenage girl. He truly had no idea how to handle anything of a female nature, though he tried. He had raised five sons all on his own after his wife had passed away from cancer; girls it would seem were alien to him.

Jacob and I managed to clear the school building without encountering trouble, swinging by our lockers for the emergency kits we kept in them, and swung by the bathroom to fill up our water bottles before leaving. We kept our locker kits in small day packs that were easy to carry and wouldn't bring unneeded attention to us. I turned to take a last look at the South Desert Rose High School sign as we crossed the far edge of the parking lot, and headed for the truck we had taken to parking in the hardest area to see from the school. This area of the parking lot was usually unmonitored as it consisted of the oldest parking area that had been left is disrepair. The pavement held many years' worth of cracks and humps from tree roots left to their own devices. It was probably the original parking lot from when the school was first built, way back in who-cared what time. I sure didn't. We always parked way out here on the southern side. In our minds we had always known that if something happened, we could escape this place without notice so long as we could clear the school building. I guess now… that horrible idea and foresight was coming in handy. I hadn't truly thought we would ever really have a need for that plan. Until now.

We slipped through the partially wooded area that helped hide the forgotten parking area and made our way to the truck. My father's truck. The truck he allowed us to drive to school because it was stout, sound, and powerful. It was so large you had to give yourself a small hop just to jump up into it, and though you couldn't be sure of the original color – it now resembled the color of rust. He'd always said that if we were ever in a car accident, the truck wouldn't even scratch. We would survive. Survive… that word had new meaning now.

"The truck won't start. I knew it wouldn't." Jacob said as he hit the steering wheel with his fist and dropped his head into his hands. He ruffled his short dark hair, grabbing fistfuls in frustration. "That is all the evidence I need. It must have been an EMP. We need to start walking."

"Emily isn't here yet. Bet her grandfather's car won't start either." I stated matter-of-factly as I tried to see through the trees, looking for Emily. "No telling how strong it was or what got fried out. The truck should have started."

"Fallon... we can't bring her with us. She can take my bike and ride home. She can do at least ten miles right?" He asked as he jumped from the cab and pulled his mountain bike from the bed of the pick-up, resting it on the side of the bed. "She can alert our folks that we made it out alright and that we are sticking with the emergency plan."

The plan. The big plan. It was something my father had come up with in the event of emergency. There were particular times during the day that my mother went to town to either drop the other children at school or to pick them up. If something happened during one of those times, we were instructed to head straight for Compound. However, this was not one of those times. This was the time of day she would still be in the garden and not even considering heading to town for another hour or so. In this event, the adults at Compound had placed Jacob and me on the emergency cards for the other schools. Our job was to round the children and bring them home with us. If it was in fact an EMP that struck. Which, surely this was. My parents wouldn't be able to leave the compound if they couldn't get the cars running either. We were closer to the children than anyone else right now. We were their best bet home.

"I'm here!" Emily yelled as she burst through the trees, running for us with her kit in her hands. "I filled my water bottle too, just like you always said to. Does the truck work?" She asked before watching Jacob shake his head. "Then I guess there is no reason to check the car?"

"No. Check your car please. We don't know what this EMP did. It will be hit or miss as to what works. Check anyway... always check everything." Jacob said as he pulled his seventy-two hour bag from behind the seat and placed his locker kit inside. "Looks a lot like a Carrington type event, either solar flare are weapons attack. I suspect solar though... Compound has been a little on edge about a possible glancing blow."

I located my seventy-two hour bag and placed my locker kit inside as well, double checking everything was in order before strapping it to my back. "If your car won't start, Jacob said you can take his bike. Go straight home and check on your grandfather. Then take him to the property tonight for super. We should be able to dig up some information on what is going on by then. If he isn't there then my folks already got him."

Emily nodded and tried to start her car only to be met with silence over and over again after each click. With a huff, she tossed the key into the passenger seat and pulled the trunk release handle. "Thanks. Do you want me to tell your folks you made it out of the school?"

"There is a large blue flag hiding in the brush by the northern gate. Just stand it upright. They will see it and know everything is alright. If you find they have already taken your grandfather to the property, then don't worry about the flag at all. Just get to the northern gate and make a fuss…," Jacob informed as he grabbed her bag from the trunk for her. "Someone will come down and get you. They'll be expecting you if your grandfather is there anyway."

We said goodbye to Emily and watched her bike toward the road that would lead her out of town and into the desert, heading for her home. We were headed in the opposite direction, off to the other schools to round everyone up. We managed to take what we could from the truck. It was useless to us now anyway. We walked in silence for about half a mile before Jacob asked if we could make a pit stop at the corner store. He knew the register would be down, but the cash in his pocket would work for what he wanted. I waited outside while scanning the street and thinking about Emily and what would be going through her mind. I was pretty sure I had helped prepare her for just about every emergency possible, but there was no way of knowing if any of the information I had ever given her would be helpful. I hoped so. I hoped she could keep her head about her and not panic. Did she remember what I said about how to use the water purification tablets in case she needed them? They would take too long to work in this event. She would have to ration her water in her pack until she made it there. Any water she found along the way would be pointless.

I thought about how she had managed to hit the road before

anyone figured out the situation we were in. She could easily clear town while everyone thought this was a standard power outage. At least... those people indoors. The people in the stalled out cars up and down the roads would be standing around in confusion. The road to our property wasn't well-traveled; there wouldn't be any obstacles to contend with. My parents had made sure of that many years ago. Only two homes sat on that road. Any property after them was nothing more than empty desert land as far as you could see. I found myself relieved that we were so far from the town of Baker, Nevada, and far from the main highways and roads around it. The last thing we needed now was for people to travel our road looking for supplies. Most people would stick to the main roads and highways, not wanting to risk a walk through a dusty desert road that could lead them to nowhere. A dangerous walk with little water. For the first time in years, I was thankful I wasn't a normal teenager after all. Everything my family had taught me over the years would come in handy now. All the training, the classes, the survival skills... this was my new life now not just training exercises. Emily's new life too.

Jacob came bounding out of the corner store with a huge grin on his face, before passing me a chocolate bar, a spare water bottle, and a bottle of diet cola. I winced at him and his unnecessary spending on pointless junk when we were in survival mode. He could have spent his money on things we could actually use right now, though I couldn't wrap my head around something our packs may have been lacking.

"Who knows what is going to happen right? If this thing is as bad as I think it is, you won't have chocolate or cola again for who knows how long. Just enjoy the damned things... and freakin' smile for me? You are totally freaking me out right now." He smiled before taking a huge bite of his chocolate bar and closing his eyes in pleasure. "Damn I'll miss this."

"What the hell is wrong with you Jacob? Are you making light of this? All of this?" I motioned around us as I scolded. "Sometimes you are so leveled headed and other times you are flat out the stupidest guy I have ever had the displeasure to know."

"A displeasure to know huh?" He snickered. "Fallon, just enjoy it alright? You'll need the sugar rush for this journey." He said quietly, his dark eyes looking defeated. He wasn't coping well with what was happening. This seemed to be his way of trying to handle the stress we both knew we would be under for weeks to come. For a fraction of a second, I held pity for him.

"Whatever." I stated as I adjusted my pack and began walking again. We had a long way to walk. Just up the road about a mile away, Jacob would be splitting off and heading to the Junior High School to pick up his brothers. I would keep going for another two miles to the Elementary School to grab my little sister Jade. I wondered if Jacob and the boys would wait for me at the end of the road or just head out of town without us. I secretly hoped they would wait, but I didn't want to have them caught in the hot afternoon sun in the desert if they didn't hit the road as soon as possible. Nevada was no place to be walking when the hot hours hit. I was already looking at a long journey with Jade. How I was going to get an eight year old to hoof it better then fifteen miles was beyond me.

As we neared Jacob's detour, I noticed two young men running down the street toward us. They looked as though they were escaping prison or ditching school, whatever the reason for the speed, they were at a full run straight at us. As they neared, I noticed that one of them was waving at us. Jacob laughed and returned the wave, excited to see his little brothers had made the break to save him the trouble.

"Matt! Travis! What the hell did you guys do huh? Just grab your bags and run?" Jacob yelled as he ran to meet them.

I managed to make it to them shortly after the knuckling bumping, which I was thankful for. Travis began explaining how he was in the bathroom when the lights went out and met up with Matt in the hallway. "...We were just standing there talking when this car couldn't stop and smashed into another car right out front! We saw the whole thing from the window. Everyone ran outside to find out if the driver was alright. When a few people started talking about their cell phone not working to call the police... I kind of put two and two together and we grabbed our shit and left." He breathed as he adjusted his thin glasses.

"Watch your damn mouth Travis." Jacob played. "I'm glad you saved me the trouble of having to sign you out. I always dreaded that part of the plan."

Travis Dunn wasn't a large fourteen year old, but he stood stoutly and proud the same way Jacob always did. His slightly heavy-set frame and dark blond hair was a shocking contrast compared to both Jacob and Matt. If it wasn't for similar mannerisms, stance, and walking style, a person wouldn't believe the brothers were ever truly related.

"Is this an EMP?" Matt asked as he took a draw from his water bottle. "I mean... this is what this is right? Nothing is working. People were so distracted they didn't even notice our jail break." He grinned, as he apparently relived the moment in his mind.

"Looks that way." I said more to myself than to them. I was in a hurry to get back to walking. I needed to get my sister as soon as possible. "You guys head back home. I have to get Jade. I'll meet you there."

"No way in hell! The beginnings of panic will start showing in the street at least. Not sure how many are figuring it out just yet. I figure by the time you ladies make it back this way, it will be worse. We are going with you." Matt said as he slapped Travis in the arm. "Jacob is coming too. Trust me. People are starting to head to their cars in boredom with the power out. As soon as they start finding the cars won't turn over, this whole place is going to be chaos. Not to mention the number of car accidents we have seen. No power and no car means no medical attention. Desperate and confused people are going to be on the loose."

There wasn't a point in arguing with the Dunn brothers. I'd grown up with them my entire life. They were stubborn and bull headed. Life on Compound made everyone family, even though none of us were related. My parents started Compound before I was born, recruiting their closest and most trusted friends. The Dunn parents had grown up with my parents and became the first family to agree to move to the property. They were raised on a similar compound nicknamed Haven, when they were children. Their grandparents were friends with my grandmother Ginny, founder of the Haven compound. Generations of preppers as they joked. My father often called us Generation Compound, a nickname for survivalist children, born and bred.

Four other families also called Compound home. The Simon Family, that simply consisted of Brian and Sarah Simon with no children. They had never managed to get around to it when they were younger. Now the years for that were over, leaving them with nothing more than several hound dogs they called their children. The Jackson Family, consisting mainly of Angela Jackson and her three year old twin daughters Cassidy and Cassandra. Her husband left her shortly before she had the girls and she moved to the property while pregnant and alone. It was my understanding that she was a friend of my mother's from high school and that she had kept in contact with my mother over the years. They had a couple of barn cats on the property that loved to taunt Mrs. Simon's dog children on a regular basis. Then there was David Ratcliff, he was a family all on his own. No children and no pets to speak of. Just an old hog he brought with him when he moved to the property, that he jokingly named Bacon. The Sanders Family consisted of a very pregnant Megan Sanders and her two young children Bobby and Becky. She was recently widowed as a result of her husband's military career. In fact, she had laid him to rest just a few months ago. I had helped her with watching Bobby and Becky while she made his arrangements.

I snapped out of my thoughts in time to see the Dunn brothers stop at the street corner and sit under a shade tree, here they would wait for me to return with Jade. Best not to invade the school as a group of Compound Kids. It could cause someone to take more notice than necessary. I nodded as I kept right on passed them and right through the parking lot to the double doors. I had never practiced this plan to this extent. No dry runs, just conversations on how this could play out and how it could go wrong. The only way this would work perfectly is if I could make it here before people began to worry about what was really going on.

The elderly receptionist behind the office desk was trying to sort papers when I entered the room. "Fallon Henley? My goodness child you have grown." She came around for a better look at me, instantly making me feel uncomfortable. "Some power outage huh? What can I do for you today?"

"I'm here to sign out Jade. I'm on her emergency card as an emergency pick up contact. Here is a note from my mom saying it is alright too." I said as I handed her the note my mother had written many months ago and forced me to keep in my seventy-two hour bag should I ever need it. The note would likely explain that my grandmother Mary on my father's side had passed away and that my mother was busy and sent me to get Jade. It might also say we would be going out of town for the funeral. I wasn't really sure exactly what was in the note, only the general idea of what my

Darkness Falls

mother had explained. The term "Grandma Mary" was our emergency term for SHTF or Shit Hit the Fan as it is better known. "Mom said she tried to call but couldn't get through." I lied, knowing their phones were down.

"So sorry to hear about your grandmother sweetheart. I never had the pleasure of meeting her. Please let your parents know I am keeping them in my thoughts." She turned to the desk and scribbled on a piece of paper before handing it to me. "I would call her room on the com unit but it is down, you see...," She said as she pointed to the intercom system on the desk. "Take this note to her teacher and I'll handle signing her out on the book today. I'll go ahead and write her in for not being here tomorrow either. Just tell your mother to get a hold of me as soon as she knows when Jade will be coming back."

"Sure thing." I said as I left the office and headed down the hallway toward Jade's classroom. Yeah right, depending on how bad this is... Jade won't be coming back. *You'll figure it out soon enough*, I thought to myself. It didn't surprise me at all that she had never gotten the chance to meet my grandmother Mary... I didn't even have one. My grandmother lived in Utah and we rarely ever spoke with her. She cut ties with my father when he was a young man, angry over the fact he was leaving Haven to start Compound on his own and taking her daughter with him. Her name was Ginny anyway, not Mary.

I stepped into the open classroom door in time to see the children playing board games and reading books with the light from the windows. The sound of giggles and chatter filled the room as the teacher went table to table trying to calm them down. She looked up at me and came jogging over, handing a book to a little boy as she went. "Are you taking Jade from us for the rest of the day?" She asked, as I handed her the note from the office. Her eyes scanned the note and she sagged slightly before looking up at me. "I am so sorry to hear about your loss. I'll gather all of her things from her cubby for you, including her homework. But don't feel pressured to do the homework right away. I understand completely. It is just to be handy in case she feels she wants to complete it." She smiled sadly and turned to the wall of cubby cubes to find Jade's things.

Jade saw me from across the room and ran over to me. Her brown hair in bouncing pigtails with small pink ribbons dancing with every bound. She was the picture of beauty in her silky pink dress, ribbons and missing front teeth. She slowed to a near stop as she noticed I was wearing my seventy-two hour bag and not my normal backpack. Almost in fear of what to say or think she crept closer with more caution, her eyes questioningly staring me down. I could see the events replaying in her mind and her expression changed several times while her mind mulled over every moment that had taken place in the last hour.

"Jade." I said as I bent down to her level, taking care that my voice wouldn't carry farther than I wanted it to. "I don't want you to get upset alright? But Grandma Mary has passed away. Mom sent me to get you. We have to go home now. You understand?" I asked as I noticed the teacher listening in on our conversation.

Jade's face lit with instant shock followed by fear and then understanding. I was thankful in that moment that we had prepared her for this situation many times in the hopes she could control herself should the real thing happen. "I'll... I need to get my stuff. Right? All my stuff then." She said as she turned to look at her classmates.

"I've gathered it all for you Jade. I'm sorry about your grandmother. We won't be doing anything interesting the rest of today anyway. You go be with your family."

Jade took her backpack from her teacher and grabbed my outstretched hand with a firm grip. I thanked the teacher and quickly got out of the school building with my sister trotting at my side. As soon as we were out of sight from the school yard I stopped and hugged her as tightly as I could. I knew she would think this was some sort of elaborate drill until I had the chance to explain further. Before I could say a single word she began to cry, heaving wet sobs against my lightweight sweatshirt. She had noticed the Dunn brothers sitting in the shade. Everything was becoming clear for her now, for that I was sure. In that moment, I began to cry a little too. Life from this moment on was going to be very, very different for all of us.

Matt pulled himself from the grass and gently rubbed Jade's back as she wept in my arms.

CHAPTER TWO

Jade whimpered as we strolled slowly back to the main road we needed as a means home. We would have to cut back through the way we had come in order to get to our road. From Jade's school to Compound was roughly fifteen miles, and the day had already begun to heat up. Living in the desert brought you freezing temperatures and scorching heat, all in the same day. I pulled my sweatshirt off and stuffed it in the loop at the top of my bag before strapping my bag back on. Jacob had helped briefly sort Jade's bag, tossing things she didn't want or would no longer need. If we had any hope of getting home before nightfall, we had to keep everything on our backs to a minimum. Less weight always meant easier travel. My father taught me that tip after telling me to pack my own bag and had me walk a mile with it. I learned quickly that weight made all the difference when it came to being on foot.

I wasn't exactly sure how long it would take us to make it back to Compound. After calculating the numbers, situations, and taking into account the distance an eight year old girl could travel without complaining, I ended up giggling to myself about the math film I had ignored. Yet, I still managed to draw the conclusion that it could very well take us until tomorrow to reach Compound's north gate. Frowning at my math and kicking a pebble, I quietly crunched more numbers and determined that we would need more water. Now!

"Jacob. Do we still have that case of water under the shrubs? You know, about halfway home?" I asked as quietly as I could, being sure my voice wouldn't carry.

"Last I checked. Although, I have been crunching the numbers on this one. We can't put all of our trust in the fact the water is there; it could be missing or destroyed since then. We need to get more before heading out. If the water is gone, we won't make it home." He informed in almost a whisper.

"How much water do we have on us right this minute? Total." I asked as I glanced behind me at Jade.

Jacob thought for a moment before speaking, "I am packing a gallon total if you count the bottles I divided the weight into. Matt and Travis told me at the tree that they have little over a gallon each. You are packing at least a gallon with you, and none of that counts the water we bought for Jade earlier. She doesn't have her own emergency bag. It is divided up into your bag and mine."

I frowned, "That won't be nearly enough. We need to grab more water just in case. Do we still have the gear at the shrubs?"

"Yes. Sleeping bags, medical gear, and even food. Your dad wanted there to be a full on camp at the halfway point. Just in case we ever needed it. If we can make it there, it puts us just seven miles from Compound."

We walked in silence back to the corner store we had begun our journey at earlier in the afternoon. All three Dunn brothers collected the emergency money from their bags and disappeared into the store, leaving Jade and I sitting on the curb with the bags. Jade leaned against me, now with dry eyes. Her little body sagging into me more exhausted emotionally than anything.

In the distance I could hear crying, glass breaking, and even an argument. Why is this place in chaos already? Shouldn't it take a few days? People were beginning to put the pieces together. Jade and I watched in silence as a woman wondered down the center of the street, obviously injured. Her clothing was torn in several places, dried blood crusting into massive brown stains down her left side. I wasn't sure the blood on her clothing had even belonged to her. The only real injury I could see was the drying gash on her forehead. I called out to her, asking if she was alright. She stopped and looked at us in deep confusion before slumping down on the street in shock. Whatever it was she had been through, she had walked long enough. I watched her begin a soundless sob. Full body heaves ripped through her and she crumpled into a quivering mass in the middle of the street. I turned just in time to see Travis

Darkness Falls

bolt through the door of the corner store and out into the street, Matt close behind him.

"Ma'am? Do you need help? Are you seriously hurt?" Jacob called as he bolted out of the store, collecting his brothers' bags before running to her aid.

We reached her just as Matt tried to pass her a bottle of water which she refused. Though they had managed to get her into a seated position, her body shook uncontrollably as tears ran from her eyes. "I couldn't stop...," She heaved, staring at the pavement. "The airbags. They didn't go off."

"Are you badly hurt?" Travis asked as he did a once over of her gash. "Where is all this blood from?"

The woman stopped shaking and just lifted her gaze to the direction in which she had come. "I couldn't stop." She repeated. "I couldn't stop."

Travis stood and pulled me aside. He seemed to have some real concerns he didn't want the others to hear. "Fallon. The only injury she has is her head. That blood isn't hers. I caught a glimpse through the rips in her blouse. Her left side isn't injured. That amount of blood...," He looked back at her before continuing, "She had someone in the car with her. My guess is they bled out. She must have held them until they died. She is in shock."

My heart suddenly dropped right out of my chest. This woman's nightmare began with watching someone die. Not simply a power outage. "We have to get her head bandaged or it will get infected. Is there some place we can take her to work on her? We can't leave her in the streets."

Travis shook his head. "Not really. Maybe we can get the store attendant to allow us to bring her inside and patch her up. But we can't take her with us when we leave. She will have to stay here."

The store attendant seemed more than willing to take her in for care, even helping to pull her from the street. Jacob cleaned her wound as she continued to repeat how she couldn't stop, obviously still in shock. From the bits and pieces we could gather from her babbling, she was driving into town from the South when her car died. There was an accident. She wasn't alone. By the way she burst into tears every time she looked at Jade, I could only assume her passenger was a child. The idea of it turned my stomach into knots, threatening to bring what was left of my lunch right out of me. The sheer amount of blood that covered her informed me without words, the child did not survive the crash. I secretly hoped in that moment that if it was indeed a child, it was a quick death with little suffering.

Jade sat in the corner on a small table, kicking her feet and staring at the floor. Whenever I had pictured trying to make this journey back to Compound, I never envisioned the hell we might find as well. Why did I assume this would be easy? Why didn't it cross my mind she would see? Always so innocent, Jade would now be forced to grow up much sooner than she should. This new world would be hard for her to swallow. We had already passed several accidents this afternoon, yet all yielded minor injuries. This would forever embed itself as a horrific memory in her mind. Her first fatal car accident images, paired with the changing of everything she had ever known.

"Hey little lady? How about you pick any candy in the place you want? Huh? Anything." The aging store attendant smiled at her.

Jade smiled and jumped to the floor with a giggle. She knew right where to find her favorite candy. Our mother would bring her here sometimes to allow her to buy candy with her allowance money.

He turned to me with a smile, "If this is what I am thinking it is, I won't need any of it anyway. I see your mom in here all the time. We are good friends. I know how far you all have to walk in order to get home. Take whatever you need. I'm closed."

"I thank you, very much." I whispered as I watched Jade fill the tiny pockets of her dress with packages of gummy bears. "It means so much to us."

"As soon as we are done here, I'll drop this woman at the hospital before heading home. People will loot my store in no time... it isn't safe here." He turned to Travis as he continued. "Boy, you are a good young man. I can trust you to take only what you need? I would rather it go to good kids like you folk, rather than someone trashing the place."

"You have our word." Travis said with a nod.

"Good then. I guess I should take what I need as well. I have a ways to walk. Like you. Opposite direction though. You'll be alright I trust?" The man turned to watch Jade. "Traveling with

Darkness Falls

someone so young... it won't be easy."

"We have to try. It is the only choice we have. If we can clear town before things get out of hand... we will have an easier go of it." I replied.

"There is an old pull wagon in the back. It belonged to my grandchildren once. I use it to move around the beer and water in the walk in refrigerator. Take it. You can pull your bags or even the child if the going is rough." he said as he pointed to the employee door behind the counter. "I have plenty stored up at home. I've been preparing for something like this for years. You can have your money back too. You might need it later, who knows. You'll be alright once you clear town. I know where you live and how far you have to go. Be safe and be smart. It is likely your mama told you long before now the things you might see out there. Level heads make for safe trips. Bless you all."

The store attendant turned back to the sobbing woman and spoke softly with her and Jacob, informing her that he will take her to the hospital on his way home. Travis ran to get the wagon and prepare us for our departure, which I could only assume would be within minutes. We couldn't stay here much longer. Getting to the half way camp would make all the difference. Early evening would creep up on us quickly, forcing us to make camp in the dark. I couldn't have that, not in the dark.

Ten minutes later, we waved goodbye to the attendant as we started back down the road with Jade in her red wagon. We could already smell smoke in the air. Something was burning on the edge of town, in a completely different direction than we were heading. We had roughly another couple of miles to go before we would clear the town completely, freeing us from the hell that would befall in the next few hours. This town had become progressively worse at a quicker rate than any of us had predicted. Things could very well take a deadly turn on us, if we didn't pick up the pace. Jacob tapped my shoulder and quietly pointed down a side street with a weak smile played out across his face. I knew what he was suggesting and I wanted no part of it, as I shook my head and continued my stride. Matt and Travis exchanged the same soundless conversation with Jacob, unlike me however, they seemed to agree with him.

"You can't Jacob! It is considered looting! We weren't raised to be looting bandits." I threatened.

"It isn't looting. It is survival. We don't have any weapons on us except for some knives and pepper spray. Things are getting much worse around here. I don't know why things are going south so fast, but I don't like it! If we don't do this now while we have a chance...," He insisted, "We need guns. Now, before we are caught in the dark and in the thick of it all!"

Travis and Jacob darted off down the side road at a hurried pace while Matt insisted on quickening our speed on the road. I didn't like leaving the boys behind to do a gun run on the Army Surplus and Firearm store, but they had been right. No one had looted the place just yet and it was our only chance to gain a few firearms for the walk home. Jade was our responsibility and her safety became our main priority. Knowing Jacob as well as I did, I knew he wouldn't risk bringing unwanted attention by breaking any windows. He would break down the backdoor of the place. Good thing it was closed today as well. I wouldn't want them to run into anyone inside. Breaking into the front of the building would be the worst idea possible. A smash and dash would become an uncontrollable situation once other people caught on to what we were up to.

We had been trained with firearms from a rather young age, yet school rules wouldn't allow us to keep them in our vehicles. My father always insisted that we knew all there was to know about safe handling, respecting, and firing many kinds of firearms. As well as carrying them on our person around Compound on a regular basis. Out in town was a whole other story entirely. A firearm was the one item our bags had always been lacking, for obvious reasons. Truth be told, I felt almost naked without one on my hip or in my bag. I knew the brothers were right, but looting guns from a store just seemed incredibly wrong to me on so many levels. However, after witnessing some of the chaos I saw the need for such a move.

Jacob and Travis caught up to us a half an hour later, sporting a couple of rifles and some handguns stashed in their bags. We didn't have much farther to walk before reaching the cutoff that would take us off the main road and far from town. To other small bands of people heading for the center of town, we must have looked like a motley crew. A small group of armed teenagers with survival packs and a candy chewing child in a wagon trailing behind them must have looked horrifying. One man we ran across, informed us that there were car accidents all up and down the highway. There were bodies, and badly injured people flooding into the street looking for help. We pointed him in the direction of the hospital and told him we would be careful. We weren't headed for the highway, but we didn't want him to know that. We would have to be cautious of the eyes that may watch our journey, so as we weren't followed home.

The obstacles slowed our progression much more than I would have liked. We managed to clear the cutoff without being noticed by taking a shortcut, shaving a little time off of our trip as well as hiding us from prying eyes. Just before dark, we hit our stash location. This marked the halfway point between the town and Compound. Working quickly, Jacob and I dug with our pack shovels behind a large brush pile that obscured our camp at almost every angle from anyone who may walk the road. Matt excitedly dropped his pack when my shovel struck metal. Just three feet under the sand sat my dad's large metal box, containing everything we would need for a temporary camp set up.

"There is water here… dated just last week. I guess your dad came out here to check it after I did my last rounds." Jacob stated, as he took a quick stock of what supplies the box contained. "A couple of sleeping bags… some MRE's and food pouch enough for two meals each, easy. Plenty of water and a medical kit too." Jacob began to pull everything he could from the box, placing it on the ground. "Some knives too it looks like. Everything I remember from my last check. Except for this." He said as he pulled a small folded paper from the box and handed it to me.

Dear kids,
I came out today to check the box after a news report said we might take a glancing blow from a solar flare. If you are finding this note than the water is fresh and there is a small stock of jerky that Dave made up for you. I hope you never have to use this camp, but if you do it has everything you need.
Love, Mom

I read over my mother's note twice. It was dated for yesterday. So it was true… the parents had suspected something would happen. I knew the dirt had been freshly dug here the second we arrived. Now I knew why. I tossed the note at Travis who gave it a once over and handed it to Matt. At least we knew at this point there was a greater likelihood the EMP was sun related and not a weapons attack.

Jade wasted no time rolling out a sleeping bag and crawling inside. She fell asleep before we even had the chance to finish setting up or getting a meal together. I wasn't sure if it had anything to do with the many pounds of gummy bears she must have eaten, but the child didn't at all seem to be starving. We allowed her to sleep and skip a meal for once. Come morning we would force food in her if we had to. For now… sleep.

Travis decided to take first watch and ate the jerky before heading out to scout around camp. Matt would take the second watch, followed by Jacob. This would leave me to get camp ready in the morning for the seven mile trek to Compound. We all agreed that Jade would need a full night of sleep lest we want a crabby little girl all day. She loved her sleep more and anything. To wake her even accidentally meant we would likely pay for it. Though she seemed to favor our mother with her green eyes and charming smile, her personality must have come from our father. He was a grizzly bear in the morning if he didn't manage to get a full night of restful sleep.

Jacob dug through his bag until he located the small bottle containing the alcohol soaked cotton balls he would need to help start the fire, and one of the many lighters he always kept on hand. After I handed him three large handfuls of broken brush, we dug out the small logs we kept stocked under the brush pile. Within minutes, Jacob had our fire going while I made a quick meal for everyone who would be eating tonight. This consisted mainly of powdered drink mix, and small pouches of dehydrated food of random varieties. I managed to keep the beef chili macaroni for myself, eating both portions as we had very little to eat much of the day. I tried to remember what it was I had eaten for breakfast, but it seemed a distant memory. Lunch had been light as I really hadn't been in the mood for sloppy Joe mystery meat and rock hard corn bread. All of this walking had placed my hunger in overdrive, and I made quick work of my pouch.

I wasn't ready for sleep just yet either. For the first time sense the EMP wiped out the power, I realized just how quiet everything was. How dark too. My eyes were drawn to the distant horizon

Darkness Falls

where on a normal night you could see the lights of town. All I could see was darkness and the hint of an orange glow that indicated a fire blazed just West of downtown. Knowing the layout as I did, I knew on that side of town there was a preschool, food market, an auto parts store and the movie theatre. I wasn't sure what building was burning to the ground, but I wondered if there was anyone trying to stop the fire... or just leaving it to burn. It is true that I had been floored by how quickly town fell apart. I guess I had more faith in mankind. Maybe I was just naive in my young age.

Jacob poked the coals of our fire with a stick in silence. He had been watching my gaze toward town, apparently seeing the blaze as well. He smiled weakly at me and continued to poke the coals.

"Jacob? Is everything alright?" I asked as I curled my knees up and wrapped my arms around them. "You seem really distant. I know it is a completely stupid question after the day we just had. But I am not sure exactly what to say."

He set his stick aside and went back to watching the small fire. "Nothing will ever be the same. Everything has changed. Just this morning... we were happy teenagers with happy lives. We were thinking about things like Prom and Graduation, the end of the year party... all those things that will never happen now."

"You don't know that for sure Jacob. They could get the grid up." I stated as I tossed brush on the coals.

"They won't Fallon. Not for a very long time. You know that, don't you?" He removed his shoes and began to take his socks off, hanging them on the brush. "We are entering a whole new age Fallon. Think about it. This morning we were still children in the eyes of society, now we are adults in a world of survival. People are dying around us even now." He stretched his feet closer to the fire to warm them. "Think about how many people died just seconds after the EMP. Car accidents of course, we have seen that much. But the planes too, Fallon. Any plane that was in the air the moment that fucker hit... came crashing down. Entire families were on those planes. In cities and suburbs across the country, those planes came down on people. Fires and explosions wiped out many people in just minutes. Our town may be chaos right now, but nothing like the cities."

I squeezed my eyes closed at the thought. I hadn't even

allowed my mind to think such thoughts until he had brought them to light. Why was his mind so dark tonight? He had always been the level headed one with the personality of a class clown. I was beginning to think it was all just a cover to hide what really went through his mind.

"Here," Jacob smiled as he reached into his bag and handed me a bottle of beer. "Don't give me that look. The store attendant slipped it to me and told me I had to be a man now. I would like to share it with you."

"Is this our coming of age ritual?" I giggled at him with a confused smile.

"I guess you could call it that. Things are forever changed now. In that first second when it hit...," He whispered as he handed me a bottle opener from his bag, "...We aged without knowing it. No longer teenagers. No longer children. Now we fight for survival as adults. When things rebuild... if they rebuild... the new world will be looking to us for a way to keep it stable. A way to rebuild society using the wisdom of the younger generation. Those who lived through it and learned from not only their mistakes, but the mistakes of the generations before us."

I popped the bottle open and sipped the warm and disgusting liquid before making a face and sticking my tongue out. "Crap this stuff is bitter!" I whispered as I shook my head in an attempt to somehow shake the flavor it left behind in my mouth. "You need to stop being so doom and gloom huh? That has always been my job anyway. I am the one that isn't happy with my life."

"My parents left this morning for Haven." Jacob stated, taking the bottle from my hands. "They were trading goods with them."

"Oh my God Jacob, I didn't even know." I whispered.

He took a large swallow from the bottle, never once making a face. "I have no idea how long it will take them to return. At least I know they will be safe at Haven." A small smile crept across his face and he drew another large swallow from the bottle before passing it back.

"I am sure they are alright. Is that what has been bothering you all day?" I asked while taking a second sip and watching him nod. "I could tell there was something on your mind other than the EMP. You haven't been your smartass self, since this morning."

Jacob shrugged. "In all honesty I have had tons on my mind today. When we left Compound this morning, I started thinking about trying to figure you out."

I gasped and passed the bottle back to him. "Why me?"

"You never did fully embrace what Compound has done for us. I watched you trying to ignore the morning meeting like a sickness you didn't want to catch. You've fought for so long to be a normal girl. Why? Do you know what normal girls our age are doing right now? They are totally freaking out. They have no idea how to handle what is going on, and may not even have the foggiest idea what is coming. But you…," He downed another swig before continuing. "You need to redefine what normal means to you. You are prepared for times like these. You think being normal is being ignorant of the world around you and embracing the stupidity of being a mindless sheep. In all reality, they are the ones who aren't normal. History has taught us time and again that not paying attention will get you killed. You are closer to being normal than any of them are. You are smart. You have a mind about you that hasn't been tainted by an egotistical lack of knowledge. They are so wrapped up in technology and social structures they don't fully understand. The second they lost that part of themselves, they were faced with not knowing how to property communicate and relate to each other on a very human level. They latched onto a society built entirely on the false notion that nothing would ever happen. We could continue to reap the glory without some form of consequence."

"You are getting far too deep for me now," I offered.

"There is that deep seeded defense you use to hide the fact someone is right. You do it all the time. Changing the subject doesn't change the facts." He shook his finger playfully in my direction. "Shame on you."

"In all honesty? Sense we are being adult about all of this… yes. Yes I want to be normal. I never wanted to grow my own food and live a life like this. Once I got old enough to see what those on the outside were doing, I realized how little they had to worry about. I wanted to live that stress free life they led. To be able to worry about other things all the time and not whether or not I could purify water or make medicine out of silver. I wanted to grow up in a big house with a family that thrived in their ignorance. All those guys we go to school with can laugh at things because they have a completely different perspective. They could enjoy life without some sort of hidden fear. I wanted that. I didn't want to see the world the way we do. To constantly have a watchful eye on the world. That was my dream." I said.

Jared smiled before shaking his head. "Don't you understand what you were wishing for? We were never taught to fear the changes that would come. We were taught to be prepared for them so that we wouldn't be afraid of it. What you wanted most... was to live in a false world like a drone and pretend everything was normal... only to live the worst fear of all later. Today we didn't panic. We knew exactly what was happening and instinct took over. We left the school, got the others, and began our journey back to Compound. Not once did we freak out or hide from the truth. We did what most kids our age wouldn't. That is the reason we have a better chance of making it through this. We have a leg up. A gift our families have fought to give us that is better than a large house, cell phone, or a new car. They gave us life when we were born... and they continue to give us life even now. They taught us how to survive and thrive in ways most parents don't think about."

I smiled weakly. "What you are saying is that what I wanted most was a fake life?"

Jacob laughed before offering the last swallow of beer. "I'm not saying you have to completely embrace and understand our way of life. But right now, we are living in a world we have spent our entire lives preparing for. At Compound we have everything we need to continue that life. We could very well be one of those families over there...," He pointed toward the dark horizon. "We could be cuddled in a corner with a can of beans and a flashlight. We could be looking at truly horrible fears we couldn't even fully grasp. Instead, we are at a camp in the desert with a bottle of beer and an open mind."

I laughed. "How the hell did you grow up in the last couple of hours?"

"What can I say," He smiled before draining the last of the beer. "Must be the beer talking. At least, that is what I plan to use as an excuse for this whole conversation."

We both laughed then. Of all the conversations I had ever had with Jacob, I had to admit that not one of them had ever been like this one. For the first time, he finally opened up his walls of protection and let out some real feelings. Right here in the light of the coals, I saw the man in him for the first time. Not the boy I had loved like a brother my whole life. In this moment he had transformed right before my eyes. There was wisdom beyond years bubbling to the surface. Jacob had truly grown up in a matter of hours. In the time it took us to get this far... he changed. *Maybe I had changed too*, I thought as I climbed into the sleeping bag beside Jade. Jacob had given me something to think about. Tonight however, I would dream of the false world and not the world we faced. Just this once, I would pretend none of this had ever happened. Come tomorrow I would open my eyes to a whole new world I wasn't sure I was prepared to face. I never had enough confidence in my ability to handle what was just over the horizon. For now, I'll dream of a peaceful life of ignorance.

CHAPTER THREE

I found myself wondering aimlessly through a bustling metropolis. Glass towers rose high above the skyline glistening with the morning rays dancing across the glass. The air only slightly chilled, gave a fresh morning scent with a hint of sea salt. Crowded sidewalks moved quickly with people busily rushing to the destinations they desired. Dogs barked in the distance and the many sounds of cell phones ringing and people chatting were almost too much to bear. I could smell the ever present scent of traffic, trash and foods I could not identify. As I watched everyone move about their day, I found myself panicked. Something wasn't right and I could feel it in my bones. I screamed at the crowds to catch their attention. Only a few stopped and shot me a glance of irritation. I screamed again, this time for everyone to seek shelter. Those who stopped to listen shook their heads and began to move on. I ran as quickly as I could toward a woman pushing a stroller. Her slightly greying hair in a tight bun high on her head with small curls popping out from the tight confines she insisted on forcing them into. What I could only assume was her small daughter playfully babbled away in the stroller, her brown eyes occupied by a fluffy stuffed teddy bear. Though I was running as fast as I could muster, I found myself barely moving as if I was running on a moving sidewalk in the opposite direction. The woman stopped moving and turned to face me with tears in her eyes. I screamed to her that she needed to take shelter for the sake of both her and the child. The woman slowly shook her head, defeated.

Darkness Falls

Then I heard what sounded like thunder and looked to the clear skies for any sign of stormy weather, finding nothing. A shock wave like a torrent from a tornado ripped through the streets as people screamed and scattered behind me. I glanced back for a fraction of a second to see a wall of debris heading straight for us. Buildings shook and rattled themselves to the ground with thunderous power. I turned back to the woman and her small child, seeing nothing but an empty and charred stroller. Their smoldering remains lay beside it, filling the air with the fowl sweet smell of death. I screamed without a single sound escaping me. The world around me completely silent, I tried again. I heard a voice call my name in the distance and instantly bolted toward it. Someone is in the silence? Someone is alive out there? I called out to the voice but nothing came back to me. I screamed again as I ran passed burned bodies and charred remains of the world I once knew. The voice became louder within my ears as I struggled to gain enough ground to locate the direction the voice was coming from. It called out again and again as I searched, screaming...

"Damnit Fallon! Wake up!" Jacob shouted as he smacked me across the face with force.

"What happened?" I asked, as I rolled onto my side in a fog of confusion and pain. The sting on my cheek burned deep to the bone, blazing white hot fire across my skin. Blinded by the pain and the predawn light, I blinked repeatedly as I began to search for Jacob's face. I almost wished I hadn't found it with such clarity as his brown eyes glared at me.

"You apparently had a nightmare. You screamed loud enough to wake the dead. Poor Jade jumped out of bed crying, Matt had to catch her because she took off and hid in the brush. I think it best you pull yourself together." Jacob declared as he turned to his bag, "We have a long walk ahead of us. If anyone heard your voice carry across the fields, we could be in for some trouble. You sounded like you were being murdered or something."

"Is that why you smacked me like that? Hasn't anyone ever taught you not to hit girls?" I joked painfully as I pulled myself to my feet and began to roll up the sleeping bag. "You have a lot of nerve you know. That hurt like hell."

"Sorry about that." Jacob now looking concerned handed me a small cup of coffee. "I tried shaking you and everything. Nothing was working. Your screams were about to give away our location. We can't have that you know. The morning brings fear to those in town. People are starting to understand all too well that something is wrong. Yesterday was a day of shock for most people, today the fight for survival begins out of fear. There is no telling what is going to happen out there and we still aren't clear of it completely. Seven miles left to go and if we can just make it there in one piece, we have tackled today's largest battle."

I placed my rolled sleeping bag into the wagon to give Jade something soft to sit on. Yesterday's travels had given her sore feet from walking, as well as a very sore rear end. I took a tentative sip from my small coffee cup as I winced in reality. I wasn't awake to get camp going. I had slept in. Perfect. They let me sleep and did the work themselves. Sleeping bags were rolled up and placed into the wagon, bags had been packed up and all trash had been secured in a day pack to be brought to Compound. Besides the still smoldering coals of the fire, the vision before me didn't suggest the slightest hint that anyone had spent the night behind the shrubs. Our best bet was to bring everything from camp home, save for the large metal box. That would have to be put back in the ground for now. We didn't need people finding this camp and figuring out someone traveled through here before. Compound had to be secured. Many of the town folk knew about Compound and some even knew how to find it. That thought made me nervous. When desperate people remember where we are, they will come looking. We have enough supplies to pass out, but to how many? My parents always made sure there was plenty to handle the neighborhood if need be. Many of them at least. I couldn't be sure of how many refugees would come looking for help in the end.

The sound of a shotgun in the distance snapped us to attention. I suspected a rapid downfall would happen in town, just not this quickly. My father said once that the media has fueled the rapid decline with television shows and printed media for years, showing people what would happen in a downfall. EMP was no longer an unknown term to the general public. Those who have been blind to the world around them are now panicked, and looking for answers.

"We need to hit the road now. I'm not sure what the hell that was about, but we don't want to be a part of it." Travis stated as he picked up a shaken Jade and helped her into the wagon. "I'll pull

Darkness Falls

the wagon for a while. Camp is secured. Also, I saw a car accident on my watch. It was too far away for me to investigate without leaving my post. I think we need to check it out."

"Alright, you and Jacob handle Jade. I will take Matt and check it out. It could be dangerous, but this far out from town I won't be expecting much. Take Jade and head for the dry creek bed. We will meet you there shortly." I informed as I turned to Matt, "How many rounds do you have in this magazine?"

"Locked and loaded. Two full ones on me, one ready and one on my side." Matt said, as he motioned to his hip.

"Good. Let's get going and make this fast. If there is anything in that accident that might be helpful, let us hope we don't have to fight for it." I mumbled, as I started walking in the direction Travis pointed. I wasn't sure why I had agreed to investigate this thing. We had plenty of supplies to get us back to Compound. Travis had a soft spot for helping people; he must be being eaten alive by the thought that someone could be hurt out there. His internship at Compound's medical wing had made him a little too helpful. With my drive to gain some brownie points after the nightmare, I didn't have much choice except to check it out for him.

It didn't take long to find exactly what Travis had been so concerned about. Just one half mile from our overnight camp location sat a blue rumpled pile of metal. We had managed to walk passed it without notice when we took the short cut the night before. Backtracking wasn't exactly what I was in the mood to do today. The closer we got to the accident, the more nervous I felt. Matt could sense it as well and walked slowly at my side, both hands on his 9mm handgun. I couldn't even tell from which direction the car had been traveling but it was obvious to me this wasn't a local's vehicle. It had to have been trying to take the highway back roads to avoid traffic. If that had been the case, the driver at least knew a fraction of the area as not a soul traveled that open road which cut across ours and headed West. A person could avoid the highway as well as downtown with a straight shot to a lesser used connecting highway. This rumpled metal would never make it. Not now and not ever. It's final resting place wrapped around a tree.

"Matt, do you hear that?" I whispered as we were almost right on top of the accident. "Is that crying?"

"Someone is alive in that!" Matt whispered back in shock as he quickened his pace.

This was something I wasn't prepared for. I half expected the vehicle to be abandoned or the driver dead. Whoever this driver was, survived not only the crash but a long cold night and chilly morning alone. I began to mentally survey my first aid kit while taking in the sight of the accident. "Matt...," I whispered. The rest of my sentence cut short as he noticed the same thing I had. Lying on the ground just feet from the driver side was a four ounce sized baby bottle.

Matt reached the driver door before I managed to close the distance. A dark haired woman covered in blood and extremely pale rested her head on the steering wheel, eyes barely seeing and whimpering softly. She was young, maybe early to mid-twenties at most. Her hair so badly matted with dried blood I could barely tell where her head injury was located. A quick survey of her condition told me instantly that moving her would kill her; though it was obvious to me she wasn't going to survive much longer either way. I touched her face gently as her eyes fluttered and blinked.

"My son." The stranger began in barely a whisper, forcing me to get as close to her as I could in order to hear her words. "He ... quiet... morning." She shuttered and coughed her words as her badly pinned body jerked in protest. "Check ... him."

I watched as Matt looked into the back seat and ran around the car to find the best way in. A small car seat sat in a rear facing position, blocking my view of the child the driver worried about most. I hadn't even noticed the car seat before that moment. The stranger struggled with her words again though I could not understand what she was trying to say. With Matt fussing in the backseat I tried to pay most of my attention to the driver and doing whatever it took to make her feel comfortable.

"Dying...," She stammered. "Like... me."

"Fallon! He is alive, barely though. He needs care right away." Matt called loud enough for the driver to hear, her body relaxing instantly. "He's very young Fallon. Ask her how old he is?"

"Two... weeks." The injured woman whispered before struggling to sit upright. Her back had been broken in several places making her efforts pointless. Giving up in pain she relaxed against her wheel before continuing, "Take him... help... prom... promise." She fought as a tear rolled down her cheek softening the crusted blood.

"What is his name? Hang in there alright? You'll make it." I lied, watching Matt slowly release the restraints that held the newborn within his seat. I blinked back tears as for the first time, the boy whimpered in protest and fear.

"Bentley...," She whispered as her eyes began to close. "Tell him... I waited... for you."

"I will." I said as I fought back tears. Breathing had become difficult for her as I watched her fight to take a breath. She wasn't going to win the battle she was fighting to win, and she knew it. I placed one hand on her face and grabbed onto her hand with the other. A true testament to a mother's love, she fought to stay alive long enough to see her son get help. What hell that must have been for her to hear him cry and not be able to do anything to help him. Once he had gone silent, she must have been scared to think he was either dead or just sleeping. Her last hours on earth were spent in a mother's nightmare. "Matt! Is he stable enough to bring him to her? She's fading fast!"

"It is a goddamned miracle he is alive. Not a scratch on him one! He's dehydrated though, and cold." Matt answered back as he rounded the car with the infant in his arms. The tiny bundle barely moved as he lowered the boy into the vision on his mother.

We watched her smile weakly before her body convulsed and fell still. Her eyes now unseeing, gazed directly at the last image she would ever see, her son alive and in the arms of a complete stranger. I slid down the driver door and sat staring off in the direction of Compound, silent tears streaming down my face like a torrent of hot flood waters. The child fussed in Matt's arms as he began to squirm. We were now in the possession of a child we knew nothing about.

"What the hell do we do now?" I asked in shock.

"Hold him while I search the car. There has to be a diaper bag or something in here. He needs to eat and at this point I am just praying he isn't breastfed." Matt answered as he gently handed me the squirming bundle. "Not a single mother at home is breastfeeding right now and he wouldn't make the trip without eating."

For the first time I gazed down at the tiny child in my arms. He was pail and fragile as he looked at me with searching eyes. Up until now, besides the Compound babies I had never seen another child this small let alone held one. I wasn't sure how he managed to survive but had heard stories of newborn children surviving all sorts of crazy things. This had to have been one of those cases. He lived through the car accident, and several hours without food. The cold at night alone should have done him in, but he had to be a fighter like his mother, for he was alive!

"Thank God!" Matt yelled. "There is a can of formula in here and a bottle too!"

Bentley ate the entire bottle quickly, spitting up only once. Matt had managed to locate a fully packed diaper bag and a wearable baby sling on what was left of the backseat floorboard. While I changed Bentley's diaper, Matt informed me something had to be done with the mother. Her body could spread disease and attract wildlife if left within the car. We spoke of setting the whole car on fire, but that plan was unrealistic. A fire would quickly become out of control and left unchecked, would burn thousands of acres endangering everyone. We decided the best option would be to dig a grave for her and mark it. If the grid ever came back, we would tell someone where she was and give her a proper burial. Almost an hour had passed as I sat caring for Bentley while Matt dug the hole and struggled to pull the woman from the wreckage. It wasn't an easy feat as the vehicle was so badly mangled it made her removal nearly impossible.

As soon as I knew he had eaten his fill and had fallen asleep, I strapped Bentley to my chest in the sling and helped to fill in the grave. It didn't take nearly as long to bury her as it had been to dig the grave itself; however it was nearly noon as far as we could tell. The others would be worried about us if we didn't hit the road quickly.

"Mrs. Stephanie Monroe, age twenty-four. She was from Palmdale originally according to her driver's license. There was a blood soaked letter in her purse I could barely read, but it looks like she may have been heading back home a widow." Matt stated as he handed me her belongings. "A Navy guy looks like. He died overseas before Bentley was born. I found a box of cremations on the passenger floorboard after I pulled her out. She must have been headed home to lay him to rest. That was the box I placed in her arms earlier. I figured they should be together."

"That is very sweet of you Matt. We will take her purse with us. Her driver's license might help us locate a family member if the grid ever comes back." I commented as I set my pack and secured Bentley to my chest. "We need to hit the road quickly. Jacob and the others are waiting for us at the dry creek. I am sure they are wondering what has taken so long. Be assured that Jacob is probably backtracking by now and is on his way here to see if we are dead or something."

"We've done all we can here. I'll carry the diaper bag and purse. Let's get this wee one out of the elements and passed onto someone at home that can help him. We could still lose him from exposure." Matt stated as he began to move.

We walked in silence the half mile it took to get back to our camp, and kept going without a word for another mile. Bentley slept quietly tucked to my chest in his sling. He didn't make a sound or fuss the entire walk, which made me think the movements had rocked him into a deep sleep. I hoped he wouldn't awaken again until we made it to Compound. I wasn't sure we would make it before dark if we had to keep stopping to care for him. The heat of the day would be on us in no time. If we didn't gain some serious ground we would end up trapped in it. I was already tired and sore, but stopping to rest anywhere was completely out of the question. *Just keep sleeping little one, let us get to Compound in one piece*, I thought to myself.

After we crossed another mile off the travel, I spotted Jacob with rifle in hand trotting in our direction. Even from the distance I could see the concern in his stride. It couldn't have been easy to leave Travis and Jade alone to come find us. Then again, he had no idea what we had just been through. As he neared, he began to slow down as panic washed over his face.

"The blood on you! Are you hurt? Are you alright? What happened out there?" Jacob yelled.

I hadn't even noticed all of the blood on Matt and me until that moment. "We are fine. We aren't hurt at all. There were two survivors in the accident. One of them died after we got there." I stated as Jacob reached us.

"Dear God. What about the other one?" Jacob relaxed slightly.

"Right here...," I offered as I pulled back the sling enough to give Jacob a good look. His eyes widened in shock at the tiny form snuggled in deep sleep. "His name is Bentley and he is only two weeks old. How he managed to survive is beyond us. I'll tell you all about it later. Right now we need to keep moving."

Jacob nodded in agreement. "Travis and Jade are still on the move. I sent them on ahead as we weren't far from Papa Perez. It was only a couple of miles off. I figured they wouldn't be met with trouble being that close to home. I made sure Travis had a gun though, just in case. They should be nearly there by now."

With only five more miles to go, I quickened my pace while Jacob spoke. We didn't need any more distractions or stops. "Matt, you run on along ahead of us. They might panic everyone at home with news that we went missing and Jacob came looking for us. You can fill them in on what happened today and get things ready for Bentley. He will need to be evaluated at soon as I get there."

"You got it. I'll have Sarah get a room ready." Matt agreed before handing the diaper bag and purse to Jacob and taking off at a dead run, his bag bouncing on his back.

At only thirteen years old, I knew Matt could make the journey with greater speed than I could; especially toting a baby along. Without Jacob's mother, Sarah Simon was Bentley's best chance of survival. She was a nurse in the NICU before she retired five years ago. Compound had a medical trailer set up to handle most any emergency with two primitively stocked rooms should the need arise. We all had been preparing to use at least one of those rooms for Megan Sanders as she was due to give birth in the next month. For now, Bentley would need one. He would need to be evaluated to make sure there wasn't some horrible injury my untrained eye failed to notice. I was already in an almost constant worry over every move he made. Surviving the accident was the first step, surviving the trip home was the second. If I could get him that far, then my mind could be at ease knowing he would be in good hands.

I was still deep in thought when we reached the Perez property line. I hadn't even noticed the lack of conversation between me and Jacob. I did at one point explain the entire accident, the mother and what had happened. Then we continued in silence. He must have noticed my concern over Bentley, for we had picked up our pace and arrived at the Perez property quicker than I had expected. Maybe I had just been lost in thought for the last few miles. I couldn't be sure. Either way, it didn't matter now. We were only half a mile from the northern gate and Bentley was still sleeping. With the news of what happened I was almost certain there would be a wagon waiting at the gate to rush us to Sarah as quickly as possible. I was beginning to think he should have woken up several times to eat by now and it concerned me he hadn't eaten sense we buried his mother a few hours earlier. Jacob had tried to make small talk but I wasn't really in the mood. He took to surveying our route looking for any dangers. This close to home however, there wouldn't be any.

As we passed the Perez house, I could tell someone had been there several times in the last twenty-four hours. There were bags and boxes packed up into the back of a small wood hauling trailer. The flower pots that normally sat alongside the rocking chairs were missing as well as the chairs themselves. My family must be moving Papa and Emily Perez onto the property to offer them better protection. The old rundown house had been in need of major repairs before the grid went down. My father must have thought it best to abandon it for the time being. From the look of disarray, the move had been cut short. Probably due to Bentley's arrival and the need to see we have all arrived safely. I made a mental note to help cut down the overgrown grass for Papa Perez as it was normally my chore… and I hadn't done it in a while. That was, if the grid ever came back up and he wanted to move back into his family home.

We were barely to the northern gate when I caught sight of Dave Ratcliff waiting impatiently, tapping his foot yet sporting a grin from ear to ear. He was slightly older than what I would have called middle-aged with a long, heavily greying braid of aged hair down his broad back. Dave was a wide man, always in flannel shirts and faded jeans I could only assume used to be blue many years ago. His unruly grey beard was twitching with the facial expressions he tossed our way. I didn't need to see his mouth through the forest of fur to know he was smiling. Like I pictured Santa Claus as a child, Dave smiled with his eyes. Dave sat leaning against the old farm tractor with the flatbed utility trailer attached behind it, one hand on a beer and the other on his hip. This must have been our ride up the long driveway to Compound.

"I heard yawl got you selves a tiny stow-away." He grinned. "Best let me have a gander, but don't you be a thinkin' I am gonna touch it or anything. I ain't much for the crying and pooping things." He played with a laugh.

"Dave you are a sight for sore eyes. Did everyone arrive alright? Did Emily arrive as well?" I asked as I pulled the sling back enough to show Bentley off. "I am worried about Bentley. He has been asleep most of the trip and hasn't eaten but once since we found him."

"Everyone be here just fine. Sarah be waiting on you in the med'cal building. She insisted I drag my butt down here and give a ride." He turned to climb onto the tractor. "Best go slow she says, don't bump the baby around she says...," He trailed off as he started the tractor.

Jacob and I climbed onto the flatbed and chose to sit as close to the middle as possible. The last thing we needed was to fall off the flatbed and get injured right after arriving home. Not to mention Bentley would probably have been hurt as well. We bumped and thumped up the road enough for Dave to stop and close the gate behind us. The tractor was louder than usual making me wonder what sort of trickery they had used to get it running when nothing else seemed to be working after the EMP. I could barely hear Jacob as he yelled over the sound of the engine, telling me to hold onto Bentley tightly.

The first sight of home took my breath away. For the first time I saw my home with new eyes. Older eyes. Wiser eyes. The stables with our two lazy horses sat just north of the main compound structure. Next to them, Jacob's half acre pasture with Nigerian Dwarf goats chewing and watching us pass with curiosity. Two of the goats were missing and must have meant they were butchered out sometime in the last twenty-four hours. Not out of the ordinary here at Compound. I closed my eyes and took a deep breath before passing the slaughter house. Though it probably doesn't smell anymore after the cleanup, I didn't want to tempt my weakened tummy in case the slaughter was in current progress. I had been so wrapped up in the baby I hadn't eaten since we left camp. In fact, I didn't remember eating anything at all. Even just picturing the slaughter house right now made me feel ill as I thought about the mass amounts of blood and accidently compared it to the accident. I fought to hold composure until the trailer tires hit the pot hole I knew well, meaning we had turned the corner and was heading toward the chicken and rabbit house.

Darkness Falls

I opened my eye and scanned the compound. Just after the chickens, rabbits and pigs, we would come to the expansive gardens being prepared for planting season. The compost piles that had rested for a year or more would be ready to spread soon as well. Four tiny homes faced each other in a large square sharing a massive deck with an outdoor kitchen. This was the center of Compound. The main house which my family lived in consisted of seven hundred square feet with a loft bedroom for me and Jade to share. It was painted a pale green with chocolate trim, two of my mother's favorite colors. On the left sat an eight hundred square foot tiny home owned by the Dunn family, painted light brown with what I had always thought to be gold trim. Across from the Dunn house was the home of Angela Jackson on her twin three year old daughters Cassidy and Cassandra. It was an amazing little home with three bedrooms, and five hundred square feet. I always loved how it was painted light blue with trim that matched the sea. Megan Sanders' home was just across the deck from my own, and was equally the size of Angela's place yet matched the paint job of my own. Brian and Sarah Simon put their small home out by the medical building to be closer to the herb garden and the facility. Dave preferred to sleep in the loft bedroom in the barn as he could see above the compound and keep his eyes on the animals from up high.

As we pulled alongside the barn to park the tractor, I could see everyone in deep conversation on the expansive twelve hundred square foot deck. I could smell my father's steak on the grill and saw something cooking on the outdoor stove in the deck kitchen. They must have known how hungry we would be. Bentley began to stir in his sling as I held him close to my chest. His tiny eyes opened and closed several times and he looked up at me. My head began to swim as I looked down at him and tried to focus on his sleepy face.

"Welcome home tiny one. Welcome to Compound." I whispered just before everything around me went black.

CHAPTER FOUR

I slowly rolled and stretched, searching for even more comfort than I had been previously curled into. Not finding it, I slowly opened one eye. I wasn't in my loft like I had thought I was. I'm in the medical building. Blinking several times against the fog in my mind, I tried to piece together the puzzle of scattered memories. The EMP happened and wiped out the grid. Since I could see lights in my room I knew that my father had his solar panels and battery bank working overtime. I had obviously made it back home and I was alive, that was good. I couldn't tell what time it was as the shades in my window were down. What I could tell was that I was in the recovery room and not the surgical room. The medical building only had two rooms, one on either side of the single-wide trailer. The center mass of the structure housed all the supplies, a washing station, and a triage with several chairs. The Simons and the Dunns ran the place like a well-oiled machine. Everything had a proper place, everything constantly sterilized and picture perfect.

I sat up slightly to get a better look around. In a small pink vase in the far corner sat a beautiful handful of wildflowers picked from the first blooming patch behind the barn. I smiled as I knew they had come from Dave. Still trying to shake the fog from my mind, I began to remember something. Something important. A panic began to well up in me and I knew what that was something was...

"Bentley!" I screamed as I searched around me on the bed, tossing sheets off of me. He wasn't on the bed next to me. I rolled out and onto my feet, losing balance I slumped to the floor and looked under the bed. Surely he was here, right? Did he roll off the bed? Do newborns roll? Is he hurt? With lightning speed the memories came flooding back to me. All of them. At least up to the point of arriving at Compound. I still had no idea how I managed to land myself in the medical building. "Bentley!" I screamed again as I managed to stand and stumble to the door. I was in a gown and not the clothing I came in here with. There was no telling how long I had been in here and for what reason.

I flung the door open to find the triage of the medical building completely deserted, no one around to interrogate as to his whereabouts. I thought about the surgical room and figured he had to be in there. Sarah must be in with him tending to whatever injury he must have suffered that I hadn't found originally. With my legs less shaky than before, I jogged to the door and flung it open. Empty. The bed had been freshly made with clean sheets looking very much like no one had been seen today. I wasn't sure Bentley had even been in here at all. The sinking feeling in the pit of my stomach told me the reason he wouldn't have been seen, and I blinked against the thought. Bentley was my responsibility. I had to find him quickly.

I bolted through the door onto the porch of the medical building. "Bentley!" I screamed, running down the ramp. I didn't care that I was still wobbly and weak in the knees. I screamed for him a second time before catching sight of people on the shared deck between the homes. Sarah turned with a look of shock on her face as I bolted across the dirt and up the steps to the deck. "Where is Bentley? What happened to him?" I screamed as tears threatened to well from my weakened eyes.

"Dear God child, you've ripped your IV right out of your arm!" Sarah informed as the look of shock and concern on her aged face slowly changed to playful warmth. "I was wondering when you would finally join us. You fainted when we tried to help you off the flatbed. You've been asleep for two days. Dehydration we reckoned after Jacob told us you didn't have a drop of water yesterday. Let's get you cleaned up again. You shouldn't have ripped the IV out. You have blood running down your arm."

I hadn't even realized I had an IV. I had been asleep for two whole days? I shook my head against the fog. "Where the hell is Bentley?" I urged.

"He's fine sweetheart. He was dehydrated but otherwise in perfect health. You did well by him. He wouldn't have lasted much longer out there. Getting him here as quickly as you did, saved his life. I released him this morning but I am going to continue to evaluate him a few times a day just to be sure. Jacob took him down to see the goats. He hasn't left your side or Bentley's since you both arrived." Sarah smiled.

"He is alive?" I sagged in relief. I was exhausted though I wasn't sure why if I truly slept for two days.

Sarah giggled as she reached for my arm. "Yes. He is quite the handful too. He seems to get rather upset if anyone holds him, except for you and Jacob of course. He had the biggest fit the evening you arrived. I brought him in to see you and he calmed right down again."

I walked over and slumped down into a chair on the deck, placing my face in both hands. Bentley was going to live after all. I had managed to get him here within enough time to save him. The fear now turned to overwhelming joy, releasing the tears I fought to control. I had instantly become and emotional mess and I didn't care in the slightest. Sarah insisted on taking my arm while I cried, in order to clean up the blood and check the damage. It wasn't bad thankfully. A little clean-up and a bandage would do just fine. When I managed to calm down and look up, Angela was smiling at me. Her long blond curls lay loosely and untamed across her shoulders. Her blue eyes sparkled with a knowing smile causing me to grin sheepishly. I panicked like a mother who had misplaced her child. I must have looked like a manic freak to everyone within five hundred yards. Sarah and Angela exchanged a glance and a giggle before helping me to my feet and leading me back to the medical building for a change of clothing and a hot bowl of soup.

I continued to interrogate Sarah as to Bentley's health the entire time I changed into a new set of clean clothing. Chosen for me was a dark, figure hugging pair of blue jeans with rhinestone hearts on the back pockets paired with a black tank top covered in rhinestone hearts to match. I tossed my long auburn curls into a shaggy ponytail after I managed to rip my brush through it several time to untangle what the journey home had done. I refused a shower as Sarah had been nice enough to clean me up once she admitted me to the medical building. I wasn't in the mood to spend

Darkness Falls

time away from Bentley. I had to see with my own eyes that he was safe and no longer knocking on death's door. Sarah had even brought my make-up case. I didn't even care about putting make-up on. After the EMP there really wasn't a point anymore. Maybe I will feel differently months from now when I am depressed and need to lift my spirits. For now anyway, the only person I could be looking good for was Jacob... and that was not what I had in mind.

Sarah gathered my belongings while I busied myself with putting my military issue boots on and working the laces. I loved these boots and wore them almost daily. One of the greatest gifts my father had ever given me; save for the many rifles and pistols I had in my gun safe. When I finished with my boots, I put on my belt, checked my firearm and placed it in my hip holster. With nothing left to do, I turned to Sarah for the all clear sign indicating my freedom from the medical building. Plopping down on the edge of the bed I watched her clean and ready my bags for my release. Her long grey hair in a tight braid down her back almost to her waist, slid back and forth with every twirl she made from one side of the room to the other. She wore a faded dress made entirely out of blue jeans she recycled from old Compound clothing, covered by a thin, white apron she wore daily without fail. Her heavy set frame swayed back and forth as she quietly hummed to herself a tune from her nursing days. I almost didn't want to bother her, but I couldn't get my mind off of Bentley and the thought of Jacob taking care of him.

Once Sarah and Angela had finished, we returned to the deck where I was forced to sit and wait for everyone to come and greet me. The stalling became almost unbearable. Jacob rounded Megan's house before anyone else managed to arrive, carrying a tiny little bundle of blankets in his arms. His face lit up the second he saw me sitting there. His brown eyes smiling even before his lips caught up to the action.

"You are up! He has been looking for you. I gave him a tour of the place but he didn't seem interested in the least." Jacob informed as he handed me the squirming blanket bundle with a smile.

"He's only two weeks old Jacob. All he cares about is food, sleep and pooping." I laughed, taking Bentley back into my arms for the first time in two days. I could feel his warmth even through the faded blue blankets. He had begun to fall asleep again until I had wrapped him into my arms. His tiny eyes fluttered open, saw me and closed again. I kissed his head and snuggled him into me. "He has so much more color to him now."

"It is weird to say this, but I think he has chosen you as his new mom. He barely lets me do anything with him at all. He seems to like Matt a little more than most, but he doesn't shut up unless he is around you. Like a puppy or something." Jacob poked fun as he sat in the chair next to me. "I think you have been adopted."

I thought about it calmly and as odd as it sounded, it didn't bother me as much as I thought it would. I had rushed Bentley here as quickly as I could in the hopes of passing him off on either Angela, Megan, or my mother. When push came to shove however, I couldn't get him off my mind and knew there was something special about him. I would need plenty of help figuring out how to take care of him. I didn't know the first thing about babies, and being only sixteen I hadn't had plans to become any sort of mother for years yet. I felt more like his much older and extremely protective sister. Whatever the bond between us, Bentley and I had something special I had yet to be able to find the words to explain. I couldn't imagine having the strength to let him go. As odd as it sounded to me, I felt the need to have him by me every minute of every day. I felt a duty to his mother as well; something that couldn't be ignored. She had stayed alive long enough to wait for someone to save him. That someone was me. She told me that herself. She died only after making sure he was safe and in good care.

The first to arrive to welcome me home had been Megan Sanders with her two small children Becky and Bobby. They weren't yet school aged and their entire attention had been on Bentley sleeping peacefully in my arms. Megan seemed massive to me. Her black hair in two tight braids kept them out of her way as much as possible. The extremely large pregnant belly reminded me of just how little time she had before her third child would enter the world. She hugged me, commented on how adorable Bentley was and spoke highly of my bravery in his rescue. She told the tame version of his rescue to her children as they listened with full attention. When the story was over, they both kissed Bentley on the head and hugged me before running off to play. To them, life

Darkness Falls

here never changed. We had been living off grid our whole lives. The EMP meant very little to them.

Sarah returned with her husband Brian just as Megan was heading out to collect the wash. Brian smiled brightly at Bentley and then at me before informing me that I was much too young to be a mother, but Megan could only handle one newborn at a time and Angela wouldn't have the time with her Compound duties. Sarah nudged him in the side with her elbow, interrupting him long enough to inform me that though I may be young the right help could get me through in the responsibility I had been entrusted with. Brian seemed rather uncomfortable seeing me with a baby in my arms, making me wonder about his thoughts on my maturity. Several times he ran his thin hands up and down the legs of his black jeans as if looking for his keys, a nervous habit he had that alerted us to his desire to run away from something he didn't want to deal with. If no one caught on to this nervous habit, he would run a hand through his salt and pepper hair. I promptly gave him the excuse he needed by informing him that due to my medical stay, I hadn't been feeding the rabbits and worried about their wellbeing. Both of us knew that any one of the people on Compound handled it for me, but he was willing to use it as a means to get away and I didn't mind.

Angela Jackson and her twin daughters were next in line. Though not as excitable as Megan's children, they seemed rather interested in Bentley and when he would be old enough to play tag with them. Jacob laughed and explained newborn habits to them while Angela held Bentley and told me about all the things that happened at Compound while I was knocked out for the last two days. She seemed overly comfortable holding him; a naturally born mother in every sense of the word. He woke up and fussed in protest but she refused to cave into his will and continued in our conversation. Angela had always been a gentle woman, lean and soft all at the same time. I couldn't understand why her husband had left her when the news broke they were having twins. His lose I guess, she always said he just wasn't into being a father.

By the time everyone had cleared the deck I found myself exhausted. I could barely keep my eyes open though the grip I had on Bentley never faltered. I had yet to see my parents, my sister or even Jacob's brothers and I was already losing my battle. I gently handed the baby to Jacob and told him I needed to see my family before I fell over. He agreed without hesitation and sent me to my room, telling me that not only would my family be in to see me shortly, but that he would take Bentley for a while.

I barely made it to my family's tiny home and up the small wooden ladder to the shared loft bedroom before falling over. It didn't even matter to me that I hadn't seen my family at all in days. All I wanted to do was sleep, deeply. Sarah had told me I would be exhausted for a while and if I needed a nap to go sleep it off for a while. In the beginning I fought it. Now I welcomed it. I removed my gun belt and locked it into my small safe near the bed. I didn't keep my large safe in my room, but the small one worked wonders for my everyday carry weapon, also known as my EDC. Slumping into my bed boots and all, I buried my face in my pillow and drifted off to sleep.

When the dawn broke across Compound the light licked at the walls of my bedroom through the window. I didn't realize I had slept not only all afternoon but through the night as well. I opened one eye and glanced at my bedroom window. It was morning alright... only the morning sun shines through like that. I knew I wasn't alone in my room, I could feel there was someone watching me.

"I am sorry about the other night at camp. I didn't mean to scare you like that." I whispered. I knew all too well that the invader was Jade, watching me sleep. I could not only sense she was there, but I could smell maple syrup.

"You always know it is me." She frowned as she crossed her arms. "I've never been able to sneak up on you."

I rolled onto my right side facing her. "Don't feel bad kiddo, no one can sneak up on me. Many have tried."

"I want your super power." She smiled.

That was the term she had always used for it. My super power was to see the unseen; as if I was some sort of superhero that had eyes in the back of my head. Every chance she had, she would put me to the test just to see if I had a hidden identity I was keeping from her. When she was younger, she would do whatever it took to try and catch me flying off to fight crime. It annoyed me to no end in the beginning. Now I just feed her curiosity.

"So If you really are feeling lots better your powers will work again. So what is for breakfast then?" Jade teased.

Darkness Falls

I sat up in bed and placed both hands on my hips, closed my eyes and sniffed. Once I could smell the ever delicious smell of the meal I knew all too well, I pretended to think as hard as I could trying to envision the meal for Jade's benefit. I placed my fingers on my temples and squeezed my eyes closed making Jade giggle. "Breakfast is... pancakes with maple syrup, biscuits and gravy, coffee, bacon, and eggs with sausage and chopped bell peppers in them too. I think I can even sense Miss Megan's apple pie she is secretly preparing for after supper tonight."

Jade jumped to her feet. "Really? Are you sure?"

"It is cinnamon and apples which I can sense, so it must be true." I grinned as I opened my safe and grabbed my gun belt. "Where are mom and dad?"

"I wasn't supposed to tell you, but with your super powers working I am sure you already know." Jade teased as she stood and gave me a tested look. "Are you testing my super powers now?"

I stood as straightly as I could. "I know what they are doing... but do you?" I teased, knowing all too well that she was about to spill the beans.

"They are out by the garden building your house. They are almost done too. I was told they were going to come to breakfast and surprise you with the keys."

I wasn't exactly sure how to take that information. If I showed outwardly the same shock I was feeling inwardly, Jade would know she blew the whole thing. I decided my best bet would be to nod and congratulate her on her skills as a superhero. "You've done well Jade. Let's get to breakfast."

I still had on the outfit I had worn the day before and I didn't care. I would change later if need be, but I hadn't done anything to get it dirty. Once I figured out what was going on I would get cleaned up. For now, all I wanted was a hot cup of coffee and a hot meal. Pancakes weren't exactly what I had in mind but they would have to do. Jade was the first to shimmy down the ladder and run out onto the deck as I tried to follow behind her as quickly as possible. Still groggy from my recovery, I could barely keep up with her energy. Jokingly, I thought about how I was going to manage to keep up with Bentley if we never managed to find his extended family.

The large banquet table that stretched down the center of the shared deck was overflowing with food. Several plates stacked high with pancakes sat every few feet on the bright white table cloth normally used only for special occasions. A jug of Brian's homemade apple cider had been placed dead center in the fifteen foot wooden marvel. Dave had built the table many years ago as a gift to everyone at Compound as his way of saying thank you for allowing him to move in; and for agreeing to never eat his hog Bacon. He was rather handy when it came to wood crafting and had built much of the furniture on the property. It kept him busy which was something he always insisted on. Heaping piles of bacon balanced precariously in mounds in four locations alongside large serving bowls of scrambled eggs. The sight of such a spread had yet to be seen since Christmas.

Angela was standing at the stove seemingly toasting homemade bread while her daughters were having a pretend tea party with a pile of teddy bears. She was humming a tune to herself and giggling at her daughters when she caught sight of me. "Good morning sunshine. How did you sleep?"

"Well I am guessing alright. Didn't think I would sleep for that long. Where is the coffee?" I smiled. "I can smell it but I don't see it."

"That is because I maxed out the useable space out here making all this food. Megan had to use the tiny kitchen in her place for coffee and tea. She was rather irritated about it as she needed the space to make a pie for tonight. Bobby and Becky are getting dressed and should join us shortly. Dave, Brian, and your dad are busy and probably won't come around for a few more minutes. Your mom is in with Megan if you want to see her."

I sure did. I hadn't even seen my mother since the morning before the EMP hit. From my rough calculations I could only assume it had been five days. With the dehydration and sleeping for two days, plus the passing out yesterday I wasn't even sure what day it was anymore. I watched as Jade sat down to the tea party with Cassandra and Cassidy while I walked to Megan's door and gave a little knock before opening.

Megan sat in the chair at her small table hunched over a cup of decaffeinated tea, my mother across from her sipping her coffee between words. They seemed to be deep in conversation about something important. My mother's long auburn curls had been pulled into the familiar bun I had seen her wear almost daily my entire life. As I entered the room her green eyes flashed with excitement and a bright smile grew across her face.

"Mom!" I giggled happily, hugging her as hard as I could. "I'll tell you my story if you tell me yours. I want to know all about the last few days around here."

"Ladies, let's talk over breakfast. There is so much to talk about." Megan stated in a hushed tone as she rose to her feet and collected her tea cup.

My mother sat next to me at the banquet table and began to fill me in on all I had missed. The news had been reporting for a couple of days that a glancing blow from a solar flare might hit and that an EMP blast powerful enough to wipe out the grid hadn't been expected. The reports had been pouring in saying that some disruptions in electronics may have been seen but that it would be monitored and minor. My father had used his laptop to get online and check the current conditions on space weather; only to then report back to the adults it seemed the flare would be stronger than the ones that had been repeatedly hitting us for months. Sarah had put in a call to Haven and insisted on speaking with grandma Ginny in an effort to double check emergency medical plans. Ginny wanted Jessica and Robert Dunn to leave Compound as soon as possible, to drive out to Haven and pick up military medical supplies uncle Charlie had given to her. These supplies were to have been delivered to us over the weekend when he was to take leave from the military. However, his leave was denied at the last minute for unknown reasons. Jessica and Robert left with nothing but their bug-out bags and a few gallons of water. From my mother's calculations they would have reached Haven before the EMP struck. My father insisted on sending everyone to school as normal that morning in the hopes the flare truly would be a glancing blow; though the decision had greatly bothered my mother. When we all had left, my parents collected all of the electronics including the satellite internet dish and took them to the underground shipping container they used as storage, locking them in a faraday cage they had prepared for just this sort of thing.

In the minutes and hours leading up to the blast, everyone at Compound secured the property and double checked the solar panels could handle what might have been coming. Then it hit. My mother was standing in the garden when the lights went out. She hadn't noticed right away of course, but Megan had cranked the handle on the emergency siren. The sound could be heard from one end of Compound to the other. My mother said it was in that moment she began to worry about whether or not I could manage the plan for picking everyone up from school. My father apparently walked down to check on Papa Perez only to then bring him here to talk about moving in for a while. It hadn't taken long for Dave to get the tractor up and going again, though mom said many curse words had been exchanged between him and the machine. My family had spent all afternoon moving Papa and his belongings into the Dunn home temporarily.

Emily caught them all in Papa's yard moving boxes and informed them of our journey to pick up the younger children. That was when my mother knew I would be alright in getting home. Emily told her I knew exactly what happened before anyone else did, and helped keep her calm. When Travis and Jade arrived the next day without us, my mother set to work putting together a rescue mission and prepared to head out in search of us. Matt had met her at the gate as she was leaving and explained everything. From that moment on, Compound rushed to get everything ready including digging a grave in the small cemetery just in case Bentley didn't survive the trip. When Jacob and I arrived, he had taken Bentley from my arms just before I went down. Dave carried me into the medical building. When news broke that Bentley was going to live, apparently everyone cheered except for Dave who just grumbled playfully about diapers.

Sarah hadn't lied when she told me Jacob refused to leave Bentley and me. My mother informed me that he ran home long enough to grab a spare blanket and took to sleeping in a chair by Bentley's bed or mine depending on who fussed more while sleeping. Though I had no memory of doing so, I apparently told everyone in an exhausted haze that beer tasted nasty. After the laughing had died down, and everyone sat down to dinner, Jacob explained about the entire journey from start to finish. Matt and Travis filled in the blanks that Jacob hadn't been present for. That was the only time Jacob had left the medical building and only did so after he was assured Bentley and I would be alright.

"That poor boy was in an all-out panic the entire time. With his parents currently at Haven, he has taken on both his brothers and now apparently you and Bentley. It is almost as if he wants to worry about everyone else in an attempt to squash the worry he has for his parents." My mother whispered. "He has even offered to

Darkness Falls

help Dave with his current projects just to stay busy."

I sipped my coffee before leaning back in my chair. "What on earth could Dave be doing now?"

"Ah." She giggled. "He's been building a cradle for Megan's new baby, though he has grumbled about it the entire time. I think he secretly loves babies and just doesn't want to destroy his manly persona."

Both of us laughed at the thought. I hadn't realize how much I had missed my mother over the last few days. It was nice to sit and enjoy a cup of coffee together, forgetting for a while that our world had changed. Here at Compound, nothing had changed. Like any normal day, Compound ran as usual.

"Miranda!" my father called from the steps as he bounded onto the deck with excitement. "We finished the project in record time. Looks like Dave is finished too. We still have a busy day ahead of us, but at least we made great headway."

"That is great news Jared. Call everyone to breakfast would you? Their food is getting cold and there is much to talk about." My mother smiled as my father nodded and rang the large dinner bell that hung on the corner post.

Three loud chimes rang out across the grounds before my father turned to me. "Feeling better kiddo? Sarah has been evaluating Bentley this morning in case you are still panicked about him not being attached to you."

"I wasn't worried. Angela told me when she filled my coffee cup earlier." I stated as I took another draw from my mug. "I do believe I am fully recovered now."

"Good because we are having a meeting this morning and I need your insight."

I smiled and gave a nod that was met with a smile. He loved including me in all things Compound. Now that most of us save for Jessica and Robert, were all accounted for we could finally get down to business. There was much to be done around here and security measures would need to be reviewed. The last thing we needed now was to have a couple of strays find their way to our gates in search of supplies. Food stock reports would need to be reviewed as well as safety protocols, weapons assessments, power and gas reserve would need a nod as well. There was so much to discuss I thought for sure we would conference until lunch rolled around.

My father handed over my notebook and pen. "Hope you can handle what is coming today. You better have that writer's cramp under control. Get ready kiddo. This will take a while."

CHAPTER FIVE

I slipped a spoonful of eggs into my mouth and chewed slowly, listening to Dave Ratcliff give his report of current resources he is normally in charge of. Frantically taking notes, I glanced up every few lines to inform him with a nod that I had gotten the information down. We had twenty cords of firewood left after the winter season's end, six of them in the seasoning process and the rest of it being stored in the barn crammed into the old stalls we hadn't been using. Little over five hundred gallons of gasoline stored in fifty-five gallon drums still sat untouched in the fuel house, along with four hundred gallons of diesel fuel and four hundred gallons of kerosene. Even barrels of fuel stabilizer had been counted, enough to handle the lot of it. Two of the four Compound tractors were currently operational, but one of the nonworking ones had been in need of a new tire, something Jessica and Robert Dunn were to bring back with them should they return home. The furniture and tool crafting shop was also operational as well as the generators used to run the place. Dave had spent much of the last few days tinkering with things that had been damaged in order to keep Compound running smoothly.

Brian Simon was next to stand and give his report. I always loved hearing about his duties here at home; he took such great pride in making sure he did the very best job he could. Our six hundred square foot root cellar had suffered with our winter usage. However, we still had plenty to get us all through the spring if we went easy on it and pulled a large enough harvest from our first round of spring crops. The underground storage room we used for canned foods didn't suffer from much usage. There was enough food in that storage room alone to last Compound for six months. Brian had spent much of canning season working overtime to restock some of the goods we had traded to Haven over the summer. He did manage to gain one hundred size ten cans of freeze dried milk out of that trade, just in case something happened with our milk cows and goats, something he took much pride in. Brian had also gained one hundred size ten cans of powdered egg mix to put in the deep storage for emergencies. I smiled brightly at him when I finished writing it all down. I was excited and proud of his efforts.

Since Robert Dunn had been detained at Haven, Jacob and my father took a quick stock this morning of the armory in his absence. Jacob stood to give the report almost nervously, and explained that we had in fact gained a few extra firearms during the journey we took to get home. My father hadn't been too terribly pleased but understood our need and seemed to relish in the knowledge we knew how to obtain these items in a civil manner. Jacob had left a note on the office desk explaining what we had taken and that we would pay the owner handsomely when the grid came back. One hundred firearms filled the armory along with enough ammo for each to last for several months or even years depending on usage, and this didn't include what everyone had in their personal gun safe or on their person. Robert had also managed to score a few compound bows and harpoons which we had been unaware of until Jacob began his report. What we would need with harpoons I couldn't imagine, though my father was overjoyed by the thought of having a few. There were fifty-five gallon drums full of brass and though we probably wouldn't need to use them, all the reload stations had been set with enough to create more ammo for each firearm should the need arise.

Sarah Simon had been quick to inform us in her report that some much needed medical supplies would be on the way from Haven with Robert and Jessica, including some items she felt we would need for the coming birth of Megan's baby. However, the medical building remained in perfect running order and completely stocked with everything Compound would need, though we were low in Novocain and flu shots, something that would be arriving with Jessica. The generators the medical building used to run certain equipment had been repaired as needed by Dave yesterday. The solar system for the building was unharmed and operational. The stay Bentley and me had taken had used up a few bags of IV fluids, some bandages, and some of the stock of baby formula that had been stockpiled for Megan's baby should she be unable to breastfeed. Overall though, the medical building was in sound order and could do everything from stitches to burns and everything between. Jessica and Travis were normally in charge of helping at the medical building, but with Jessica gone, Sarah felt it important to remind us she was down one set of hands and for all of us to please remember not to hurt ourselves. We giggled at her worry before letting her know we would do our best.

    My mother gave the gardening report next as I slugged down the last of what remained in my coffee mug, which Angela was quick to refill with a smile. The western most corn patch had been set to rest after last harvest and the patch next to it we have rested for the last two years would be ready for this year's corn crop. Due to the fact that the field's water well was set to a hand pump last spring, we wouldn't have any trouble keeping this year's food watered. Compound was currently working on filling one compost box while another was resting, giving us a box for this year to use on the garden. The move Compound had made years ago to composting toilets had been very wise for our food growing processes and for that, she was truly thankful. Our harvest had grown steadily over the years allowing for the stockpile of reserves we now maintain. Our emergency seed vault currently overflowed with preserved seeds, as well as our normal seed vault used to replant this season's food supply. Potatoes, carrots, watermelon, pumpkin, squash and tomatoes had already been planted last week and plans to fill the rows of green beans and peas were set for later this afternoon. The late winter had pushed our normal planting dates and we were being forced to plant later than we had wanted to.

    Megan Sanders slowly stood though we had told her to stay seated for her report. The stubborn woman remained on her feet reading the notes she had created over the week. Compound currently had a supply of fifteen gallons of homemade liquid laundry soap and fifty pounds of dry laundry soap. Our stockpile of soap making supplies could keep us in soaps for at least a year. Due to her pregnant state, she had been unable to keep up on the bath soap and shampoo supply without Jessica's help. This left us with a supply of ten gallons of homemade shampoo which didn't include what everyone kept in their personal stash, and only forty bars of soap in the storage. Megan had also taken to giving us Jessica's report on homemade candles and yarn in her absence. As far as that was concerned, it was business as usual.

    Angela Jackson informed all of us that the everyday food supply was in great order, and that Emily Perez had been lending a hand with milking and egg collecting duties. Together they discovered that six of the meat rabbits were ready to be culled, and two of the breeding does would be ready to deliver in ten days or less according to the breeding charts. Twelve of the chickens were ready to cull as well, along with one of the goats that Compound was unable to get to when we had arrived with Bentley. In the last couple of weeks, Compound had managed to butcher out two goats, six chickens, four rabbits, two pigs and a steer. Along with the new finding, once the jobs were completed, we had more than enough meat to last throughout the year and leave enough for trading.

    My father gladly agreed to take his turn next and began with promising to add the culling duties to his list of things to complete in the coming days. He then gave a status report on all home repairs that had been required according to the work orders. Jessica and Robert Dunn had requested their wood burning cook stove be looked at for fear that the temperature sensor might have gone out. My father informed Jacob that he had replaced the sensor and all was back to working order. Brain and Sarah's broken pipe for grey water had been replaced and the holding tank it drains into as well, due to its age and failing state. Angela's broken window had been replaced as well as the squeaky board in her kitchen floor. Then the solar power and wind report followed as we all had expected. All solar was currently running smoothly and wind was also up and running again. Nothing seemed to take damage and the over preparing had managed to work in preserving batteries. North Gate and South Gate were both secure and all alarm set ups had been checked and rechecked for damages. Some repairs had been needed, but Compound was back to being as secure as ever. Both the garden's water well and the main well were functioning as normal, and all water holding tanks have been checked for water levels. The underground bunker complex complete with deep earth farming capabilities had been checked as well, to make sure they were fully stocked and all air filter systems were operational in case of emergency. Family from Haven had come down and built the entire bunker system for us five years ago in trade for some work that needed to be done and fifteen head of cattle.

Just as my hand began to cramp up from the pages of notes I had been taking, Papa Perez stood from his chair in true Compound fashion. This was his first camp meeting and we were eager to hear what he may have wanted to add. He smiled brightly and let out a gruff giggle before he began. "You have all been very kind to Emily and to me for a long time now. I want to thank you for allowing us to stay in the safety of your household, though I don't think I will ever get used to so much storage you need a meeting to handle it all. I haven't done a lick with my gardens in a long time and I have no animals to add to your herds. Everything I had was butchered out or sold before winter with no plans to bring any back in. I'm just too old to do that crap anymore." He shifted his weight before continuing. "But I am happy to add whatever I have to this little shindig you have here. I am not too good with my hands at this age, but I can do whatever you need."

"Papa, I could use your help running the smoke house. With all this meat, we need to keep it running for some time to come. If you are interest in the smoke house job?" My father smiled. "We had a couple of the chest freezers go down when the EMP hit. We aren't sure why some went down and some didn't. We have a lot of meat to handle or it will go bad on us. Brian is going to be running those pressure canners into the ground with all the meat canning he has been doing to keep up. He's been salt packing too, but can't handle it all at the moment."

"I'll be happy to help." Papa smiled as he took his seat again at the table.

"Dad, I have been meaning to ask you something. What went down and what didn't? It seems to me that Compound is running far too smoothly to have even been effected by the EMP." I asked.

Dave laughed loudly before playfully slamming his fist onto the table. "Damned EMP took out a couple of chest freezers and a refrigerator I now be fightin' to repair if it be even possible. Two tractors went down too. Yawl don't even want to know what I had to do to get them beasts running. We ran all over this place takin' e'ery battery we had and storin' it in the cage just in case. But you can't be too sure what these things will do or what ends up being affected. All of them computers and medical equipment we be findin' went in the cage too along with the small generators. All of them came out fine. Anythin' with a computer that didn't get in the cage was fried. Anythin' we thought would be alright seems to have taken a fifty-fifty hit. Thank the heavens for spare parts and junk piles. O' course, I am none too happy to be workin' overtime on this. Why some things be fine and others are not is a complete mystery to me."

"I'll lend you a hand Dave, together I am sure we can figure it out. If it can't be fixed then maybe there can be another use for it." Matt stated as he pushed his empty plate away from him. "So long as you keep that hog of yours from sniffing my pockets every time I come out there."

Dave pointed, "Bacon be lookin' for those jerky snacks you boys keep eaten. I swear yawl keep pockets full. Hell I make enough of them for you boys... eatin' your weight in beef."

I sat back in my chair with a giggle and looked over the notes from the morning meeting. The survey was now in my hands as to what would be needed. This was a responsibility I had taken just a few months ago and took great pride in my ability to handle it. I closed my eyes and rubbed my forehead as I thought about what was to come. It wasn't like I could send anyone to town to buy items we needed or wanted. It wasn't like I could have anyone call up Haven to schedule a trade day with a list of items we needed. We were now completely on our own. At any normal meeting I would be creating a list right now, and speaking with everyone about what we would need. I would be going over the four homesteads and farms we normally trade with and what goods we would need to make deals for. Now that everything has changed, my major focus had been to listen carefully to what we already had in storage and paying close attention to how long each thing may last. I jotted down a few notes of my own on the list of things from the morning meeting I felt important.

I took a deep breath before standing. This would be the truest test of my abilities to run Compound. I knew if I made a mistake, my father would step in without fail though I would feel I hadn't done the duties up to par if he did. "Everything seems to be in good standing. However, when Jessica and Robert return they will want their home back. We need a more permanent solution for

Papa and Emily's living situation if they will be staying here full time." I glanced at my father for support in my thought process and was met with a wink and a nod. I continued with a smile. "Also, we need to assume that those in town who are familiar with what we do here will eventually come to our gates for help. We need to consider opening the overflown storage container on the south side of the property that houses the goods we have set aside for just this purpose. It also houses the goods we have set aside for trade as well as boxed food supplies for refugees. These will need to be gone over very well to make sure we can handle the influx. Please remember though that we cannot help everyone that arrives here... and always be prepared that if anyone does show up, not everyone is going to be nice about it. Violence may well become a form of survival now for most people who did not prepare for hard times. They will want to take what we have. For this reason I would like everyone to carry their everyday firearms on them at all times and double check they have plenty of ammo in their personal stockpile. If you need to check some out from the armory please remember to log it so that we can better keep track of what needs to be restocked as soon as possible."

Jacob interrupted, "That shouldn't be a problem. I'll make sure to take over the armory duty until my dad comes back."

I smiled back knowing all too well that it was a duty Jacob had been wanting to handle on his own for months. "Thank you Jacob. Now, because Jessica and Robert aren't back yet and we have to assume they probably won't make it back in time, we have to make double sure that we can at least make do with what we have to handle Megan's birth. Sarah, if you need an extra hand in the medical building in Jessica's absence I would like to have Megan if she is interested, take over in her place. I can take over soap duty in her place. This can help make sure she is as close to the medical building as possible in case she goes into labor, and we can all make sure she isn't lifting heavy buckets of soap and not telling us."

My mother's laughter broke the brief silence, followed by that of Megan and Angela. We had in the past caught Megan doing just that, and though she had promised not to repeat it, none of us could be completely sure she was keeping the promise. From the look on Megan's face I knew she would gladly accept the new duties without trouble. Sarah seemed to enjoy the new hands as well.

"In final, seeing as school has been canceled...," The cheering from Matt and Travis interrupting my thought causing much laughter around the table until my father raised a hand to calm them. "...sense school has been canceled, I think it is best that we try to keep a learning schedule for the family? I think it best that we continue with our studies. We have all the books we need here, my mom made sure of that. There are textbooks to handle every grade."

"My little girl is growing up." My mother laughed. "Yes, we have a stockpile of textbooks and other school supplies. We shall come up with a plan to keep the education going. I think it is a wonderful idea." She smiled as she patted me on the back.

My father stood and clapped his hands together with a smile. "We've had a great meeting this morning and I feel that Fallon has done an amazing job of covering the important issues. We will be sure to address each one of them as soon as possible. Sense we are not in any place to be trading or bartering with others at the moment thanks to the EMP, we won't even touch on that right now. Our main concern is sustaining what we currently have. I would like now for Brian and Dave to help Papa and Emily move the last of their belongings into the shed. Let's get them moved out of their home as completely as we can. We don't want them to lose important memories or supplies if they end up looted by people coming out to our property and not getting what they want from us. We will begin construction on their tiny home starting tomorrow. We will need the extra time to make sure we have enough supplies after the recent projects we completed. Dave, I believe you have something for Megan?"

Dave stood with a broad grin and patted the chest pocket on his dusty flannel shirt. "I have two gifts to give! A cradle for Megan's new bundle of poo-n-tears, and a last minute one for Fallon... for that infernal lump of blankets she be callin' Bentley."

I was sure in that minute the shock on my face was the reason for all the excited eyes burning into me. He had made a cradle for Bentley. Surely the child would need a place to sleep; I just wasn't sure why the news of a cradle would surprise me so much. My infernal lump of blankets? Bentley was now being referred to as my child? I had known there wasn't a single person here that had the ability to take him. Not that I would be willing to part with him anyway. I also knew that his care had been entrusted to me by his birth mother. Though I had known the responsibility would be my own, it still came as a little bit of a shock to hear the others agree to such a thing.

Jacob pulled Megan's cradle from under the table and slid it over to Megan. It was a beautifully hand crafted piece like none I had ever seen. A pair of teddy bear holding each other tightly in loving embrace had been burned into the headboard piece just above where her child's head would lay; baby booties burned into the other. A cherry wood stain brightened the piece yet gave the feeling of calm and warmth. A hand knit blanket obviously done by Jessica, had been laid into the cradle adding a touch of green and blue to the gift. Megan beamed with joy as she hugged Dave, thanking him for such a beautiful job. When Jacob slid Bentley's cradle toward me, my mouth fell open in disbelief. Instead of teddy bears, Bentley's name had been burned in brilliantly bold letters along the top. Two open hands holding a heart with wings adorned the other end, perfectly cut and burned. The job had to have taken hours to complete, and with love. Inside the cradle lay an old blue knit blanket with tiny dark blue bows stitched randomly, adding a unique touch of beauty.

"I gave it a maple stain figuring it would be more his style. I wasn't sure...," Jacob mumbled as he pointed to the wood. "I thought heck, it might as well have his name on it. Dave cut all the wood and stuff. The blanket isn't new though. I know that if my mom were here she would have made one. That is my old blanket. She made it for me when I was born."

"You made this?" I whispered as my eyes trailed the length of the gift in disbelief.

"Well, Dave was busy with Megan's so I had asked him to cut the wood for me. I watched him build her cradle so I built this one alongside him. I had him double check it though to make sure I had done everything right and that it was safe. I knew you would want a safe one. He can use my blanket for as long as he needs. Hell, he can keep it."

I smiled, "Jacob, I have no idea how to thank you."

"Just don't let him barf all over it or something." Jacob laughed as his face colored in embarrassment. "I am sure he will though. Babies do that sort of thing."

I slid my hands over the cradle and into the bed, touching the worn blanket and feeling something under it. Moving the blanket aside I noticed a small wooden box with my name carved into the top. Puzzled, I picked it up and slowly opened it. A key attached to a single ring lay inside all alone against the dark wood bottom. This must have been the key to the home that Jade had blabbed about earlier that morning. A tiny home all my own.

"We had started to build the place weeks ago as a guest house for Grandma Ginny as you know, in the hopes she would come and visit knowing she had a place to stay. After the EMP we decided it best to make it the Perez house. When you arrived with Bentley and word got out he would survive... well, we couldn't have him crying in the house and waking your dad or Jade. You know how those two can be if they don't sleep well. After a conversation with Papa and Emily, they agreed the house should go to you and Bentley. You are much too old to share a loft with your eight year old sister anyway." My mother beamed as she wrapped her arms around me from behind. "You are close enough to everything you need including help with Bentley if you need it. Think of it like having your own room with the benefit of a kitchen."

After a few stunned moments in silence, Jacob grabbed my hand and pulled me out of the chair and across the deck. Everyone jumped to their feet and followed behind, giggling and whispering as we crossed the yard toward the garden. There, between the watermelon patch and the pumpkin patch sat a small cabin painted a deep forest green with jet black trim. Black planter boxes lined the small front porch adding a home like feeling to the entire look of the place. Someone had created a river rock path leading from the front of the garden patches clear to the front porch; a good twenty feet of pathway. My name as well as Bentley's name, scrolled across a wooden plank hung from two metal rings on the railing of the porch, and my father's old rocking chair had been set near it with one of my mother's old throw pillows added for a seat cushion.

Jacob led me down the pathway and onto the porch, pushing me at the door. "Well, you have the key, open it up!" He insisted.

I placed the key into the freshly oiled lock and turned, hearing a click before turning the handle and opening the door. It wasn't a large place by any means. Compound was never big on the idea of large homes with wasted space. The idea of freeing your life by letting go of useless material items had been adopted by my parents after years of living at Haven and watching people lose all they had to economic downturn. Watching so many families lose homes to foreclosure during the first big closing boom in recent history, cemented this value into my parents and helped their hand in convincing all Compound members to go small. The plan had worked. In the beginning even Angela had bucked the notion, coming from a large family home to Compound. In the end, those like her who had made the transition found they were happier this way. Less it seemed, was always more.

    I stepped into a small room with a wooden dining table and chairs for four people. I had guessed it had been made this way in order to give guests a place to eat as well as myself. The same small pink vase full of fresh wildflowers from the medical building adorned the table atop my mother's white table cloth. Each chair seemed to have been hand crafted by bending branches impossibly into swirls and curled edges. It was though I had stepped into the home of fairytales. I couldn't see how such beautiful chairs could be made in such a way to suggest they had actually grown that way. Beyond the dining set sat a small sofa fit for two, crafted in the same manner as the chairs, with handmade cushions filling the useable seating space in deep greens and blues. The wood cooking stove my parents had used when they first created Compound, sat against the far wall. The stove, a gift from family at Haven to commemorate my parents' wedding had been used for years before being placed in storage, only to find its way into my home. It was a sentimental touch they knew I would adore more than words could properly express.

    A small bedroom sat just to the right of the living space with a large window looking out over what would be the green beans, peas and cabbage patches. The bedroom sat empty except for the large bed with handmade headboard and footboard matching the motif of the chairs and sofa. Curtains matching the blue and green bed set hugged the large window, hanging the length of the wall to touch the wooden floor.

    "Dave had been making all the furniture to sell at the county fair this summer. Sense I am sure there won't be a fair now... he thought it best to let you have it all. The linens we bought on a heck of a sale last spring to add to the sleeping quarters of the bunker complex. In fact, we pulled the mattress from there as well.

There is a loft bedroom above this bedroom but it doesn't have anything in it right now. You won't need it for a while so we didn't bother much with it. It is an open loft though and looks out over the rest of the house, a lot like Megan's own loft. It was her idea. She thought you would like it as it makes the space seem more open and inviting. The bathroom is finished but only has a composting toilet and a shower. The plumbing runs from the water tank and through the wall behind the woodstove. The heat will transfer to the pipes so you will need to start a fire if you want hot water. Same with the sink in the kitchen, you'll need to start the fire for hot water." My dad began to ramble as he walked around pointing at everything in explanations. "Your solar system is completely set up. Like your mom said, we started this project with the idea it would be for Grandma Ginny if she ever decided to grace us with her presence. The entire solar system set up was purchased before the blackout, but it was stashed in the cage for weeks. I gave you some oil lamps as well in case we have bad weather and your batteries aren't charging well. I figured you wouldn't need the wind power back up, but if it gets too bad I will tie you in."

"We will move your belongings for you if you like the place. There should be plenty of room for the cradle in the bedroom. We dug out all the radios from the cage and oddly enough they all work perfectly. I put one in each house to help with communications in the event of emergency. Your radio is by the door on the shelf." Brian stated as he pointed to the radio.

"This is too much guys." I whispered, still in shock that all of this had been finished for me. "This is like, the coolest thing ever!"

"How many sixteen year old girls get a house?" Jacob jokingly mocked. "Seems to me… this is a dream come true?"

Obviously Jacob was touching on the conversation we had at the camp, and my desire to be a normal girl in a normal world. I am not normal. *Normal teenagers don't get a house*, I thought to myself. Normal girls aren't raising a child they found in a wrecked car either. While the world falls apart outside the gates of Compound, inside we were thriving. I hadn't even thought much about the outside world since my arrival home. I wondered in that moment how the other teenagers from my high school were doing. Are they confused? Do they have a way to cook food without power? My mind began racing with thoughts of how all this time I looked at them all as spoilt brats that were handed the world. Now, they suffered. Yet here I was, thinking we had been suffering all along within the lifestyle we had chosen, to only be proven that indeed, I am the spoilt brat. For I thrive. We cook. We grow. We live. Our own little world may have taken a hit when the blackout struck… but we are doing more than just getting by. Compound lives on.

"Thank you. All of you." I smiled as I scanned the faces of the most amazing family in the world. Every one of us that made up Compound, were a family.

Emily squeezed through the door, still holding Bentley in her arms. "Pretty awesome place you got here Fallon." She laughed as she passed Bentley to me. "Matt and Travis went to get your things. If you like, I can go make sure they aren't touching your underwear or something."

"Thanks Emily." I said as I lightly bounced Bentley in my arms.

I hadn't noticed Jacob had snuck out and retrieved the cradle from the main Compound deck. I watched as he walked in and placed it in the bedroom near the bed. One by one, everyone hugged me and left the small cabin to return to their duties. My cabin now sat empty except for Jacob and myself, looking out the window overlooking the front walkway and porch. He seemed deep in thought as I watched his dark eyes scan what was now my front yard. The hint of a nervous smile began to grow across his face when he realized I had been watching him. He ran a hand through his brown disheveled hair and down the back of his neck.

"So here you are Fallon… a cabin for you and Bentley. Does it feel weird at all?" He whispered as he turned toward me, his eyes seeming to look deep into my soul.

"I wouldn't say it is weird I guess." I whispered back as I avoided his gaze by looking down at Bentley who slept in my arms. There was something in the way Jacob looked at me in that moment that made me a little uncomfortable. "I am still trying to figure out why everyone thinks I am so capable of handling Bentley on my own. I am only sixteen for Pete's sake… and I have no idea what I am doing."

"Your mom and Angela will be a huge help as far as that is concerned. The entire family is helping in his care, so it isn't just you. But I think you need to have more faith in yourself. You can handle him with help. Somehow I always knew you would make a good mom."

"Cut it out! I am not his mother. He is just a little boy who needs someone to help him out. I feel more like his sister anyway… a much older sister." I joked as I walked to the bedroom and placed Bentley in the cradle to sleep. "I still can't believe you made this for him."

"It was nothing. I admit I have grown attached to him. Unlike you though, I don't see myself as his older brother."

I turned to see Jacob standing behind me; eyes clouded in emotion as his gaze rose from Bentley's cradle and met my own. I couldn't be sure if he had been thinking about his parents being stuck at Haven, the blackout, or something else entirely. There was something so very different about him and I couldn't put a finger on what that difference was. Then as if he awoke from a dream, he blinked several times, turned on his heels and walked out of the cabin before running to the main deck of the complex; leaving me stunned and confused.

CHAPTER SIX

Dear Diary,
As far as I can figure, three weeks have passed since the day I was handed the keys to my new cabin. This also means, that it has been about four weeks since the blackout. No one has ventured off the property to see how the people in town have been doing. Jessica and Robert haven't returned either. I looked at the calendar for the first time this morning while I was on my way to collect my new text books from my mom. She has been running a homeschooling program for us to help keep our education up. Between studying, the duties I have here and caring for Bentley, I haven't had much time to do much of anything else. I haven't had any contact with anyone off the property and it is beginning to make me feel a longing to talk to someone that isn't family. An update on life outside the gates would be nice about now.

Megan has been in and out of labor for the last week, though Sarah says she isn't dilating at all and the baby could be born sometime next week. Jacob has been avoiding me since the night I moved into the cabin. He comes by to see Bentley almost daily and has taken him for several hours at a time, but I feel like he doesn't really want to talk to me. I am worried that the fact his parents haven't returned yet is making him more nervous than ever. He came over last night to drop Bentley off and I invited him to stay for dinner, but he just frowned at me and said he had to get back to his brothers. I probably should have joined the dinner going on at the main kitchen like normal. I just didn't feel up to it after such a long day. Now that the Perez cabin is finished, I guess I should get back to my normal chores. Jacob has Bentley down at barn probably annoying Dave about now.
Fallon Henley

The radio on the shelf squawked to life, beeping a few times before a slightly panicked voice bled through the static. "Jared, we have company at the northern gate. The guy from the corner store and two other men I have never met. They want to barter some goods with us on their way out of town."

I jumped off my bed and grabbed the radio in anticipation of my father's response. Company at the gate meant two completely different things: someone wanted to make contact in a friendly manner and also that they could have been followed here, which would be very bad.

"Thanks Brian. If it is only the three of them, let them in. However, stay down there and make sure they weren't followed. It would mean trouble." My father spoke.

Bolting out of the cabin, I ran to the main deck in time to see Megan and Angela exit their homes with radios in hand. There was a buzz of confusion and excitement as my mother rounded the corner with her radio and Emily beside her. Matt and Travis made quick work of setting the table with the leftovers from lunch and a fresh bottle of Brian's homemade apple cider. Dave and Jacob came up from the barn with Papa to see what the commotion was all about.

"I want the women to go indoors and take the children please. Keep your radios with you at all times. Jacob, go with Fallon and Bentley. Her house is the farthest away and if there is any trickery to be had, I don't want them alone. Matt you can go with Megan and Travis with Angela. Miranda, take Emily and Jade into our house and wait this out in there. If this truly is a trade mission I will let you all know by radio contact. We can't take chances with safety." My father spoke confidently as he rushed everyone off the deck. No one fought his decisions when it came to overall safety of Compound.

Jacob grabbed my arm hard, and pulled me off the deck and down the pathway to the cabin. In the distance I caught sight of three men walking up the long driveway headed in our direction. In seconds, I was standing in my living room stunned as I watched Jacob bolt my front door and close the curtains. "What the hell is this about? We know the corner store guy! He isn't a stranger to this family."

Jacob turned to me with a look of confusion and passed

Darkness Falls

Bentley to me. "I think the concern is with the two gentlemen he has with him. We all know he lives alone. Why would he bring two strangers way out here if he were indeed leaving town? We aren't even in the right direction to leave town!"

Until that moment I hadn't thought about the dangers he was suggesting. Jacob was right; the situation didn't make much sense. He lives alone at the far end of town. If he were bugging out he wouldn't have come this way at all and he wouldn't have dared to bring others way out here. I pulled Bentley's cradle from the bedroom and placed it next to the dining table so that I could better watch him while he slept. Thankfully, he was sound asleep and didn't stir when I laid him down. Jacob stood at the window peering through a tiny gap in the curtains, soundlessly watching the event play out on the deck.

I plopped down into the chair at the table and placed my head in my hands, closing my eyes tightly against the welling fear inside me. For many long moments we waited in silence, hearing nothing but Bentley's soft breathing as he rested unaware of the commotion outside. I tried to think of the good things this meeting could bring.

"Fallon...," Jacob whispered from the window, never taking his eyes from the gap in the curtains. "I am sorry I have been so distant lately. I am sure it hasn't been easy."

"I thought you were mad at me for something, though hell if I know what that might be. That or you are worried about your parents, I completely understand if that is the case." I said.

Jacob turned from the window to look at me. "Mad at you? How could you think that? I couldn't be mad at you." He ran both hands through his hair in frustration as he crossed the room and sat in the chair next to me. "You just don't get it is all."

"I don't get it? Get what?" I questioned as I slid my chair closer to Jacob. If this was going to turn into an argument I didn't want it above a whisper, for fear of waking Bentley.

"You are Bentley's new mother, like it or not. You are doing a great job with him too. But I only get him a couple hours every day and it isn't enough." Jacob complained, his eyes on Bentley.

I sagged into my chair in shock. "You are mad at me about how much time you get each day with Bentley? Like some sort of parental visitation issue? Look if you want more time with him then by all means, come by more often! Hell, take him to your place a couple nights a week if you want!" I was now laughing at his plight. "Seriously do what you have to do if he means that much to you."

Jacob frowned, "He needs a strong father figure in his life. I have a connection with him. I have no idea why. I just want to be a part of his life. I want to be a part of your life."

"You are a part of his life and you are a part of mine! You are like a brother to me, Jacob. Can you not see that? We have only grown up here our whole stinking lives together." I joked as I leaned in trying to see Jacob's eyes through his confusing tears.

"I don't want you to see me like a brother." He choked as he placed both of his hands on either side of my face. "Have you ever looked at me in any other way, Fallon?"

Before I could consider what he may have been suggesting, his thick lips were on mine with enough force to make a statement, but gentle enough to show a passion I had no idea he had harbored. For a few brief moments I pushed against his chest in an effort to break free. He left his hands on my face as he pulled away, still questioning me with his eyes, searching for answers. My mind swirled in confusion as I blinked several times in an attempted to clear my mind and make sense of what just happened. Did he seriously just kiss me? Why on earth would he do that? My mind began to swim uncontrollably in directions I had never let it wonder in.

"I... I am sorry Fallon. I shouldn't have done that." Jacob stammered as he let go of my face and stood. "Like I said, you don't get it. You probably never will."

I watched Jacob walk back to the curtains and peer through the gap investigating the meeting happening between the strangers and my father. I sat in stunned silence, unable to take my eyes off of him. He seemed to be lost in thought standing there with his shoulder against the wall, one hand on the curtain and one on his hip, just inches from his firearm. He looked older than I had ever seen him before. He aged the day the blackout happened, and as far as I could tell, he was aging again right before my eyes.

The radio squawked, beeped, and then my father's voice came through the static. "I need Brain to report to me as soon as possible. Dave is on his way to relieve you. Everyone please sit tight." Then it fell silent again.

I stood and walked to the window to see if I could get a

glimpse of what may have been going on, but couldn't get around Jacob to catch a peek. He shifted into my way like a massive wall of protection, as if looking outside would somehow harm me.

"Jacob, move over you big idiot. I want to see what is happening out there." I said while pushing him.

"You aren't even going to answer my question are you? Are you that shocked to find out I have feelings for you? Or are you trying to figure out how to get rid of me?" Jacob questioned sternly as he turned around to face me, his back to the window. "I have waited for you to figure it all out on your own but you never have. I am sorry I kissed you! I didn't know what else to do to make it any clearer. You are dense as hell, Fallon!"

"I am the dense one?" I asked my voice now above a whisper. "You are such an idiot Jacob Dunn. A big fat stupid idiot! When we were little I had the biggest crush on you but you were only interested in throwing handfuls of pig shit at me every chance you got! Hell, you still do it!"

Jacob's laughter shattered the tension as he doubled over in hysterics, one arm around his waist and one hand on my arm trying to keep from falling on the floor. He laughed hard enough that sound no longer escaped his lips and tears began to fall from his closed eyes. Bentley began to stir and fuss, forcing Jacob into gaining some control of his laughter and the volume back down to a whisper.

The all clear signal came through the radio as we fought to control the sporadic fits of giggles from both of us. I picked up Bentley as Jacob unbolted the front door, and together we walked back to the main deck to meet with the first people to visit Compound since the blackout.

Everyone at Compound gathered around on the deck, picking chairs or sitting on the ground as my father introduced the corner store owner as Mr. Glover, and informed us he had a story to tell. The old heavy set man hugged my mother and handed a small bag of gummy bears to Jade before taking a seat of his own. Jade jumped for joy and ran to Cassidy and Cassandra to share the booty.

"Good people of Compound...," Mr. Glover began as the last of us took our seats on the deck. "...I want to thank you for inviting me into your home this afternoon. I wish my visit had been under better circumstances to be honest. As some of you know, I have done some trading in the past with you, and I am friend to your very own Miranda Henley. This is the reason I have come here today. I brought two gentlemen with me as you can see. This is Anthony Cooper and Jeremy Cooper, friends of mine and working hands on my ranch. I brought them with me as bodyguards and extra eyes to make sure I wasn't followed out here."

Anthony and Jeremy both nodded to the crowd and laughed. Anthony was tall and lanky with blond hair as long as mine, pulled into a pony tail at the base of his long neck. He wore faded blue jeans a few sized more than he needed to wear, and what I could only assume had been a white tee shirt once upon a time. Over his shoulder he carried an automatic weapon on a sling. Every bit of ammunition the trio carried had been removed and placed on the table of their own doing. A sign of trust my father took as seriously as a good old fashioned hand shake and the word of a good man. Jeremy's thick frame and round face barely held brotherly features enough to match that of his sibling. His eyes were the same shade of hazel as Anthony's own eyes and his hair was almost identical all the way down to how he wore it. Besides these two features, nothing about the brothers seemed to suggest relation. Even Jeremy's clothing seemed to fit him better and didn't look as disheveled either.

Mr. Glover rubbed his hands together nervously as Angela passed each of the trio a cup of coffee. After a long draw from his mug, he continued. "Last week my home was attacked by a band of thieves. Up until that point, I had no need to have contact with anyone from the outside. I have lost everything now. They raided my place and took everything they could carry. It wasn't worth the violence to try and defend the place, so the boys and I ran. We headed to my bug out location but apparently someone set the place on fire and burned it to the ground. I picked through what I could, but there wasn't much the fire hasn't taken from me. We are currently heading up the highway and into Utah to see if my brother is alright. We decided it best to take a detour first and inform you of the condition of downtown.

"Most all of the stores have now been looted. Just about every window is busted out of every business in Baker. Nothing of any good is left out there, not a scrap. Looks just like a war zone too.

Darkness Falls

The smell is horrible like you wouldn't believe. Idiots have no idea how to handle their dead. If people aren't already getting sick out there, they will be soon. Best for you guys to keep your eyes out for anyone who looks sickly. Also, we saw two different bands of looters in town. Apparently they are having some sort of turf war. They are heavily armed and some seem to be trained well in how to use the weapons they carry. You would be wise to stay out of downtown at all costs if you can. They won't think twice to kill you on site. I watched them gun a man down over water. Nothing I could do. There is just far too many of them for the three of us to handle."

"How many are we talking about here, Gordon?" My mother asked as she held Jade in her lap and watched her eat her gummy bears.

"One group looked like maybe ten men and eight women. Those were the ones that attacked my place. The other band is roughly twenty men or more. I didn't see any women with them at all, though that is not to say they don't have some hiding out somewhere. We didn't see a single kid as we passed through town either, at least not alive anyway." Mr. Glover closed his eyes. "Did manage to see a small group of teenage boys ransacking what was left of the jewelry store on the corner of 5th and Patrick Creek."

"I am not sure what you need from us Gordon, but we are willing to help in any way we can." My father said.

"Well, I was hoping you could give us a place to sleep for the night, some supplies for the road and a hot meal or two. In trade of course, for not only the information I just gave you, but for more I will share only with you, Jared." Mr. Glover stated before tossing a small leather bag onto the table in front of my father. "Not to mention the contents of that bag."

"That wouldn't be what I think it is, would it Gordon?" My dad smirked.

"It is just that. What I am asking for can only be properly paid in silver. I need enough food and supplies to handle three people for at least a week or more, enough ammo to keep us safe for the trip up the highway and over the ridge into Utah, and some supplies for our first aid kit. That is if you are willing to part with it. We don't have much else in trade, but if you have a set of wheels that can run, I have something else you might be interested in I would be willing to trade as well."

My mind began to run down the list of items I knew we had in each and every stock room and shed across the property. Surely according to my calculations we had enough food to spare these men. We had an entire forty foot shipping container full of supplies for refugees alone. But I could tell by the look on my father's face he wasn't about to let on to anyone that a stash like that even existed. No matter how much trust there seemed to be between my father and Mr. Glover, my father would be keeping the aces in his deck top secret. I watched my father's eye pan from one face to another and back again.

My father smiled, "As far as the silver in exchange for the goods, you have my word. It will take some time however to get everything in order as you know. You are asking for enough to get you through and my family has to be sure we can handle such an order. There is a small bunkhouse out by the horses you can stay in for the night. I'll have someone run down fresh linens for each of you. There is a small bathroom there as well with a shower to get cleaned up. If you don't mind, I'll be holding onto your ammo for the length of time you are guests here. No offense, but my family and their safety is my top priority. You will get a hot meal tonight and one in the morning. Hopefully by then not only will your goods be ready, but you will be rested enough to be on your way?"

Mr. Glover nodded, "I have no problem with your terms. I know you are a good man, Jared. As far as the other matter at hand, we shall speak of it alone if you don't mind."

An hour after the meeting on the deck broke up and I watched my father take a walk with Mr. Glover, I found myself sneaking off to the refugee storage with Emily to see about gathering the supplies as needed. Matt and Travis escorted the other two gentlemen to the bunkhouse with linens in order to distract them. The last thing any of us needed was for someone to figure out how much we had or where it had been stored. To the untrained eye, I was simply taking a walk across the yard to the large chicken coop with a bucket of feed for the chickens. A daily duty no one would think twice about seeing two teenage girls doing. I popped the latch to the gate leading into the large chicken yard and motioned for Emily to go in first. Secretly I giggled to myself about how she had been in charge of chicken care since the moment she moved onto Compound property, and right below her feet hid a vast storage of food she had no knowledge of. I quickly secured the latch behind me and made my way across the yard, pushing chickens out of the path with my feet. When we reached the chicken house Emily opened the large door to allow us to walk in, and closed it behind us.

"Fallon, why did you drag me way out here anyway? It isn't like we are going to give them some of the chickens, right?" Emily's eyes burned with confusion.

"Trust me. Have you gotten the chance to do any coop cleaning duties yet?" I asked in a teasing manner. Emily nodded slowly and looked about the coop as if to check the need for another round. "Didn't you ever wonder what the ring bolted into the floor is for?"

"Angela told me it was bolted there to strap down feed buckets back when the goats used to be out here with the chickens. It kept them from knocking over the food." Emily informed with a confused smile.

"Well, part of that is true. Look, pull all the straw away from that end of the floor and pull that ring as hard as you can." I teased, knowing all too well I was about to blow her mind.

Emily's eyes widened in surprise as her mouth fell open, searching the floor. "There is crap stored in here?"

I laughed aloud, "Not in here, but under here. That ring opens the floor to a hatch cover. Open that and climb down the ladder into a small hallway. There is a forty foot shipping container under you right now packed ceiling to floor in boxes of goods for refugees."

"You are shitting me! Are you serious?" Emily whispered as she frantically dug the straw away and found the ring.

"You'll need a flashlight to see where you are going." I informed as she yanked the floor up to reveal the hidden hatch door. "Now that you are a full-fledged member of our crazy nuthouse life, you should know that under almost every inch of this place there is something hiding out of sight. In fact if you pull up the floor of the goat house you will find a twenty foot shipping container of nothing but sugar, salt, coffee and beans."

"Nothing of any of this has been talked about at the meetings every week. Why is that?" Emily asked as she opened the hatch and peered inside into the darkness.

"Common Compound knowledge. We don't include any of it

in our weekly calculations or reports. It is just one of those things that we know about but don't count on having." I laughed as I climbed down the ladder and turned on my flashlight. "My dad has always been big on having multiple layers of storage for different purposes. This particular refugee storage was originally set up to handle a crashing economy. We could pass out the goods to people in town if we have to, in order to keep people from starving to death I guess."

Emily climbed down the ladder and stood next to me as I moved the light across the small hallway to find the container doors. I quickly dug into the pocket of my blue jeans and found the small list I had made with my mother just after the meeting with our guests. There were items in this container she wanted me to bring up for her as quickly as possible. I handed Emily the flashlight and released the handle on the set of double doors and pulled. Both doors protested before squealing open to allow enough space for two people to fit through easily. From behind me I heard Emily gasp and I smiled at myself, relishing in her shock and amazement. There before us sat a wall consisting of white boxes from floor to ceiling just behind the doors. I unhooked a spare ladder from the inside of the door and leaned it against one of the columns of boxes. I climbed up and quickly grabbed one of the boxes from the top of the wall and passed it to a very astonished Emily before grabbing a second one and climbing back down.

"We only need three of these. It might be best if we make sure we aren't noticed when we haul them back." I smiled as I passed the next box.

"You got it! I'll start hauling these up into the coop and you can close the doors." Emily said as she set the flashlight down and shimmied back up the ladder.

I passed up each box one by one and closed up the storage container before heading back up the ladder myself. We shut the hatch and the floor before pushing all the straw back over the area in order to cover our tracks. Once Emily double checked the coast was clear, we set out across the chicken yard, through the gate and across the property to deliver the boxes to my mother. My father and Mr. Glover were still off in conversation somewhere and the two other men were nowhere to be seen.

Megan sat in a chair at the large banquet table with her head in her hands, rocking slowly back and forth in her chair looking increasingly uncomfortable. Cassidy, Cassandra, Becky and Bobby were sitting on the deck having a tea party next to Bentley's cradle while my mother and Angela rubbed Megan's back. This looked very much like a situation we didn't need with extra guests hanging around the property. I set the boxes down on the table and ran to check on Bentley who was sleeping peacefully even with the noise from the children. He didn't seem to mind them much as long as they weren't touching him of course.

"Emily, can you please go alert Sarah of Megan's condition? She is in second phase by now and things could move very quickly from this point on." My mother spoke with a gentle tone.

Emily nodded and ran as fast as she could off the deck and across the dirt to the medical building. Seconds later she bolted back through the door with Sarah close behind her. At the moment they reached the stairs I heard a noise that resembled that of a massive water bucket being turn over on cement, followed seconds later by screaming children who scattered in every direction possible. Megan's water had broken. This situation had now become critical. I handed Bentley to Emily and instructed her to collect the children and head to my cabin to read stories to them. In a blink, she was gone. I had only seconds to make it across the yard to the emergency siren and yank the crank a few times before heading for the medical building ahead of Sarah to prepare the room. The siren rang a long and loud blast from one side of our complex to the other.

Darting up the ramp and into the building I found Travis frantically digging through a cabinet. He looked up only briefly and smiled from ear to ear. This was the moment we had all been waiting for. The most glorious and stressful day of all of our lives was finally happening. I heard Megan scream just as the sound of feet hit the ramp. I looked out the window to see my mother let go of Megan and run the large yellow flag up the flag pole in the herb garden. This was the signal used to alert everyone that Megan was in labor and no one was to enter the medical building until it was over.

In a matter of seconds, Megan and Sarah barreled through the medical building door with Angela and my mother close behind them. I managed to get the water running in the birthing tub housed in the recovery room's bathroom while Sarah helped

Megan out of her clothing. I stepped out of the room and into the waiting area in time to see a frantic Travis breeze past me with a box of gloves and a handheld fetal heart monitor.

"She is dilated to eight and thin as paper! Travis, where are you boy!" Sarah called out from the bathroom just as Travis stepped into view.

I took this as a cue that my assistance was no longer required. Everyone had a duty in line for the day Megan's baby would be born. Mine was to hit the siren, fill the tub and return to let everyone know the latest and juiciest news on how long it would take. I was also to help Emily with the younger children. As far as my duties were concerned, my job here had been completed.

I gently closed the medical building's door just as chaos erupted inside. As far as I could tell, Megan was having another contraction and was being told to breathe.

CHAPTER SEVEN

"You kissed her?" Matt laughed in a whisper as he sat down next to me. "What the hell were you thinking, Jacob? Did she punch you?"

I smiled to myself remembering the shocked look on her face; her eyes wide in confusion. Everything had happened so quickly that I hadn't even thought about what I had been doing, until my lips were on hers. "Shut up Matt. She didn't hit me. She just looked at me as if I had single handedly just brought the grid up or something. I'm not even sure she knew what to say."

Matt boomed with laughter. "You left her speechless. That's perfect." He shifted his weight on the edge of the log, looking around to make sure we weren't being heard. "The ball is in her court now. She needs to do a lot of thinking. Seriously, you have been laying it on pretty thick! I can't believe she hasn't noticed. I think Jared has though, watch out for him."

The last thing I needed was to have her father sit me down for a long conversation on being a man. I suspected he was well aware of my intentions with his daughter, but because she is extremely dense the relationship might be seen as safe. So far, Jared hadn't even made a move at me save for the occasional sideways glance or two.

Across the property, an emergency siren began to blare. I jumped from the log and ran up the long driveway toward the main complex, Matt running beside me. Two things could have happened to cause the siren: Megan was in labor, or we were under attack and Bentley and Fallon were in danger. As we neared, I caught sight of Emily darting this way and that, collecting the children and rushing them off to Fallon's cabin. *The same cabin I kissed her in*, I thought to myself. Little Cassidy had taken off down the driveway and right at us, her blond curls bouncing off her shoulders with each step her tiny sneakers had taken. I caught her around the waist without missing a step and kept running for Fallon's cabin. Obviously these children were scattering for a reason. The three year old girl struggled in my arm in protest, but there was no way I was going to let her go.

"Cass... what is happening?" I asked.

"We were having a tea party." She yelled as she fought against my grip. "Miss Megan popped her water balloon all over the place! So gross! Don't let it get on us!"

"She popped her what?" Matt asked just as the realization hit him. "Her water broke! Oh God. The baby is coming!"

As we reached Fallon's cabin, Emily looked frazzled as she fought to get Bobby to listen to her. She struggled to hold Bentley in one arm and drag Bobby with the other.

"Jacob, trade me rug rats." She yelled. "You take your son and I'll take Cass!"

It was the first time I could remember anyone calling Bentley my son. Though I had figured the term had slipped out in her state of panic, I welcomed it more than she could ever understand. For that was how I viewed the Compound stow-away, as my son. I quickly took Bentley in my free arm and passed the squirming three year old with the other.

After Emily managed to push the entire herd of children through the cabin door, she turned. "Thanks guys. Megan's water broke on the main deck. Fallon rushed off to the siren and hauled off to fill the tub. Everything happened so fast."

Matt frowned. "I'll get started on cleaning the mess. I am sure someone is going to ask me to do it anyway. Might as well beat them to the punch, right?" He spun on his heels and headed for the deck.

I lightly bounced Bentley on my shoulder. The chaos and noise had woken him from his nap and he was fussing again. I nodded at Emily as she disappeared into the cabin to read stories to the children. I decided at that moment it might be best if Bentley and I stay out of the way. A visit to Bacon would be in order. I

Darkness Falls

crossed the yard in an attempt to make it to the barn without being run over by everyone trying to get to the main deck. Bentley liked hanging out with me and visiting Bacon. The hog had the ability to capture his interest in a way I have never seen. This was how I normally managed to calm him down. A bottle of milk, a fresh diaper and a visit to Bacon worked every time.

I sat on the usual bench we used in our daily pig watching duty, and turned Bentley around so that he could get a better view. In a matter of seconds he calmed down when he caught sight of Bacon, Dave's old and grumpy hog. The beast snorted and turned, lumbering over for his usual treat and pet fest. Bacon was a huge animal of what pig breed no one could be sure. To Dave he was a dog-hog. A huge porky pig who thought he was a large breed dog. Dave had originally bought him to raise for meat purposes, but had grown attached to him after living alone for so many years. Bacon, he said, began to act more like a dog then a hog… and Dave doesn't eat dog meat. Bacon was then spared a trip to the freezer and instead was given a large dog bed and toys to entertain him with. In the event he escapes the barn, he finds joy in meeting up with Sarah's hound dogs for a little cat chasing around the property. Nothing made me smile as quickly as seeing Bacon chase cats.

"Listen here little guy, I thought you told me you would have a talk with your new mom about me." I whispered to Bentley as I handed a treat from the box on the wall to Bacon. "You spend more time with her than I do."

Bentley curled his nose and stuffed his fist into his mouth, eyes wide as he watched Bacon sniff at him. Both the animal and the child made a sound that resembled a grunt. I still found myself looking at Bentley in amazement. How he managed to survive that accident, then the trip to Compound, still had me thinking that somehow he was meant to be a part of the family. That day, when I saw Fallon in the distance and covered in blood, I thought for sure she was hurt. My heart pounded hard enough to hurt my ears. It was in that moment I realized my feelings for her went far deeper than I had ever known. Then, she introduced me to Bentley and my whole world tilted on end.

"I don't know what to do with her, Bentley. She's brash, dense, and completely out of touch with reality at times. She hasn't even realized that I am the only person her age that understands what she is going through."

Through the barn doors I heard a sound I hadn't heard in almost a month. A vehicle is coming. It can't be that, nothing much can run now. I grabbed the radio on my hip and hit the on switch. I normally left it off during our visits with Bacon so that we had as much peace and quiet as possible. That was how I liked it; just the two of us in silence. Whatever was coming was still far off from Compound's northern gate. Maybe someone is still manning the outpost and will be calling in, that is if they aren't wrapped up in the birth of Megan's baby.

The radio snapped on with a click. "Jared, you better get down here!" The panicked voice of Brian blared through the static loud and clear. "We might have a huge problem! There is a convoy coming our way! Two Hummers and a deuce and a half military transport are headed straight for us. They are coming in hot and fast." I sat bolt up on the bench. Either Mr. Glover had been followed after all, or we were about to intercept something much worse.

A second voice cracked over the radio, "Brian quick! Look through your scope and see if they are flying any flags from the convoy. If so, I need to know what they look like. Now!" Jared yelled.

I jumped to my feet and being careful not to bump Bentley too much, ran to the barn door to take a peek outside. Jared was standing on the deck, rifle in one hand and the radio in the other. Fallon looked stunned as she stood on the steps and spun to look into the distance. *Fallon is out there? She needs to take cover that stupid girl!* I screamed in my head. Brian's voice came cracking over the radio. "They have flags on all three vehicles Jared. They are blue with a yellow H on them... and they are waving at me!" There was only one thing flying that flag meant. Haven was coming. Not just Haven... but my parents!

Jared's voice filled the radio, "Stand down Brain, it is a Haven convoy. Check the vehicles to make sure they aren't being held at gun point and let them in. I'm sending Dave your way right now. Don't let them in until you have proper back up. And keep your eyes on the road... a convoy like that could have been followed."

My heart jumped into my throat as I flung the barn door open and bolted for the main deck, dropping my radio in the dirt to use my free hand to support Bentley. If my parents were in that convoy

I needed to know about it. I hadn't seen them since the day the world changed. They had left for Haven before I had left for school that day, a month ago. Matt stood slightly shaking in excitement on the deck, eyes glued in the direction the convoy would be arriving in. He must have had the same thought I had. I made quick work of the stairs and ran to my brother's side, Fallon right behind me. I quickly squashed the thought of passing off Bentley. If the Haven transport had been intercepted somewhere on the journey, then those vehicles weren't friendly. My hold on Bentley tightened as my eyes scanned the roadway in the distance. Fallon, Jared, Matt and our guests all stood in silence. After what felt like a lifetime, Jared's radio cracked. Our eyes snapped onto his radio in one fluid movement. "Yeah Jared...," A very happy Dave laughed. "It be Haven a callin' and all is well. They have Jessica and Robert with 'em. They be on their way up now."

My mother's voice interrupted Dave with laughter. "Hand me that damned radio you old fart.... Hey Jared, slap that damned hog, Bacon on the grill. We are starving!" She played as the sound of Dave's reprimand came through seconds before the radio fell silent.

Cheers rose up from not only the deck, but they could be heard coming from the medical building as well as Fallon's cabin. They must have had their radios on as well. I nudged Fallon and handed Bentley to her before turning to my brother to give him a hug. A second set of cheers rose up from the medical building as I turned to see my brother Travis bolting through the door and run down the ramp. I had never seen him move with such speed. The sound of the convoy grew louder, as did the cheers from the vehicles we now heard. The first behemoth rounded the curve and came into full view. The lead vehicle in the convoy was a military HV decked out in enough weapons to take out an entire city without trouble. I couldn't tell who was driving the beast, but it didn't take long to see my old friend Jasper Montgomery hanging off the side and waving frantically at us. Jasper was a Haven Kid. His parents were friends of all of us and longtime residents of the Haven complex. The only time I managed the chances to see him were on the rare occasion I had been invited on a trading mission. He had never come out to see us before.

Jasper jumped off the side of the Hummer and ran across the dirt. "Mr. Henley!" he yelled as he came within ear shot. "We left the tail vehicle at the gate in case we were followed. We didn't see anyone though. They will take the gate duty. Brian and Dave are in the transport coming in now."

Then I saw it. A two and a half ton monster rounded the corner and into view, my father behind the wheel. It didn't surprise me in the slightest that Haven managed to keep beasts such as these running. Not only were they a more militant compound, a deuce and a half military transport could run on any fuel you fed it. It made for the perfect bug out vehicle if you knew how to drive one, which Haven members did. What did manage to surprise me was the sight of seeing my father behind the wheel, and looking mightily proud to be there. The massive beast pulled alongside the tractor by the barn, making the tractor resemble a child's toy in comparison. Within seconds, everyone was running off the deck and across the dirt.

My mother jumped out of the vehicle first. She looked thinner than usual and her long brown hair had fallen from whatever style she had it in before she arrived here. Her blue jeans showed twice the damage they had before she left, and two new holes in the knees proved it. I couldn't tell what shirt she was wearing or if it was the one I had seen her in when she left. The vest she wore over it took up most of her upper frame. Automatic weapon in hand and enough gear in her tact belt to suggest she had been to hell and back gave her a look I hadn't seen on her before. She resembled a soldier returning from ground zero, excited and dirty with a story to tell. Behind her, Dave and Brian climbed out laughing, patting each other on the back with smiles from ear to ear.

"Boys!" my mother yelled as she ran across the dirt and scooped us each into her arms. "I knew I would see you all again! I just knew it! Having no contact with you turned me into hell on wheels!" She kissed us one by one before continuing. "Dave said Megan's in labor? Did I miss it?"

"You sure did!" Travis beamed. "I caught the baby myself with no help! She had a boy. His name is Michael, after his father. He came in at Seven pounds four ounces."

My mother laughed, "Shit. I missed it? I am glad you got to catch him though. How does it feel to be part of the medical wing?" She played as she patted Travis on the back for a job well done. "I need to talk to Jared right away. Something has come up and it is important. Promise, we will talk more later."

Without another word she breezed by us and headed for Jared. My father climbed out of the beast and jogged to me with a fist pump. "Did you see me boy? That monster is our newest toy! It is a gift from Fallon's uncle Charlie. This is what he was going to take leave and bring to us before the military denied his papers. Scrapped it up somewhere as usual, just like everything else he finds for us."

My father wasn't lying, Charlie never told us where he managed to score the items he continually had a habit of sending our way. No one dared to ask him either. This vehicle had been on the Compound wish list for years. Charlie kept his eyes out but until now, there wasn't hope of scoring one. I didn't want to know how he got his hands on it and frankly, I didn't care. He probably didn't steal it but knowing Charlie like I did; I knew he had to have done some haggling and trading in order to get his hands on it.

"We left Haven little over a week ago. Can you believe it? Little over a week to cross four hundred miles. That is nuts." My father informed as he ran both hands through his dark blond hair to knock the sand out. "We had to keep stopping to set cars on fire. There are bodies all over the highway. The smell out there will put hair on your chest, I tell you."

The thought turned my stomach upside down. It took my parents several days to reach us because they were cleaning up the mess on the highway, burning the dead to keep disease down. It was a disgusting thought to put it mildly.

It didn't take long to introduce the convoy to not only the members of Compound, but also the guests we had over for the night. Jasper wasn't the only member of Haven to join us for the evening; two former army ranger friends of Charlie's, and the newest members of Haven, also came along for the ride. A former FMF Corpsman named Edward Masson joined us now as well. Unlike the rest of the Haven members, Edward would be staying with us at Compound permanently. Apparently he was another one of Charlie's gifts and would be helping in the surgical area of the medical building. The convoy would be on the move again at dawn, save for the monster my dad had been driving, with all the weapons and supplies it had been loaded with. Ginny had hand selected the members of Haven that would need to protect the convoy in order to safely deliver the payload, and expected them back in a timely manner. Already the journey had taken longer than expected.

Jared, Miranda and Angela had set before us a glorious fest of smoked turkey and ham, and enough fixings to feed an entire army for a week. Due to the special nature of the gathering and the fact Megan had a safe delivery of her own, Brian opened several bottles of his homemade liquor. While we ate, one by one people stood to tell their side of the story, filling us in. My mother went next and told a tale beginning from the moment they hit the highway on the journey to Haven.

"...We were flying so fast I thought for sure Robert was going to get nailed by the cops." My mother laughed as she continued. "When traffic got heavy, he actually hit the emergency lane and flew right by everyone! I thought I was going to die. He drives like a damned maniac!" She laughed again and patted him on the back. "We got there though, and in one piece. We drove through the gates and parked in the western lot thinking we might have time to do a quick turn around and begin back. We hadn't been there but maybe an hour before the blackout happened. My biggest fear at that moment was the thought of the boys being in school and if they could make it back home safely. We agreed to spend some time at Haven to help them back on their feet before we took off. We had hopes to bring Charlie back, but no one has heard a word out of him since before the blackout. We waited to see if he was going to show up, but he didn't."

Bentley let out a whimper as I bounced him against my chest. Fallon had just fed and changed him, but apparently he still chose to fuss. It must have been all the commotion happening around the banquet table. More people than usual were in merry spirits tonight.

"I've been meaning to ask you guys, who the heck is that?" My father laughed as he pointed to the baby I held in my arms.

Jared boomed with laughter. "Well Robert that would be your new grandson Bentley. Seems on the journey home the day of the blackout, your boys and my Fallon rescued him from a car accident that killed his mother. Fallon and Jacob are raising the boy now. Congratulations grandpa!"

"Oh hell no! Don't you dare refer to me by the name Grandpa you old dirt bag! If I am one then so are you." My father

Darkness Falls

laughed as he stood and walked over to take a peek.

I pulled back the blanket enough for my parents to get a good look at the baby. "His name is Bentley." I whispered as my father looked down with an odd smirk on his face.

"Well I'll be damned my boy… that is a baby. I'm not ready for this grandpa business, but I guess if you are claiming responsibility for him then I have no choice." He whispered as he patted the top of my head.

With that, another round of alcohol was ordered and the celebrations continued. My mother asked to take Bentley and cooed at him as she spoke with Fallon about his rescue and current care. Fallon smiled brightly as she spoke in hushed tones, gushing over Bentley with the pride of a new mother. I watched the two walk off to the farthest corner of the deck and sit at a small table normally used for the children. Oddly enough, my mother had taken the idea of Bentley far better than I had expected.

Mr. Glover stood for his turn and retold the tale of how he managed to make it here, including the information about the gangs forming and turf wars in downtown. This became something of a hot topic as the Haven members were more interested in the gang activity than the meal that had been prepared in their honor. From what I gathered, gangs had become a problem in every small town they passed on their travels to Compound. Droves of hungry people had been resorting to extreme violence to feed their families. The criminal element had begun to thrive in all areas, forcing small bands of people to become violent themselves, or get the hell out of town. Refugees fleeing into the more rural areas were becoming more and more common. The biggest battle in the last couple of weeks had been over water. The desert was no place to be caught in without water and the town and city water pumps were no longer operational. Those that owned large water supplies held the control and used this power to get anything they wanted.

I couldn't hear another word of it and decided to take a walk. Though I had wanted to know how the world outside the gates had been coping, I discovered I was much happier before I knew the truth. I couldn't go visit Bacon again, not without Bentley. The visits weren't the same without him and right now, my mother wasn't going to hand him over. Visiting the goats was out of the question as well for the same reason. I just wasn't in the mood for it. I decided that maybe I would occupy my time with a check of

Fallon's firewood supply. She just didn't have the time to refill her ring of wood what with her constant care of Bentley and all. Every couple of days I would secretly fill it for her, hoping she wouldn't figure out who had done it. It was just another way I could make sure that her and Bentley were staying warm at night.

I walked around the side of her cabin and noticed the ring was already full. Frowning, I snatched up a couple of chunks and walked back to her porch. *She'll want to have a warm cabin here shortly. It is already getting chilly,* I told myself as I opened her front door. The cabin was chilly, as usual. Even in the spring the weather in the desert could confuse a person. Hot days and cold nights could last clear until June. I popped the stove open and packed it for a large enough fire to take the chill off, but small enough to not bake them as she slept. *Stupid girl never thinks to light a fire before the chill hits, only after,* I scolded in my mind. With summer coming, she wouldn't have to worry about a fire too much. But come next winter she better watch her wood and her fire or Bentley will freeze.

Once the fire began to take on its own, I slammed the last of the wood onto the floor and pulled up a chair to watch the flames. I wasn't about to leave until I knew without a doubt the fire wouldn't go out on her. Twice in the last two weeks I walked into this very room in the middle of the night while doing my rounds and saw the fire had gone cold. She would kill me if she knew I had been in her cabin while she slept, but I wasn't going to tell her. I had been out walking and the lack of smoke coming from the cabin had tipped me off. I walked the property most nights, unable to sleep. In fact, I hadn't been sleeping well at all these days. In truth, I checked on everyone's cabins, though Fallon's had been the only one I had ever entered in the middle of the night.

I rubbed my eyes with the palms of my hands, placing my elbows on my knees. The lack of sleep must have been getting to me lately. I just seemed more exhausted than usual.

"So this is the place huh? Looks pretty good. Wish I could have been here to help you guys finish it." My father said as he walked through the door. "I have to say, the job here is top notch."

I groaned when I looked up to find my father and Jared entering the room holding three glasses. One of them I knew would be mine... and they were alone. This could only mean one thing: they saw me come down and check the wood, and they knew the best time to catch me alone would be while I started the fire for

Fallon. *Damn my luck*, I thought. I wasn't ready for what I knew they wanted to talk about.

"I see you are starting my daughter's fire again. She has never been good about remembering to do that herself." Jared offered as he pulled up a chair alongside my father and across the table from me. "You fill her wood ring for her too."

"I do. She doesn't have the time to do it herself." I stated, trying not to take my eyes off the fire burning within the stove. I was now cornered with no escape. There was no way to even get to the door as they had chosen to sit in such a way as to block it from me. Not that I wanted to run really. They wanted to talk to me about Fallon and Bentley, and I knew it. "I don't want Bentley to get cold at night."

My father slipped one of the glasses in front of me and laughed. "A father always does whatever it takes for his kids. It is part of being a man, son. I can't say I'll ever get used to the idea of you stepping up to the plate like this at such a young age, but the world is a different place now. I am proud of you for helping make sure that baby made it here safely. Rescuing that child took guts and heart." He took a sip from his glass. "You don't have to take Bentley on like you have. If he is too much…"

"You aren't talking me out of this, are you Dad? I honestly don't care how anyone feels about it. Bentley is part of my responsibilities around here. I chose that for myself. Screw my age. I am not going to pawn him off on someone else just to make life easier on myself. Nothing is easy after the blackout. Nothing will be the same either." I argued.

"I am not trying to talk you out of being a father. Hell, I would have done the very same thing you did. You are much more mature for your age then most boys." My father smiled, "We also both know how you feel about Fallon, which is why we are here."

"Oh holy hell. Shoot me. Just shoot me!" I slumped down in my chair in an attempt to hide. "Please for the love of God! I kissed her one freaking time! I won't touch her ever again. Just please don't try and have a sex talk or something because I will seriously die where I sit."

Jared laughed. "Well hell boy I was unaware you had kissed her. Did she hit you? Rumor has it she punched the last guy that tried to kiss her." I shook my head making Jared laugh even harder. "Then you are a lucky man, Jacob."

My dad nudged Jared with a grin. "These kids will be the death of us old man. Mark my words."

"Give me a break Dad. She didn't kiss me back and probably didn't punch me only because I surprised her with it. Regardless, it doesn't look like anything will ever come of it anyway. She doesn't see me like that. I'm like a brother to her." I frowned.

"Ouch, that is harsh." Jared grinned. "Well thank you for being honest with me about kissing my teenage daughter. Of course, you know now that I have to warn you against ever laying a hand on her again. I have to threaten you; it is in my job description."

I laughed. "Mr. Henley, I promise I won't harm a single hair on her head. By the way, what the hell is in the glass? It smells foul."

Jared smiled at my father, and then looked at me. "That would be Brian's super-secret zombie killing brew, also known as gut rot and cola. We mixed it for you to take the edge off. Powerful stuff it is. You may be a man now, but even your dad can't handle it straight up like I can."

"You damned dirt bag! Insulting my manhood in front of my son like that? You are such an ass, Jared." My father laughed as he motioned to my glass. "He is man enough to share a child with your daughter; he is man enough to down that glass without gagging on it."

"Watch your words there, Robert. That is my daughter you are talking about." Jared played before taking a swing from his glass. "I admit though, I am not sure what he is making this crap out of but it tastes like pig shit."

All three of us roared in laughter. I was thankful the topic of conversation had changed at that point. I knew the effects of the zombie brew had a huge hand in lightening the mood between the two and distracted them from digging any deeper into my feelings for Fallon.

CHAPTER EIGHT

I moved slowly to be sure I wouldn't roll right off the earth and fly off into space. My head pounded with the sounds of a million marching bands multiplied by ten megaphones. I couldn't be sure exactly, but I was beginning to think I had been hung by my ankles and beaten like a piñata all night by crazed children hyped up on sugar and cola. Even the sounds of the crickets chirping made me want to beat them with the largest sledge hammer I could find; probably the very same sledge hammer some idiot had used on my head last night. If I ever found that bastard I was going to skin him alive. Promise.

I lifted one hand to my head in an attempt to find whatever head injury had been causing the massive amount of pain. I felt hair. Nothing but hair. Now my head was swimming, right along with my stomach. Did I… am I on a ship? Everything is moving! I rolled again until I was no longer on my side. I needed both my hands to hang on to the earth. Two hands. If I didn't make it…

I opened one eye, the one that wasn't hurting as much. Through the fog I could see Fallon's face just inches from mine with the biggest grin I have ever seen. Her bright green eyes glistened in the light like emeralds. The bright rays of the dawn licked across her soft skin, dancing off in all directions like reflected fire. I squeezed my eyes closed praying I wouldn't vomit and opened them again. She still lay there, just inches from my face; her warm, sweet breath caressing my face like a gentle wind on a warm day.

"Did you sleep well sexy?" She spoke in barely a whisper. I slowly nodded, closing my eyes so that the world wouldn't spin. She giggled and got closer before continuing. "Good! Rise and shine you jerk!" She screamed right into my face.

Sheer terror ripped through me as I sat bolt up, smashing my head on the underside of the banquet table. Now even my vision blurred as I fought to focus. There was laughing all around me. I opened my eyes again and waited for the tilt-a-whirl in my head to slow down enough to take it all in. I wore only my navy blue boxers and hiking boots, unlaced and without socks. *What the hell? Where are my pants?* I thought to myself. I looked around me and found only the wooden floor of the main deck, the underside of the banquet table above me, and a sea of legs around me. I looked to where I had seen Fallon lying beside me and she was no longer there. Instead, she was standing beside the table tapping her foot in irritation. The laughing continued.

I slowly pulled myself up the edge of the table to see who I would need to apologize to later. Enjoying their morning coffee around the end of the table as usual, sat my mother, Miranda, Angela and Fallon. Perfect. The hen house caught me in my underwear. I would have some explaining to do later, that was, once I remember what the hell happened to me last night. Obviously Fallon had been well aware of my misdeeds by the look she was currently giving me.

"You...," Fallon scolded, as she grabbed my arm and pulled me out from under the table. "Do you remember what you did last night?"

"No ma'am, but I am sure you will gladly yell it at me later." I murmured as I tried to stand up. Even more laughter came from the peanut gallery, this time even louder. I stood as straight as I could, dusted myself off and continued. "Ladies, if you don't mind... I am off." I walked off as quickly as I could in the direction of the last place I remembered being last night; Fallon's dining room. My pants must have been there for some reason, though how I lost them in the first place was a mystery to me.

I tried to piece it all together as I walked. My father and Jared had a talk with me about Fallon and Bentley. They challenged me to drink the glass of gut rot without gagging and I did it without flinching, just like a man they said. They celebrated my coming of age by fetching me another glass. After that, things got really fuzzy.

I thought I remembered a few challenges going down last night but I couldn't remember a thing clearly. Since I couldn't find my pants anywhere in Fallon's house, I decided I would at least use her shower in an attempt to not only wake up, but clean up enough to be considered a living being. However, in my condition I had forgotten I needed a fire to heat the water. Ice water blasted my face like being pushed into a polar lake naked and in the dead of artic winter. I screamed and jumped back, but it was too late for that.

The laughing just outside the shower curtain had caught my attention. "It's freezing in here! For the love of all thing woman! Start a fire!"

"Not on your life." Fallon laughed and flung the curtain open.

"Damn you!" I yelled as I tried to cover myself with my hands.

"You are the biggest idiot I have ever met. Do you want to know what you don't remember? By the way, I laid your clothing out on my bed. Don't start thinking it will become a habit or anything." She teased as she closed the shower curtain. "You came down here to kindly light a fire for me and got into a conversation with my father and your father. Obviously the three of you idiots had been drinking that crap Brian has been brewing because you moved your little party back to the deck and joined the other guys. Before any of us knew what was going on, you jumped onto the banquet table and declared your love for me in front of everyone."

I flung the curtain open in shock. "I didn't!"

Fallon crossed her arms. "You sure did! Not only that but you told everyone that Bentley will now and forever be your son. Then you asked me to marry you! To make matters much worse, our fathers both jumped onto the table and declared the whole thing acceptable! They agreed with you and elected Dave to do the ceremony. You then tried to convince everyone you were a real man by taking your pants off and wearing them on your head... chanting and dancing around like a maniac about some sort of coming of age thing and how you were now a man."

The shower curtain still open, I leaned back against the shower wall and put my face in my hands. "Dear God no. Please say you are lying."

"Wish I were sweet cheeks, because you weren't the only one. Our fathers were wearing their pants on their heads as well. Dave played his banjo for the three of you. I even think Edward got in on the party after I left. I found him sleeping out by the chicken coop. Hell of a way to be welcomed into Compound. I found my dad passed out with your dad down by the goat house. I don't even want to know…"

I opened my eyes and caught her gaze headed south of the border and quickly covered myself back up. "I… I'm sorry?"

"Don't mention it again. Apparently Brain took you three out to taste some of his newest creations at some point last night. We have all decided to blame Brian for the whole mess. However, you would be wise to sober up quickly and be ready to face the masses." She declared as she spun on her heals and left the room.

Asshat. That was the new name I was giving myself… for the rest of my life.

I stepped onto the main deck of the complex less than an hour later, feeling much better than I did when I had been so rudely awakened earlier. Angela giggled as she handed me a cup of coffee followed by a kiss on the cheek and a hug. I took a seat next to my mother who giggled into her coffee cup before taking a sip. Megan had managed to make it out of the medical building with her son, and rocked him slowly in her arms as she whispered with Sarah about how adorable he was. Miranda sat with Fallon, both sets of eyes on me and giggling like school girls as they slowing began pointing over their heads. I followed their finger pointing only to find the source of their glee: my pants were on the roof of my cabin just behind them, my socks were hanging off the gutters, and my shirt hung from my mother's hanging flower box from the loft's dormered window. I rolled my eyes with a groan and ran my hands through my hair before giving up and toasting them on their find. I raised my coffee cup with a smile and took a sip while they laughed at me in true school girl fashion. Today was going to prove to be a day I will never live down. My whole life will be boiled down to the one memory of the night I made a fool of myself because of homemade hooch. *Thanks a lot Brian*, I thought to myself.

Jared and my father stumbled onto the deck in a haze of groans and curse words. Jared too was in nothing but his underwear and boots. However, my father was wearing one of Sarah's gardening dresses. A flash of a memory flooded my mind.

Brian had given it to him after we had finished tasting his latest creations because my father apparently drinks like a sissy. I had a blur of a memory of my father playfully cursing out Dave and Brian, yet agreeing to wear the dress. After that, everything becomes fuzzy again and flashes hit of the four of us singing show tunes. *And did we actually try to go cow tipping last night?* I asked myself.

My father pulled up a chair next to me without a word spoken to anyone as Angela passed him a cup of coffee. Jared sunk into a chair on the other side of my father and groaned before giggling and looking at the ladies around the table. The hen house erupted in laughter when Angela commented on the color of the dress matching my father's eyes. At least I wasn't the only one to make a fool of myself last night. I couldn't be sure of the rest of the men on Compound, but the three of us must have been the life of the party.

"Did you throw up yet this morning son?" My father whispered from the corner of his mouth.

"No, at least not that I can remember anyway." I whispered back.

"Well then you are doing better than I. That new brew we were trying last night happens to be a selection of moonshine Dave and Brian have been tinkering with." My father whispered as he rubbed his head with one hand.

That would explain the lack of memory and the upside down spinning in my gut. I once helped Brian and Dave taste some moonshine they made several months back. I barely remember the three of us tasting some new recipes and then I threw up on my shoes and fell asleep. Though we had agreed never to tell anyone about that incident, I suspected that my father had found out. I also suspected that he never told my mother about any of it. That was a good thing, the less she knew the better.

"Mr. Masson is in the shower. Since he was located in the chicken coop this morning, I take it you boys had given him the old Compound Welcome. He looked nearly just as bad as you three do. I would however like to know how such a large black man ended up in such a small dress? He looked to be busting at the seams in that thing." Miranda giggled.

"It is simple. They are sissy drinkers!" Brian boomed as he rounded the corner and cleared several steps at a time onto the deck. "Sissy drinkers wear dresses. Good morning everyone, it is a beautiful day today."

Brian's excitement was more proof that he must sample his moonshine more often than the rest of us. He didn't look hung over in the slightest, and smelled of fresh soap and aftershave hinting at his recent shower. Fresh blue jeans hugged his thick legs so tightly they reminded me of sausage casings and his clean grey shirt looked freshly pressed. Obviously he had taken to great lengths to rub it in our faces that he survived the night without looking like a train wreck. Even his salt and pepper hair had been brushed back and gelled to perfection. He smiled at me and winked before walking over to the table and pulling up a chair.

"The Haven crew is preparing to leave. They would like you to go meet with them and Gordon before they depart. Anthony and Jeremy are down there with them. It looks to me like they might be giving our guests protective cover to the state line." Brian smiled as Angela handed him a cup of coffee. "Though, you might want to go clean yourself up Jared before you head down there... you are still in your under shorts."

Gordon, Anthony, and Jeremy would indeed be heading out along with the crew from Haven. After the private meeting the night before, Jared had apparently given them one of the old pickup trucks that Dave had set up to run on wood gas years ago. Dave hadn't been happy to part with the truck but Jared had been insistent that Mr. Glover made a far bigger trade for it. Fallon and Matt helped to load the supplies they would need into the back while Jasper and Travis checked the truck over with Dave to make sure it could handle the trip. Word around Compound was that the group would be leaving in less than half an hour. My parents delivered a few boxes of supplies to the crew from Haven and wished them luck and safety in their travel home. Though I wanted a longer visit with Jasper, I was assured the crew had taken longer to reach us than expected. With the tight timeline they had no choice but to do a quick turnaround or Haven would send a secondary team to search for them.

After a couple of rounds of well wishes and a triple check of the gear, the vehicles roared to life and headed down the hill to the northern gate while I watched from the roadside. Once I was sure they had passed through the gate and were on the open road, I turned for the main deck with the intention of having a conversation with the Compound council. The last twenty-four hours had been a blur of chaos. Touching base with the council would be a priority especially now that my parents had returned. I rang the dinner bell that hung on the post and promptly sat in a chair at the empty table.

My father must have had the same though as seconds later he pulled up a chair next to me. "Calling a council meeting I see. Good idea."

"I thought so." I managed, as I watched Jared, Miranda and Fallon heading in our direction. "If acceptable, I would like for Edward and Papa Perez to join us this time."

Once a week the entire community of Compound would gather to talk about resources and duties that would need tending. However, the primary council consisted of only certain people: Jared Henley, Dave Ratcliff, Brian Simon, and my father. Fallon and I had recently been asked to join the council before the blackout, though we had only attended one meeting before our world went dark. These meetings were rare and usually only required when new information came in that had to be discussed privately.

My father explained to Miranda that a council meeting was being called and instructed her to inform the others not to attend, but that Papa and Edward had been requested. Fallon ran to her cabin to fetch her notebook and ask Emily to babysit Bentley during the meeting. Dave took his sweet time to arrive and was still grumbling about the wood gas truck that apparently had become is favorite tinker hobby. Everyone took a seat around the table as Brian arrived with a jug of something I couldn't be sure of, and began to fill glasses.

"My son called the meeting." My father stated proudly with a playful glance at Jared. "He wants answers."

Jared leaned back in his chair and rubbed his chin with his fingers. "Well then, that is something new! Alright Jacob... you have the floor."

Instantly my mouth went as dry as the desert around me. Clearing my throat obviously wasn't working. Slowly I reached for the glass Brian handed me and cautiously took a sip. It wasn't alcoholic – excellent. "The last twenty-four hours have been chaotic for all of us. I think it best that we touch bases and get down to some serious business. With the arrival of my parents, we now know without a doubt that the blackout wasn't just local as Haven went out as well. This tells me that it could very well be wide spread. I think we all have questions and maybe together as a group, we can put the pieces together."

Jared nodded his head and leaned into the table. "Yes, the blackout is wide spread. How wide we are not sure. When your folks arrived they brought a letter from Ginny detailing an incident involving another community they trade with called Bunker Creek. It also explained that Edward Masson would be staying with us. Maybe he should begin by sharing some information."

"Yes Sir." Edward spoke in a deep yet silky voice, before clearing his throat. Even when seated, his massive frame towered over even Jared's. "I haven't had the pleasure to meet some of you yet. I am Edward Masson. I am a friend of Charlie's and the reason he scored that transport for you. I only became a member of Haven a few months ago, though I have known Ginny and the Haven council for much longer than that. I was sent here by Charlie in the hopes that I could help you in the long term with your medical department....among other things."

"Why would Charlie think we would need help with the medical department?" Fallon asked softly with a hint of confusion. "Did he know something we didn't?"

"Actually ma'am... we both did." Edward answered before taking a draw from his glass. "Bunker Creek is a compound very similar to that of your own. The biggest differences are that the people who run the place are former military soldiers, and the entire operation is underground. From air and surface you can't even tell they exist. Very few people know they are out there. Charlie and I have connections at Bunker Creek. We helped Haven set up a trade deal with them. It was that trade deal that earned me a place at Haven as a temporary home until I could be sent here. The Commander of Bunker Creek gifted the transport to Compound as a peace offering and in good faith."

"Why would they do that? They don't even know who we are... and what sort of trade deal?" I asked, now more confused than ever.

Edward glanced at Jared who nodded his approval. "Haven traded food, supplies, and goods to them in exchange for military intelligence. The transport was meant to be delivered by us, along with information a while back. They trusted Charlie's word when he explained your need for it, as well as your need for the information."

Military intelligence. Charlie and the members of Haven had been trading goods for military intelligence. I wasn't sure why that information alone came as a surprise to me. Charlie had informed Bunker Creek that Compound not only existed, but that we could also be trusted. Whatever this information was that he felt we needed, must have been important enough to risk our safety.

"When we left Bunker Creek with the transport, our goal was to drop supplies off to Haven on our way through to you. However, everything happened far too quickly and we couldn't make it here. Charlie was called back and I haven't seen him since. I sent a message to Bunker Creek to let them know the connection had yet to be made with you and that Charlie had been detained, but the messenger never returned. We suspect that is due to the blackout." Edward informed as he rested back into his chair. "Charlie and I suspected he would be detained, so we had a backup plan in place."

"What kind of backup plan?" Brian asked.

"I am the backup plan." Edward stated, "You see, I am not just here for the medical department, I was sent to deliver intelligence and help with your security needs. I am to take Charlie's place in the event he was detained. I am here to safely escort you to Sanctuary."

Sanctuary was the name we used for the top secret bunker complex deep in the north-western Rocky Mountains in Montana. The retired military complex had been purchased back in the 1950s by Haven and promptly restored. Over the years, the complex grew with renovations and had been set aside as an emergency bug out location for both Compound and Haven, to be used only in the event of complete government takeover or societal collapse. A small group of Haven members traveled to Sanctuary twice a year to check on supplies and securities in order to keep the place in running order. Though all members of Compound had an emergency map and instructions, not everyone had been there to see it. Sanctuary was thought of as the end game... our last shot at survival in a world destined to die.

"Dear God...," Brian whispered as he ran his hands through his hair, resting his elbow on the table.

Silence fell for many long moments as members of the council absorbed the shocking words Edward had spoken. My eyes moved first to my father who seemed to have been aware of this information before the council meeting. He must have had this conversation with Edward while back at Haven. That alone would explain why he had yet to say a single word since the council meeting started. Jared had the same look of determination on his face that my father had. The letter from Ginny must have explained the plan to leave Compound.

"We be a leavin' why?" Dave yelled in shock. "We gots a bunker right unda yo feet Mr. Masson."

"That bunker cannot protect you from what is coming. You see Sir, the United States government knew the EMP was coming and suspected it long before the public caught on to the possibility. Bunker Creek managed to get their hands on top secret information that detailed that not only was this information known, but that the media would be fed misleading information. This wasn't a glancing blow from the solar flare... we were hit dead on by an X-Class solar flare that made the Carrington Event look like a party trick. There was plenty of warning to alert people about it in order to prepare. Apparently activity on the sun not only didn't stop after it ended its eleven year cycle, but picked up in speed and frequency. Several massive flares have been detected happening almost daily for the past few months."

"They didn't want to tell us?" Brian asked in a panicked tone.

"No Sir. The government went to great lengths to prepare for themselves but chose to keep the flare as secret as possible. Originally, we suspected it was to avoid wide spread panic. However, the Commander at Bunker Creek assured us differently. Over the last few years, Patriot Militias have formed across the country with the intention of restoring what they feel is a failing government and justice system. They have made many attempts to take on the government in a war to return control back to the hands of the American people and out of the control of the corrupt. Not informing the general public allowed them to keep the information out of the hands of the Patriot Militias as well. The militias without an informer didn't have time to prepare."

"So, with no time to prepare they are disoriented and unorganized due to the flare... which means...," Fallon began as her green-eyed gazed turned toward me with a look of shock. "A prepared government against an unprepared militia is..."

"War." I stated matter-of-factly. "They can strike against the militia forces, and with the blackout the general public would be in the dark about the entire thing. The forces could be crushed before the grid is restored and no one would be the wiser."

"Smart kid you have there Mr. Dunn." Edward grinned at my father. "The blackout buys the government time. Bunker Creek is known as a Patriot Militia Survival Compound, former military and government officials who have pledged to fight for the people. An agent for the cause intercepted the documents for Bunker Creek. Though the actual date and time for the flare wouldn't be known until just hours before it struck, the plan detailed that in the event the flare hit, to immediately begin preplanned maneuvers to systematically wipe the known militia compounds."

"We aren't part of the Patriot Militias. This is not our war!" Brian screamed.

"We fully understand that. The reason for the exodus is to get the families to safety before the war spills onto your streets. Your current bunker can offer some protected and probably hide you for a long time, however it is not equipped to endure some of what is coming, not even Bunker Busters. Please take into account that many people in this town know you live here and what you are. When the government pours into the streets, this will be the first place the people will retreat to. You won't be able to fend off that many people and if some of the soldiers even remotely suspect this compound as a Patriot compound they will kill you and burn it to the ground without question. The safest thing to do is stow what is important to you in the bunker and head to Sanctuary. When it is all over you can come back. The chance that the people in town or the forces searching for the Patriots find your underground storage is small. It will be a constant influx of smash and dash activity."

"That might explain why chaos erupted so quickly in town after the blackout. There could have been hidden government cells in town?" Fallon asked.

"If they suspected Patriot forces before the blackout... yes." Edward nodded. "It has been a month since the blackout though, and a small band of government spies can't report back quickly enough to get forces here in that time frame. Our hope was to remove you before the blackout and now the only hope is to remove you as quickly as possible."

"Gordon bought us a little extra time." Jared spoke as he

leaned into the table and folded his hands. "He is an informant for Patriot forces. There was a cell in town. He sent them on a wild goose chance to the Nevada-California border. Once he was sure they were gone, he came here to let us know before he went east out of town. That is why I traded the wood gas truck. He bought us plenty of time to get out of Nevada and on our way Sanctuary before they figure out what went wrong and come back."

Papa Perez leaned back in his chair and huffed loudly. "Listen here boy. Here you are spoutin' off about government conspiracies and none of it makes any sense. You are trying to tell us… that the government knew this whole time that we would be caught in a blackout, decided not to tell the American people, and then planned an attack on some rebel forces while the power is down? It is a load of hog wash through and through! To top it off you want us to escape to some super stronghold location to keep us safe from this war that is going to happen that we aren't even a part of? Had you told us there was a huge gang in town of sixty men who were planning to attack us… maybe I would believe your tales! How are we to trust you anyway? We don't know you. For all we know, you infiltrated our home in an attempt to force us to leave and the rest of your gang will sneak in and take everything we have!"

"You don't have to believe me if you don't want to Mr. Perez. Regardless of the rebel wars… there are bands of people who believe that the government is just as disabled as the general public and are forming their own governments and justice systems. If one of them happens to gain enough power, it won't be long before they overthrow your home and even go so far as to have you executed for hording medicine and water. This compound is well secure and your security is tight, I've seen it myself. How many weeks or months do you think you can hold the fort? How long do you think it will take to get the grid back up?" Edward sneered. "Charlie himself sent me here with a military transport vehicle that can run and any fuel you have. If he didn't feel this family needed it, he wouldn't have risked sending me here. Haven is headed for Sanctuary and their compound is one of the most secure I have ever seen. No one wants to take any chances on this. Even if you feel the information is hog wash… better safe than sorry."

I had to admit Edward was right. Compound was built for situations such as these; however we were far too undermanned to handle a very large mob. With all of the weapons training and man power, we were still a small community compared to the massive size of Haven. "He is right. If Haven doesn't want to risk it than we shouldn't either." I leaned back in my chair and found Fallon's green eyes on me, tears welling up behind her long lashes. "You have already said yourself Jared that we have gone out of our way to stockpile goods at Sanctuary several times a year. When we prepare here, we are also preparing there."

"What we have here is only half of our stockpile. We will take as much as we can when we leave… but the fact remains that we need to stash everything and lock it down for our return. We need to get to higher ground before the valley floods with the violence." Jared said. "We just don't have the man power as it stands. We are mostly women and children. For their safety… I say we go."

"Wait!" Fallon choked. "Do we even get to think about this a few days? You are talking about a change. A huge change! You are talking about uprooting everything we have built here. Aren't we capable of taking a stand?"

"No." Dave whispered as he took a drink from his glass. "I be too old to be a fightin' like some young buck. Brian and Papa ain't young neither you know… Dunn boys be young like bucks. Can't be holdin' off nuttin' large. We go down fightin' like that, and not survivin'."

I stood from the table and pulled Fallon to a standing position, holding her to me as she melted into heavy sobs. I turned to the council before continuing, "Then I guess we need to inform the rest of Compound. We have a change of location. Jared… when do we leave?"

Jared stood facing the sad and shocked faces of the council, "First wave should leave no later than two weeks from today. Second wave will follow shortly after. That should give us plenty of time to butcher any livestock we can't take with us and preserve the meat for travel. We will move everything of value into the storage containers and bunker. Hopefully that will keep them safe until our return. We will cross pack the vehicles with supplies in case something happens along the way. I am sorry for this guys… you have my word, this is only temporary."

With that, the meeting ended. We would be leaving to Sanctuary with the hope of returning.

CHAPTER NINE

With the dawn came the silence of breakfast as no one felt the need to speak. It was quickly consumed and the table emptied, leaving only Fallon and I to enjoy our coffee in peace. Several members didn't even arrive for breakfast. The news that we would be leaving Compound for the long trek North had caused such an uproar the discussion lasted well into the night. I did my usual nightly rounds and had heard several people crying in the privacy of their own homes. When I made my way to Fallon's cabin, I didn't hear her crying. Instead I heard signing. I leaned against the wall closest to her bedroom window and listened to her sing song after beautiful song to Bentley. I wished more than anything to have been in there with her and rocking Bentley to sleep while she sang to him. She always had such a beautiful voice, yet refused to allow anyone to hear it. Now as I sat at the table picking at my bacon, I watched her sip her coffee in contemplation. She absently pushed an unruly curl behind her ear before her eyes lifted to meet my gaze. The sheer sadness across her face cut through me like a hot knife through butter.

"I am not marrying you, Jacob Dunn." She joked half-heartedly as she pushed her empty plate to the center of the table.

"That wasn't what I was thinking about." I answered as I repeated her action with my own plate. "Your dad sent Dave and Brian out before dawn to herd six head of cattle to the Parker Farm this morning in the hopes to make a trade with them for something useful in our travel to Sanctuary. I believe he is trying to score that old car trailer behind the barn."

"Oh." She frowned as she took another sip from her mug. "Six head huh? Sounds like a fair price for a trailer they have no use for. We haven't even spoken nor done any trading with the Parker Farm in little over a month. How does he know they are even still there?"

That was a good question that I didn't even know the answer for. Jared must have had some information on them recently or he wouldn't have sent Brian and Dave on such a mission. The Parkers regularly traded with us and had for many years. To my knowledge, we hadn't had any contact with them since before the blackout. If we could get our hands on the trailer, we could haul more food and supplies with us on the journey North. I had still been doing my rounds when I caught sight of Brian on horseback and Dave in one of the farm trucks leaving through the northern gate with the cattle meant for trade. The Parker Farm was a sixteen mile journey but with cattle slowing them down, I couldn't calculate the time of their return.

They weren't the only ones I saw leave this morning before the sun. I caught Miranda and Angela loading a few items into the boxes attached to one of the quads we kept on the property. When they were done, Angela returned to her house and Miranda left with the goods seemingly headed for town. I assumed she was heading out to alert the Parker Farm about the incoming cattle deal, as well as head east to Casper Ranch. Casper's place was only ten miles out from Compound and on a quad it wouldn't take nearly as long to return as it would for Dave and Brian, even with having to backtrack from Parker's. Miranda was packing with her a rifle and two side arms as she left alone through the gate. I wondered briefly at the time if she would be trading the quad which was no longer a necessary item on Compound. If so, she would be walking back alone and on foot.

I still hadn't slept and the exhaustion weakened my entire body. My third cup of coffee had helped temporarily to keep my mind alert enough to think straight, but my body protested against every move I tried to make. Blinking against my watery eyes, I caught a glimpse of Travis and Matt heading for the chicken coop in the clothing they reserved for days of slaughter. They hadn't even had breakfast yet and they were already working to cull a large portion of the flock. I pulled myself to my feet armed with my coffee cup and stepped around the edge of Megan's house to watch them enter the coop. One by one, they chose the largest birds and placed them into a wooden cage on wheels they managed to drag down with them.

"Chicken time." Fallon whispered beside me. She had managed to sneak up on my right side without my noticing. Maybe Jade had been right all along and Fallon did have super powers. "Some are for trading and some are for food storage I heard. Dad told them to leave the best layers to be brought to Sanctuary with us. We will do the same with the rabbits."

"It might take the better part of the day to do just the chickens if those two are the only ones doing the culling." I played. "There are a good sixty birds in that coop. They will hog up the slaughter house too. No one else will be able to get in there and do any butchering."

"Angela is culling rabbits later today out by the barn and feeding scraps to the Simon hounds. She thinks she can get through forty before someone else takes over." Fallon whispered before taking another sip from her mug. "She won't need the slaughter house for that. We are only taking two bucks and six of the does with us. My dad wants to trade the nursing does with litters as it is too much good meat to cull so early just for dog food."

"We are only taking two of the milk goats, the pregnant one, and a buck. Your dad said that he could trade the other bucks along the way if we can't find someone to take them here. That or butcher for dog food. Haven is apparently bringing their goats as well. We can start the breeding program up again when we get there." I said as I turned to face her. "We are going to be alright. You know that don't you?"

Her face fell as her gaze sank from my brothers to the dirt just below the edge of the deck. "The hardest part of it all... is thinking that we built the perfect property to protect all of us, but it isn't enough. I just can't see leaving something we created with the idea of standing our ground and staying. Making that journey with two babies... one of them barely two weeks old by then. It is a risky move that could put us all in danger."

I took a deep breath but decided I wouldn't argue with her. Staying here was an even riskier move on our part. There were just too many children to care for and still manage to man the gates to the North and South in the event of attack. Fallon, Angela and Megan had been trained in weapons and survival but if they were needed at the gates, only Emily could hide and protect the children with Miranda. I ran my hand through my hair and walked back to the table to refill my coffee cup. I could hear Fallon moving behind me this time, as she walked to her chair and sat down.

Today was the day we began the preparations to flee Compound. Livestock would be traded, sold or slaughtered. Belongings would be locked away into the bunker complex beneath us. All vehicles and tractors on the property would be worked over to see which ones could make the journey to safety. Fallon and I had been tasked with the inventory of Fallon's cabin. Every item would be labeled with colored strips of tape indicating whether they would be stowed in the bunker or packed into the caravan for the trip. For now, we were taking a moment to enjoy some coffee while Emily and Bentley were in the medical building visiting Sarah.

Fallon motioned behind her, "We should get started on the cabin before it gets too late. There isn't much there. If we are quick about it, maybe we can take Bentley back and give Emily the afternoon."

There really wasn't much in her cabin. As the wood cooking stove belonged to her parents when they got married, we labeled it with a red strip of tape. Red meant it would not be traveling with us and needed to be taken down to the bunker for storage. The handmade dinning set and sofa had also been labeled with red tape. There wasn't much need for them as we had been informed that not only was packing room limited, but Sanctuary was fully furnished. I had managed to dig up several empty boxes from one of the storage rooms to pack out what we could. Miranda's favorite table cloth that Fallon had been using, the curtains, and wall hangings, were neatly packed into a box that we promptly labeled with red tape before setting aside. With the agreement all meals would be as a group from now on, we packed away her dishes and cast iron cookware as well.

In the boxes meant to be packed with us to head to Sanctuary, Fallon placed her photo albums, the jewelry box her dad had made her for her eleventh birthday, and a few survival items she cherished. Watching her sort her life down to just a few boxes wasn't an easy thing to do. I tried to make it less stressful by labeling the boxes with her name and blue tape. We agreed that the cradle should probably be stored for its safety as it may not survive the journey unscathed. Bentley had been growing rapidly and soon wouldn't need it anyway. The nursery at Sanctuary had large cribs just waiting for the children who would arrive. The baby blanket I had given to him would head to Sanctuary as well as all the clothing my mother made for me as a baby, and the hand-me-downs from Megan that were still too large for her son Michael. To my surprise, everything that Bentley owned had fit into one box neatly with room to spare. I made a mental note that I would have to make or find him some toys as he got older.

"So if everything is moved, I am down to one box for me, one for Bentley, and my bedding. I can sleep him with me at night on the floor if need be. I sorted my closet and the dresser. Better than half of this is staying." Fallon called from the bedroom as she darted back and forth across the doorway. "Well that and the duffle bag for clothing and gear while traveling. I figure I only really need a couple of weeks' worth of clothes. Sanctuary has a way to wash them after all. The less I take the more food and water we can pack."

I opened my mouth to tell her she had a workable plan in place, but before I could say a word the sound of the farm truck pulling up the road broke the conversation. Not simply because the truck was loud and obviously towing something large behind it, but also because the sound was accompanied by screams and crying. With a quick glance at Fallon, I jumped from my position on the floor and ran out the cabin door and across the dirt. Looking back only briefly to see that Fallon had the same thought I had, and wasn't far behind me. Jared had been on gate watch waiting for the others to arrive from their trade missions. However, he was currently standing at the top of the road restraining a fitfully hysterical Emily who fought against him. She was screaming and punching him though he refused to let her go. The truck Brian and Dave had taken this morning was coming into view towing the car trailer the cattle had been traded for this morning.

"Sarah, what is going on?" I asked as I watched her hand Bentley to Fallon.

"Oh child...," Sarah whimpered before wiping her eyes. "It is Papa. He walked down to his place this morning to grab a few

Darkness Falls

things for Emily to take with her that hadn't been moved yet. Brian stopped in on his way home to see if he needed a ride back up the hill." She whispered as she gazed down the road. "Brian and Dave found him sitting on the porch steps alongside the box he had packed. Jared ran back on foot after Dave told him what happened... to prepare Emily for the news."

"Is he alright?" Fallon asked in a hushed tone as she gently bounced Bentley.

I already knew the answer before Sarah could give it. I turned away from the sight of Emily in hysterics and watched the farm truck with trailer pull gently to a stop in front of us. Miranda slowly climbed out of the cab, eyes red from a long spell of crying.

"He is gone, Fallon." I whispered as I pointed to the bed of the truck where Brian sat crying and holding the body of Papa Perez, gently covered in sheets.

"He was gone when they found him dear. Nothing they could do. He'd been gone a while." Sarah cried softly as she walked off in the direction of the truck.

Dave walked around the cab and off to the medical building. I could only assume he was fetching a stretcher for Papa to be taken in on. Sarah wouldn't be trying to save his life, only cleaning him up for his funeral. I pulled Fallon and Bentley into my arms and watched my mother do the same with Emily. With four uncles who refused to care for her when her parents died, Papa had been the only member of her family willing to take her in. Now that he was dead, we were all she had left.

It was deemed that Papa must have died of natural causes alone as no foul play had been suspected. No autopsy had been given. Sarah and Edward had taken great care in preparing Papa Perez and placing him gently into the wooden coffin Dave constructed in time for his service. Though Dave had never built a coffin before, he did an amazing job crafting a thing of beauty. Every detail had been handled with skill and perfection. It wasn't extravagant as Dave had figured Papa wouldn't have wanted it that way, but simple and beautiful with a carving across the top detailing a fish jumping from the water. Jared had retrieved an outfit for his burial that Emily had chosen for him to wear: a pair of black jeans, a dress shirt he wore only when the occasion called for it, and his best boots. It had been decided that Papa wouldn't be buried on

Compound land, but instead buried on his family land under the tree in his backyard. The same tree he once hung a swing in when his wife was still alive and his boys were only children. He would have wanted it that way.

Brian, Travis, and Matt had dug the grave before we arrived. My mother led a beautiful service in his honor, allowing everyone to take turns in speaking about him. Fallon and Jade sang Amazing Grace so beautifully that even those of us who had yet to cry, shed a few tears when they finished. Emily told us stories about the day she moved in with him, how stubborn he could be at times, and the funniest moments she had with him the last couple of years. We laughed, we cried, and we hugged each other tightly. My father helped Emily toss the first handful of dirt into the grave after Brian and Dave lowered Papa Perez. She kissed the first handful before letting it fall through her fingers. Travis hugged her tightly as she cried into his chest on the walk back to the truck.

Over dinner, the atmosphere was somber. Angela and Megan sat with the children and explained softly for a second time what had happened in terms they would understand. Brian brought out a jug of homemade apple cider, making a toast to the life of Papa Perez. Everyone sat in silence for many long moments just pondering the turn of events before anyone spoke.

"My uncles made it very clear they didn't want me after my parents died. If you don't mind... I would like to live with you." Emily said softly as she picked at her dinner plate.

"We would never toss you out Emily. You know that." Jared reassured her. "Our bunker here on the property has an extra wing for guests. If you like, we can go to your place tomorrow and pack up a few things to be stored there for you when you return."

Emily nodded before burying her face into his chest for another round of tears. Before long, she had cried herself to sleep against his chest, sagging into him with exhaustion. He pulled her into his arms and carried her into Megan's house to lay her on the sofa. The same exhaustion weighed heavily on the rest of us as well, though I was sure I wouldn't be able to sleep. Bentley didn't seem to have much trouble in that department. After his last bottle he burped a milk bubble at me and slipped into what I can only describe and a food coma, and lay in my arms with eyes half closed and snoring. I wiped the milky drool from his chin with the edge of his burp rag before kissing him gently on the nose.

"We need to figure out who will be in each group when it comes time to leave." Miranda spoke softly as she poured herself a second glass of apple cider. "We are taking this in two waves. Each group will leave at different times and days. Emily told me she would like to leave in the second group… it will give her a little more time to say goodbye to Papa and the property."

"Then I am leaving in the second group too." Travis stated and he crossed his arms over his chest. "I am traveling with her."

"I want Fallon, Bentley, and myself in the first group if at all possible." I offered.

Jared returned to the deck and handed Fallon her notebook and pen. "I'll need you to take some notes if you feel up for it kiddo."

Brian and Dave had traded the six head of cattle to the Parker Farm, who were not only home but had decided to bug in and stand their ground. They excitedly made the exchange as they had been having a family reunion at the time of the blackout. With the twenty extra mouths to feed, the cattle would be desperately needed. Miranda had managed to talk the Casper Ranch into buying some of our moonshine and the quad for some silver and gold she thought we might want on the travel north to Sanctuary. In the event we needed to buy something that paper money just couldn't purchase, gold and silver could be used as currency.

The two groups had been decided on based on function and need. My family would be divided into both groups to handle any security issues we may encounter along the way, and would be in charge of making sure any supplies from the armory made it into both caravans. My father, my brother Matt, and myself would go in group number one. Travis and my mother would go with group number two. The Henley family would also be split up as both Jared and Miranda had made numerous trips to Sanctuary. This was also a security measure Jared insisted on. It would keep the groups from pulling out maps that could fall into the wrong hands. Each group would have someone who knew the way without a map, and a secret map would be hidden in the event of emergency. Miranda, Fallon, and Bentley, would be traveling with my group leaving Jade and Jared to travel in the second. Jade cried that she wanted to travel with Fallon and Miranda, but Jared assured her they would be right behind us.

Angela, Cassidy, and Cassandra would also be traveling with us. This left Megan, Becky, Bobby, and little Michael for the second group. This was thought to be a good idea as each group would contain two small children and an infant in each, spreading the children out between the groups. Sarah wanted to travel in group two with the youngest of the infants in case her medical training was needed. Brian agreed to travel in the second group as well in order to be there with his wife. Edward would travel with our group so that we had someone with medical knowledge in our caravan as well. This left Emily to her wishes of traveling in the second group, and Dave to travel in the first group. Eleven people per caravan now that Papa Perez was gone.

The first group to leave would also take Angela's three barn cats that she absolutely refused to leave behind, Dave's hog, the remainder of the breeding rabbits, and several laying hens and one rooster. Jared would be taking the goats, a couple of calves, some piglets, and the three hound dogs belonging to Sarah and Brian. All others would be butchered or divided when the time came to leave. We were still unsure about the horses but thought we could give each caravan a horse if we had too. Everyone agreed the trip would be slow and dangerous. All supplies would be equally divided between both groups.

"It is safer to travel in two groups. Each group will have two vehicles. Leaving as one large group in a four vehicle caravan is asking for trouble. Those in the first group should take the military transport and the small truck with the small wood utility trailer. You can put your group's livestock in the wood trailer. This will leave the farm truck towing the car trailer and the tractor with the flatbed. We can build sides for both trailers and use one for supplies and livestock." Jared informed as he looked over Fallon's notes. "The military transport is large enough to help clear the way in front of us. We won't be far behind you. That tractor is a beast."

"Bet'ta be. It's the fastest one in the West." Dave smiled. "Won't be there ifin it gives yawl trouble. Best show you how to be talkin' to it. I find cussin' and kickin' work most times."

A round of giggles rose up around the table before we decided to call it a night. As everyone hugged and left for their homes, I walked with Fallon back to her cabin carrying Bentley as carefully as I could. I didn't want to chance waking him so I moved carefully in the dark feeling every step with a light foot. Fallon stumbled in the dark ahead of me in an attempt to get the solar porch light on and light my way. When I looked back at the main deck, only Jared stood watching us silently in the light of the deck. He nodded at me before turning on his heels and disappearing into the Henley home. I took the gesture as a pat on the back for making sure his daughter had been safe every night, and for wanting to make the journey with her and Bentley in the first group. Though I couldn't be sure that is how he meant it... that was how I was going to accept it.

I slid by Fallon in the doorway of the bedroom and placed Bentley into his cradle as gently as possible. Being careful not to make any noise, I slid the bedroom door closed being sure to leave it open just a couple of inches so that we could hear him. Fallon was sitting at her now naked dining room table running her fingers along the wooden table top. Grabbing the chair next to her I sat and reached for her other hand, holding it tightly between both of mine. We sat there silently listening to the sound of crickets and the soft breathing sounds of Bentley.

"You haven't slept in days." Fallon whispered. "You are such a stalker... hanging around my house at night and sneaking in to keep the fire going. Do you ever sleep?"

My mouth dropped open in shock. *How the hell did she know?* I thought to myself. "Not a stalker...," I finally answered, "...just a worry-wart I guess. You are right about one thing, I haven't slept. Not in days."

"You are welcome to sleep here on the sofa. You'll sneak in later tonight anyway to work the fire... you might as well be allowed to sleep here. You won't have to sneak around. I have a spare blanket in the chest and you can have the second pillow from the bed." She whispered softly as she turned to face me. "Tomorrow will be a busy day. We will be taking all my belongings to the bunker. If we have time, maybe even my parents' place too."

I placed my forehead on the table, feeling the chill of the wood against my hot face. "I think we need to send someone to check on your dad's truck. It is still in the parking lot of the high school. Maybe Dave can get it up and going again if someone hasn't ruined it or taken it by now. We could give it to the second group and it can tow one of the trailers instead of having the tractor do it. It makes a lot of sense to me. Thank you for allowing me to take your sofa, my house is crammed with people right now. I'm too tired to fight it all right now. There is just so much to do. I don't know. I need sleep."

Fallon smiled, "I'll get the pillow."

I didn't remember tending the fire, but when I awoke the next morning the coals had been allowed to die down. I could hear Fallon speaking gently to Bentley as she dressed him for the day in her bedroom. I sat up slowly and looked around her cabin. This place would be emptied today save for the bedding and boxes to be loaded into the truck for the trip North. I hadn't even had the chance to box up my own belongings and I didn't care. My biggest concern had been Fallon and Bentley. I didn't care what items of mine ended up in the truck, so long as the two people I cared about most were protected. I would need my guns as well; I would need them on a trip like this. All of them would be needed to protect the caravan. There was no way I was going to allow something to happen to Fallon or Bentley.

I folded the blanket and placed it neatly on the edge of the wood framed sofa and tapped gently on Fallon's bedroom door before entering. Her green eyes lifted to meet mine as she smiled brightly. She was dressed in a pair of dark blue jeans that has been lightly distressed as was the fashion for teenage girls. They made her legs look thinner and longer than usual. Her long auburn curls had been tossed up into a mess of a flip bun pile with long strands hanging on either side of her thin face. It reminded me of the photographs of painting in our history book of Greek Gods and Goddesses who had been worshipped by the ancient people they ruled over. I forced myself to look away when I noticed how low cut her green blouse was, as it instantly attracted my gaze. I didn't want to make her uncomfortable… or catch me looking. As always, she had donned her military boots and belt with firearm. She looked like a beautiful warrior standing there holding a pair of baby shoes and smiling.

"I am taking him to see Sarah and Edward today for a checkup and maybe some shots. He won't be happy with us." She giggled before tending to the shoes.

"He will be mad for a little while, but he will get over it. Want me to go with you?" I asked as I stepped into the room.

"Please! I am not sure I can handle watching him cry again like that. Last time I took him in he acted like Sarah was trying to kill him." She laughed as she lifted Bentley from the bed and bounced him in her arms. "I have to be heading over there in a couple of minutes. Can you grab the diaper bag?"

I picked up the bag from the edge of the bed and followed Fallon from the bedroom and through the house. There was still a slight chill in the air as the sun hadn't had the time to warm the earth beneath our feet. I readjusted the bag on my shoulder and looked around the compound for signs of life. I expected to hear the songs of crickets and birds, but instead was met with the distant sound of the hound dogs barking as they chased Angela's barn cats. We smiled at each other as we heard Dave yell from the barn for Bacon, who obviously had gotten loose and had joined in the fun.

We crossed the little yard on our journey to the main deck to grab some coffee before heading to the appointment. Sarah and Edward were likely already in the medical building checking over Bentley's file and preparing for his visit. I wasn't well versed in well baby checkups, shots, and health concerns, but I was pretty sure we would receive a little forced education from Sarah. That had been the way of it since he had come into our lives. Impromptu parenting classes seemed to follow every checkup appointment Bentley had since the day he had arrived here. I didn't mind them so much; it helped us to understand his every need. My mind wondered to our school mates and I giggled at the thought of what their reaction would be should they ever find out I was a new dad, raising an orphaned child found after the blackout.

Jared was sitting at the table when we reached it, breaking apart and cleaning his firearms in preparation of the mass exodus that would be coming at the end of next week. I counted at least three rifles and four side arms displayed in front of him, not counting the one he was presently attending to. His brown eyes lifted and met mine, though it was a brief exchange, I gathered the display of firearms had been placed in such a way as to sever as a warning for my sake. I quickly set the diaper bag into a chair, gave a nod of morning greeting, and gratefully exchanged a smile with Angela as she handed me a cup of coffee. I had a feeling I wouldn't be attending today's appointment with Fallon and Bentley. Something told me the look Jared had given me the night before, and the display of potential force would be followed by a discussion of an adult nature. I decided my best course of action would be to get it over with as soon as possible, by offering my help in the cleaning process.

I whispered into Fallon's ear that I would be rather late and might miss the appointment all together, and that it looked like her father wanted to talk. She glanced over to the table, rolled her eyes, and nodded at me before taking a cup of coffee from Angela and continuing her conversation. Turning to face Jared, I saw a small knowing smirk stretch briefly across his face, his eyes never lifting. I was done for. I pulled out the chair next to him and sat with my coffee, wondering what ungodly discussion this had been planned to become. I had kept my promise to him. I hadn't touched his daughter. It was then that I remembered I not only hadn't taken my nightly walk of the property, but that I had slept in his daughter's cabin the night before. Granted, I had slept on her sofa... but he wouldn't have known that unless he had gone in and seen me there. For all I knew, he assumed the worst of me.

"May I be of assistance?" I asked, far too formally than I had wanted it to sound.

Jared smiled before sliding a 9mm across the table to me. "Good morning Jacob. I trust you slept well?"

I knew I needed to take this opportunity to set him straight as quickly as possible. "I think so. Her sofa is quite comfortable. I am glad she insisted I not go on my walk and sleep for once."

Jared glanced up at me before returning to his cleaning kit. "I knew you would take the sofa. You didn't have to tell me that." He said as he pointed and dry fired his pistol into the distance. "I trust you and know you wouldn't do anything to break that trust. That... and I know my daughter better than anyone. Had you done anything to make her feel uncomfortable she would have slapped you. Since you don't have a black eye or a hand print across your face, I have been assured you were on your best behavior last night."

I gulped my coffee instead of the sip I planned, scorching my throat with hot liquid. I tried to pretend I didn't just boil my insides and set my cup down gently before me. "She asked me to sleep on the sofa and I was too tired to argue. She slept with Bentley in the bedroom." I informed as my sore throat cracked my words.

Jared smiled before rolling his eyes at me and setting his weapon onto the table. "I wanted to talk to you privately while everyone was off doing other things this morning."

I nodded as I glanced around the deck. Angela and Fallon

were no longer with us, leaving us alone on the expansive main deck. They must have taken the moment of distraction and snuck away to the appointment. I secretly wished I could have gone with them but knew this would be my chance to speak with Jared away from Fallon. He wasn't the only one who wanted to speak privately these days.

"When the time comes for us to leave this place...," He spoke softly as he gestured at our surroundings, "... You will be in the first wave of people, along with my daughter, the baby, and my wife. You will have your father with you as well as Edward and Dave. But this journey won't be an easy one and if something should happen to anyone, I need to know you will do whatever it takes to get my family to Sanctuary safely. I am counting on you as a man, to do whatever it takes. You are going to come across things and situations that will test your maturity and your will to survive. I hate to pressure you but you have to understand that there may well come a point where you will have to fire your weapon to save a member of your team. Though we do not believe in taking a life, you have to be prepared that if your dad, Dave or Edward cannot take the shot or are injured... you can take it." He leaned back into his chair. "If the lives of your team are threatened, you need to consider the fact you might have to do something about it. Not saying it will happen... just saying to prepare for the worst possible outcome and pray for the best."

I took a sip of my coffee. "I know this trip won't be easy. I have been thinking about this for the last couple of days. If something happens to Dave, Edward, or my dad, I will be the only one left to protect Fallon and the children. You have my word Sir... I won't allow anything to happen to those within my team, not on my watch."

"You love my daughter. You are raising a child together that isn't even yours. I have to come to grips with the fact that you are not children anymore. As much as it pains me to admit, the blackout has forced us to look at things differently. This doesn't mean I want you shacking up with my daughter... but it means that I need to stake more faith in both of you, and accept that you are young adults with more responsibilities than before. This is why I am going to give you some information I trust you will likely need for this trip." He picked up a rifle and began breaking it down for cleaning. "Gordon gave us a little more information than what came out at the meeting the other night. He gave me the directions to a secret place where the caravan will be safe. About halfway between here and Sanctuary is a cave he has spent years stockpiling with supplies and weapons. He hasn't been there in about six months and isn't heading in that direction so it is ours for now. Miranda and Robert have been informed of it, but they haven't been told everything. I want no one else to hear what I am about to tell you. No one in your team is to know the place even exists until we meet up there. It is your job to get the team safely to it... and wait for my arrival. Do I have your word?"

I nodded. "You have my word."

"It is important that no one in your team knows about any of this. If it falls into the wrong hands or something goes wrong, it could jeopardize the lives of our entire community. People will die... and we will never make it to Sanctuary in one piece."

I nodded again slowly as he leaned across the table, motioning for me to get closer. Suddenly I felt as though the fate of the entire compound rested on my shoulders. I was about to be entrusted with information he didn't even tell his own wife about. The thought had me rather uncomfortable to say the least. I could sense that what was about to be shared with me would be a double edged sword – helpful and harmful at the same time. Jared pushed the guns out of the way and pulled out a tattered piece of paper displaying a map and a list. As I picked it up and look it over, the shock of what I was looking at ripped through me.

"Is this...," I whispered as I tore my eyes from the paper. "This can't be..."

Without missing his chance, Jared proceeded to spin me a tale so outrageous he captured my complete attention.

CHAPTER TEN

For the last four days as I watched the preparations for our departure, I couldn't stop thinking about my conversation with Jared. There was more to this cave then just a few supplies and a safe harbor for travel. In fact, there was more to it than just a simple cave in the middle of nowhere. Two military transport vehicles similar to the one Edward had brought with him were sitting in the cave with our name on one of them. That was just the tip of the ice burg. There were weapons in crates: rocket launchers, automatic rifles, grenades, and even mines. There were enough supplies to arm a sixty man army and keep them fed for months. The stockpile had been created by and for the use of Patriot forces, all of it stolen from the military. I didn't even want to know how they had gotten their hands on any of it. Maybe it was best that part of the story hadn't been shared with us. It didn't matter anyway, our job was to take what we would need and get the hell out before any Patriots remembered the long forgotten stash. Gordon had informed Jared that the Patriots who formed the stash had been killed or lost years before, and that its location had not been disclosed to other forces within the area. Only Gordon and his brother knew the location and neither one of them had use for it now. He couldn't guaranty that word hadn't eventually made it to other ears however, but to his knowledge it still sat as top secret Patriot information and his brother wasn't likely to share it with anyone.

I stood with my coffee cup in hand as I watched Dave and

Brian stock the smokers with the last of the goat meat. The entire herd had been butchered, save for the ones that would be traveling the road with us to Sanctuary. Dave and Brian had spent the last four days pressure canning or smoking the meat for preservation. Both the caravans would be taking forty quart sized jars of raw packed goat to be made into soups or added to other dishes for the trip. They were currently working on fifty pound feed bags they wanted to fill with goat jerky for each caravan. I secretly knew they wouldn't get a full one hundred pounds of jerky from my goats, even with butchering out all the Nigerian Dwarf goats and the eight Boer goats. Not when they canned up so much meat in tightly packed jars, although I could have been wrong when making my weight calculations before they started harvesting the meat. The hanging weight of a few of the Boers had surprised me.

    Sarah and Edward had been busy the last four days as well, preparing medical boxes for each of the four transport vehicles. Taking into account they would need as many supplies as possible to stay in the medical building, they came to the conclusion that the building would be the last on Compound to be dealt with. Certain things had been set aside to be stored in the bunker, but for the most part everyone agreed that everything would stay in case something happened before we left. Even Travis had spent most of his time in the medical building sorting supplies into each box and labeling medications. Each vehicle would carry a box packed tightly with medications, bandages, and surgical and stitch kits… in the event we would have to patch someone up during the journey. There had even been kits put together for the animals that would be in transit. Each group would carry a kit made for just the livestock within their group. Since we would be taking one horse, the cats, rabbits, chickens, and Bacon, our livestock kit had been designed with simple bandages and wound ointments.

    Jared and my father had agreed with my idea about trying to retrieve the old pickup truck we had left at the school the day of the blackout. The morning after our conversation about the cave, I explained my idea to both of them. After a quick stop off at the armory, they left in the smallest farm truck to look into it for me. If anyone could get that truck running again I knew it would be Jared. I had expected them to return the night before, but they had yet to make it back to Compound. We had all kept our eyes out and hoped they hadn't run into trouble, but the longer they were gone the more everyone worried. Dave, Edward, and Matt had taken shifts watching the northern gate with a radio in order to relay messages at the first sign of them.

Miranda and my mother dispatched the last of the meat rabbits before taking up the job of pickling the hides of not only the rabbits, but also the other animals that had been butchered. It had been a lengthy process of salt rubs, soaking, and softening in repeated motions. Some would be stored in the bunker when finished but most would be coming along in the caravans to give a bored person something to stitch into blankets or covers along the way. Each caravan would be carrying twenty jars of rabbit meat and ten pounds of rabbit jerky, all of which had been waiting on Dave and Brian to finish the goats. For now, the meat rested in large bins of ice water to relax before handling. Only the second caravan would carry the extra meats we used to make our dog food, which was generally a raw food diet. During the journey however, there wasn't a way to keep the meat in good condition without it going bad unless we left it on the hoof... which wasn't an option. My mother had a plan to have Dave salt pack the dog food.

Megan and Angela took on the chore of helping Fallon empty her cabin into the bunker. Brian had to disassemble the wood cook stove and hauled it down as the ladies couldn't move the piece by themselves. I was surprised to see them finish the job within a couple of hours. I had offered to help them several times but had been met with irritated expressions and told to leave. Even Fallon had explained that I had lent a hand with labeling the items and that I had done enough to help them pack the place out. I had decided my best course of action was to just leave them alone to finish the job. The cabin sat completely empty now like an abandoned yet beloved shack. The vent hole for the stove as well as the windows had been boarded up on both sides in an attempt to keep wildlife out and protect the glass in the windows from breaking.

Emily and Jade had spent most of the last four days with the small children in the garden, picking what had either been ready or nearly ready for harvest. When it had been decided that we would no longer stay at Compound, nothing new had been put to seed. It wouldn't have been ready anyway and the seeds would have been wasted. Instead we held onto them with the idea of salvaging what was left of the seasons when we reached Sanctuary – providing the trip didn't get us there in the winter months. I had gone out to the garden the day before and screwed plywood down onto several of the empty boxes and drilled holes throughout the top for the bugs, but protecting the soil from being needlessly scattered in the wind. The boxes would dry out without someone to keep it moist and care for it, creating dry dust that would be lost across the pastures in the first big gusts to rip through the property. I am not sure why I bothered to try and save the soil. I had guessed we would be in need of it on our return.

Matt and I had been on armory duty, boxing up weapons for the caravans. Most of the time we floundered between working parties, doing everything from clean up duty to babysitting when our assistance had been required. We didn't need four days to figure out which of the hundreds of firearms and ammunition would go with each vehicle. In truth, it had taken us just two days to separate everything into piles and begin boxing them. Matt had come to the conclusion that whatever was left inside the armory would have to be divided in the event someone stumbled onto the shipping container we used for weapons storage. Half the stockpile would be stored within the bunker complex where we knew it would be safe. Our favorite weapons that could not make the journey had been the first to be taken to the bunker. Each caravan would take extra ammunition for each of their personal firearms, along with six automatic rifles, ten extra side arms, a bow and a harpoon... though we weren't sure there would be a need for it, it definitely would make a great addition bolted onto the transport vehicle. I tried to talk Matt into taking one of the large homemade flame throwers but he protested, saying it would be far too much fun to play with which would attract unwanted attention. I guess I had to agree, however I still felt we needed the smaller handheld ones for each group – in the event we had to set bodies on fire or something else nearly as disgusting.

"What the hell are you doing you old fart? Lay off the sauce before you burn down the smokers!" Brian yelled playfully as he yanked the bottle of moonshine from Dave's reluctant hands. Their squabble had interrupted my mental wonderings. "Keep your eye on that meat and not on the shine...," he laughed, "... you bloody drunk!"

"I ain't burn' nuttin' down... you overgrown bag o' pig shit! Ifin you didn't want me to be a drinkin' it, you shouldn't be a brewin' it!"

My radio squawked on my hip and I turned my gaze in the direction of the northern gate. Every member of Compound likely had their radio turned on in anticipation of the arrival of Jared and my father. I stepped to the edge of the large main deck and lifted the high powered binoculars I had come across in the armory the day before. Matt had come onto the radio to say he could see a dust cloud on the road and needed a stronger set of eyes to identify it as the distance was too great for him to get a good look. I peered out and panned the roadway stretching from the northern gate down passed the Perez property, finding the dust cloud in question. Two vehicles barreled down the road at a high rate of speed. As they neared I could just make out Jared's giant truck, the one we had left at the school yard the day of the blackout.

I smiled to myself before replying to my brother's request, "It is them. They are coming in hot though, not sure why yet. I am sending Brian down to meet you." I didn't need to tell Brian as he must have heard the conversation on his radio. He gave instructions to Dave before jumping onto his quad with the moonshine in hand and headed for the gate. "He is on his way now." I laughed.

I took a second look with my binoculars, being sure to scan the dust cloud left behind by the trucks. I strained to see if they were being followed but didn't see anything that would suggest it. I set the binoculars on the edge of the table and took a sip from my coffee cup. I made a mental note to be sure to ask about any trouble when the privacy allowed. The caravans would be bypassing town by taking the highway down by the split. Even then, I was sure Jared had scoped the place out from the road to check for hazards or roving gangs of people looking for supplies.

When the trucks pulled up near the barn, Jared jumped from the cab and ran toward the main deck before my dad had time to park. His jeans and tee shirt were covered in grease and what looked like a month's worth of dirt. One of his hands held an automatic rifle; the other was bandaged and covered in dried blood.

"Jacob!" he yelled before he cleared several steps at a time onto the deck. "We hit a snag out there. A big big snag... be expecting trouble and lots of it."

"What happened to your hand?" I asked as the panic began to grow inside me.

"The trouble happened. I need your radio for a minute." Jared said as he reached out his good hand after setting the rifle down.

I quickly handed over my radio as I saw my father run to the armory. Whatever was coming wasn't going to be pretty. I pulled my sidearm and double checked my clip. I had a full clip and one chambered for the ready.

"Attention all Compound residents...," Jared blared into the radio. "All women and children are to report to the bunker complex immediately. Drop what you are doing and go now. We have hostels incoming! I repeat hostels incoming! Dave, Brian, and Travis are to meet me on the main deck. Matt is to follow the women and children. Edward, I need you now!"

Rapidly the property resembled a hive, with screaming bodies running this way and that, collecting everyone they could and running for the entrance to the bunker complex. I bolted off the main deck and ran for Fallon who emerged from her cabin with Bentley held tightly in her arms. The fear showing in her eyes made my blood run cold. I screamed for her as our eyes met and together we ran toward the barn. By the time we reached the farthest stall in the corner, Miranda had pulled up the floor and had opened the hatch. I watched as Sarah and Megan began to usher the children down the stairs.

"Fallon...," I said as I turned her to face me. "Do you have everything you need?"

She nodded frantically, clutching Bentley to her chest. I grabbed her face in both my hands and kissed her hard. I could feel every ounce of fear between us blaze through our lips. "If something happens to me...," I began as I looked into her panic stricken eyes.

She blinked against her tears and hugged me, "Just don't die or I will kill you."

I smiled at her joke and kissed her hair as I watched Emily head down the stairs with Michael in her arms. Megan quickly followed, tugging a screaming Jade down with her. Miranda yelled into her radio that The Sanders and Jackson children were accounted for as well as Emily and Jade. I kissed Bentley on the head before pushing Fallon toward the hatch. Angela and my mother pulled up the rear of the pack, my mother stopping to hug me and tell me she loved me before she ran down the stairs. Mentally I was taking notes and counting those I had seen

Darkness Falls

descending into the bunker complex.

"I got them." Matt said as he grabbed my arm and nodded in the direction of the hatch.

Matt gave me a knuckle bump before he headed off to the hatch himself. I walked over to Miranda who promptly handed me her radio and climbed down the stairs closing the hatch behind her. I quickly dropped the floor back into place and kicked the straw over the top of it to hide the entrance. "Bunker... we need a body count!" I called over the radio to make sure my mental count had been accurate. Though I had already seen all the women and children had made it down safely, I needed another count to make myself feel better. Fallon's panicked voice confirmed my count and replied, "Deck... bunker is accounted for."

I nodded into my radio though no one could see. "Entrance secured. Requesting radio blackout from bunker. Bunker do you copy?" I called before I placed the radio on my hip and ran through the barn door, closing it behind me. "Bunker copy. Going dark now."

By the time I made it back to the main deck, my father had returned from the armory and was passing out a variety of automatic rifles, ammunition, and the like. Seeing them in flak jackets and tactical vests I quickly turned off Miranda's radio and tossed it into a bush, fearful that having more radios than men would somehow tip off the hostels to the whereabouts of those we were protecting. Travis was packing spare clips into his tactical vest and firing off questions about what would be coming. I promptly donned my flak jacket and tactical vest that Edward passed to me and checked every clip that had been packed with ammunition and placed onto the table. One clip in my 9mm, three clips in my vest pockets. I grabbed a loaded .22 firearm and stuffed it into my belt followed by extra ammunition before slinging an M16 over my shoulder.

"We've got two vehicles heading this way. Not sure when they will arrive but we were definitely followed here... no way they were going to let us get away that easy." Jared stated as he passed a loaded .22 to Brian as a backup sidearm. "These aren't the kind of people you are going to want to be friendly with. They are armed and dangerous."

"Why didn't we keep Miranda and Jessica to help us with this? They are a better shot than any of us are, guarantee it!" Brian replied.

"Because when we stumbled onto them they were raping a woman in the street." My father spoke through angry clenched teeth. "We didn't make it there in time to save the first woman, but we saved the second one."

"What happened to the first one?" Travis asked as his eyes widened.

Jared racked his shotgun, "When they were finished with her, they beat her head in."

My blood began to boil as anger spread through every fiber of my being like molten lava. I could see why they wouldn't want my mother or Miranda on point. If something went wrong they would be sitting ducks for a pack of monsters like these.

"Listen up. I want Brian, Jacob, and Edward with me at the gate. Travis and Dave, you two stay up here. Robert you have the bunkhouse. If they get through us you are the last defense the families have. Do not let anyone through. If one of these bastards manages to make it up here it means we went down fighting. Shot to kill." Jared informed.

Travis turned to Dave with a look of shock. Dave slowly nodded and grabbed Travis by the shoulder. In a flash, both of them ran off the deck and toward the barn, Dave taking shelter just inside the barn door and Travis behind the tractor.

Edward and Brain ran to the quad and jumped on, sharing the seat. Jared tapped my shoulder as we ran down the stairs and pointed to the small farm truck. Brian fired up the quad and barreled down the road toward the gate as we dove into the truck and fired it up.

"If anything happens to me boy, I am counting on you to protect my girls." Jared said as he kicked the truck into gear and hit the gas pedal, aiming the truck to come alongside the corner of the main deck.

My father jumped off the main deck and into the back of the truck as Jared neared, still barking orders at Travis and Dave to stay hidden and protect the bunker. We rounded the corner heading for the straight away when my father beat his fist on the top of the cab. "There they are!" he screamed and pointed across the desert. In the distance I could see a small cloud of dust rising up into the sky. I choked back the vomit that threatened to explode from my trembling body. My father jumped from the back of the truck and took shelter behind a water barrel on the side of the bunkhouse we use for seasonal farm hands or guests. When I was sure I couldn't see him anymore I glanced at Jared who had been watching from the rear view mirror. "Don't worry boy... he is more trained for this than you know. We were children of Haven after all." He said with a sad smirk as we approached the northern gate.

Jared pulled the truck around and positioned it to span across the roadway in order to help block access to Compound, and jumped from the cab. I caught sight of Edward taking point several yards passed the gatehouse near the dirt road as I jumped from the cab and ran toward Brian. "We saw them coming!" I yelled as I watched Brain dive into the gatehouse and position his rifle through the small window facing the roadway. I decided after watching Jared stand in front of the gate that I would probably do best at the other end, opposite from Brian. I ran to my position and quickly checked my flak jacket and the tactical vest I wore over it. If they managed a head shot at least my death would be quick.

We stood there silently for a couple of minutes before we saw Edward signal to us and point down the road, and then hold two fingers in our direction. Shortly after, the sound of two vehicles could be heard in the distance. I thought of Fallon and Bentley at that moment, tucked away in the bunker. My brother and Fallon would likely be armed and guarding the inner most steal door, pushing the children toward the back of the bunker complex. *Protect her Matt. Don't let them get her.* I thought to myself, pleading for my little brother to hear my thoughts. *Protect them all.*

Jared picked up his radio. "Gate is going dark. Robert and team two, maintain radio contact." He said into it before shutting off his switch and placing the radio back onto his hip. Brian and Edward followed suit, turning off their own radios. I double checked my hip before realizing that I had given my radio to Jared, and the one Miranda handed me had the power turned off and was lying in a bush by the main deck. "This is it. Follow my lead. I am going for a nonviolent approach if possible. Keep your weapons on it and cover me. If all else fails... open fire." Jared declared as he widened his stance and unclipped the strap on his hip holster before hoisting his shot gun.

My heart pounded in my ears so loudly I no longer heard the sound of the incoming vehicles. I had been trained for a situation just like this one, but nothing could prepare me for the actual event. I went through the reactions in robotic motion, dropping to one knee to the left of the post, pointing my weapon toward the road. Attention to detail. *Don't fire until the enemy moves aggressively. Always assume they are armed and dangerous. Always suspect and never let down your guard.* The words from years of training repeated within my mind. *Don't squeeze the trigger. Exhale and gently pull toward the back.* Over and over again the words repeated until I was no longer afraid of what was coming our way. I took a deep breath and let it out slowly as I watched the first truck appear in my scope.

A small silver pickup truck came into view before slowing down slightly. *One driver... two passengers... three in bed,* My mind ticked off as I panned across them. *Driver weapon status unknown... Passenger weapon status unknown... two firearms seen in the bed.* I panned to the vehicle trailing behind them. As the red pickup pulled into my line of sight, I surveyed the vehicle as quickly as possible. *One driver... one passenger... bed unknown... weapons status unknown.* I glanced up at Brian who silently counted to himself with lips moving. We were grossly outnumbered. All the members of the invading party were male and all had been assumed armed. *There are always more guns than you can see at first glance,* my father's words from years of training played in my head. I swallowed hard and took another deep breath as the silver truck pulled to a stop several feet from where Jared stood blocking the gate.

A young man not much older than me stuck his arms out the driver window and opened the door from the outside. Slowly he climbed from the cab and kicked the door closed behind him. "Gentlemen... gentlemen... we mean you no harm. We just want to talk." He grinned as he turned his hands back and forth to show he was unarmed. His short blond hair had been spiked straight up on his large head in almost a rebellious sort of way. I watched as his thin frame slowly danced in circles as he laughed. He turned to face Jared lowering his hands to pat loudly at the pockets of his faded blue jeans, an obvious display to further prove he wasn't armed. "Please... can you allow my brother to join us? He is right there in the truck." He pointed toward the passenger side of his vehicle.

The second truck pulled up slowly beside the first one, but both men stayed in their vehicle during the exchange. The firearms I had noted earlier that had been displayed with the three men in the bed of the first truck... were no longer in sight now. I wondered to myself if the others had noticed them earlier in their scopes as well. I mentally crossed my fingers and hoped they had. Then again – everyone would be treated as armed and dangerous.

"What is your business here?" Jared called out loud enough for all of those present to hear.

The young blond man sneered, lip twitching. "Come on now. You know why we are here. It wasn't easy to follow you of course. You led us on a two day goose chase all over town. You are a smart man!" He laughed as he shook his finger at Jared. "Maybe not that smart though. You got involved in something that wasn't your business. I just want to talk with you. Can you call off your dogs?" He asked as he pointed toward the gatehouse and to me. No motion has been made toward Edward, and as I could no longer see him I wondered if they even knew he had been out there.

"Not on your life. You must understand that we trust no one. After the business we interrupted… we have no reason to even trust you." Jared called out again. "What do you want?"

"Just to talk." The blond ran a finger down a long scare stretching from the top of his forehead down the length of his right cheek to his jaw. "You put a huge damper on our fun the other night." He said softly as he took two steps toward Jared. "She owed us for a trade and couldn't pay the price. We just wanted to teach her some manners." He laughed as he took another step.

The man identified as the brother opened the door the same way the driver had, and stepped free of the vehicle. He looked nothing like the driver and I suspected they weren't even related. He slowly turned in circles with his hands raised. The men standing in the bed of the truck stifled laughter at the display. Their reaction angered me and my eyes trailed from one to the other. My mind spun one option after another, feeding me numerous outcomes as the situation played out before me. Jared could take the blond one without trouble, Brian would likely go for the brother as he was the closest to him, leaving Edward and I to clean house on the guys standing in the back of the pickup truck. That would leave the two men in the red truck and there was no telling if they were armed or if there were men lying down in the bed. At the angle they had parked, I couldn't get a clear enough look. I didn't like the feeling of being outnumbered.

"One more step and I will instruct my men to open fire."

Jared said as he stepped back against the gate to gain more room. "Why are you here?"

The blond laughed and raised his hands in the air. "She never got the chance to properly pay me... you see, you stopped the transaction. As I figure it... since you were the one who stopped it... you owe me."

"I owe you nothing." Jared called out.

"Oh really?" The man laughed again. "Well... the way I hear it from my brother over there...," He pointed to the man standing by the edge of the truck. "... that you have more than enough for a fair payment. I was told you have food... water...," He grinned deeply, "even women and children here. Tell me, do you have women and children here?"

My blood pumped heatedly through my body and into my ears as my finger slowly slid closer to the trigger. The longer he played this game the more furious I became. I could tell by the body language display that Jared was just as furious as I was. I didn't dare take my eyes off the action long enough to catch a glimpse at Brian, but I assumed Jared and I weren't alone in the frustration and anger brewing in the situation before us. I continued to keep my eyes on the men in the bed of the truck.

"There are no women and children here. We are a group of men fighting for survival the same as you. I understand I disturbed your fun, but rape and murder is no way to live a life. What you did to those women is disgraceful and against the law. I could not allow you to murder another person." Jared called.

"There is no law!" the blond screamed as he buried both hands into his hair, doubling over in laughter. "You think there is law? Bullshit!" He stood up and took another step toward Jared. "I know you have at least one woman in there you can't stand... right? How about seeing as you took my woman, I take one of yours off your hands. One that maybe you could do without?"

"You've come to the wrong place for that." Jared growled.

"A child then... my brother tells me you have two beautiful daughters way out here in the middle of nowhere. If the teenager is too valuable to you, I am just fine with taking the other one. One less mouth to feed for you." The man laughed as he took yet another step closer. "Let us make a deal here. You owe me and you have something I want. You could hand over the little one or...," He grinned, "... I just take her. Your choice."

"Screw you," Jared sneered. "I warned you about coming any closer. There will be no more warnings. You have two choices right now. You can turn around and leave this place... or die."

"You are outnumbered old man. You don't have what it takes to play this game. I am giving you one more chance to hand over your youngest daughter... or my men will take her by force. If we are forced to take her... be assured we may take a likening to the others as well. Do you want their blood on your hands old man?" The blond man laughed.

Out of the corner of my eye I caught movement seconds before the sound of gun fire filled the air. A bullet shattered the windshield of the red pickup truck followed seconds later by another one. Both men in the truck slumped over, eyes wide open yet unseeing. I couldn't tell where the shot had come from but knew it had been justified. One of the men slumped over in the pickup had apparently drawn a weapon, which fell from the open window and clattered to the ground. In a matter of seconds the situation turned from a standoff to a firefight. I trained my weapon on one of the men in the back of the pickup truck that had momentarily dropped from view only to return with a weapon trained on Jared. I pulled the trigger and watched the bullet slam into his chest, knocking the weapon from his hand and toppling him off his feet and over the side of the truck. A second blast followed shortly after mine, fired from one of the men in the back of the truck. The bullet slammed into Jared's chest moments before my own bullets dropped the shooter, preventing his second shot. Flipping to three round burst, I placed three rounds in rapid succession through him as he screamed and fell backward into the bed of the truck and out of sight.

I was no longer able to hear a sound as the ringing in my ears grew so loud that all I could hear was a deafening high pitched screeching like the brakes of a freight train. The man identified as the brother fell forward, arms flung out to his sides as he stumbled and fell face first onto the dirt. The entire situation seemed to flow in silent slow motion as I moved in a half crouch from my previous position and made my way to Jared. The blond man had ducked behind his vehicle and had left my line of sight. I heard the distant sound of gunfire as the last of my hearing left me. All I had left was the feeling of what could only be described as a shockwave hitting me every couple of second to remind me to keep my head down.

Jared struggled to breathe as he laid on his back in the dirt, frantically firing his pistol under the truck with one hand, the other clutching his chest. I quickly scanned around me before touching Jared with one hand. I didn't dare pull my eyes from the truck to look at him for reassurance that he was alright. Instead I waited for his universal signal that he was uninjured... and was met with a double tap of his fingers on top of my hand. I knew exactly what that double tap meant, he wasn't breathing well but the vest had taken the shot.

    I made my way to the brother lying face down in the dirt and trained my firearm on him as I kicked him over onto his back. I didn't have to question whether he survived the shot... he was probably gone before he hit the ground. Quickly I searched the ground around him to make sure there wasn't an unattended firearm before moving on to the edge of the truck bed. Before I had time to make another move, something hit me in the back with such force I fell forward into the dirt. My hearing already having left me, I now struggled to breath, unable to catch my breath. My eyes caught sight of Brian stumbling toward me, his leg pouring blood onto the dirt as he neared. I could tell he was screaming at me but I couldn't hear a sound. I felt as though I was suffocating as my vision began to blur. I rolled onto my back and fought with the zipper of my tactical vest, frantically trying to remove it to allow access to my flak jacket. I closed my eyes as Brian reached me, pushing my hands out of the way and taking over with the zipper.

    Unable to breath, I felt myself begin to slip into darkness. I fought against it with everything I had in me, but the effort had been pointless. Brian looked panicked as he struggled to get the zipper to let loose. I had just managed to catch sight of Edward dropping to his knees next to me before my world went dark.

    Darkness fell around me as the last of my senses slipped from my control. There was nothing left for me except the inky blackness.

CHAPTER ELEVEN

I felt the weight lift from my chest but was unable to tell where the weight had come from or why it had been there. I continued to swim in the open darkness that surrounded me. Something struck me in the chest and then across the face. I continued to swim. Another blow struck me in the chest jerking me so hard I was forced to stop swimming. Suddenly I felt the urge to surface for air. I struggled to swim toward the surface, unable to tell what direction I was going in. Then I opened my eyes and inhaled sharply. Confused, I frantically choked on the air that entered my lungs, vomiting into the dirt as I fought to regain control of my breathing. Edward knelt over me, patting me on the back gently with one hand while the other helped to hold me onto my side. He smiled down at me and spoke though I was unable to hear him.

I closed my eyes briefly to slow the spinning of confusion, only to feel the sensation of floating. Not floating. I was being carried. I opened my eyes to see my father and Edward lay me in the bed of the pickup truck, Brain speaking into the radio in a blur of silent motion. I spoke but no sound left my mouth. I screamed as loudly as I could yet still... my voice stayed silent. I rolled onto my side and vomited again as the truck bumped up the road rocking back and forth, bringing me into a motion induced wave of sickness. I fought against the waves as well as the blurring in my vision. Blinking several times as I tried to steady my breathing, the high pitched sound returned to my ears and I clapped both hands over them as I tried to scream.

I fought against the urge to sleep, though I was unsure as to why I was fighting it. The sound of the freight train barreled through my head and then slipped off into the distance leaving me in silence again just before I vomited. With no options left and knowing it might stop the vomiting, I allowed sleep to claim me completely. I closed my eyes and gave into it as the darkness wrapped around me and pulled me under. My last thought had been of Fallon and my need to make sure her and Bentley would be safe.

"Jacob?" A soft and low voice slipped through the darkness, barely audible. "Jacob? Can you hear me?"

I was suddenly aware that I was not alone in the depth of the nothing. I slowly opened one eye only to see a blur of light streak through my vision. I blinked against the pain it caused and fought to find my barring.

"Jacob? Can you hear me?" the voice repeated as my eyes settled on the massive form of Edward standing next to the bed. As our eyes met, a smile played out across his broad face. "Your hearing took a hit. You'll be alright but I am going to give you some ear protection. Don't take it off for several hours alright?" He looked to be yelling but the sound was only a whisper. He motioned to a white board and marker sitting on the table, indication we could use it to communicate. I quickly grabbed it, wincing in pain as it ripped through my back and down my left arm. Edward stopped me, grabbing my arm hard with one hand and grabbing the board with the other.

You injured your back so try not to move, he quickly scrolled across the board before showing it to me. I nodded in reply and lay back against the pillow behind me. As far as I could gather in the short amount of time I had been awake was that I had lost my hearing, I felt sick to my stomach, and my back and arm were out of commission as well. This did not bode well with me. I also didn't know how long I had been asleep. I gently tapped my wrist at him and hoped he would understand. He quickly nodded and put several liquid drops into each ear before writing on the board. The drops felt like heaven, rapidly numbing the pain as it journeyed deeper into my ears. *You have been asleep for an hour. Brain took a grazing shot and needed stitches. Jared has a couple of broken ribs. Everyone will be alright,* he smiled as he turned the board to me allowing me to see what he had written. Quickly he erased it and began to write again. *We got them all. All eight of them. The one who got you was hiding in the bed of the red truck.* He beamed at me as I read the board.

So my instinct had been true, there was an eighth man hiding in the red truck bed. I remembered taking two of the men out myself, which left six men for Brian, Edward and Jared to handle. I remembered the details of the battle up until the moment things went dark. Edward leaned in and showed me something in his hand before he pushed it into my ears and slide a heavy headset that resembled sound eliminating headphones over my head, adjusting them to my ears. When he spoke again I heard nothing but silence. I smiled and gave him a thumbs up which he promptly returned. I tried to speak, asking about the bunker and the people inside. He frowned and quickly scrolled another note. *Still safely in bunker. Needed to be sure there wasn't another group. Wanted to dispose of the bodies before the children were brought up.*

My stomach promptly turned as I thought of them trapped in the bunker during a radio blackout. The entire gun battle and the hour I was asleep, they sat in worry right under us with no idea whether we were alive or dead. I trusted they would stay put until someone came for them, but was unsure how long they would wait if they suspected Compound had been overrun. Edward patted me on the hand softly before turning off the light and leaving the room, signally to me to get some rest by placing his large hands under his tilted head and closing his eyes. I nodded slowly as he closed the door with a smile.

There wasn't anything I could do now except to sleep. I closed my eyes and gave into it willingly as images of Bentley in Fallon's arms filled my mind.

The gentle scent of lavender and oatmeal slowly took control of my senses as I began to stir. To me, it smelled like heaven as I knew exactly where I had smelled it before. I opened my eyes as I inhaled again, this time more deeply. The room was dark save for the light from the small lamp on the end table by the bed. The soft light only slightly lifting the darkness from my field of blurred vision, like a nightlight in a child's bedroom. Fallon sat in a chair pulled to the edge of the bed; her body slumped over on my legs in a soundless sleep. She wore the same outfit I had seen her in before I escorted her to the bunker for her safety, only now her hair was down and her clothing dirty. I gently reached over and with one finger moved a strand of hair out of her face. Tear stains ran from her swollen eyes down the length of her puffed and pinked cheeks to her chin, disappearing forever. One arm had been tucked in close to her body, her hand close to her face filled with crumbled tissues, while the other arm lay stretched out across my legs limp and unmoving. She had been crying while I had slept and by the look of it, she had cried for many hours.

I watched her slow breathing and ran my fingers through the strands of hair that repeatedly fell back across her face. She stirred slightly and sniffled causing me to pull back quickly and wait. I held my breath as she wiped her nose, eyes still closed before settling back down. I glanced around the room trying to gain an idea as to what time of day it was, but there was nothing to clue me in. It was then that I noticed I could actually hear her breathing though the sound seemed slightly muffled. I reached up with both hands and felt my ears. The heavy headset and been removed as well as the gauze ear plugs. The only thing left in each ear was a large wad of gauze that fit into the opening of each canal and had been taped to my head. Smiling, I moved her hair again and ran the back of my finger down the tear stain on her face. She slowly opened her eyes, blinking the sleep away and smiled at me softly.

"Hello." I whispered.

"Hi." Fallon whispered, as she rubbed her eyes with the heel of her hands and sat up slightly. "I wasn't sure you were going to wake up until morning. Can you hear me alright?"

"Yeah... muffled a bit, but at least I hear again. Hurts a bit though." I replied softly as I leaned back against the pillow. A sharp pain stabbed through my back causing me to wince. "What time is it now?"

"Three in the morning," Fallon answered as she checked her watch. "Try not to move. You took a shotgun blast to the back at close range. You are lucky to be alive. Edward said the shooter popped up behind you out of nowhere. By the time he saw him and fired... it was too late."

I rubbed my temple as I tried to recount the last seconds before I had gone down. I had come down alongside the silver truck, positioning myself between both vehicles to supply extra cover. My goal had been to round the backside of the pickup and get a clear shot at the blond. Brian was behind me in the gatehouse.

Jared was behind me on the ground trying to find a clear shot. Out of the corner of my eye I can remember seeing Edward moving up alongside the bushes to my left. I moved. I tried to get into position. I left my back exposed to the truck behind me. Both of us targeting the blond… we never noticed the secret shooter.

Frustrated, I balled up my fist and punched the edge of the bed. I should have known better. I had been trained better. "He could have gone for a head shot being that close." I spat in irritation.

"I know." Fallon whispered almost too softly for me to hear. "Like I said… lucky."

"It knocked the wind out of me." I replied almost as softly.

"I know." She said as she moved closer to me. "Hurt your ears too. Your dad said that might have been his fault." She smiled before continuing. "He could tell you guys were outnumbered from his position. He snuck down toward the gate using bushes for cover. He said he was attempting to go around you guys and come up behind the second vehicle when he saw a gun being drawn. When he fired… he was too close to you." She said as she slowly shook her head.

"Where is Bentley?" I asked, in need of a change of subject.

Fallon smiled sleepily. "Your mother spent several hours here with you. Scared her to death you did. When I arrived to take the late shift she insisted on taking Bentley for the night." She rubbed her eyes again. "You need sleep. I suggest you get some while you have the chance. Move over. This chair is killing me."

I gently moved, being careful not to hurt my back, to the far side of the bed as she climbed in next to me and lay down on the covers. She reached over to the end table and turned off the light, forcing the room into complete darkness before she curled in next to me placing her head on my shoulder. "Thank you for everything." She whispered before kissing me gently on the cheek and drifted quickly off to sleep.

Once I was sure she was asleep, I lifted her head and wrapped my arm around her, placing her head on my chest. I stared off into the darkness that surrounded us and smiled. Fallon and Bentley were safe. I wasn't sure how long it had been before someone let them out of the bunker. Choosing to leave the families tucked away out of fear of a second round of attacks had been a smart plan. None of us could have been sure as to whether the men had been part of a larger group or not. I hugged Fallon tightly to me as I thought about that moment when I let her go and pushed her toward the hatch door. As I watched her and Bentley head down the stairs, I couldn't be sure I would ever see them again.

I didn't fire the first shot, but my hand had taken two lives. Two men lost their lives with the pull of a trigger. My trigger. In a fraction of a second, I aimed and fired on two men I didn't even know. I shuttered as the realization set in. I killed two people. Both of them had taken aim at Jared. He had been the target. My life was not the one in danger in that fraction of a second before I pulled my trigger... Jared's life was. I did what I had to do to save a member of my team. *Still, your life was in danger too Jacob*, I thought to myself as a single tear ran down my cheek. It was exactly what Jared had tried to prepare me for... making the decision to do whatever it took to save a member of my team.

I tried to twist the situation over and over in my mind as silent tears rolled from my eyes in the darkness. I shot the first man before he could get a shot off. Had the second man shot Jared with a head shot and not in the chest, he would have been killed. I got the second man before he had time to turn on anyone else. With Jared down, the other men would have turned on me as I was in the open. I would have been the next target. If Jared had been killed, I likely would have been as well. With me down, they would have turned on my father who likely would have tried to come to my aid. For several minutes I thought about every possible outcome and came to the conclusion that Compound would have lost the gun fight had I not fired my weapon when I did.

Everything happened so quickly there wasn't time to think about what I was doing. I just did my job. I did as told and I saved lives... by taking lives. After wiping my eyes with the back of my hand, I turned my hand over and over in front of me in the darkness, looking at it as if it were a stranger to me. Before the blackout, my hand could write essays, clean weapons, wrench on cars, harvest food and care for livestock. Now, it could still do all those things but it can also be gentle enough to care for a baby, and deadly enough to kill. I hadn't been outside the gates since the world had changed. If those men were the sort of people that now had control of Baker, this journey north would be more dangerous than I originally thought. The men I shot had killed at least one woman that we knew of, and brutalized two. I clenched my fist and placed it on my lips. Animals. Animals ruled the outer world. Beasts. Demons.

Fallon shifted against me. The people of Compound had been protected from the hell that thrived outside the gates. Locked away up here in our own paradise, we had lived everyday as if nothing had been happening outside. Maybe we had been too naive. Maybe we should have feared the situation more than we have been. We had full bellies, laughter, electricity, and loved ones. Things like coffee, shampoo, and toothpaste which were likely in short supply outside, hadn't been much of a thought here. *Are we prepared for this... for suffering?* I thought as I bit down on my fist to keep from sobbing loudly. I inhaled sharply and winced when white hot pain shot through my back and down my left arm. Fallon could have been one of the women those animals attacked. The fact they wanted Jade made my heart drop straight out of my chest as I thought about how many children on the outside could have been destroyed by those monsters.

Related or not, Compound was considered family. If I was going to do my part and make sure my family would make it to Sanctuary, I would have to dig deeper. I couldn't be weak. The confrontation at the gate wouldn't be the last one we would come across on our journey. That ordeal was just the tip of the ice burg as far as I was concerned. I would have to change my way of thinking... be more like Haven, and less like Compound. I would have to be the very thing Jared himself had fought against when he left Haven to create this place. Compound embraced a more relaxed lifestyle with focus on a collective unity where everyone did their part as a whole for the betterment of the entire community. We shared duties, learned from each other, and though everyone had a specific job – all of us pulled together.

Haven led a completely different society, one where when a young man reached the age of thirteen he joined the ranks of the Haven army. He would be trained in warfare, strategy tactics, and hand to hand combat. Those that showed great promise were promoted at seventeen to the special security forces. Those that did not, were released into the community with further training in specialty fields such as brewing, baking, and farming. Young girls normally had only been taught basic self-defense and use of fire arms for personal protection. Strict laws against dating and marriage had been put into place to keep the young soldiers from having their vision clouded and their priorities in line. Groomed through life to be the perfect warrior, these young men would never have broken down in tears over having to take a life. They were born and raised to do just that. Shoot first and ask questions later. Kill the enemy before they have a chance to kill you. Protect the Haven society with your life.

I never agreed with the structure of the Haven way of life. I never understood why it had been so important to them to keep such a large force, until now. The friends I had made while on trading missions to Haven wouldn't have thought twice about doing any job they were instructed to do. Many times they would ask me about the way of life Compound led, laughing when I explained before calling us a hippy commune. Even my friend Jasper often complained about how I wasn't properly prepared for the end of days and that being raised on Compound had weakened me. Every time I pulled through their gates I felt like I was stepping into another world, a world where war was an expected outcome at any given moment.

Jared had bucked the Haven government by falling in love with the founder's daughter. He had been promoted early at sixteen to join the Special Operations unit, an elite group of the Haven Guard meant to clear entire towns in the event of war. They were the first ones sent in before other forces would be allowed to deliver supplies or food to surviving locals. When someone asks him now about his military days or his duties to Haven, Jared simply says that he was nothing more than a street sweeper. Jared had been what Haven considered to be one of their finest and most dedicated soldiers. A top marksman and a decorated member of the Haven Guard, Jared gave it all up for a woman. Miranda and Jared dated secretly so as not to break Haven law, and were eventually married with the blessings of the Council. Once they were married, Jared turned on the Haven rule and left the Guard, arguing that his specialty was no place for a married man. Though they had granted him his request, they only agreed with the constant pleading of Miranda. Not wanting to see their children become soldiers, they fled soon after he left the Haven Guard and ended up in Baker, Nevada.

In the beginning, Haven disowned the young lovers and broke all contact with them. Eventually Miranda returned to Haven to plead their case and beg for understanding. Her mother agreed though it had taken months of repeated trips, and began a trade deal with her daughter to supply Compound with everything they needed to start their own society. My parents fled Haven after the deal had been made, following Miranda back to Compound. The four of them built Compound from the ground up with their bare hands. Fallon and I were the first children born within Compound, setting the stage for a Haven free generation… one where we wouldn't be recruited to serve as soldiers. I had never been forced into being a soldier. Fallon had never been forced into more domestic roles. Few girls served within the Haven army. Most who tried had to be put through extensive testing and gain approval from the Council. We never had to live that life.

Compound trained girls and boys alike, though we were never forced into it. I had been trained in survival skills, foraging, hunting, and fishing. Weapons training, hand to hand combat, and team work had been on the forefront of the lessons everyone had been expected to learn. Though the focus on security and armament had always been similar to that of our parent society, we never formed an army here. Children were not required to serve as soldiers for the community. We learned much more than the children at Haven had ever been allowed to learn. Along with the military training we also taught human relations, animal husbandry, food preservation techniques, and herb ology. Women and children were to be protected, but they would never be weakened by a lack of training.

Jared had aimed for a more well-rounded community where all members could share the skills they naturally possessed. Those who had been naturally gifted in the ways of brewing alcohol took to brewing duties, sharing their knowledge by teaching classes to others within the community. People who wanted to become part of our society had never been turned away. Miranda and Jared made it clear that new people had new skills and a sharing community would better prepare us all for a thriving community. When Angela Jackson arrived at the gates pregnant and alone, she had been welcomed with open arms. She turned out to be a stellar chef, breathing new life into every meal prepared for the masses. She excitedly taught her skilled and shared her knowledge with many of us who were willing to listen. Angela also possessed a way of dealing with the animals that no one at Compound could compete with. Her arrival brought a plethora of information that became beneficial to the overall wellbeing of our community.

Though I had been trained to be a soldier, I had never been raised to expect a war to befall us at any given moment. I hadn't been raised to fear change, instead I was raised to adapt to it. Right now, I was adapting to the changes within me. Every aspect of my upbringing had been to prepare me for dangerous changes in the world. I could survive alone or within a community… and thrive. I could build a shack with my bare hands, run solar electricity, plumbing, and breed animals for food. I could stitch a wound and dig a well. These skills I learned by being a child of Compound. I had the freedom to learn any skill I felt I needed in order to prepare for any situation that might come my way.

The door to my room slowly slid open, filling the room with light from the main corridor. Sarah poked her head in and smiled brightly before walking over to the edge of the bed. "How are you feeling this morning Jacob?" She asked as she playfully shook her head at the sight of Fallon curled into my side.

"Much better, thank you for asking. When do I get clearance to leave?" I asked.

"You can leave today. Now actually if you like. It is six in the morning and everyone is up and working. Dave and Brian have been up for the last couple of hours working on the meat." She answered as she checked my chart. "There is a rush to leave for Sanctuary ahead of schedule. Jared is worried that we are no longer safe here. He is worried about someone bringing a group to look for those men you boys handled."

"Then I need to check out of here now. Can you let Fallon sleep? She is exhausted." I smiled as I gestured at Fallon in the light filtering in from the door. "She doesn't sleep well most nights and without having to worry about Bentley, she can catch up on some lost sleep."

Sarah nodded with a soft giggle before walking over to the other side of the bed. I slid out from under Fallon as carefully as possible, climbing out of the bed with the help Sarah had offered. Tiptoeing through the door and into the short hallway, we slowly closed the door behind us, sealing off Fallon in darkness to sleep for a few more hours in silence.

"Now then…," Sarah said as she clapped her hands together and rubbed them. "You will need to get cleaned up. You can use the bathroom by the surgical room. I'll have your brother run you in some clothing. Don't wash your hair; I can't have you getting your ears wet yet. Then meet me at the front counter for your medications."

"Yes ma'am." I laughed before saluting her and playfully marching off in the direction of the shower.

The best solar system within Compound supplied all the power for the medical building. This allowed for enough power to do things like run most of the equipment that didn't need the generator; including the heat on demand water heater. It was one of the few places on the property where you could take a hot shower that didn't need to be fueled by burning wood. I made quick work of washing up, being careful not to get my head wet as was requested. By the time I stepped out of the shower, my clothing had been delivered in a neat folded pile on the edge of the counter. My favorite pair of blue jeans slid up my legs with ease as I smiled. I had spent months breaking them in to be the most comfortable pair of pants I owned. I pulled my black tee shirt over my head and ruffled my hair in the mirror before I brushed me teeth.

Sarah was waiting at the front desk for me when I emerged feeling like a whole new person. "Good to see you looking better, Jacob! Alright here is the deal. We need to check your bandages and probably remove them now. I just have to make sure you aren't seeping. You injured both eardrums, rupturing one of them. You'll have to use some ear drops for a while and take some preventative antibiotics to stave off infection. I'll put you through a hearing test in a couple of days to make sure the damage hasn't caused hearing loss. In the meantime, no loud noises for you mister! This means no firing range, no gate duties that could end in a fire fight... and no working with Dave on any projects he has going. Between his cursing and starting up loud equipment, you'll be deaf by the end of the day."

"You got it." I laughed softly as she pulled the bandages from my ears to examine them. "Am I the only one with busted ears?"

"No. All of you have damage though to varying degrees. You shouldn't have been out there without ear protection. Your dad and Jared suffered for a few hours with ringing in their ears, but they seem to be fine now. Edward's ears rang for a bit. He seemed to be the least affected. Brian has one ear that is almost as bad as you." She stated as she finished. "You look good. Don't get water in them. I bagged up your medications and wrote you a note about how and when to use them. You are good to go. Watch for wind and water and cover your ears if it seems loud out there to you."

I hugged Sarah and thanked her for taking such excellent care of me before slipping out the front door and into the coolness of the morning. The sun had already raised high enough to provide adequate light around the grounds. I inhaled as deeply as my back would allow without pain and made my way to the main deck. I passed by Dave and Brian as they worked over the meat. They waved and nodded at me as I went by. I wasn't sure how they managed to do it, but they had proven me wrong when it came to the goat jerky and total weight. I laughed when Dave smugly pointed to the two feed bags busting at the seams with preserved meat.

Angela was already hard at work making breakfast when I wondered onto the main deck. The table had been set with oatmeal, fruit, toasted homemade bread with butter, and a pitcher of orange juice. She smiled at me, poured me a cup of coffee, and set a plate of eggs benedict in front of me... made just the way I liked it. Avocado sliced thinly sat across the top with sated mushrooms and onions made for the perfect combination to tease my taste buds. No one else at Compound ate it this way and only she could make it the way I like it. Though rare as it was, when she managed to hit a deal in town for crab meat, she would surprise me with adding it to my plate on benedict mornings.

"Angela... you are amazing as always." I said as my mouth began to water.

"Well after the day you guys had yesterday you deserve a good meal. My thanks for helping to protect my kids." She said as she hugged me gently. "Eat up. I won't be sounding the bell to call anyone to breakfast. Don't want to hurt any more ears. I'll be calling it in on the radio. Grab what you want before we are flooded with hungry people."

She quickly turned on her heels and returned to the stove as I grabbed a spoonful of fruit to be added to my plate. She clicked her radio and called the group to breakfast as I listened. Everyone had been out tending to their duties before dawn. They would likely be hungrier than I was. I took a small sip of my coffee

Darkness Falls

followed by a large bite of fruit. Remembering what Sarah had said about my medications, I quickly dropped my fork and tore into the bag to see if I needed to take one with food. Sure enough, two different pills needed to be taken this morning with a meal. I gulped my orange juice taking both pills at once and placed the bottles back into the bag before sliding it across the table.

"Good morning." Jared said as he stepped onto the deck. He was shirtless with a large bandage wrapped several times around his chest and middle. A large bruise stretched from just below his collar bone and disappeared underneath the edge of his bandage. "Hurts to lift my arm to put my shirt on...," he said as he noticed me looking at him, "... figured I would just take it easy... with the ribs."

Jared pulled out the chair next to me and slid into it slowly. He smelled of shampoo and aftershave. I nodded and stuffed a forkful of food into my mouth as Angela delivered Jared his morning coffee and plate. My father arrived and pulled up the chair on the other side of me just as Dave and Brian came walking up the stairs. My brother Matt stumbled out of Megan's house with his arms full of apple pies which he quickly recovered after tripping over the threshold; Megan yelling at him from inside.

"Don't you dare drop those pies!" Megan called as she followed him out the door carrying several more. "You drop them; you will be the one eating them."

"Yes ma'am." Matt said as he rolled his eyes and winked at me.

I smiled as I watched the exchange between them. Yesterday we fought for survival, but today it seemed to be business as usual. The transition had been flawless. I stuffed another bite into my mouth as I thought about what the next few days would bring us. Depending on when we would be leaving, this might very well be the last normal moments within Compound. Our last breakfast as a complete family might be this one. I took a sip of my coffee in silence.

"Jacob...," Jared said before swallowing his food and wiping his mouth. "We took care of the cleaning up while you were in recovery last night. We chose to keep the silver pickup truck. Not only does it run but it has a full tank of gas. Dave checked it out and said it will work perfectly. When it comes to your group, I want Dave to drive our small truck, your dad to handle the transport vehicle, and Edward to drive the new truck. You'll be a three vehicle caravan but it allows you to carry more supplies. I'll need you and Matt in the transport handling security." He sipped his coffee before continuing. "I want your team on the road earlier than we had planned. How soon do you think you can get your team ready to leave?"

I set my fork down on my plate and crunched the numbers quickly. "I can have us on the road by the end of the day today."

"Glad to hear it." Jared said flatly before stuffing a forkful of food into his mouth. "The sooner the better as far as I am concerned."

Dave pulled each vehicle up to the fuel house one by one and filled the tanks with fuel before lining them up in the order they would leave in. The transport truck would lead the pack, followed by Dave and Edward. Breakfast now seemed like a distant memory as everyone in Compound pulled together to quickly pack up the team. Due to the added vehicle, it had been decided we would not be taking the horse. In fact, both horses had been taken by Miranda and Dave and delivered to the Parker Farm as a gift of thanks for many years' worth of faithful trading. The second team would also be leaving ahead of schedule as Jared insisted there had been no other option.

Cassidy and Cassandra managed to catch their barn cats with the help of Emily, and placed them into a small carrier to be delivered to me. The underside of one of the long benches in the transport had been transformed into an enclosed animal cage, sectioned off for each group of animals with enough room to allow for a little roaming. I knew it wasn't an ideal situation for the barn cats as they had spent their lives roaming freely around the property, but we didn't have much choice if they were to make it to Sanctuary safely. I carefully slid the door open on one of the cage sections and placed each cat one by one inside before closing and locking the door. Even with three cats sharing a section, there still seemed to be enough room for them to at least make the journey without getting mad enough to rip my face off when trying to feed them.

Matt gathered the chickens we would be taking and after I consulted Angela on the animals and their normal behavior, I placed the chickens in the cage section closest to the back of the

Darkness Falls

vehicle, leaving the last and center most cage for the six female rabbits. I had been unaware the chickens and cats normally didn't get along, so I was thankful I had taken that extra couple of minutes to ask her before I made my choice. Because our buck rabbits couldn't be housed with the does, I slipped them into a special cage built under the edge of the second bench near the front of the transport and across from the cats. This helped to make sure we wouldn't be overrun with baby rabbits due to accidental breeding by the time we reached Sanctuary.

Once all the animals chosen to ride in the transport had been secured, I began to fill the rest of the spaces under the bench near the rabbit bucks with the water containers Brian filled and delivered. Originally I had been leery of placing so much weight on one side of the transport, but Jared assured me that when the vehicle packing had finished the weight wouldn't be an issue. When it came to storing the animal food, I figured the best place for it would be closer to the back of the transport so the animals couldn't get into it. I stood up and looked around at the job I had done, and smiled.

"Are you ready for the refugee boxes?" My father called as he tossed his duffle bag into the cab of the transport.

"Yes dad, have an area ready for them now." I yelled back as I jumped out of the transport.

Slamming the door, my father turned to me, "Good... because we leave in less than an hour."

CHAPTER TWELVE

I had no idea so much gear could be packed into three vehicles. We double checked everything had been secured into place before gathering by the vehicles for our last goodbyes. The second group would stay behind for a few days, just long enough to board up the houses, finish their own packing, and secure the property before heading out behind us. Jared and I managed to find a moment alone to go over the cave at the halfway point and go over how I would convince my team to stop there. The only thing left to do was to load the members of the team and hit the road running. Even Bacon had been loaded into the back of Dave's small farm truck. Dave had used wood and wire fencing to build sides and a roof that completely enclosed the truck bed and stood three feet above the cab, and filled the back of the truck with thick straw. Bacon would be forced to share the space with one of the roosters we had planned to take with us as well as our Nigerian Dwarf goat buck. Dave looked more like a traveling petting zoo than someone preparing to journey hundreds of miles in a caravan. He would also be towing the small utility trailer packed with gear and supplies.

Edward would be traveling alone as he pulled up the rear of our caravan. He didn't mind the idea saying it would give him plenty of time to think as well as keep his eyes on our tail. Each vehicle had been not only loaded with weapons but also mounted with weapons. My father and Jared both congratulated my brother and me for a job well done. Jared had been sure to create mounting brackets into every vehicle to hold our radios allowing each vehicle to communicate with each other.

"I really am going to miss this place." Fallon whispered as she looked off toward her cabin.

"I know. We will be back though. We need to hit the road as soon as possible. You better go say goodbye." I informed as I held Bentley in my arms, intent on letting my mother get one more cuddle moment with him before we left.

Jade cried into Miranda's shirt as they stood near the military transport vehicle. Miranda stroked her hair and begged her to be a big girl and take care of Daddy. Jade nodded as tears ran down her face. Cassidy and Cassandra though only three years old, couldn't understand why they wouldn't be allowed to ride with Becky and Bobby. Emily had to explain to them that we were such a large family we needed two big groups just to go on vacation. Listening to her tell it, we would have so much fun together once we made it to the mountains.

I helped Angela, Fallon, and the children into the back of the transport being sure to show them the tiny makeshift living space I had created for the children to play in. Angela thought the idea had been brilliant and promptly handed the girls some coloring books and crayons to keep them busy for a while. I had even taken the time to create a small sleeping space for Bentley to take his naps in. Miranda jumped into the cab of the truck followed quickly by my father and fired up the engine. Dave climbed into his, started it and did a radio check to be sure we were all satisfied with our radios. Edward climbed into his truck and replied that his radio was working perfectly.

Screams and hollers for a safe journey rang out over the sound of the engines as we roared down the long driveway toward the northern gate. Matt and I sat at the far end of the truck in order to open and close the gate, as well as watch the road. Jared had given me a small box and told me not to open it until we arrived at the supply cave. I slipped it under the seat between a container of water and a box of food. Cassidy and Cassandra cheered the start of our vacation as we pulled through the gate and onto the road. I watched us pull away from Compound, my eyes on the area of the gun fight we had the day before. Hints of blood still stained the dirt around the tire tracks. Jared told me he had buried the men in the field across the street in a mass grave they had dug using the tractor. I knew the exact location by the look of the freshly turned dirt. I closed my eyes against the memories.

When we passed the Perez house I could hear Fallon inhale sharply before whispering a goodbye to Papa. Everything we knew we were now leaving behind. A month and a half ago, we walked up this very road trying to make it back home after the blackout. We never thought we would be leaving our only home. Compound had been built to be secure... and somehow it no longer was.

"Fallon... we are coming up on it." Matt whispered as he glanced around the edge of the transport to see ahead of the vehicle. "Do you want my dad to stop or just keep going?"

"Don't say anything. We will be back." She whispered as she moved next to him and pulled back the edge of the canvas cover for a look.

I moved up alongside them in time to see the car Bentley had been found in. The driver door still sat rumbled and open. Scraps of metal and trash from the original accident still scattered the area and dark brown staining could be seen down the side of the door, on the steering wheel, and on the seat. I could just make out where Bentley's birth mother and cremated father had been buried as Matt and Fallon had marked the grave, though the dirt no longer looked disturbed. I hadn't been there when they had found Bentley alive and rescued him. I wished I had been. As we passed by, I realized this would be my first and probably last look at where my son had been found on the day he came into our lives. I leaned over and kissed him on top of his head while he lay half asleep in Fallon's arms, before reaching over and grabbing my brother's hand. Matt watched as we continued onward, the accident slipping into the distance behind us.

"Thank you for saving him." I whispered as I squeezed his hand.

"Hey... I am glad he made it. I can't picture not having him around anymore." Matt replied as he sat back into his position at the back of the transport to watch the road.

My radio cracked and my father's voice came over explaining we would be coming to the split shortly and would be turning right to get onto the highway. There was no need to go left and head into town. I sat back into my position opposite my brother. I would likely not see what happened to Baker, Nevada until after we managed to make it back from Sanctuary. For that, I was glad. I knew the town looked nothing like it used to, I didn't want my memories tainted with the images of suffering. I could gather that every business in town had been looted, vandalized and without trash service… it wouldn't be the beautiful place it once had been.

"I hope they enjoy dinner. I cooked something extra special and left it on the stove." Angela smiled as she opened up a large plastic bag she has brought with her. "I know you didn't get lunch so you must be starving by now. I brought some dinner for us too. I boxed some up and gave it to Edward, Dave and your dad. This bag is ours."

"You took the time to make dinner?" Matt asked excitedly as he grabbed a small white box she pulled and handed to him.

"Why wouldn't I? Megan even sent the leftover pies from breakfast with us for dessert."

Angela handed me a small box that I reluctantly accepted with a nod. I hadn't been very hungry since breakfast. I set it next to my feet with the intention of eating it later. Not only wasn't I hungry, but I was slipping into protection mode. We would be hitting the highway in a matter of minutes and there was no telling what we would see out there. I couldn't be distracted by food when there would likely be danger lurking around every corner.

As I turned to look out the back of the transport I caught sight of Dave giving me a wicked grin and shaking his finger at me through his windshield. My radio cracked and without missing a beat, Dave came on to tattle on me for not eating, saying the best time for it was now. Angela gave me an irritated look prompting me to at least look at what she had painstakingly prepared for our meal. Inside I found a pulled pork sandwich dripping with barbeque sauce, homemade garlic fries, and two small containers, one with vegetables and one with fruit. She had even gone so far as to apparently raid the supply stash and include utensil packages containing our plastic ware, napkins, salt and pepper, and hot sauce. As I flipped it over in my hand I realized why it looks so familiar. Angela, Sarah, and I had put these together last summer when we started building our own MREs. Angela had been disgusted at the quality of military grade MREs, saying the only good items in them had been the candy. We enlisted Sarah's help to make sure that nutritionally we had covered all the bases in their creation. We took our cues on the utensils from an MRE we can collected from Fallon's uncle Charlie, and replicated them all the way down to the toilet paper and coffee. The only thing we had added to customize them for our community was the tiny foil package of water purification tablets – enough to purify two liters of water.

Knowing I was being watched, I devoured my sandwich and fruit as quickly as I could with my bare hands. I could tell Dave was laughing at me from his truck when I opened the vegetables and dumped the container straight into my mouth. I wouldn't be opening the utensil package as there was no reason to do so. Instead I slipped it into the upper pocket on the tactical vest for later. I grabbed my M16 from the floor by my feet and proceeded to rest the butt of the firearm on my thigh, pointing it toward the sky while I stuffed my face with fries from my free hand. Dave had been frantically stuffing his face as well, making the exchange more of a game as to who could finish eating first by the time we reached the highway. Though he had eaten his sandwich as quickly as I had, he couldn't get passed the flavor of vegetables and made faces at me as he tried to chew them and swallow. I smiled and shook my finger at him.

Angela reached over and grabbed my radio. "Slow down you two! This isn't a penis size game. You will choke to death eating like that. No speed eating while we travel!"

Dave roared in laughter loud enough I could hear him from his open window. I couldn't help laughing either as Angela handed the radio back and walked back to the children to deliver their meals, obviously no longer wanting to watch the testosterone fueled display of competitive eating. I held up my last garlic fry to show Dave that I would finish my dinner before him, and popped it into my mouth with a winning grin. He shook his head in defeat and smiled as he held up a large handful of fries.

"Winner winner chicken dinner." Matt laughed and gave me a knuckle bump in celebration while laughing at Dave.

We began to slow down as we made the turn onto the highway, heading east toward Utah. The transport rumbled beneath me as it shifted and groaned onto the ramp. Straightaway I became flooded with a million scents at once like a wave smashing against my face. I twisted my nose as I watched out the back, knowing that all too soon I would see the cause of the stench. Taking a peek ahead of us through the edge of the canvas cover, I managed to get a good look at what lay ahead of us.

Cars and trucks littered the highway facing every direction

possible. In some areas they had been left in the multicar pile ups from the accidents that followed the blackout. Windows had been smashed out in many of them. Some cars sat like burned out relics, reminders of a time that was now lost to us. Fossils of the old world, left to rot on the roadside in the middle of the desert. Evidence of small encampments now abandoned sat sporadically along the road. Shelters built from scrap junk, burn piles that might have once been debris, and the stench of human waste turned my stomach upside down. People tried to survive out here for quite a while by the look of it. Their encampments hadn't been but ten miles or so from Compound, but not a one of them ever found their way to us.

We managed to make good time as we had found the path carved out by the Haven team. My father had driven the transport from Haven to Compound after all, and knew the path he helped to carve. Both Edward and my father had made the trip, but for the rest of us this was our first true glimpse of the downfall. I turned and watched the road behind us, my eyes on a stray dog as he darted between burned out vehicles and junk piles looking for food. He may have been a chocolate lab in his past life, now he looked more like an unloved and starved street mutt. Dave had noticed him too and tossed some fries out his window. The dog hadn't noticed as he darted behind an overturned minivan, obviously scared by our vehicles. He would find them eventually and by then we would be long gone.

"It is nearly six now. Prepare for an all-night run if we can help it. We need to get as far from civilization as possible before we stop for the night." Fallon said as she came to sit on the floor at my feet. "We can't camp around here and need to get as far as possible." She placed her hand on my knee. "Are you going to be alright with being on guard for that long?"

"I am prepared. I even made sure I took my medicine." I smiled playfully.

Fallon patted my knee and moved to the back of the transport, leaving me to my security detail. We drove on for several miles, covering plenty of ground at a high rate of speed. At some point we would venture off the path carved by Haven and the speed of travel would slow to a crawl. For now anyway, we would push on as fast as we could muster putting as much distance between us and Compound as possible. Jared had given specific instructions to make it as far as we could and push for the state line. Miranda wanted to bypass Salt Lake City completely as the city would be too dangerous for us to travel through. This would also allow us to follow the route the Haven caravan had taken home by putting us on Highway Two Thirty-Three. I had suggested we take the cut off for Highway Ninety-Three, but eventually we decided to stick with the route nearest to Haven. Highway Eighty to Salt Lake would be disastrous. Our trip would take us through Utah and Idaho before we would reach Montana.

Though we had managed to make great time, there were some areas we had to slow down through as obstacles managed to be placed within the roadway. An hour into our trip and we were nearly at the state line. The hair on the back of my neck began to prickle as I made note that some of the vehicles looked to have been moved. The path slowly began to get thinner, dirtier, and more dangerous as it slowed us to nearly a crawl.

"I don't like this. Something isn't right here." Matt whispered as he checked his rifle.

I grabbed my radio intending to alert the caravan that something didn't seem right about the area when I heard Miranda scream from the cab of the transport. I motioned to Angela and Fallon to get down. I couldn't tell what the commotion had been about without swinging around the back of the transport, possibly putting myself in danger. I looked to Dave for any sign he could give me. His mouth hung open in shock as he leaned out the window of his truck. Seconds later the transport stopped in the roadway and the engine growled as it shut down. Matt and I instructed the children, Fallon, and Angela to stay down as we jumped from the transport with our M16s drawn. Matt covered the left side of the vehicle without being told, and I instinctively took to the right side.

As I rounded the side of the vehicle Miranda flung the door open and jumped from the cab, slamming the door behind her before running off ahead of the transport. It was in that moment I finally caught a glimpse of what we had come across. Partially blocking the highway about fifty yards in front of us lying in its' side was our old wood gas truck. Another fifty yards from the truck sat the burned out reminisce of what could only have been one of the Haven escort vehicles.

"Gordon!" Miranda screamed in panic as she ran for the

truck. "Gordon!"

"Miranda...," My father yelled as he jumped from the transport and ran for her. "Miranda, stop!"

Miranda reached the wood gas truck before anyone had time to stop her. She was already gagging from the smell before she even had time to confirm what we all had known. Gordon Glover was dead. His body still sat within the wood gas truck that lay on its' side abandoned on the road. The moment she found him, she fell to her knees scampering away as quickly as possible before vomiting into the street. I could smell the death in the air from my position on the side of the transport. My father grabbed for Miranda, desperate to pull her from the ground and lead her back to the vehicles. She retched and screamed, fighting against him to be let go.

"Dear God...," Dave whispered as he and Edward came along side me. "Welp 'at be my truck. Gordon gone I reckon?"

"I can smell it; someone was left in there alright. At least one...," Edward whispered. "Keep your eyes peeled. They were ambushed."

I scanned the side of the road around us, seeing nothing. "Edward, I helped fill that truck. All the boxes from the back of the truck are missing."

"I see that." Edward said as he pulled his rifle from his shoulder. "He didn't get very far did he? Likely died the day they left. Someone had to have seen us roll through on our way to you... waited to see if they would come back this way. Someone waited them out. The other Haven escort is missing. Dave, stay here. Jacob, come with me. I need cover."

Edward pulled his rifle up and in a crouch scanned the area as he moved quickly for the wood gas truck. With one hand on his shoulder to guide me as I panned around us, we moved as one fluid unit. I trusted his judgment as I let him lead us toward the wreckage. He tapped my fingers and I dropped off, moving into a kneeling position and covering the areas behind us. There was no sign of ambush around the caravan, which sat still on the highway with a screaming woman being detained in front of it. Edward rounded the truck, surveyed and moved on to see about the escort vehicle. We worked like a well-oiled machine, taking subtle cues and one word answers as we moved. When he finished his sweep of one area, I moved to cover his sweep of another. Once he finished his sweep he came up behind me and placed his back against mine.

"The pickup is stripped. They took all the gear, food, battery, and what they could from the wood gas system. One body in the driver seat... obviously Gordon. The Cooper brothers are missing. Escort vehicle was stripped and set on fire." He informed as he held his rifle in front of him. "Five body count, Gordon in the truck and four bodies on the other side of the transport... one of them Haven Guard. The other three look to be bandits of some sort. One of them by the transport but the other two are in the bushes."

"The smell is horrible." I choked as my eyes watered.

"That smell will never leave you kid... sticks with you for life. Just be glad we were the ones who found this and not Jared." He replied. "Time to move."

This time I led the way back to the transport with Edward's hand on my shoulder. He kept his weapon trained on the wreckage, eyes constantly scanning around us as well as behind us. When we got back to the transport vehicle, Miranda had quieted down allowing my father to finally let her go. "What the hell happened here?" My father asked as he pulled Edward and me aside.

"The caravan seems to have been herded like cattle to this spot. Surrounding area suggests an ambush. Plenty of cover to allow a large group to hide. They raped the caravan of what they could and set the escort truck on fire. I have no idea why they didn't set fire to the wood truck though. Hell of a battle it was. One dead Haven Guard on the other side of the escort, three dead bandits. This area became a war zone. One escort truck is missing along with the brothers, and the rest of the Haven soldiers. You know as well as I do... they leave no one behind." Edward whispered. "I have no idea if the rest of them are alive or not."

"We can't bury Gordon; his body is too far gone to be handled. We have to set the wood gas truck on fire. The other bodies need burned as well. Are you sure there is nothing we can save here?" My father asked as he looked off toward the wreckage.

"Not a damned thing here. We have to burn it to the ground and get back on the road before the smoke alerts someone of our position. One thing is bothering me though...," Edward spoke softly. "Haven was to send a second team to collect this one if they didn't arrive on time. Even if the entire first team had been wiped out before the second arrived, they won't have left a member of the Guard lying in the street like that."

"So where the hell is the second team?" My father whispered deep in thought.

"Exactly my point." Edward replied and he shouldered his rifle. "We need to clear out of here now."

We moved swiftly to retrieve the handheld flame throws from the caravan. I handed one to my father who promptly headed to the wreckage with Edward. I climbed onto the side of the transport to get a better view and scanned the area for any signs of trouble.

"Pst... Jacob." Fallon whispered as she peered out of the canvas. "What the hell is going on out there?"

"Just stay down and I will explain once we are moving again." I replied.

After we set fire to the wood gas truck and the bodies, we backed up our caravan far enough to drive off the highway and through the dirt in order to go around the wreckage in a wide arc. Once back on the highway we found a clear shot had still been carved out by my father when he had made his way back at Compound from Haven. I quickly explained to Angela and Fallon what had happened as Matt listened intently. He spent most of his time guarding the caravan and hadn't been able to catch more than a glimpse of the destruction, though he had gathered enough information to figure it out. Fallon cried as Angela held her. The news of Gordon's death had hit her rather hard.

I sat back in my position at the back of the truck to watch the road. I couldn't help but wonder where the second team from Haven had gone. Edward had been right; they wouldn't have left the body of one of their own in the street like that. They also wouldn't have left without cleaning up the mess by burying or burning the bodies left behind. Something must have gone wrong as it looked like the second team had either never been dispatched in the first place, or never made it to recover them. Edward had assured me the Haven soldier had not been my friend Jasper Montgomery. At least I could rest knowing he didn't spend all this time lying forgotten in the street. With the second escort vehicle missing as well as the rest of the travel party, I prayed they somehow made it out alive and that Jasper hadn't been killed.

I watched Dave driving behind us obviously crying but trying to hide it. My entire team had been turned into an emotional mess. Everyone that is, except for me. I was numb. Numb from the tip of my hair to my toenails. No tears fought to free themselves from my eyes. I just sat and watched the road in robotic motion, scanning every area that came into my field of vision. Sitting up straighter in my seat, my back pinched in pain causing me to wince and grit my teeth until the wave left me. Even my ears began to bother me again as the sound of the transport's roaring had become a constant irritate. I fought against the pain as I tried to remain composed.

"You are hurting again dude. No lies." Matt said as he tossed me the bag of medications prescribed by Sarah.

I reluctantly took the bag and checked my watch. I should have taken my pain pill about the time we found the wreckage, but had obviously been too distracted to remember. I grabbed my canteen and a pill, chugging it down before putting everything away and thanking my brother. Then I had a thought that captured my attention. Suddenly I pulled out my radio.

"Dad, do you copy?" I asked.

"Yes, I am here." He replied almost as if he were confused.

"The second team never made it out of the gate. Haven never would have sent them if they had been under attack. They would have waited until the community was secure before sending a team out to retrieve them." I spoke calmly. "They were attacked shortly after your team left. They knew the team would be coming back that direction and waited for them because they watched you leave! Those weren't bandits in the street… those were survivors they had been trying to help."

The radio went silent for several seconds before my father's voice came through, "What are you saying?"

"I am saying that someone let you through before attacking Haven. They let you through so they could follow you and find the location of Compound, Dad… they hit Haven and they are going to hit Compound!"

Matt inhaled sharply and reached for the radio. "Our forces are split into two. Compound cannot hold off attack with half the force gone. Dad… they had to have ambushed from both sides on that caravan, which is why they couldn't fight back! They let you through again… we are pulling into a trap!" Matt obviously must have understood my train of thought as he knew exactly what I had been about to say.

"Shit!" My father yelled.

I stared at my little brother as we put the rest of the pieces into place at the same time. The local people around town wouldn't have been organized enough to challenge Haven. Not to mention it is more than just biting the hand that feeds you. Someone was in place early on after the blackout. Someone watched them leave knowing they would be traveling to another community to make a supply drop. The team not only cleared the road to allow for easy follow, but unintentionally led them right to Compound's door. Waiting to hit the team until they began to head back meant that specially trained Haven soldiers wouldn't have been at Compound during the invasion. Ambushing the caravan kept them from returning to Haven to help in the effort. Haven's returning team was a sitting duck the second they left Compound that day. Ambushing far enough away from both communities made sure that word wouldn't make it back to anyone… the strategy had been brilliant.

"They must think we are Patriot!" Edward yelled, as the same thought struck all of us at once.

"Fish in a goddamn barrel." My father replied.

"Miranda, get on a map and find us a way off this goddamned highway. We cannot head anywhere near Haven. The boys are right… this is a trap and we are surrounded. Find us a way out of here now!" Edward yelled.

"There is no way out of here! There are no towns or roads off this highway. It is a straight shot to the cut off leading to Haven. We are in the middle of nowhere." She yelled in a panic.

"We don't need a road." I interrupted on the radio. "Hit the goddamn dirt and cut across the desert. Back track West and cut up through Idaho that way. Once they realize we figured it out they will think we tried to find a way around them to Haven or found a way back to Compound. Hit the dirt and get us the hell away from Utah!"

As the transport made a hard left off the highway and into the desert, darkness had begun to fall around us. I looked out at Dave to make sure he managed to make the turn as he had been carrying livestock and hauling a trailer. He smiled at me and gave me a thumb up as he hit the dirt without trouble. I leaned back in my seat and took a sharp breath before blowing it out and taking another.

"We aren't out of the woods yet. They could come after us." Matt said as he sat back in his chair to watch out the back.

"They won't." I rubbed my eyes as I thought about the strategy. "They won't bother with us now. We were the bonus. Once they see we figured it out and took off, they will turn their attention to their main objective. What they really want is in the second caravan... the man who started it all."

"They want Jared!" Matt whispered. "Son of a bitch Jacob, they will hit the second caravan either while still at Compound or on the road!"

"On the road will be the plan. Catch them off guard and away from the weapons stash. Surround them from all sides. Once they finish the job... they will hit Compound and burn it to the ground." I closed my eyes as tears ran down my face.

"Oh god... Mom and Travis." Matt whispered.

"Yeah... Mom and Travis...," I whispered back. "... and everyone else we love."

Though I hadn't been sure Angela had heard the exchange, I knew Fallon had as I could hear her whimpering behind me. I wanted to turn around and hold her but all I could think about was my mother and brother. They would be trapped and butchered along with half of our Compound family. I gave in and allowed myself to cry. I allowed myself to grieve their deaths though I knew as of this moment they were likely still alive. They wouldn't see the trap coming. Fallon's cries became a wail as she fell apart behind me. I frantically tried to figure out a way to save our second caravan but nothing came to mind that didn't result in the complete destruction of Compound. Everyone would die, not just half of us.

The entire caravan pulled to a stop somewhere in the middle of the desert, forming a tight circle to help protect us from all sides. Edward and Dave built a small fire in the middle of the circle and helped pull the sleeping bags and bedding from the vehicles. I sat in the back of the transport holding Fallon until she had cried herself to sleep in my arms. I gently slipped out from under her, tucking a pillow under her head. As I turned to leave I remembered the small box that Jared had told me not to open until we made it to the supply cave. That cave would be our only salvation now.

Darkness Falls

Getting the caravan to the cave as soon as possible might actually save our lives.

I grabbed the box and walked over to the hood of Dave's truck and climbed on it. Except for Bentley, Fallon, and the twins, everyone was gathered around the fire speaking in hushed tones and hugging between random tears. I set the box next to me and pulled out my highway map, hoping to find the quickest route to the cave. After several minutes and much thought into the different outcomes, I tossed the map down and looked out at what would be the only survivors of Compound. Dave Ratcliff and his old as dirt pig named Bacon consisted of a family all their own. They would survive. Me, my father, and Matt, would be the only surviving members of the Dunn family. The Henley's would lose nearly half of their family as well. Angela and the twins would survive... but we would be losing Megan and her kids, as well as Brian, Sarah and Emily.

Tears ran down my face as I began to sob into my hands. I didn't know how to fix the situation. I didn't know how to cope with the idea of losing my brother and my mother. I grabbed Jared's box and held it. He had always been like a second father to me. I turned the box over several times in my hands. He would want us to go to the cave and not turn back for him. In fact, if he had been here right now he would have told us to drive all night, but none of us had the energy after today. I decided I wouldn't wait to open the box at the cave, I would do it now. There might be something useful inside. If not, there might be a note that I can give to Fallon as the last words her father had ever written. I pulled out my pocket knife, cut the tape seal, and opened it. Inside sat a map, a radio, and a note addressed to me. I set the box down and opened the sealed note.

Dear Jacob,
I know you well enough to know that you did not listen to my instructions and wait to open this at the cave. I am not angry at you for it. Sometimes, we have to listen to our intuition and not the orders our commanding officers give us. It is the reason I left the Haven army and began my own community. I could not do something as ordered when my intuition told me the situation was wrong. I have spent many years encouraging you to follow your gut and listen to that inner voice that tells you when something feels horribly wrong. You listen to that inner voice more often than anyone else I

know. It is what makes you such a good kid and what makes you one hell of a soldier. It was that quality about you that made me feel proud to have you protect Fallon and my wife on this dangerous trip. If I know you as well as I think I do, you have opened this the same night your team left Compound. You have likely pushed your team to cover as much ground as possible. For this reason, I suspect you would have made it into Utah before you realized what was happening. I am a smart man Jacob. I wanted you to wait to open this so that I could be sure you would be as far away as possible and wouldn't turn around. You are far too smart for your own good. I am sure it didn't take you long to put the pieces together. You have likely made it through and are off the highway crossing the desert. If so, you have made the right decision. I am who they are after. I am well aware of the trap. For this reason, I have secretly left Compound shortly after your caravan did. I led my team out the southern gate and have a plan to lead them up through the center of Nevada in order to avoid the trap all together. When they get here, the place will be empty and we will have managed a great head start. Do not fear for us. Like I have said – I am a smart man. Get your team to the cave as fast as possible. I have included a map with marked out directions that will take you through on unmarked roads. You should have enough fuel to make it to the closest small town to where the cave is located. We hope to see you soon. Turn on the radio when you reach the area located on the map but only after sunset. Not before then. Seriously!

No more tears now... take care of my girls.
Always,
Jared Henley

My hands began to shake as I reread the note a second time just to be sure I read it correctly. I pulled the map from the box and flung it across the hood. The exact path we had taken had been marked off in red, with a line leading off highway Two Thirty-Three and into the desert. A second route had been marked off in blue, detailing the route the second caravan would be taking up through the center of Nevada and Idaho. Both routes came very close to each other in one location on the map that had been marked with a star. I quickly compared my highway map to the one Jared had placed in the box. They had been different. Jared's map did not include just highways and roadways. It detailed off road trails, logging roads and ghost towns all along our route. I calculated we would most likely have radio contact within twenty-four hours if we made it to the location indicated, but that we would stay on two different paths until the moment we met up at the cave.

"Dad! Dad!" I screamed as I jumped off the hood of the truck with the map and note in my hands.

"What is it?" My father yelled as he jumped to his feet with a panicked expression.

"Jared and the rest... they are alive! We have a new route to travel and I have a note to prove it." I laughed as I passed the map to Miranda and the note to my father.

"Jesus Christ," My father whispered as he scanned the note. "That smart son of a bitch did it... he really did it!"

Cheers and laughter split the tension as everyone fought to see the map and the note. Fallon rubbed her eyes as she poked her head through the canvas. I ran to her, jumped into the transport and hugged her as tightly as I could. "Your dad is one smart man Fallon Henley." I laughed as I swung her around in a circle.

"What is going on?" She asked.

"They left when we did. They are way off course and very safe."

Together we cried as we stood in the back of the transport vehicle. In a matter of minutes what had been tears of grief had been replaced with tears of joy. Though there was still a chance that Compound had been raided shortly after we had begun our journey, there was a better chance that the second team had been long gone before anyone realized it. If they stuck to their map, they went south and cut west before shooting up on the other side of Baker, Nevada.

"Dave... I know you have a bottle of moonshine in that blasted truck." Edward laughed as he gave Dave a pat on the back. "Pour us all a nightcap."

Moments later we gathered around the fire and rose our glasses.

"To Compound!" We cheered, before we chugged the foulest homebrewed moonshine we had ever had the displeasure of tasting. Amidst the couching, gagging and spitting... we laughed as a family. A family that might just make it to Sanctuary after all. A family that stood a fighting chance.

CHAPTER THIRTEEN

I stood on the hill closest to the main deck and watched the first caravan leave Compound carrying with them my father and both of my brothers. Knowing that it could be days or even weeks before I saw them again made me nervous. In fact, the last twenty-four hours had made me nervous. Having to hide behind the tractor by the barn and listen to gunfire at the gate almost ruined me. When they had brought my injured brother up to the medical building I found myself in a panic. It took both Edward and Sarah to convince me that Jacob would be fine. Now as I watched them leave, I worried for my brothers more than ever.

"Jared, they have just passed by the Perez place." Brain called, as he stood on the main deck looking through his binoculars.

Jared smiled faintly with a look of sadness in his eyes. His daughter and his wife were on that transport truck. He turned and walked onto the main deck and took the binoculars from Brian. Scanning the road ahead of the caravan, he panned slowly and then smiled before setting them on the table.

"I need everyone assembled right now." Jared called out. "This is important."

I picked up Becky who squirmed in my arms as I carried her to the deck and set her into a chair at the smaller children's table. Emily quickly brought Bobby up with her onto the deck and handed him a coloring book. I watched the children argue over crayons while we waiting for everyone to assemble. There would be chores that would need completed before we could leave, including boarding up the homes and medical building. With half the community on the journey already, this could take a while.

"We are leaving now. Right now. Gather your bags and get into the caravan." Jared informed as he motioned to the vehicles.

"What? Why? We aren't even ready!" Megan complained loudly in shock as she bounced Michael gently in her arms. He had been slightly fussy since this morning and now he wanted nothing more than to cry.

"Our situation has changed. There isn't time to do anything else. Brian filled our water and packed food while he helped the first group. We need to be out of here as soon as possible. All homes have been emptied into the bunker already so what else is there left to do here? Brian, please fuel the trucks as well as fuel cans. Jessica, I need you to load the animals. Sarah, please lock down the medical building and grab any last minute items you think you might need. Emily and Travis... get the kids loaded and do a last check of the food. We are on the road as soon as the trucks are fueled." Jared said as he grabbed a couple of duffle bags from under the table. "Don't worry about the first team and their safety. They are a diversion meant to distract while we sneak away out the southern gate. They are buying us the time we need to get out of here. We've been watched from the outside."

My heart pumped loudly into my ears as I stood, eyes fixed on the wooden floor of the main deck. A thousand thoughts blazed through my mind in that moment. Before another word could be spoken, I ran into my house and climbed the ladder into my loft. I had already packed the clothing I wanted to take, but I had to grab a few personal items from both my room and the medical building. One of them I had no intention of leaving behind, my medical notebook. Everything I had ever been taught here at Compound about medical practices had been noted down to the smallest detail. I quickly crammed the notebook and my other items into my bag and stripped my bed of my comforter before tossing them off the landing of my loft into the living room below. Turning for one last look at my bedroom, a single tear fought to break free. Jared's words repeating in my head as I went, I climbed down the ladder grabbing my bag and comforter and ran from the house toward the trucks.

"Leave all the animals we had planned to butcher." Jared yelled as he tossed a bag into the cab of the large rust colored truck he usually lent to my brother. "We won't have time! Trust me when I tell you they won't suffer to death out there. The people planning to take over Compound will be finishing the job."

"You are going to feed them!" My mother yelled back as she was loading the milk goats into the utility trailer. "Are you insane?"

"We can't do anything about it. We need to leave right now." He yelled as he ran off toward the main deck.

The entire property erupted in panicked frenzy with everyone running to gather what they could at the last possible minute. In a matter of minutes both trucks had been loaded, the engines now running.

"Travis, get into the cab of my truck." Jared yelled as I helped Becky and Bobby into the back of the pickup to sit alongside their mother. Brian and Dave had taken the time to build an enclosure, bench seat, and small bed to allow for passengers to ride safely. It seemed to make the children excited to see what resembled a little house they could play in.

"Yes Sir!" I yelled and ran around the vehicle and climbed in.

Jared jumped into the driver seat and shifted into gear, stomping on the gas petal. The truck lurked forward hard. We quickly rounded the front of the main deck and circled houses, cutting between them and Fallon's cabin, before heading down behind the property. Brian stood at the gate leading into the cattle pastures obviously intent on closing the gate behind us. We barreled through it and kept going without slowing down.

"Jessica, pick up Brian and meet us at the southern gate." Jared shot into the radio. "I am blowing through."

He set the radio onto the seat before looking at me. "Travis, I know this is sudden and probably rather confusing. I am sorry for that." He said softly as he shifted the truck. "Since the day the Haven team arrived I have suspected they were followed. When we left to retrieve the truck from the school, I scouted the highway before anything else. I had been right... they were followed. They have been watching us from afar. I forced your brothers and father to leave early in order to take the attention off us."

"You fed them to the wolves." I spat angrily.

"No. There is much more to it than that. I wish I could explain everything but right now we have to get out of here. Just know that I did not place them in harm's way. They have to face their own dangers on this trip just as we will... but in doing what I did I helped to make sure we all survive." Jared said before slammed the truck into park, exiting the vehicle, and running for the gate.

Once the southern gate was open, we pulled through and off to the side of the road to wait. My mother drove right on by him to pull up alongside us. Everything was happening so fast it still had yet to sink in completely. I quickly put my face into my hands trying to quell the anger welling up inside me. I heard the door open and felt Jared climb into the driver seat and kick the truck into gear. I looked out the window and watched my home slip out of view as we barreled down the dirt road in the opposite direction of Sanctuary.

Jared's truck led our caravan carrying me in the passenger seat, and Megan with the children in the enclosure in the truck bed. Emily and Jade had decided to ride with us as well in order to help with the smaller children. This left Brian, Sarah, and my mother to handle the second truck and the trailer hauling the livestock. Brian and Sarah's hound dogs had been loaded into the second truck's bed. We didn't take the tractor or have a third vehicle like the first group had. We were smaller and quicker than they were. Maybe that had been on purpose… to allow us to get away as quickly as possible.

Half an hour later, our caravan made a right onto another dirt road leading us West across the desert and farther away from Compound. We continued on in relative silence as we moved quickly into a direction that didn't make sense to me. Moving South and then West took us out of our way if we would be heading to Sanctuary. I had to trust that Jared knew what he was doing and had a plan. I worried about my younger brother Matt working security for the first team. He wasn't as skilled as Jacob; then again… none of us have ever been as skilled as Jacob.

"Jessica, do you copy?" Jared asked into his radio.

"I am here." My mother replied.

"We will be making a right onto Prescott Road and taking it all the way out. It will lead us parallel to Baker by several miles. We shouldn't be detected that far outside of town. Still, I want Brian to keep his eyes peeled for any signs of trouble. There will be no slowing down and no stopping if we can help it… not if we plan to catch up. On these back roads we should have smooth sailing all the way out. People don't normally travel these roads so be leery of any vehicles parked on the side of the road. Chances are… they don't belong there."

"Yes Sir." My mother replied before the radio went silent.

Jared set the radio down and laughed aloud before shaking his head. "Your brother…," he said through his laughter. "That boy is going to open that box tonight."

"What box?" I asked confused.

"I gave your older brother a box and told him not to open it until he made it to our halfway point. Within the next few hours he will think we are in serious trouble. Probably about the time they hit the state line. I would say that he opens the box tonight in camp… about the time everyone thinks we are lost." Jared roared in laughter. "I wish I could be there to see the look of shock on his face when he realizes we left right after they did and that we are safe."

I sat pondering this new information and smiled. "Wait. You mean you gave him a box and told him not to open it… knowing he would open it?"

Jared smiled and glanced at me. "He is a very intelligent young man. He will trust his instincts more than usual on this trip. His instincts will tell him that something isn't right and turn the caravan off course and into the desert. He will open the box to look for guidance and answers as to what to do next and any sign that we are all safe. I put my life on it."

I sat back against my seat and looked out the window at the desert flats as we passed by. I didn't like the idea that there would be the chance my brothers and father would think something bad happened to us. It turned my stomach at the thought of it. I readjusted my glasses on my face and turned to look through the little window into the truck bed. Becky and Bobby were curled up and sleeping in Emily's lap, looking peaceful and content with no worries or fears. They were so young they would never remember the days before the blackout. I secretly prayed they would never remember the days shortly after it as well.

We hit Prescott Road and barreled North right through the center of northern Nevada. My brothers' caravan had been heading east toward Utah, but by the look of our route we were headed north and into Idaho. At some point we would have to cross the highway that ran from West to East. Jared had said it would be a

Darkness Falls

while before we would have to worry about that section and that I could take a nap if I wanted to. We were nowhere near civilization and wouldn't be for a while. I closed my eyes and sunk down into my seat intending to take full advantage of the opportunity. Time slipped by as I drifted in and out, lulled by the motion of the pickup truck and the silence of the open desert.

The sound of gunfire startled me awake. I sunk deeper into my seat and reached for my M16. We had been caught off guard. Jared screamed into his radio as he shifted the truck and swerved. Emily and Megan began to scream in the back of the bed for everyone to get down.

"Travis! Gang snipers up there in the ridge...," Jared screamed at me. "Fire!"

I blinked the sleep from my eyes and turned in the direction he had been pointing. The orange of the evening sky seemed a striking contrast to the darkening of the earth around us. Up on the ridge not far from our current location sat two armed men opening fire on our caravan. I pulled my knees up under me in the passenger seat in order to help steady my hand, trained my rifle and opened fire. One man dropped his gun and fell backward while the other kept shooting at us.

"Jared!" My mother screamed through the radio. "Brian has been hit!"

Now fueled more heavily in fear I opened up to full automatic and let the second man have it. Several rounds in rapid succession slammed into him forcing him to drop his gun and fall on his side.

"Travis, climb into my lap and take over. I need you driving!" Jared yelled at me as he slowly moved closer to the passenger side of the pickup. "Don't stop! Just blow through and keep going until I tell you to stop. Go around or even through shit if you have to!"

I quickly slid onto his lap, taking control of the wheel as he slid out from under me. I had never driven the truck on the road before, only in the fields around Compound. I didn't even have a license, though I had guessed it wouldn't matter much these days. I glanced into my side mirror and saw my mother's vehicle behind me as it gained speed. I shifted and slammed my foot down on the gas petal. The engine roared and lurked. Gunfire rang out again as Jared leaned out the passenger window and opened fire. Ahead of us in the distance sat two pickup trucks blocking the roadway with several armed men.

"Get low!" Jared screamed, just as the passenger side of the windshield exploded.

I swerved hard to the left before correcting and aimed the truck down the center of the road. I dropped down into the seat, unable to see the armed men or the road ahead of me. I glanced at Jared to see the bullet had grazed his leg but hadn't fazed him. He still kept firing out the window. I peered out over the edge of the dash just enough to make sure I was keeping the truck steady, and saw two men fall dead. I shifted again and buried my foot into the petal. "Jared! Blow through or go around?" I cried as we neared the blockade.

"Blow through! Aim for the center!" He cried, before several rounds hit their mark on another armed man.

The trucks had been placed with the cabs pointing outward, obviously to allow for a quick exit once they managed to get what they were after. I would be smashing into the gap between both truck beds, forcing them to give way. I could hear Jared screaming at Megan and the children to brace for impact. I grabbed for my seatbelt and clicked it closed before sitting upright and pushing myself into the seat. The passenger seatbelt clicked seconds before I closed my eyes. Watching the impact might have caused me to release my foot from the gas petal, and I didn't want to chance it. The harder I hit the beds the better.

I took a deep breath and held it. For the briefest of moments I heard people screaming. Seconds later I felt as though I had driven right into a brick wall as the truck slammed into the target. My body jerked forward hard before slamming back into the seat. The deafening sound of broken glass and twisting metal flooded my ears with intensity. The truck rocked and jerked as I fought to hold the wheel steady and keep my aim down the center of the roadway. When I opened my eyes we had blown through the blockade.

"Good job! Keep going." Jared screamed as he climbed out the passenger window and onto the top of the cab.

He moved with speed onto the top of the truck bed enclosure and opened fire again at the blockade behind us. I checked my side mirror in time to see my mother's truck clear the blockade behind us as Jared added cover fire. Then everything went silent. The sound of my ragged breathing filled the cab as I continued to push on. Jared moved above me on the roof and slipped down through the window into the passenger seat.

"We need to get to a safe place to check for injuries. Are you hurt?" Jared asked as he slid across the bench seat toward me to inspect my head.

"I am fine." I stated flatly, more concerned about Brian than myself. "Who were they?"

"Desperate people looking for food and water...," Jared frowned. "... They are fighting for survival."

The radio crackled several times before my mother's voice came through. "Jared... we are losing him!" She cried as Sarah screamed hysterically in the background. "...He won't make it!"

"Stop the truck." Jared yelled as he leaned out the window to see behind us.

I quickly slowed the truck to a stop, turned off the engine, and dove from the cab into a dead run. I desperately wanted to check on Emily and the children but knew I had to make it to Brian as quickly as possible. I cleared the back of our trailer in time to see my mother jump out of her truck, running to meet me.

"He took one to the chest!" She screamed as we ran around to the passenger side. Jared had the door open and was pulling Brian out of the truck and down onto the ground. Sarah screamed uncontrollably within the cab as she fought to climb out.

I grabbed the blood covered first aid kit that had been sitting at Brian's feet inside the truck and fell to my knees on the ground next to him. Brian gasped for air as he lied there shaking and coughing blood. I quickly tore his shirt open and found a single bullet wound to the right side of his chest. He choked and strained against Jared who fought to hold him still.

"Jessica... go check on the girls!" Jared yelled before turning his attention back to Brian. "Stay still buddy. It is going to be alright."

Sarah dropped down next to Jared and grabbed Brian's hand. "Hang in there baby. We have to get a look at it." Sarah choked.

I knew the second I saw the wound that Brian wouldn't last much longer. A quick glance at Jared confirmed it as the expression on his face told more than a thousand soundless words. Brian would drown in his own blood. The sucking chest wound would fill his lungs with blood before we could do anything to stop it. I shook with fear as I fought with the clasps on the first aid box before opening the box and digging inside.

"Travis...," Jared said softly as he put his hand on my shoulder. "We've got this. Go check on the animals would you?"

Before I knew what I was doing, I jumped to my feet and ran. Even with all the medical training I had been put through over the years, I couldn't handle the thought of losing a member of Compound. I rounded the back of the utility trailer and retched into the dirt, falling to my knees. I buried both hands into the dirt in order to stabilize me for fear I would fall face first into the mess as the tears began to fall. I glanced up into the utility trailer to see the faces of both milk goats watching me intently. One of them had blood spatter down the left side of her face. I jumped to my feet and flung the small gate door open. Both milk goats moved away from the door, allowing for me to climb inside. The pregnant goat lay on her side, blood dripping from a bullet wound to the neck. In a panic, I dropped down next to her as she slowly blinked but refused to move.

"Damn...," I whispered as I ran my hands down the length of her body. "... sorry old girl."

She was only days away from birth. I pressed gently and felt a kid move against my hand. The kids were alive. Quickly I pulled my survival knife from my tactical vest. If I had any chance of saving the babies, I would have to work quickly. Trying to remember everything that Angela had taught me about emergency caesarians on livestock, I gently set the blade of my knife against her chest. One swift motion would kill the goat and end her suffering. I didn't want her to suffer through what I knew needed to be done in order to save the kids. Every motion would have to be done as quickly as possible. Time could not be wasted. I gently ran my hand across the top of her head, and plunged my knife into her chest just like Angela had taught me to do if the animal had no chance at life. The goat jerked only slightly and went still.

With Angela's words playing from memory, I set to the task of carefully opening her up without injuring the kids inside her... who now fought for their own survival. I didn't care about how messy the process would be or whether the mother could survive what I attempted. She was now gone, her pain ended with the thrust of my blade. Within seconds the belly of the goat began to swim as I opened enough space to have a look inside. I couldn't tell how many kids there were but knew they didn't have much longer if I didn't get them out. I opened up the goat as much as possible before dropping my knife and pulling on the kids. With a couple of firm tugs I managed to pull free the kids, spilling them out onto the trailer bed at my knees. I reached back in and did a last feel around to make sure I had pulled them all free. Three small kids lay squirming at my knees.

"Well hello there...," I said as I cleaned their faces with my hands. "Welcome to the world."

After a brief sexing of the kids, I managed to figure out that Compound had gained two does and a buck, all three with similar coats to match their parents. I slowly showed the milk goat the kids as I moved to allow them a line of sight. The largest of the does stepped forward to have a sniff at the squirming pile of kids. Angela had fostered newborns to them before, but I didn't know the first thing about how to do it. I crawled backward to give her room, but tried to stay close enough to rescue the babies if she decided to stomp them. She sniffed them all several times before she surprised me by licking them. I crawled toward the gate door as I watched both milk goats take to the care the kids needed.

I couldn't be sure the goats wouldn't decide to kill them after all, but they would die without a mother anyway. Their best shot at life would be the two remaining goats fostering them. I climbed out the back and closed the gate. Pulling the dead mother from the back would take more than just my hands. I turned to run around the end of the trailer and almost ran right into Jared. I couldn't be sure how long he had been standing there watching.

"Good job, Travis. Saving those kids was a good deed. The girls will accept them, you can tell." Jared whispered as he dried his tears with the back of his hand. "We tried everything we could... we couldn't save Brian. He's gone."

Tears fell in a cascade of emotion as I fell back against the edge of the trailer and leaned into it. "Everyone... else... alright?" I stammered as the shock ripped through me.

"No...," Jared whispered as he placed both hands on my shoulders. "We lost the goat, one of the dogs... and Megan."

"Wh... what?" I asked in a panicked tone.

"The bullet that came through the cab of the truck had gone through into the bed. She had taken her flak jacket off and wrapped it around Michael. Wouldn't have mattered... the bullet struck her... in the back of the head." Jared said as the tears began to flood from his eyes. "She was leaned over on the children trying to protect them. At the angle she was in..."

"No!" I screamed as I buried my face into his chest.

"I am sorry kiddo. Emily and the kids didn't notice right away. They stayed down trying to hide from more gunfire. Your mother went to check on them, that was when they saw."

For several long minutes, I let it all out against Jared's chest. Every painful emotion poured from me in a torrent so great, it couldn't be controlled. Brian and Megan, we had lost them both. This morning in the comfort of Compound, we had all sat around the breakfast table talking about our journey to Sanctuary. Now we were divided into two groups at different points within the state... and some had lost their lives. I had helped Megan give birth to Michael. I had spent my whole life with Brian and Megan. Now the thought they were gone tore my soul right out of me, leaving me an empty shell of what I once was. Everything had happened so quickly. One minute we were traveling peacefully and the next minute two people were dead.

"We have to be strong Travis...," Jared whispered. "The children are confused. They don't really understand yet."

"I don't understand yet!" I screamed as I punched Jared in the chest several times, trying to break free. "Why did this have to happen? Why are we running away? We should have stayed at Compound and hid in the bunker instead of running away like cowards! Now they are dead... dead! You killed them! You did this by making us leave!" I pushed myself from his grasp and fell back against the trailer gate. "I... hate... you. I will never forgive you for this, any of it."

"It is okay. You are allowed to hate me." Jared said dejectedly as he dropped his arms to his sides. "It wasn't supposed to happen like this. I never intended for this. You have to know... this trip is dangerous. We headed out knowing we would meet trouble along the way. I had no way of knowing..."

My eyes burned with grief as I watched Jared slump against the bumper next to me. Fueled by the high emotions of the day, the death of two beloved members of Compound, and the high energy of saving baby goats, I began to shake with anger. I stood and turned toward Jared, my fists clenched in fury. Before I even realized what I was doing, I punched him square in the jaw with everything I had in me. His head fell back and bounced on the trailer before he rolled to the right and fell off the bumper and onto the dirt.

"You sick bastard... I hate you!" I yelled, before storming away to find Emily. I felt as though I had shattered my hand as the pain ripped through it and up my arm. I stuffed it under my other arm as I marched, unwilling to admit that I had probably just done the dumbest thing I had ever done in my whole life. I fought the urge to turn around and tell him that I didn't mean it and that my actions had been fueled by pain, but I was still so furious I knew it might end just as badly.

"What happened back there?" My mother asked confused as she walked toward me.

I couldn't tell her that I had just punched our fearless leader in the jaw, so I brushed her off with the wave of my good hand. "We have work to do. We can't handle this situation here... we are still too close to the blockade. We need to load the remaining dogs into the back of the big truck with the children, and move the dead into the back of the other truck." I said with much less emotion than I wanted to. "We need to get back on the road and find a safe place to take care of this."

My mother's eyes fell to look at the ground. "Travis...," She whispered. "I understand you have been through a lot today, we all have. Do you want to talk about it?"

"I want to get the hell out of here before someone else dies!" I spat before stomping off to Jared's truck and pulling out my M16. "You see this?" I called as I neared my mother again. "This is what we have to protect ourselves right now. I want to know why those bastards had running trucks when no one else does. I want to know how they had that firepower they used against us... but I am not willing to sit around and wait for the answers! If we don't move right now, anyone still standing back there will come with answers in the form of bullets. You want that?"

"He is right, Jessica. We need to put them in the back of your truck and get us all safely out of here before we can handle it." Jared said softly as he walked up next to my mother.

"I am driving my mother's truck. I need you...," I said pointing at my mother, "...to ride in the back of Jared's truck to help calm the children. Sarah needs to ride with Jared so that he can help calm her down. Then we are getting the hell out of here. We will handle the dead when we make camp for the night.

Someplace we can give them the respect they deserve and actually maybe even mourn them properly."

Without another word I stormed off to my mother's truck and let the two remaining hound dogs out of the back. They jumped down and ran to Jared who lifted them one by one into the enclosure of his truck. I left the body of the other dog in the back, but moved it aside to make room for the others to be loaded in beside it. Jared wrapped Megan in a sheet he had pulled from the supply trailer and placed her gently beside the dog. When I saw her limp and covered form, my blood began to boil. I wanted nothing more than to punch Jared a second time, but I held my anger in check as we needed to leave the area more than feed my need to hit someone. Jared and my mother loaded Brian, then the goat before we closed the gate and headed for our vehicles.

I turned the key and fired up my mother's truck and closed my eyes while listening to the engine purr. For the rest of the day, I would be driving the truck with the dead. I shivered briefly at the thought before the anger returned to me. As our travel party pulled out and begin the journey, I thought about my brothers and whether they were alright. We had lost two people on the very first day out. I couldn't imagine what hell they had faced and who might not have survived.

For now, I was going to focus on my team and do whatever it took to keep them alive. We wouldn't lose another person if I could help it. Not today. Not tomorrow. Not ever.

CHAPTER FOURTEEN

The early morning light filtered through the door of my tent, kissing my cheek with the warmth that had been robbed from me overnight. I rolled over slowly and lifted myself up on my elbow to peek into Bentley's cardboard box. He slept peacefully as always, his little lips moved slowly while pressed together. He must have been dreaming about eating. I often wondered what he dreamt about or what he was usually thinking. Late at night I would lay in the bed in my tiny cabin and just watch him sleep, hoping he would wake up just enough to smile at me. He had grown since the day we found him in that wrecked car over a month ago. His last check up with Sarah had gone much better than expected. Not only was he on track with his growth, but he had been packing on the weight and eating like a little monster. I giggled when I thought back on how excited she had become after she had weighed him that morning.

"Fallon... are you awake?" Jacob whispered through the door of my tent.

"I am up. But hush! Bentley is sleeping." I whispered back as I slowly unzipped the zipper enough to crawl out into the early morning light.

I always slept with the tent slightly unzipped to allow for quick exit, but the two man hiking tent had seemed much smaller once Bentley's box had been placed inside. I also worried he would get cold overnight. A six inch open gap was all I felt I could manage with a baby inside with me. It had been cold, but we both managed to stay warm enough to sleep as soundly as possible. My back needed a good stretch though; I wasn't fond of sleeping on the ground if I could help it. I stood outside the tent and stretched both arms up over my head until I heard a small popping sound from my shoulder and felt my back shift.

"Coffee mi' lady...," Jacob smiled as he passed me a steaming cup of coffee. "... half a sugar and two cream, just the way you like it."

"Thank you." I smiled before taking a tentative sip. It was hot and thick like boiled pond water, but tasted like a dream come true. "Oh that is good. Tell Angela I said thank you."

"We are planning to hit the road as early as possible. My dad and Dave helped me go over the map last night and with the timetable we are facing... we need to get on the road in case there is any trouble out there. Here, I set you up a chair." Jacob said as he motioned to the two chairs placed side by side about ten feet from the tent.

I nodded before walking over and gently placing myself into the chair closed to the tent. "Jacob. Do you think the second team is alright? I mean, we have no way of knowing right now I understand that. But I don't know... I just have this feeling that something is going to happen to them."

"You can't think like that. Your dad is an amazing man and he knows what he is doing. He won't stop until they are safe." Jacob said before taking a sip of his coffee and continuing. "What we need to be focusing on is our own team right now. Let your dad handle his team... we worry about this one."

I leaned back into my chair and relaxed my head so that I was facing the sky. The sun would warm my cold cheeks and filter the warmth down deep into my soul. Combined with the hot coffee, I could warm from both the inside and the outside allowing the warmth to meet up in the middle. Spending the night in the desert in a hiking tent hadn't been how I would have chosen to sleep, but it did the job well enough. I opened my eyes and rolled my head toward the fire that had been built the night before which still sat burning in the center of the large circle our vehicles had made. Angela sat on a rock in front of the fire, obviously annoyed by having to cook on open flame instead of the kitchen we had left behind. I couldn't tell what she had been making but I could guess it would have eggs in it. Smiling, I closed my eyes again and sipped my hot and heavenly pond water.

"Everything is ready to go. After breakfast we can break down the tents and get moving again." Matt said as he pulled up a chair next to me and sat down. "I even cleaned up after the animals and made sure they had plenty of food and water. The cats aren't very happy but oh well, they will get over it."

"I am still sore from yesterday!" I laughed as I tilted my head from one side to the other in an attempted to pop my neck. "As long as we make it to the point of radio contact, I will be happy. I can't wait to hear my dad."

Angela brought us a couple of plates piled high with scrambled eggs and jerky. She shrugged as I accepted the plate with a smile. She didn't seem happy about the meal but it looked like she had tried her best with what she had been given. I stuffed the eggs into my mouth as quickly as possible, chewing and swallowing each forkful briefly. The eggs weren't as bad tasting as the look on Angela's face had indicated, although they could have used a little garlic in my opinion. I wasn't about to tell her that. She didn't need any added stress. Matt made quick work of his eggs as well, commenting at how delicious they were.

Once we had finished breakfast, and I had changed and fed Bentley, we climbed into the transport truck while Robert and Dave packed up the last of the gear. Cassidy and Cassandra had been sluggish at breakfast and quickly fell back to sleep on the pile of blankets in the back of the transport. I calculated the distance we could travel on dirt roads and came to the conclusion that as long as we didn't stop or meet trouble along the way, we could meet the radio point well before nightfall. Under normal circumstances we would have made it to Sanctuary in a single day. We had only made it to the state line and then traveled off course by the time the sun set. The engines began to turn over as Robert called out the command to hit the road. Within seconds, we began to move as cheers rose up over the sound of the trucks. I smiled to myself as I thought about how far we could go if we just stayed the course.

My father's map had marked out our route, taking us out of our way at several points yet leaving us on as many unmarked dirt roads as possible. A straight shot would have gotten us there in a matter of a couple of hours, but that had been out of the question.

The group had decided to go slowly and cautiously, sticking to the plan that my father had laid out for us in advance. We had chosen a spot on the map as a prime location to stop for lunch allowing for a little rest before traveling on to the radio point. Dave had complained that stopping would not be in our favor, placing us on the road later than we should be. He wanted nothing more than to make radio contact and wait it out at the point my father had marked. We decided as a group that even with the late start from the lunch stop, we would be there in plenty of time.

I watched the sun move across the sky as we barreled down the dirt roads, turning from one onto another. We passed what I could only assume had been a ghost town turned tourist attraction, now abandoned due to the blackout. The ruins of what must have been a nineteenth century mining town sat silently crumbling into the earth doomed to be forgotten for all time. We drove on through it without stopping, eventually coming to yet another abandoned town that looked much younger than the first. I wondered how long it had been since someone had lived there as the place sat forgotten and lost like an ancient civilization. Buildings that had once housed a bank now sat half crumbled with sand piled by wind onto the front steps. A small house with weeds growing on the roof sat nearby with the door half hanging as if someone had once broken it down.

We hit an expansive patch of dessert and drove on in silence for what had seemed like a lifetime to me. The heat of the day had begun to climb to a point that no longer felt comfortable, forcing me to strip Bentley of his clothing and rub him down with water from the container under my bench seat. He squirmed and chewed his fist but managed to smile at me when I had finished. Angela poured small amounts of water into her daughters' hair in an attempt to cool them off as well. Even the breeze coming through the areas around the canvas cover had been hot enough to cause us to avoid it. Jacob and Matt sat in their usual spots on either side of the transport gate, watching out the back as we made our way through the desert.

"Ten minutes until our lunch stop." Robert called over the radio. "We will be stopping for a stretch and a quick meal. No fires."

I smiled at Angela as I gave a deep sigh of relief. I needed to stretch my legs and go to the bathroom. I grabbed my small travel bag that carried my bathroom gear and double checked I had everything I needed.

"Jacob... swing around and tell me if you see what I see." Robert said as the radio cracked.

Jacob stood, held onto the frame of the transport and swung out to the side. He began to laugh as he swung back into the transport and grabbed his radio. "I do believe dad that we have come across a desert hermit. We might want to stop for this."

"A what?" I asked as I opened a corner of the canvas to see what the commotion had been about. "What is a desert hermit?"

On the side of the road sat a large piece of wood with the words "Welcome travelers. Hot meal ahead" painted in red paint across the front. In the distance sat an identical sign in size to the first which read "No funny business or no food for you" in the same red paint. I turned to Angela with a look of confusion as she laughed and shook her head. We were miles from any sort of civilization to speak of, and had seen no signs of life the entire morning.

"Just remember to keep your guard up just in case. It could be trouble." Robert's voice sounded through the radio.

As we neared, we passed a few more signs indicating that we would be required to park outside the gate near a large rock and honk the horn if we did not see anyone outside. I folded myself back into my seat and quickly dressed Bentley in something he wouldn't overheat in. Moments later we pulled to a stop and I heard the passenger door to the transport slam closed. I couldn't catch but a few words exchanged between Robert and my mother, but could tell they were in good spirits.

I peered out the tiny space between the canvas and the frame to see if I could catch a glimpse. There in the middle of the desert, just off the dirt road sat a building that couldn't have been much larger than a shed, and painted the same color as the desert floor. A small pen containing a couple of pigs sat just south of the structure by about fifty feet. Close enough to the house I realized, that the person who lived there probably had to deal with the smell even while indoors. The outhouse had been about the same distance from the cabin as well which likely added to the smell. There on the small deck of the house, stood a heavy set man in camouflage pants, shirtless with a look of shock on his face. His massive amounts of greying chest hair and desert tanned skin barely hid the many tattoos that decorated his upper body. His hair looked to be pulled into a messy ponytail the same color as his chest hair, but long enough the end brushed the middle of his back. In one hand he held a spatula and in the other a beer can, as he stood over a grill staring in our direction.

"Well I'll be damned!" The aged man yelled at Robert from the deck as he emptied his hands and climbed down the steps to head in our direction. He grabbed a rifle from the edge of the deck and hoisted it. "Tell me you are along for the hot meal and not to cause trouble. I don't have time for trouble."

Robert raised his hands slowly. "We are just passing through. My name is Robert Dunn and this is Miranda Henley. We were heading out on these back roads when we happened onto your signs."

The man crinkled his face and pondered briefly. "Henley you say? Any relation to the Nevada Henley's out of Baker?"

Miranda stepped forward. "Yes. My husband is Jared Henley. He may have traveled through here a time or two in order to create the map he gave us. Do you know my husband?"

The man lowered his rifle with a smile. "Sure do, haven't seen him in a lifetime though. Rolled up through here I'd say...,"He rubbed his short beard with his free hand as he thought, "... About four or five months back on his way up North. Comes through I'd say about once a year or so by this way. He normally takes the direct route so when I get the chance to see him, we talk. Don't know him well... but well enough."

"We are headed North as well." Robert said as he dropped his hands to his sides. "He isn't with our group. He is traveling with the rest of our family on a different route."

"Well I am guessing you are welcome here for that hot meal then. I don't get many visitors out this way. Have myself a young kid that drives in once a month from the nearest town North of here. Brings me things sometimes but never stays long. He hasn't been here at all since the blackout."

"You know about the blackout? Even way out here?" Miranda asked.

"My emergency radio stopped working... truck isn't running... boy didn't show... fairly obvious in the long run." He looked down at himself and ran his free hand down his bare chest. "I'm not very decent here am I? Sorry about that. I put the signs up a couple of weeks ago thinking someone might come by here at some point. Never thought to be dressed enough for company. The name is Chase McGee ma'am, though back during the war my brothers in arms called me Firefly." He said as he extended his hand. "I was just starting to make some lunch so you are right on time."

We unloaded everyone from the vehicles and after a quick introduction, followed the elderly man to a picnic table in front of his cabin. Angela wasted no time offering to take over the cooking and offered to add some of our own food to the meal in an effort to ease the burden on his food supply. Dave brought out a bottle of moonshine and offered some to Chase, who excitedly accepted a glass though I had suspected he had more than a few beers with his breakfast already. He smelled faintly of sweat, stale beer, tobacco, and gun powder. It hadn't taken long for Chase and Dave to hit it off and begin telling stories from their younger days. Chase had served in the army most of his life and through several wars. Once he retired he found he couldn't quite fit in with society and took to finding peace in being alone in the desert.

Angela combined the meals and offered us a great array of canned fruit salad, canned vegetables, fried chicken and potatoes, all of which didn't last very long once on the table. While we ate lunch, Robert and my mother told Chase the story of the creation of Compound, what happened after the blackout, and of the journey we had taken before reaching him. He sat and listened intently as he slowly chewed each bite of food, unwilling to look away as they took turns telling the tale. My mother made sure to include the story of how we ended up taking on Bentley, and Chase made it a point to wink at me and smile. Without even realizing it, we had sat in heavy conversation for several hours while Chase asked the occasional question.

"Chase, do you have enough to survive out here alone... I mean, since the boy hasn't been showing up for you?" Robert asked eventually as he pushed his empty glass into the center of the table.

"Not anymore. I grow most everything and have several wells on the property. But I have found I relied on that kid fairly heavily over the years... mostly for the drink. My food is low now though. I figured I would stay as long as possible and wait for someone to come through." Chase said as he poured himself another glass of moonshine. "Figured I could trade some knowledge for a safe passage to somewhere outside the desert... if they be good people."

"What sort of knowledge?" Edward asked as he leaned forward on his elbows.

"Traps my boy... animal or enemy depending on the need. I was a gunsmith for a while in my younger days. The army taught me everything I needed to know and then some." Chase said as he turned his arm to Edward to show his tattoo. "Army Ranger... for life."

"Why did they call you Firefly?" I asked tentatively, not wanting to upset the man who had a few too many drinks in him by midday.

Chase roared in laughter and slammed his fist on the table. "My dear... the things I was made to do for this country...," He laughed as he patted his tattoo, "... did things to me it did. But I was the best at what I had been trained to do. When I retired finally, I didn't cope well once on the outside. Lord knows I tried. Maybe the Firefly story is best suited for a different time."

"How would you like to come along with us? We can take you as far as you need to go until we reach our destination of course." My mother asked as she began to gather dishes and hand them to Matt. "We never turn away new people who have skills they might want to share. If you choose to stay with us, we can make arrangements with Jared... if you like."

Chase leaned back slightly and looked around his property before frowning. "I won't last long here without my deliveries. Guess it would be alright to go with you. Not used to being around people. We should take it one day at a time and see where it goes."

I watched Dave laugh and give Chase a pat on the back before shaking his hand. Here we were on a journey to Sanctuary and we managed to pick up a desert hermit along the way. Not just any desert hermit... but a drunken one with service connected emotional issues. Chase had skills and knowledge in things I knew my father would be interested in. Though I found Chase to be rather odd, I couldn't deny that he could be useful to us. I lifted Bentley to my chest and patted his back as I climbed off the bench of the picnic table. I would need to check for extra room within our vehicles for Chase and his belongings. In all honesty, we were tight on room as it was. Taking in an extra person would be tricky at best.

It didn't take long for Chase and Robert to pack out what little Chase would be taking along. His cabin consisted of nothing more than a bed with storage underneath, and a small desk and pantry with solar mini fridge. Chase elected to take a few sets of clothing which he had crammed into a military issued gear bag, one box of items he said reminded him of his Ranger days, some canned food and some pictures he had in tiny frames on his desk. Once the cabin had been packed out, Chase informed Robert and Dave that there was a shed at the back of the house we would want to clean out, and that if room allowed for it… he wanted to take his pigs. He hadn't bred them in a while as he needed to add new blood lines to the group and since we raised pigs as well, it would be helpful for all of us in the long term. Dave quickly agreed and wasted no time introducing Chase to Bacon, explaining that the pigs could ride together all the way to Sanctuary… so long as the rooster and the buck goat allowed it.

After handing Bentley to Jacob, I headed around the back of the cabin with my mother to empty the shed. Chase had handed us a second military issued gear bag and instructed us to grab everything we could. We cracked the unlocked door open on the shed and waited for the light to fill the darkness. Inside sat a large array of firearms hanging from hooks on the wall and boxes of ammunition stacked nearly to the ceiling. We would need more than one gear bag to haul out the loot. I walked in and flipped the switch just inside the door. The light flickered several times before emitting a high pitched buzz and lighting the entire shed.

"Dear God." My mother whispered as she reached for a bag that sat partially opened in the corner. "Grenades… a whole potato sack full!" She pulled the bag out and placed it by the door before searching through an unmarked box. "Land mines in this one."

"How did he get all these?" I asked as I pulled firearms off the hooks and gently slipped them muzzle down, into the gear bag.

"Who knows…," She whispered as she shook her head. "Gun Peppers. That is what we call them. People who stockpile mass amounts of weapons to protect their land or family in the event of collapse. I'd say by the look of this place, he has a connection somewhere that helped supply it. You just can't get your hands on some of this stuff."

We loaded every firearm we could find into not only the gear bag, but also a second bag we found lying on top of a pile of boxes and placed them in the dirt outside the door. My mother made sure to add the land mines and grenades to the pile that would be placed into one of the trailers. Robert arrived to see what had been taking so long, and after the shock of the sight before him, became overjoyed. He quickly grabbed the bags and headed for the trucks yelling for Dave and Edward to lend a hand. With the extra hands helping with the clean out, we had the entire weapons shed packed out and into the trucks in less than thirty minutes. The pigs quickly followed.

Chase decided to ride with Dave and packed a small bag to be brought with them, consisting of some of the weapons from the shed. I climbed back into the transport and placed the now sleeping Bentley into his secured box crib as the caravan lurked forward and pulled slowly onto the open dirt road. I watched Dave and Chase in deep conversation from my position in the transport and smiled. I knew Dave missed having Brian around, and knew that even with all of Dave's complaining, Chase would be good for him.

We drove on through the afternoon, trying desperately to make up the time we had lost collecting our desert hermit. We hadn't intended to spend that long having lunch and now we were sorely behind schedule. It had been decided that we would no longer be stopping and instead heading straight to the place on the map that my dad had indicated we be before sundown. We drove through the small town where apparently the boy lived that made deliveries to Chase, but the place sat like a ghost town. At some point the residents who had once called it home had left in a hurried fashion as belongings sat half packed in yards or on front steps. I wondered briefly if they had headed out on foot or horseback across the desert in an attempt to cross into Idaho.

"I don't like this. Something isn't right." Jacob whispered as he shifted in his seat. "Matt, do you smell that?"

I sniffed the air tentatively as I leaned closer to the brothers. There was something in the air, a smell resembling meat grilling on a barbeque, but there was another smell as well. "What is going on?" I asked as I glanced at Angela behind me. The smell became stronger as we neared the source, and I could now smell bread.

"If the entire town is abandoned... who is cooking?" Jacob asked annoyed. He grabbed his radio and spoke into it, "There might be trouble ahead. I smell food cooking. Someone is still here. Keep your eyes open."

I crawled over to the area where the children sat on piles of blankets, pulling Bentley from his cardboard bed as I went. This wouldn't be a desert hermit, someone didn't leave town with everyone else. Angela lay down next to Cassidy and Cassandra, whispering to them about taking a nap before reaching the radio point. I pulled the spare flak jackets over the blankets hoping to protect the children should things go sour. Angela reached for Bentley, taking him from my arms and placing him on the blankets between the children and her.

"I've got him. Go help out." Angela whispered and she lay down and covered Bentley with a flak jacket.

I checked my clip before slamming it back into my 9mm and sliding back to Jacob's side. We had been driving through what could only be described as the main road through the center of town. Out of the edge of my vision I caught sight of something moving on the roof of a destroyed hardware store just as we drove by. I reached up and grabbed Jacob's knee, squeezing hard. He tapped the back of my hand without taking his eyes off the building.

"Jacob...," I whispered.

"I know. I saw." He whispered back as he slowly lifted his M16 into the ready.

The sound of our trucks echoed off of the surrounding buildings, amplified by the silence of the town as we barreled through the streets. The hair on the back of my neck began to stand on end as I caught sight of movement to my left. My eyes darted, only to find nothing there except an overturned compact car with the windows broken. I scanned the area on both sides of the road making mental note of how many vehicles had been overturned as if to create shelters or hiding places for ambush.

The tension was broken instantly with the sound of a siren as it cut through the silence like a hot knife. Shots rang out in multiple directions as I dropped for cover by Jacob's side. I lifted onto my elbow enough to catch a glimpse of the street and attempt to count the gunmen. They came from every direction and stood on rooftops, behind cars, and in bushes. I fired my 9mm at a man as he made eye contact with me, hitting him in the neck. His hands jumped to his throat as blood exploded in all directions, stumbling backward and falling from sight as he went. Jacob screamed for Matt to open fire on the right side of the road while he covered the left. Glass shattered on vehicles and buildings as the firefight escalated rapidly. I jumped to my knees, shielding myself behind the transport truck's gate and squeezed my trigger in the direction of a gunman taking aim at Jacob. My bullet found a place in the center of his chest pitching him backward and dropping him flat onto his back in the dirt.

I watched in shock as Chase opened the passenger door of Dave's pickup and climbed up onto the cab of the truck. He was obviously still under the influence of the beer he had consumed for breakfast and the moonshine from lunch, as he fumbled to grab the handhold Brian and Dave had welding into the roof. He locked his bare feet under a couple of the handles and using a handhold on the truck bed cage, stood straight up and laughing. Two large straps crossed his bare chest stuffed with grenades. Now becoming a target, I fired on men who tried to jump from behind barriers in an attempt to fire at him. Chase quickly tied a rope around his waist, strapping himself to the frame of the cage that houses the animals in the bed of the truck.

"Nice party boys!" Chase laughed loudly as he pulled two grenades from his chest straps. Lifting them to his mouth he pulled both pins at once with his teeth and spit them out. "I brought the presents!" He screamed seconds before he flung a grenade into a pile of rubble hiding four gunmen.

"Shit!" Matt cried as he tossed himself out of his seat and onto the floor next to me.

The pile of rubble exploded with such intensity chunks of wood and concrete launched into the air as if shot from a cannon, raining down onto gunmen as they attempted to run. Screams erupted as the second grenade landed into the bushes and exploded with such power two men instantly disappeared in a flash of flame and bloody mist. Chase let out a mighty yelp, and pounded his chest in an ape like fashion before pulling more pins with his teeth. The transport truck lurked forward as we gained speed. Blinking against the smoke I frantically checked my clip. Without realizing it, I had emptied the magazine.

"I'm out!" I screamed as I dove onto the floor of the

transport and scurried to reach my spare ammunition stash. Two more grenade blasts hit back to back, rocking our truck with shock waves and debris.

"Don't know when to stop do you?" Chase screamed. "Never learn do you?"

My ears pounded with the rapid drumming of my heart as I tried to cover them with both hands. One, two, three more explosions filled the air around us with dust and smoke. Bullets punched through the canvas cover above me as I grabbed what I needed and crawled back toward Jacob. We were taking heavy fire from all sides. I slapped a fresh load into my 9mm and returned to my previous position. Matt screamed, falling backward onto the floor of the transport as blood gushed from the right side of his head. Angela scrambled across the floor, grabbing Matt under the arms as he screamed and drug him closer to her.

"Matt is down!" Jacob screamed into the radio.

I quickly recovered Matt's M16 and jumped into his seat, which was now covered in blood. I placed both feet onto the gate to help lock my body into place. Chase nodded at me knowingly as our eyes met. He was just as worried about Matt as I was. He pulled another pin with his teeth and hurled his last grenade through the front window of what remained of a diner. I braced myself against the frame as the explosion launched debris in all directions.

Without warning, we began to pass open desert as the buildings ended. The sound of gunfire continued behind us as we barreled down the road. I stayed in the blood soaked seat with the M16 ready, scanning the sides of the road for trouble that didn't come. Jacob swung around the end of the transport to see if the cost was clear.

"I need us to be a safe distance before I can help Matt!" Edward's voice cracked through the radio. "Is anyone else hurt?"

"We be fine." Dave came back, "Chase be havin' screws loose in that head o' his though!" He laughed.

I jumped off the seat and ran, jumping over Angela as she tended to Matt. Cassidy and Cassandra lay crying and holding each other in fear, Bentley wailing beside them. "Children are fine." I spoke into the radio as I sat beside them, scooping Bentley into my arms and hugging the sisters tightly. I patted each of them down and checked them over for injuries before kissing each of them on the head and whispering that we would be alright.

"He is losing a lot of blood Jacob, but the bullet grazed his head. He is damned lucky." Angela said as she continued to add pressure to the side of Matt's head.

"Edward," Robert's voice came over the radio weakly as he began to cry. "Miranda is not good... not good at all."

My heart dropped into my gut as my eyes found Jacob. The look on his face was one of shock and terror as he slowly lifted his radio to his mouth without taking his eyes from mine. As he spoke I could barely hear his whisper coming from both my radio and from next to me. "Dad... What is going on up there?" He asked slowly before waiting in silence.

The radio cracked several times before only sobs came over briefly and went silent again. Jacob dropped his radio and pulled me into his arms as the shock of what Robert couldn't say began to hit me. I fought to suck in air as I reached for the radio.

"She's gone... she's gone!" Robert choked over the radio. "I don't know... they shot her... she's gone."

All I heard next was the sound of hysterical screaming. My own screaming.

CHAPTER FIFTEEN

"Travis, I think we need to talk." Jared said as he zipped his duffle bag closed with his good hand and tossed it into the cab of the truck.

"Go to hell, Jared." I spat, turning from him and walking toward my mother's pickup truck. "I have nothing more to say to you and I have no time for your crap."

The morning sun had just begun to rise over the edge of the mountain range, touching the campsite with enough light to begin packing. I could tell by the amount of crying I had heard that no one else managed to sleep well the night before. After driving a safe distance away from where we had been ambushed, we stopped just North of the highway crossing, passing through it without trouble. Though it had broken our hearts to make the choice, we all knew we couldn't make it to Sanctuary with the bodies in the back of the pickup. They would need to be dealt with as soon as possible. After making camp for the night, Jared and my mother set to work digging shallow graves for each of them including one for the goat. Sarah had wished for the dog to be buried with Brian in the same grave so they would be close even in death. We held a small funeral for them and placed them gently into their graves which had then been filled in with dirt and had a large pile of rocks placed on top. I marked the area on the map indicating where they could be found hoping at a later date we could somehow move them to Sanctuary or back to Compound. *That is if we ever make it to either of them*, I had thought to myself.

Dinner had been nothing more than a couple of MREs which we had only opened to feed the children as none of us had an appetite by the end of the day. As the darkness fell around us, we sat around a campfire struggling with sudden outbursts of sobs and screaming. Emily had found a can of formula tucked under the bed unit that had been built into the truck bed, allowing for Michael to eat now that his mother was gone. Becky and Bobby spent most of dinner dazed and confused. They asked few questions and cried occasionally, though they did have a couple of rough mourning sessions with Emily in private. Sarah had refused to eat a single bite. She wouldn't even sit with us around the fire. Instead, she slipped off wishing to be alone at her husband's grave. I sat watching her in the light of the campfire as she stroked the rocks piled up on top of him. She hadn't cried a single tear once we had reached camp. In fact, she hadn't spoken but a few words about burying the dog with Brian.

After dinner we fell into our tents, some of them cried and others whispered. From my tent I heard Emily whisper lullabies to the children in an attempt to calm them. I had lain in my sleeping bag silently looking through the mesh top of my tent at the stars above me. For hours I laid there listening to the silence and trying to make sense of the decision to leave Compound, and the ambush that claimed two lives. We had lost two beloved members of Compound on the same day... taken from us by people fighting for their own survival. The world I had known was no longer the world I knew now. This world was harsh, hateful and unrelenting. It took what it wanted from you and laughed about it. There was no law, no rules, and no consequence. As I thought about it, it had reminded me of old movies that Jared and my dad had us watch growing up as young children. They would insist they had been classic films of their time, and that we could learn a thing or two from watching them.

I now tossed my own bag into the passenger seat of my mother's truck and walked over to take my place in the driver's seat. The caravan would be leaving for the journey to the radio point in less than ten minutes. Sarah had elected to continue riding with Jared, which I gratefully allowed. My mother had insisted I take the first leg of the trip as the driver, as we wouldn't be anywhere near a town for hours yet. Even Jade had asked if the two remaining hound dogs could ride in with the children as it calmed them down to pet them. I rewarded her with a small bag of gummy bears I had secreted into my gear as payment for helping with the children. She had smiled the brightest smile I had seen so far on the journey and promptly she divided them up between her and the other children.

"We should be able to make the radio point without event." My mother said as she climbed into the truck next to me. "It is smooth sailing from here on out."

"You can't be sure of that, Mom." I stated matter-of-factly as I turned the key roaring the engine to life. "Yesterday we thought the problem would be the freeway crossing. Instead, we were miles from it and two people died."

"Travis, I know you are upset. Losing them is horrible." She said as she rested her elbow on the door and placed her forehead against her hand. "I hate leaving them out here like this… they deserve better."

My grip tightened on the steering wheel turning my knuckles white. "We don't have a choice. We have to push on as quickly as possible. I have to get us to the radio point and then onto the meet up point before anything else can happen to us."

"It isn't Jared's fault…," My mother whispered as she reached for my arm.

"Don't defend him. He is an asshole." I spat as I shrugged her off.

"Travis Alexander Dunn! You need to watch your mouth young man, you are fourteen years old!" She scolded as she shook her finger at me.

"Not anymore… in case you haven't noticed mom…," I began sarcastically, "I defended Compound from perverts by guarding the barn, helped birth a baby, watched people die and personally killed people with my own gun. How does that make you feel, Mom? Knowing your son has already killed people at the age of fourteen!"

I watched as she closed her eyes, tears running down her cheeks in silence. Jared's truck lurked in front of me, refocusing my attention on leaving the campsite. Shifting into gear and pulling out slowly behind him. I followed Jared back onto the road headed north-east toward the radio point. My mother cried in the passenger seat, avoiding conversation or eye contact. As the miles ticked on I wondered if my words had been too much for my mother to have heard, be it true as they were. Though I had always been mature for my age, the combination of the blackout and the ambush had done a number on me. I should have been at home planning my middle school graduation and preparing for my last summer before high school. Instead I was driving through the desert leaving behind everything I had ever known and firing M16s at roving clans of bandits, hell bent on killing and robbing my family.

For an hour we sat in silence as I drove behind Jared watching Emily attempt to play with the children in the back of the truck ahead of me. Occasionally she looked up and smiled at me, which I promptly returned with a wave and a smile of my own. Several times I heard my mother giggle softly though I had chosen to ignore her. The last thing I wanted to deal with during this journey was a lecture on girls… or worse. I opened my water bottle and took a sip before passing it to my mother. She thanked me before taking a few swallows of her own.

The radio on the seat beeped and crackled followed by the sound of Jared's voice. "We will hit the radio point before nightfall and stay long enough to make contact before pushing on. It is going to be a long night. I suggest you get some sleep Jessica, while you can. I want you to drive the truck from the radio point to the meet up location."

"No problem Jared." My mother spoke into the radio before dropping it onto the seat between us and sinking into her seat to get comfortable. "Do you have this drive alright?" She asked.

"I am fine." I answered without taking my eyes off the road ahead of me. "Sleep while you have the chance."

I didn't want to explain that I wanted her to sleep merely so that we wouldn't speak to each other. My biggest concern was making radio contact with my brothers and explaining what had happened to our team in the last twenty-four hours. The worry over the safety of my father and brothers had been welling up inside me by the hour and I couldn't shake the idea that they had met their fair share of trouble as well on this journey. Missing them had been bad enough, not knowing if they would arrive in one piece had tortured me. If their own journey had turned out as ours had… someone wouldn't be arriving to Sanctuary. My stomach turned at the thought and I hit the steering wheel with my fist.

Dwelling on the other team would do nothing for any of us except to keep us worried.

Emily smiled at me again and I quickly gave a wave back and smiled, trying not to let her see how upset I had become. Originally I had demanded to travel with the second team in order to be close to her. She desperately missed her grandfather, and had seen much more loss than anyone should at our ages. Having someone around that she could relate too might help, at least I thought so. For now, she had been forced to ride with the children though not exactly against her will. The children had a tendency to lift her spirit and give her something to occupy her mind with. Once we made it somewhere that allowed for privacy, I would get my chance to speak with her. I needed to know how she had been coping with the blackout, the death of Papa, the exodus of our home, and the journey we were currently under taking.

After her parents had died and she had moved in with Papa, I occasionally would catch sight of her in the backyard of the family home watering flowers. I would ride my horse almost right up to the fence line and we would talk for a few moments about anything she wanted to talk about it. She felt most at home in the small flower bed she had once told me, as it reminded her of her mother's undying love of gardening. Talking about her parents had always been a rarity as the topic upset her, but when she did open up about them I allowed her my full attention. In truth, I fancied Emily though I had doubts as to her feelings for me. I had once accepted advice from Jacob about how to approach her with the idea of a date to the movies, but never gained the courage to ask her. With the blackout, a movie date had become out of the question anyway and with all the recent stresses, I put the idea on the back burner.

I picked up the radio and hit the button. "Emily and Jade… how are things? Did everyone get enough gummy bears?"

I watched as Jade laughed and turned to wave at me before taking the radio to answer. "There are never enough gummy bears in the whole wide world Travis!"

"Alright then… if you have Emily turn to her right and lift the small box from the corner, you will find a gift inside." I said before setting the radio down next to me.

Emily looked at me bewildered and turned, finding and lifting the box into view. I nodded with a smile. I had secreted another stash of gummy bears into the back of the pickup truck in case they needed something to lift their spirits with. Smiling to myself, I watched Emily open the box and show the contents to Jade, who happily bounced on her seat and waved in my direction. For the moment there would be joy and laughter. Brian and Megan would never be forgotten, but for the smallest of moments there would be joy among the children and Emily would laugh again. I loved to watch her laugh.

Emily raised a gummy bear in toast to my gift and promptly popped it into her mouth before clapping her hands. I bowed my head in the most gentlemanly fashion I could muster while still driving and not wanting to crash. She tossed her head back laughing briefly before her face fell slightly, picking up Michael and passing a handful of gummy bears to Bobby. The moment of joy had been far shorter than I would have liked it to be. *How long until she smiles again,* I thought to myself.

The heat of the afternoon had begun to press through the windshield and boil me like a roasted potato – inside out. We hadn't stopped for lunch, only for a bathroom break. We ate as we drove through the desert on roads no highway map had routes for. During the hours my mother slept beside me, I had occupied my time with singing to myself songs I didn't want to forget. It had begun with theme songs from my favorite television shows I would likely never see again and quickly turned to songs I love by country artists. Emily had taken my cue by watching me and began to sing with the children. I eventually lost interest in singing and focused on watching her and Jade clap and sing together. The radio sat silent beside me as no one spoke. My only source of entertainment had been watching the back of the truck in front of me.

We had been driving most of the day and now I could see the rays of the sun turning orange around us. I rubbed my eyes and squinted through the exhaustion. I had thought about the possibility of asking Jared to pull over and allow my mother to drive, but we weren't far from the radio point and I desperately wanted to get there as quickly as possible. The drive had become boring now that the signing and fun had ended. In fact, I now had the pleasure of watching Emily and the children sleep. Not exactly entertaining but it helped to assure me they had found some sort of peace.

Darkness Falls

"There it is. The radio point is ahead. We will be stopping there for several hours before heading out again. I can't believe it has taken us two days to get this far." My mother said as she leaned out the passenger window for a better view. "Normally on the highways we would have been to Sanctuary by now."

I chose not to respond and kept my eyes on the road. Jared's truck slowed down and turned off the dirt road we had been traveling on. I followed behind him at a slight distance as the road had become rocky beneath us. This particular stretch seemed to be less traveled than the rest of the journey had been. Just ahead of us sat a lonely building that resembled a shed surrounded by rocks and endless views of sand. The two small windows on either side of the door had been boarded up with planks, the door sealed by crossed boards to match. Jared pulled off the road and turned the truck off. As I followed suit, my mother jumped from the truck and headed straight for the shed. I rubbed my eyes again before stepping from the truck and stretching.

"You did a good job handling that truck." Jared said as he walked toward me. "When this is all over, how would you like to keep it? Make it your own?"

"Whatever Jared... If we all live through this I will think about it." I sneered as I slammed the truck door and walked away. The last thing I wanted was another clash between Jared and me.

"Fine." He breathed. "We are here until after we make contact. After that, your mom will drive and we will reach the meet up point before morning. We will be spending a few days there to recoup before heading out to Sanctuary."

I casually ignored him as I helped Emily unload the children from the back of the pickup. Jared understood my cue and walked the children up to the shed while my mother removed the boards on the door. Emily handed Michael to be before jumping down from the pickup and stretching. The journey had been a long one and she seemed to be stiff from the ride. I bounced Michael gently in my arms and watched him open and close his hands. He would never remember his mother or know his father, both of them stolen from him. The only family he would know is his brother, sister, and the rest of us from Compound. I kissed him gently on the head as I promised myself to tell him daily as he grew about Megan and how much she loved him.

Sarah stayed in the truck for a while, wanting to be left alone with her thoughts. I worried about her but could understand her need for private grieving. She had lost her husband, a dog which she had considered a child and a good friend on the same day. Grabbing Emily's hand, I nodded my approval to Sarah and walked off toward the shed leaving her to her thoughts. My mother would need to be told in order to help Sarah cope and find some peace. For now, she could be left to cry.

The shed had been just as small as I had thought it was. A single room with nothing more than a bunk bed, small wood stove and table. Jared sat across the table from my mother looking over a map and holding a small radio. It didn't look like the radios we carried with us and used almost daily since the blackout; this one was bigger and looked more expensive with several buttons I had never seen before. Emily sat on the bed of the bottom bunk and took Michael back into her arms.

"At sundown we flip this switch here and begin sending a tone. If they are in the area with their radio on they will pick it up." Jared explained as he pointed at the map to show my mother. "They will likely be... here at this crossing. We will have a brief window of time to make contact and must get back on the road as quickly as possible."

"What if they aren't there when we start sending the tone?" My mother asked.

"We won't have much time to wait. I told him sundown." Jared said as he ran a hand through his hair.

"Do we tell them about Brian and Megan or do we wait?" I asked tentatively as I watched their exchange.

Jared looked up from the map briefly and frowned while nodding. "We need to tell them now. From here until we reach the meet up point it will be smooth goings. They can use the time to process and grieve."

I paced toward the open door and leaned against the frame, watching Sarah cry into her hands in the passenger seat of the truck. I couldn't imagine being told by radio of the death of a loved one and then having to grieve while on the road to meet with the survivors. That news I felt, would be best told in person. A radio just seemed so impersonal and mechanical. As I thought about it, I realized that if the tables had been turned... I would want to know even if the news had to be delivered by radio. I slumped against the door frame and slid to the floor. Crossing my legs, I sat and watched the last rays of the day begin to slip away. I closed my eyes and listened to Jared and my mother talk in hushed tones about the plan to get to the meet up as quickly as possible.

I must have dozed off for a few minutes as when I opened my eyes again the sky had darkened and Sarah was no longer sitting in the pickup truck. I slid over and looked into the cabin finding Jade and the children sleeping on the bottom bunk bed and everyone else gathered around an oil lamp on the table. A low tone like that of a low hum repeated every couple of seconds. I stood and walked slowly to the table. My mother stood radio in hand, slowly counting between the pushes of the button. She would push the button and sound the tone, count for five seconds and press the button again. Sarah sat with her face in her hands whispering a prayer.

"How long has it been now?" I whispered to Emily as I came alongside her.

She wiped her tears with the back of her hand before whispering, "Twenty minutes. Apparently the note he gave Jacob said exactly after sundown. They should have answered by now he says. No word yet."

I pulled her into an embrace and fought against the tears that threatened to spill from my eyes. She sagged into me and cried softly as the tone sound continued for several minutes. I closed my eyes as the hot rush of tears rolled down my cheeks without control. The tones continued. No one spoke as silent tears fell from many of us. I watched my mother begin to shake as tears ran down her face. She continued to tone every five seconds though now she was counting louder than before. Jared slumped into a chair and buried both hands into his hair.

"What could have happened?" My mother choked out as she dropped the radio onto the table and fell into a chair in hysterical cries.

I quickly picked up the radio and took over the tones as Jared comforted my mother. I pressed the button, counted to five, and pressed it again. Nothing. No answer. No tones from the other side and no voice coming through. "We can't give up." I said as I let go of Emily and leaned closer to the lamp light. "They are out there. I know they are."

"Travis... we have waited long enough." Jared whispered. "We need to load back up and head to the meet up location."

"No." I yelled as I continued to hit the button. "I won't let you... four, five... these are ... three, four... my brothers!" I shot as I counted aloud between words.

I hit the tone again and held the radio up, expecting to argue with Jared when a different sound came through on the radio. I dropped it onto the table and stepped back in shock. Jared instantly grabbed the radio and hit the tone again. It was quickly followed by another tone of a higher pitch. My mother and Sarah jumped from their chairs.

"Do it again!" My mother shrieked. "Again!"

Jared hit the tone sound one more time and again it was followed by a tone of a higher pitch. He quickly pushed a different button and spoke slowly and clearly into the radio. "This is Jared Henley, who am I communicating with?"

The radio sat silent for few second before the voice of my brother came over, "Jared Henley... this is Jacob Dunn. You have no idea how excited we are to hear your voice."

Cheers rang up around the table as we hugged each other and cried. We had finally made contact with the other half of our family. I hugged Emily tightly, lifting her off her feet as she giggled. My brother Jacob was alive... just the thought he had survived had lifted a huge weight off my shoulders. Jared waved his hand at us in an attempt to calm us down and hunched over the radio.

"Jacob... it is good to hear your voice. You opened the box I see. Look, we have much to tell and very little time. We have taken casualties... I repeat... we have taken casualties." Jared spoke as clearly as he could muster.

"Jared... we have as well." Jacob's voice came over almost painfully.

We all stood in silence, the cheers and smiles we shared now a faint memory. I closed my eyes and mentally ran through the list of everyone in the first caravan. I prayed silently in my mind that my brother would come over and tell us Matt and my dad were alright, but the radio sat silently in the palms of Jared's hands.

"We came under fire...," Jared said finally, "We lost the pregnant goat but Travis saved the babies. We lost one of the dogs. Two member of our travel party are also gone. Please let everyone know... Brian Simon and Megan Sanders were both killed yesterday during an ambush."

The radio did not respond. Jared sat down into one of the chairs and placed the radio on the table in front of him. We gathered closer to him and waited. I knew it could take a few moments for the shock to wash through the first team and I was willing to allow the delay. Emily squeezed my hand tightly as she looked from one person to the next. My mother stood, arms crossed around her waist as she rocked back and forth.

"Jared...," The radio finally cracked as the voice of my brother Jacob came through. "We came under attack today after picking up Chase."

Jared smiled weakly, "Chase is with us? Send my love."

"Jared... like I said we had a loss of life," Jacob paused before continuing, "We came under heavy fire. Matt took a grazing shot to the side of his head but is alive. He took several stitches thanks to Edward... but we lost someone today... Miranda was killed."

"You must be mistaken or I didn't hear you." Jared said into the radio as he stood, his hands shaking.

My father's voice came over the radio, "Jared I need you to listen. Miranda was riding with me in the transport. We came through a small town and took it from all sides. We did everything we could to get out safely... hell, Chase tossed grenades in every direction but they kept coming at us. Miranda was struck... she died instantly."

A scream rose up behind me and I turned. Jade was sitting upright on the bed shaking uncontrollably and screaming. She had heard the news as we had... her mother had been killed. Emily bolted from my arms and wrapped herself around Jade. Jared dropped the radio and stepped back from the table slowly. I picked up the radio and held it in my hands.

"No... no she didn't." Jared said slowly as he ran his hands through his hair. "She can't... she isn't...," He turned toward the door and before anyone could stop him he bolted through it and out into the darkness.

"Jared!" My mother screamed as she ran after him, disappearing from view.

"Jacob? This is Travis." I said into the radio. "Is everyone else alright?"

"Yes. Everyone else is alright. Angela, Fallon, the kids... no one else was injured except for Matt. He will have an awesome looking scar across the side of his head though. He took thirty-seven stitches and lost a lot of blood. Otherwise we are unharmed. We are heading out now to the meet up. See you in a few hours." Jacob informed before the radio went dead.

I gently set the radio onto the table and turned to Emily who still held a hysterical Jade in her arms. Tears filled her eyes as she looked at me. Compound had lost three people in forty-eight hours. Miranda, Brian, and Megan were gone from our lives in a desperate attempt to make it to Sanctuary. I clenched my fists as I paced between the open shed door and the table. I couldn't be angry with Jared any longer; he was now hurting far worse than any of us had before the radio contact. He had lost his wife. Being mad at him seemed so mute at the moment in the face of everything.

"We need to get on the road. I'll ride in the back with Jade and the children. I think it best that Jessica drive Jared's truck. Emily, do you think you can go with Travis and keep him awake? You can take over for him if he can't handle it." Sarah spoke softly as she stood from the table.

"Yes, I can do that." Emily said as she stood, still holding Jade.

"Come here child," Sarah whispered as she reached for Jade. "We need to get to the truck, we can talk there."

Emily quickly grabbed Michael and followed Sarah and Jade out the door as they made their way to the truck, Jade whimpering as she walked. I watched them walk through the door and into the darkness before sitting down at the table and placing my head in my hands. I had managed to drive throughout the day without crashing the truck or falling asleep. Now I would be driving through the night as well. The drive would be boring and uneventful, lasting several hours. Rubbing my eyes I placed my head onto the table and then closed them. Just a few minutes would be all I would need.

Emily tapped me gently on the shoulder and whispered that the time had come to hit the road. She had carried Becky and Bobby into the truck by herself and everyone had been ready to leave. I gathered the map and the radio and made my way to the trucks while Emily put out the oil lamp and closed the door behind us. The chill of night had begun to set in, soaking me to the bone with a dry freeze. I hurried for the truck and climbed in without looking to see if Emily would follow. I turned the key and fiddled with the heater controls. The children and Sarah would be warm enough within the enclosure if they closed the flap on the back and used the wool blankets and comforters. The whipping wind caused by the high rate of speed wouldn't be much of a problem with the flap closed.

Emily climbed in beside me and closed the door. "I can't believe how cold it has gotten all of a sudden. We are coming into summer soon not fall." She rubbed her hands together. "I have a gift for you by the way. I have been meaning to show you but we haven't had the time."

"A gift?" I asked. "You don't have to give me a gift, Emily."

She turned in her seat to face me. A smile stretched across her face as she held up a small CD player and a set of speakers she had pulled from her bag. She giggled as she placed a CD inside and turned it on. The thumping sound of classic rock music began to fill the cab of the pickup truck as I pulled out behind my mother, being careful not to rock the goats in the utility trailer.

"How on earth?" I asked as I began to laugh.

"While we were in the bunker complex under Compound," She smiled in the darkness, "Matt showed me around trying to get my mind off what was going on. We found a couple of cages and got curious. Once we opened them up we found a bunch of CD players, CDs and even batteries. He gave me one and let me take my pick of the music. I've been saving it for a special occasion."

"This is a special occasion?" I asked as I completed the large turn around the small shed, the trucks now headed back to the dirt road.

"Keeping you awake is a special occasion. I can't have you falling asleep on me and crashing."

We laughed together as we pulled onto the dirt road and continued on toward the meet up location. The night would be a long one for both of us. I wasn't as exhausted as I had been, not with Emily there blaring music and singing beside me. Time would pass more quickly with her by my side.

CHAPTER SIXTEEN

We stood around the back of the transport in silence, everyone looking at the now silent radio as I held it in my hands. Making contact with the second team had briefly lifted our shattered spirits. With the news of their survival had come the news we hadn't expected to hear – Brian and Megan had been killed. The news had washed all of us in shock, robbing us of words and confusing our emotions. Our team had lost Miranda and Matt had been injured. Fallon had to be sedated after the news of her mother's death, and now she sat in a medicated haze as it slowly began to wear off. Tears wouldn't be falling from her worn out and swollen eyes as she now sat partially numb in the darkness.

My father had paced between the trucks, running his hand through his dark blond hair and mumbling to himself after he had to deliver the news about Miranda. His tactical vest and pants still darkened with Miranda's blood as we hadn't had the chance to clean up before reaching the radio point. We had been slowed down after it had been advised by Edward that we handle Miranda's body quickly by setting her on fire in the middle of the desert. Fallon had been sedated before the wooden platform had been constructed, still too hysterical to mourn her mother. Dave and Chase had constructed it in haste, and though it hadn't been the best it did the job well enough with the little wood we had. We gave her the best we had in such a short time, being sure she burned far enough from the road that Fallon could witness the flames but not be close enough to smell the smoke.

Edward examined Miranda briefly, explaining that she had taken a bullet to the head and her death had been instantaneous. The job of handling her cremation had fallen on everyone else as he turned his attention to sedating Fallon and patching up my little brother. Fallon had fallen asleep after she had been medicated, leaving me to sit at her side caring for Bentley and keeping my brother talking and focused. Matt had taken the injury well after being informed the wound hadn't been fatal. Edward had been forced to shave the hair that covered the entire right side of his head in order to properly care for the injury and ward off infection. The scare we had agreed would be thick and impossible to cover if he didn't allow his hair to grow back. Matt had laughed that the scar resembled that of one normally made during a wild animal attack, claiming it gave him character. A strict medication plan for antibiotics and pain management had been given to my brother who accepted it gratefully.

Once we climbed back into the trucks and continued on to the radio point, it had been nearly nightfall. My father had worried that Jared wouldn't wait on word from us and pushed on to the meet up location. We drove as quickly as our trucks could go until we reached a point near the area that had been marked on the map. I turned on the radio and managed to hear faint tones that grew louder as we neared. I had frantically fought with it to get a reply tone out but had heard no response until we hit the exact location and tried again. As contact had been made, everyone stood around the back of the transport listening as I held the radio on my hands.

Now we stood there in the darkness trying to process the information that had come through. I placed the radio onto the floor of the transport and rubbed my hands together, looking at the members of my team one by one. Dave slumped against the hood of his truck and ran his fingers across his eyes, squeezing them closed. He hadn't spoken a word while contact had been made, though he had stumbled back onto the truck after hearing about Brian's death. Angela sat crying and holding her daughters to her as she processed Megan's death, explaining it to the girls in a way they might understand.

"We need to get back on the road." Chase whispered as he cracked his knuckles. "It would seem both your teams took losses and need to recoup. Where is your base camp?"

"It isn't far from here, a few hours North if we keep going

like this. If we push we can be there sooner." I replied as I climbed into the back of the transport. "We need to get there as soon as possible."

"Alright then... I didn't know these people and am not as emotional as the rest of you. Clear mind and all... I can drive Dave's truck." Chase said as he turned and walked to the driver door.

Within seconds we loaded back into the vehicles and found our way back to the road that would lead up to the cave. There wasn't much to do now except push on until we reached it. I climbed out of my position at the gate and lay down on the floor of the transport next to Fallon, stroking her hair as she drifted in and out of sleep. The medication Edward had given her still coursed through her veins making it difficult for her to stay awake. I rolled onto my back and tossed my arms over my eyes. When I had gotten a moment alone with my father, I had insisted he inform me with radio contact the moment we came to the meet up location. I had to be awake the moment we arrived. In the meantime, all I could do was sleep. The gentle movements of the transport rocked me into a deep sleep much quicker than I would have wanted.

I managed to catch myself snoring on two different occasions as I rolled into more comfortable positions. My back still pulsed with pain from the gunshot I had taken to the back of my flak jacket. Both times I awoke, I took the chance to check on Fallon, Bentley, and my brother. Once I was assured of their safety I fell back to sleep. It hadn't been a restful sleep, but it had done me far better than I had expected... even with my constant worrying. When I woke up to check on them again, I found I couldn't get back to sleep. I brushed the hair off Fallon's face and listened to her breathing instead.

"Jacob, are you awake?" My father whispered through the radio.

I rolled toward the radio and replied, "Yeah. Are we there yet?"

"We made perfect time. I didn't want to wake you but I don't know much about this place and you insisted." My father replied confused. "I think we are here."

I sat up and rubbed the sleep from my eyes as I fought against the soreness in my back. "Do me a favor Dad... Do you see what looks like a forestry gate? It should be green and overgrown."

"Seeing it now." My father answered quickly.

I knew I would now be forced to reveal some of the details that Jared had entrusted me with. I struggled to my feet and climbed into my seat at the transport truck's gate. "Listen Dad, there is more to this place than you know. You will need to go through the gate and head down into the canyon. When we get there, pull completely into the opening of the cave. You are going to want to head deep inside it and keep left. It will open up into a large area you can park in." I whispered back.

"What is going on Jacob? How do you know this?" My father asked in confusion.

"Trust me. It was a need to know operation and no one else needed to know. Just promise me you will be careful driving down into it. We need to be on guard just in case someone got here before we did." I said before setting the radio down and checking my M16.

Seconds later the transport pulled to a stop, engine still running. The forest around us swayed gently in the breeze, the desert now gone. I tapped my M16 against my hip and chewed my bottom lip as I listened to my father open the gate before climbing back into the transport. We lurched forward and began to move slowly. Chase smiled at me as I made eye contact, giving me a salute before pulling in behind us down the canyon. I locked my feet under the edge of the gate and stood, swinging out to the side of the transport to watch our decent. The headlights danced across the dirt road and the trees, illuminating the night around us. Edward stopped at the tree line above us in order to close the gate behind him.

The opening to the cave looked rather deceiving to me when I caught my first glimpse of it. I quickly climbed up onto the metal side and using the framework for the canvas cover, worked my way to a better position for the best view possible. Locking the edges of my boots into a couple of handles, I leaned back off the side of the transport and peered out in front of us. There didn't seem to be a cave at all, but I knew it was there. At first glance no one would have seen it especially from the air as the only way to enter it was from the side. A large rock formation blocked the opening and covered the top in a large dome. I wondered in that moment how Gordon and his brother had managed to locate it in the first place.

I quickly climbed back across the framework and ducked into the back of the transport as we neared the opened. The transport slowed slightly as the opening of the cave seemed it would be a tight fit. I sat in my seat looking out the back as we entered. The dome cover slipped into view over my head, blotting out the stars and sinking us into darkness. Light from the headlights bounced off the surfaces as Chase pulled in behind us. We moved slowly, waiting for Edward to catch up to us. My father had taken my advice and stayed to the left side of the cave when the road ahead split into two different directions.

I watched the ceiling of the cave lift higher and then disappear as we entered into a large cavern. The transport turned and pulled up alongside the far left wall before stopping. I closed my eyes and took a deep breath. Leaving Compound had proven to be fatal for a few members of our community, but we had arrived with most of us in one piece. This cave wasn't the end of the line for us; we had one last push to make before we arrived at Sanctuary. I watched Chase and Edward follow suit and park along the wall behind us just as my father turned off the engine to the transport.

"Leave your headlights on for a minute. I need to find the control panel." I yelled as I quickly jumped down from the back of the transport and surveyed the cavern. Darkness licked the edges at the farthest reaches of the headlights. Walking to the edge of the light I squinted into the dark and allowed my eyes to adjust. Clicking my flashlight on I pushed the reaches of the light into the darkness, scanning the expanse of the cavern. "I'll go look for it. Don't turn the lights off until after I find it."

The cavern could easily hold two football fields with ease and a ceiling that raised above us at least three stories. Taking one step at a time and being careful not to trip, I scanned the floor under my feet in repeated fashion. I scanned the distance, scanned the nearest walls, and then the ground in front of me. Footsteps thundered up behind me gaining speed as they neared. The thundering could have only been Dave as the pattern of footfalls resembled his jogging style.

"You be a thinkin' we got power in here?" Dave asked as he came up along my right side.

I rolled my eyes in the darkness knowing he couldn't see me. "Yes Dave. There is a generator here and a power system that should not have been harmed during the blackout. There is a control box somewhere in this direction. We hit the switch... the lights come on."

"I be a thinkin' that be true. What you lookin' fer is 'at right there boy." Dave said as the beam of his flashlight moved up and settled on a large piece of equipment that was easily as large as the transport truck. He mumbled to himself about depth within the earth as we neared it. Picking up his pace, he reached the generator before I managed to.

I stood there holding my light beam in front of him as he scaled the side of the beast and began checking it. Low mumbled curses slipped between his lips mixed with groans as he searched for his prize. "Dave, once that thing is fired up... where would you estimate the switch is?"

He ran a hand through his whiskers and twitched his nose like a mouse smelling the air for cheese. "Tank be full and pump from holdin' tank be good. That be the feedin' tank." He mumbled as he pointed his light beam to a large box not far from the generator. He made a point to follow the lines from the box to the generator with his beam. "I be a thinkin'... ifin this bitch turns over... the switch here...," he turned his beam to the wall and trailed it until the light kissed the edge of a metal box. "There! Now you be waitin' until I say so. Gonna crank it a few, horrible sounds will be comin' from this beast so you wait a min'."

Dave's hands moved with speed, turning and flipping instruments on the generator that I could not see from my position. He climbed down and turned, smiling at me and pushed a few buttons I hadn't even noticed were there. It sputtered and banged loudly before going silent. Dave grumbled and repeated the process two more times before it finally began to agree. The beast groaned slowly, followed by a growing high pitched whine as if it would explode. Instinctively I took several steps back seconds before a loud bang sounded and continued to whine. I jumped with a start and looked to Dave who pointed with his light to the metal box that held the switch. Talking would have been useless as nothing could be heard over the sound coming from the protesting generator. I ran to the box and opened the cover to find the switch. One last look at Dave as he fiddled with the generator confirmed it was time to flip it. He gave me a thumb high in the air above him in the beam of his flashlight. I grabbed the switch which was nothing more than a large wooden handle and forced it up. Sparks shot in every direction hitting me in the arms as I jumped back. Light began to flicker several times in waves around us as the generator began to kick into a normal flow and supply the needed power.

I watched the wave of flickering light move across the expanse of the cavern in awe, my mouth hanging open. The cavern was much larger than I had originally thought when I did my scans in the darkness. Several football fields could easily fit into the great expanse we currently stood in. The generator sat just opposite from the transport on the right side of the cavern. I scanned the area as the light moved and noticed what looked to be a kitchen with stainless steel counter tops and cabinets at one end of the space. I made mental note to inspect the kitchen later for supplies. Several rows of military style bunk beds and tan colored metal cabinets sat not far from the kitchen space. Massive wooden crates stacked three high lined the wall closest to me. Otherwise, the entire place sat wide open with a few tables and chairs scattered about in various places.

"It looks like a replica of a carrier's kitchen to me." Edward said to Angela as Dave and I walked up beside them. "That there is a bank of ovens… not as many as you would find on a ship though. The entire kitchen is run on steam so I bet this one is too. There should be a boiler behind that far wall. A closed system is my guess… it probably runs the showers too."

Angela was already on the move, making a beeline for the kitchen to do her inspection. "What is that giant pot looking thing?"

Edward laughed. "They call them Coppers. It is a long story but they were once made from copper. I can walk you through the entire kitchen tonight, but right now I have to check on Matt's head."

With Angela concentrating on the kitchen, I decided my best course of action was to lend a hand with getting the children into bed. Both girls had been standing at the back of the transport half asleep and gawking at the cavern with their bags in their hands when I noticed them. Trying to get sleep in the transport had proven to be difficult, and with the added stress of Miranda's death they were emotionally drained. It had been a long day for all of us. I smiled brightly at them and motioned for them to follow, which they happily agreed. Cassidy whined to herself as she walked behind me, dragging her feet. I gently picked her up and carried her in my arms rest of the way to the bunk beds.

The bunks sat roughly three feet apart with bare plastic covered mattresses on thin metal frames. There wouldn't be much comfort as the mattresses were thinner than I had ever seen, but anything had to be better than trying to sleep on a pile of blankets in the back of a truck. I opened the small tan locker at the end of the bunk I had chosen and found two plastic covered bed kits. Each kit contained a pillow, sheet set, and a wool blanket. Working quickly, I cut both kits open and made up the bottom bunk bed for the girls. I knew they wouldn't mind sharing a bed for the night as they usually shared a bed at Compound. I doubled the sheets up to keep the cold plastic off the girls and laid out both wool blankets in an attempt to provide extra warmth. Once they had climbed in, I placed their small bags into the tan locker. They fell asleep quickly without a fuss.

I found Matt sitting on the hood of Dave's truck talking quietly with Edward and having his bandages examined. He smiled up at me and rolled his eyes as he gestured at Edward. He had taken his injury in stride and had proven to be far braver than I had ever given him credit for. The moment I had seen him tumble over when he was shot, I wanted to drop my M16 and dive to him. My heart wanted to help him, but my head had screamed that doing so would have meant Fallon would have been defending the transport alone. Even now I worried about him though Edward continuously insists when asked that Matt will come out of this far better than we thought. He seemed in good spirits yet inwardly I wondered if he would ever admit how scared he had been when it happened.

Fallon tumbled out of the transport giving me little warning. I managed to catch her enough to break her fall, but she still hit the floor of the cavern with a loud thud. She laid half on the ground and half in my arms, moaning loudly. Her head hadn't hit the floor like the rest of her body had, though I was certain the moaning had to do with the sedation and not the fall. I slipped my arm under her knees and lifted her into my arms. Her body sagged against me heavily as my muscles strained to hold her tight. Being careful not to drop her or trip over my own feet, I carried her to one of the bunks and set her on the bare mattress. She rolled out of my arms limp and sleeping. Once I had the bunk across from her made, I transferred her to the new bed pulling off her boots, vest, and gun belt before tucking her in for the night.

Bentley's box had begun to show some wear with the journey. Not feeling comfortable with having him use it again, I searched for a better solution. I stumbled onto a flat bottomed box with metal bars almost resembling a crib yet stood no more than two feet tall. It was plenty wide enough for a baby his size and the spacing between the bars wasn't big enough to put my fist through. The contraption lacked legs or anything resembling a mattress, though its size was small enough to fit between the bunk beds perfectly. I opened a sleeping kit and folded the wool blanket into a makeshift mattress, leaving an overlap to cover him up with before tucking in one of the sheets to keep the wool off his skin.

"Looks like a great crib for the little guy." My father whispered as he carried over a sleeping Bentley and handed him to me. "Angela wanted you to know that she doesn't have the energy to understand the kitchen tonight so those of us awake will be eating MREs and canned peaches for dinner."

I placed Bentley into the crib and tucked him in without waking him. "Fallon won't be able to care for him tonight. I'll eat over here where I can watch him and keep an eye on the girls."

"I thought you would say that so I brought one over for you." My father laughed as he passed me a tan colored package. "Apparently there are cabinets and boxes full of this stuff. They won't be as tasty as our homemade ones or the refugee boxes but it is still a meal. Dave and Edward are going to get the boiler going for the showers. Did you know they have actual showers and toilets in this place? Anyway, I plan to take a shower and get cleaned up before Jared gets here. I am still soaked in… well… I don't want him to see me like this."

I could understand where my father was coming from. If Jared and Jade were as fragile as Fallon over the news of Miranda's death, seeing my father covered in her blood would become a nightmare. I simply nodded my agreement and sat on the edge of Fallon's mattress to open my MRE. My father ran a hand through his hair and nervously shifted his weight to his other foot as if he had something more to say, then nodded before walking away. I watched him walk back to where Angela had placed matching tan packages in front of chairs around one of the tables.

I popped a small handful of spicy red candies into my mouth, feeling the slow moving burn scorch my tongue and lips. I smiled to myself as I remembered the day several years ago when my brothers and I had accepted a challenge our father had given us. We each had been given a small bag of the same spicy candies and were told to pour the whole bag into our mouths at once. Thinking we knew what we would be in for, we excitedly accepted and instantly regretted the move. A couple at a time was plenty for anyone, but a whole bag at once burned with the intensity of hot peppers. To this day I couldn't recall what the prize had been for winning the challenge; I only remembered the burning and eye watering that ensued on that day. Slowly, I tucked the bag of candies closed and stuffed them into my pocket with the thought of challenging my brothers to a candy faceoff and repeating the experience when time allowed.

Fallon shifted beside me on the bed and rolled toward me, barely opening her eyes before snoring again. Her hair sat in a messy pile of unruly curls beside her head on the pillow. I gently swept a curl off of her cheek and rubbed my thumb down her cheekbone. No one had showered since leaving Compound, yet she still smelled faintly of oatmeal soap and lavender. I set the remaining MRE package onto the floor and removed my boots, belt, and vest before climbing in beside Fallon and pulling her into my arms. *Maybe I can keep nightmares away if I just hold her*, I thought to myself. Nightmares and Fallon went hand in hand on a regular basis. I closed my eyes and quickly drifted off to sleep.

When I awoke the following morning I found I was still in the same position I had fallen asleep in. Fallon's head still rested on my chest as before, but now she had one leg thrown over me trapping my legs beneath her body weight. I slowly tested a stretch and realized she wasn't going to move enough to allow my exit. She moaned softly and ran her hand up my chest to wrap it around the back of my neck, moving her head to my shoulder. Instantly every muscle in my body tensed up at once and the air in my lungs froze mid breath. I gently rolled my head to face her only to find she was wake and looking back at me with a devilish grin.

"You moved." Fallon whispered softly, her lips barely inches from my own. "I had been hoping you would stay asleep."

I blinked down at her in shock, my eyes trailing her lips with each word. "Fallon... I um...," I began but the rest of the sentence had been lost when the hand around the back of my neck moved into my hair and her lips found mine. White hot lava boiled up inside me as I fought the urge to run my fingers through her hair. Her lips were soft and damp as they moved against mine. The intensity of her kiss and the tightening of her fist in my hair were almost too much for me to fight. "Fallon...," I gasped when her lips granted me a breath, "Fallon what... what are you doing?"

She shifted, burying her knee on the mattress between my legs and moved above me, pinning me with her body weight. "Can't I kiss the birthday boy? Or is that not allowed?" She breathed against my lips as she moved. She bit my bottom lip softly, forcing me to groan before she giggled and moved to straddle me, now completely pinning me to the mattress.

My birthday. I had completely forgotten my own birthday. Placing my hands on either side of her head, I slowly broke the kiss and pushed her up to look into her eyes. "Fallon, you are driving me crazy. Please don't because seriously...," I whispered as I tried to catch my breath, "... I can't."

Fallon licked her lips and sank into me. Her intentions hadn't gone unnoticed. I knew exactly what she had been up to and what she had planned. I watched as she frowned yet refused to move. "Angela and the girls are in the showers getting cleaned up. Everyone else hiked out to the gate to see if they can locate my dad. We are alone."

"Sweetie, I don't care. You are an emotional wreck and as much as I would love to, I won't allow you. You can't stuff the pain away and cover it with bad decisions." I whispered as I closed my eyes and fought my own inner demons. "I love you. I love you enough to know that you don't mean any of this. You aren't in your right mind at the moment. I don't want to be your mistake."

Fallon frowned and sat up on my chest, her eyes burning into mine as she moved. "My mistake? Do you think you are my mistake? After everything we have been through growing up, and then the blackout, leaving our home and my mother...," She closed her eyes.

"That is exactly why I won't do this with you." I interrupted. "You are being fueled by grief and stress. Doing this would only make you feel better for a short time. It won't stop the pain. If at some point in the future we get back to this point and our lives have calmed down... maybe we cross that bridge later. I just want to make sure you truly want to be with me and love me. For now, please move off me because I am not sure how much longer I can fight this."

"Why fight it?" Fallon asked with a smile.

"God woman… you are infuriating. You know I want this. I want this more than anything, but I can't allow it. Not here… not in a cave and not like this. I respect you more than that. You deserve more than that," I whispered, "You are better than that."

Tears rolled slowly from Fallon's green eyes as the look of shock on her face melted into sadness. I pulled her to me, wrapping my arms around her and shifting her to lie at my side. Holding her tightly in my arms, she began to sob against my chest as I rolled onto my side to face her. "You are an asshole, Jacob Dunn." Fallon cried into my shirt.

"No, not exactly." I smirked. "If I was an asshole I wouldn't have stopped you."

She laughed and punched me in the arm as she pulled back to face me. "Can I still kiss the birthday boy?"

"You already have. I have to say though, you ever kiss me like that again in the future and I might not be able to stop myself." I laughed as I pulled away from her and rolled over. I needed a shower, a cold shower, the longest and coldest shower in history. Pulling myself to sit at the edge of the bed, I placed both feet on the floor and rubbed my eyes with my hands. "I love you but I seriously need a shower right now. Can I trust you won't try to attack me while I am in there?"

Fallon laughed loudly as she punched me lightly in the back, "Oh for the love of Pete! Go shower! I promise to be good."

At some point in the construction of the cavern complex, someone had built large wooden walls in an attempt to separate one area from another. The showers had been built into a large room made of wood that lacked anything remotely resembling a ceiling. Six shower stalls lined one wall across from the curtained doorway I had come through. I closed the curtains behind me and marched off to pull the curtain for one of the stalls. Angela was just finishing up dressing the girls and smiled at me as she rushed them out to allow privacy. I smiled to myself when she left, thinking Fallon would have been caught had I not stopped her advances. *We would have been toast. That little vixen,* I thought to myself. I pulled back the curtain to find a small area with hooks on the wall and a long bench with a towel. The shower sat on the other side with another curtain to close it off. I quickly undressed and tossed my clothing onto the bench next to the bag I had brought with me.

The cold shower proved to be more refreshing than I expected as I stood there with both hands flat against the wall, allowing the icy water to hit me in the face. I had been told there would be plenty of hot water to go around, but after my encounter with Fallon I wanted the water as cold as possible. The day I had kissed her while we sat at the table in her cabin had shocked her. I kissed her as well before I rushed her into the bunker, though at the time it hadn't phased her. Her actions this morning had shocked me all the same. She had made advances this time instead of me. I scrubbed soap into my hair as I thought about it and realized I had been right all along. She wasn't in her right mind and wanted to escape the pain by using me. I wanted to be with her, but not if she didn't want to be with me.

By the time I stepped from the shower to grab my towel, I could hear voices from the direction of the kitchen. Fallon and Angela were talking though I couldn't make out what they were saying. I quickly dried off and got dressed, noticing other voices could now be heard. Jared must have arrived with his team as I thought I heard Travis talking as well. I bolted from the shower room and passed the bunk beds to see everyone gathered around the tables listening to Matt talk about how he got his stitches and new scar in the making.

"There he is!" My mother yelled with delight, running at me.

"Mom!" I yelled back excitedly and ran into her open arms. "How long have you been here?"

"Just arrived! We haven't even unloaded the trucks yet." She laughed as she squeezed me to her. "Your dad told me you kids fell asleep so quickly last night you didn't even pull the animals from the trucks, he had to."

I winced against her at her words. The day before had been so stressful I had completely forgotten we had animals with us once we arrived. "Sorry mom."

Several hugs made their way around the room. It seemed as if it had been a lifetime ago since we had last been together as one large family. Unlike meals back home in Compound, we now had missing faces at our table. Brian, Megan, and Miranda would never join us for breakfast again. We had even gained a face at our table and now everyone wanted to talk with him and welcome him along for the ride. Angela had figured out the kitchen system with the help of Edward and Chase, and managed to make scrambled eggs made from powder, fried potatoes with rabbit meat, cinnamon rolls, and fruit salad. We sat as a group, a family, brought back together. Everyone had a story to tell. One by one people rotated in and out of the showers, eating when it wasn't their turn or listening silently to someone tell their tale.

Jared sat at the far end of the large table we had created by pushing several smaller ones together. He had barely spoken a word to anyone save for the brief and tearful exchange he had with my father when he had given Jared his condolences and the wedding ring that Miranda had worn. I watched him spin the ring slowly through his fingers as silent tears fell from his eyes onto the table. In all my years growing up on Compound, I couldn't recall ever seeing him cry. Jade sat at his side picking at her food and wiping her eyes. They hadn't showered and still wore the clothing they had traveled in. Fallon brought Jared a cup of coffee and hugged him gently before hugging Jade and heading back to the smaller table where the children all gathered for breakfast.

Even with the sadness around the table, there were still outbursts of laughter from time to time. Matt had gone on to tell about how Chase stood on the pickup throwing grenades and taunting the enemy, causing everyone to laugh as Chase simply shrugged with a smile. I panned the room and looked into the faces of my family and friends. Travis sat with Emily holding Michael and talking. Fallon sat with Angela and the small children holding Bentley in her arms. My parents sat holding hands and talking with Matt about his scar, all the while my mother clutching her chest and he explained about how he was shot and how many stitches he had to have. Sarah and Edward sat quietly discussing Matt's medical needs and any injuries that had occurred during the journey. Dave and Chase sat talking about farm animals and which of the pigs they could possibly breed with Bacon. I wasn't talking to anyone. I didn't want to.

I rose from the table and walked off toward the bunk bed I had slept in the night before. Fallon had made the bed when I left for the showers. I flopped down on top of the wool blanket and covered my eyes with my arm.

"Hey." Jared said as he sat on the edge of the bed next to me,

"I want to give you something."

I sat up on the bed and swung around to sit next to him. I hadn't even heard him approach. Maybe it had something to do with the ringing I still had in my ears as the street battle with the grenades hadn't helped the healing process. "You don't have to give me anything."

Jared laughed and handed me a small box without a wrapper. "Miranda and I picked it out for you before the blackout. She made me promise not to give it to you until your birthday."

I slowly pulled the flaps open on the box and to my shock found several boxes of ammunition, two fully loaded magazines, and a Ruger SR40 Semi-Automatic Handgun. "Jared… are you serious? You guys didn't have to do this!" I said in disbelief as I ran my fingers across the nylon grip. "This is my dream gun! Thank you so much!"

"I know. She remembered hearing you talk about getting one last summer. I know it has more sentimental value than anything seeing as Miranda picked it out, but I couldn't give you a gun without ammo. That was my part of the gift." Jared smiled sadly before pulling out another smaller box from his pocket. "This one is from us as well."

Excitedly I opened the smaller box. Inside sat a half carat princess cut diamond in the center of a thin gold band, surrounded by smaller diamonds. I recognized it as being Miranda's engagement ring, the one she had taken off her finger a few years before in order to get it fixed, but never found the time. By the look of the setting, I could only assume he had managed to have it repaired and planned to surprise her with it. "Jared."

"Now before you say anything, let me explain. I bought Miranda this engagement ring when I was a boy about your age. Your father and I were serving in the Haven Guard at the time and making pretty good money. I didn't want to buy her a ring from the Haven jeweler as we fought to keep our relationship a secret. Word would have spread like a wild fire. One day, your father and I were sent off the property to make a trade run in Salt Lake City and stopped to have a look around on our way back. Robert dragged me into this jewelry store I didn't want to go into as it looked pricey… I went in against my will and I found this. It ended up costing more than what I had at the time…," Jared laughed and shook his head slowly, "… so your dad spent half his wages and I spent all of mine just to buy it."

"My dad helped buy it?" I laughed. I had never been told that part of the story before.

"Sure did. Three days later I asked her to marry me. Took all the guts I had in me. To tell you the truth... asking her scared me more than any mission I had ever taken." Jared said as he slapped me on the back gently with a smile. "When the setting broke, she locked the ring away. I thought I would have it fixed for her and planned to give it to her when we reached Sanctuary. I was your age once. I see the way you care for my daughter. I am not saying you should ask her to marry you; hell boy... you did that once already while drunk! All I am saying is that I want you to hold onto it for me and keep it safe. The ring goes to Fallon like Miranda would have wanted. You have two choices. You can give it to her simply because it belonged to her mother and is important, or you can ask her to marry you when you are both a little older. It is Fallon's ring now... when she is ready for it, you should be the one to give it to her."

I sat holding the small box in my hands, stunned. "Mr. Henley... if I were to want something more with your daughter, are you saying you approve?"

Jared locked his fingers together in his lap and leaned in. "What I am saying is that I think you are good for her. You are both more mature for your age than most. Maybe it is the way we are raised because I was the same way. You have taken on Bentley as well and raise him as if he is your own son. The world is changing around us and I can see by watching you both what the future holds. Do I approve? I guess I would say yes I approve... so long as you aren't trying to marry her tomorrow. Promise me if you plan to ask for her hand, you will wait it out until you are a just little older."

"Yes Sir... I will wait it out." I replied.

"That is exactly what I thought you would say." Jared smiled before standing up. "It is further proof of your intentions. You could have told me you would hold it for her as a symbol of her mother to be passed down to her when she is ready. You just admitted your intentions to marry her. Are you sure about this Jacob? Do you want a future with my daughter?"

I felt like I had been tricked. "Yes I am sure. I want to marry your daughter." I admitted sheepishly as I slumped over in embarrassment.

Jared laughed loudly, "Alright then… well best of luck to you in the future. I will cross my fingers she doesn't punch you in the face. You have my blessing if you survive what she does to you." He said before he turned and walked back toward the tables.

I closed the small box and slipped it into my duffle bag along with the new gun. Still reeling from the conversation and still feeling tricked into admitting how deeply my feelings for Fallon ran, I tossed myself back onto the bed and covered my eyes with my arm. My relationship with Fallon has proven to be a complicated one and though I was unsure how it would play out, I knew one day I would ask her to be my wife. The thought hit me the day before we left Compound. The day the perverts showed up at our gates and I rushed Fallon and Bentley into the bunker. The moment it hit me that I wanted to spend the rest of my life with her was the moment I found myself gasping for air on the ground after being shot.

As the haze of sleep began to claim me, I drifted into sleep thinking about Fallon and what happened this morning, Bentley and how much I loved him, and of the time we had spent together since the blackout as a family. A family I would do anything to hold on to.

CHAPTER SEVENTEEN

"Are you coming to dinner Jacob or are you going to pass out like last night?" Travis asked as he sat down next to me on the edge of the wooden crate we had been sorting. We had been tasked with the chore of prying open several crates and making lists of the contents. "Word has it that Dave and Chase found another bottle of Brian's zombie making brew in the back of one of the trailers. We are planning to celebrate his life along with Megan's and Miranda's tonight. Like a party for them."

I rolled my eyes while looking over the list we had spent most of the day making. "I'm not sure yet but I might. If I can get the rest of these crates done I might have time to check that other chamber." I said as I stood and walked to a different crate. I had noticed the items in the crates we had been checking weren't the items I had been told would be here when we arrived. There were several items Jared had told me would be here, and since I had yet to come across them I suspected the chamber we hadn't been into might hold the key. "Is everything alright between you and Emily? I noticed she has taken more of an interest in you lately. Are you dating?" I asked in an attempt to change the subject.

Travis grinned as his pen scrawled across his paper. "We kissed once… on the drive here from the radio point. Mom wanted to pull over to allow us to rest a bit instead of pushing straight through. She was in the truck with me listening to music. We never even made camp, just slept in the trucks for an hour or two. We curled up to stay warm but couldn't sleep. Then she totally kissed me just out of nowhere." He jumped down from the edge of the crate and handed me the list he had made. "Kind of freaked me out a bit because it was so sudden."

I smiled taking the list and looked it over. "She is taking over the care of the Sanders children I have noticed. Does that mean you are going to help her out?" I winked with a grin.

"If by help her out you mean playing house like you and Fallon, then no. I am not into the instant family just add orphans thing like you are." Travis snickered as he pushed me. "Besides, she is older than me and I don't have a clue what I am doing. The slower I take this the better."

I set the lists down on the edge of a wooden crate and walked down to the next crate in line. Placing my pry bar under the edge of the lid, I pushed down hard until I heard a crunch. "She is only a year and a half older than you. I get what you are saying about the kids though. There is just something about Bentley I can't put my finger on. I instantly fell in love with him and he happens to be being raised by the most amazing girl in the world." The nails on the lip gave way and I moved to another side. Travis yanked on the lid until it pulled free and fell to the floor. "I can't explain my relationship with Fallon. It is complicated."

"Oh! So it is a relationship now? She hasn't punched you?" Travis laughed as he moved a few things around inside the open crate. "She hasn't turned you down again?"

"She made a move and I shot her down. Long story and I would rather not talk about it. She wouldn't want me to and frankly it is our business. I will say however that I have made a decision about how far I want to take things." I began to scribble on the list taking inventory of every item we could see.

"No way! Are you going to ask her on a real date?" Travis mocked as he passed me his pry bar and placed the lid back onto the crate.

"No. I am going to ask her to marry me." I informed as I walked off to another crate, leaving my brother stunned.

We opened three more crates in silence, Travis just staring at me and occasionally shooting me an excited grin. I still had yet to come across what I had been looking for in the crates, but the list we had compiled would make our father and Jared happy. I helped my brother replace the last lid and sat on the edge of the crate to nibble on a strip of jerky. Travis sat and laughed, "You are serious aren't you? You are going to ask her to marry you? When? How will you ask?"

"It won't be for a while so don't say anything to anyone. I have already talked to Jared about it… in a way. I have Miranda's engagement ring." I whispered as my eyes trailed down the last list.

"You talked to Jared? Wow… and a ring! You must really be serious then! I won't say anything… promise." Travis whispered before excitedly taking a bite of jerky and chewing.

When we had finished our jerky we grabbed our lists and walked back toward the tables where the meetings of the day had taken place. Angela and Emily were sitting at a small table with preschool workbooks teaching the small children about addition and subtraction. My father and Jared were at another table sorting maps and talking about Sanctuary. My mother and Fallon stood in the kitchen chatting about food and making a list of their own. I hadn't spoken to Fallon since the second team had arrived. I had hoped to get her alone to make sure she was alright, but had fallen asleep after Jared had given me the ring. When I had woken up this morning, she had taken the bunk bed across from me on the other side of Bentley.

I set the stack of lists down on one of the tables where I knew I could be left alone, and set to work sorting them by crate number. We would likely take several boxes of the ammunition to replace what we had used leaving Compound. We had blown through more than we had thought we would use and with one last push to Sanctuary we would need them. I scribbled a note on one of the lists indicating our need for more ammunition for my team. During the morning meeting we talked about our need to take as little as possible from the cave. The supplies stored here weren't for us, they belonged to the Patriots. Gordon told us to take only what we needed… and the items I couldn't find.

Travis plopped down into the chair next to me and picked through the lists I had set aside. He scribbled side notes as well, one being the need for more bandages and antiseptic wash. I watched him as I passed one list after another in his direction. He occasionally shot a look of anger in Jared's direction, not realizing I had been watching him. I couldn't be sure what had happened to their team on the journey, but at some point they must have gotten into an argument.

"Done. I am going to hit the showers before dinner. Catch

you tonight." Travis said as he tapped the stack of papers on end and laid them back onto the table. "Good luck in the chamber when you go."

I watched him walk off toward the bunk beds and retrieve his bag, all the while burning Jared with his eyes. Travis had always been the sensitive brother who went out of his way to care for other people. This new attitude toward Jared confused me. He was changing and growing in ways I hadn't noticed until that moment. As I thought about it, he seemed to be becoming numb as well. Numb to the pain. Numb to emotions other than anger. I couldn't put my finger on it but it seemed the moment his journey into manhood began it had been fraught with the hidden horrors of the second team. I couldn't blame him, he was a fourteen year old boy trapped in a world held hostage by a blackout. Members of his team died along the way and we hadn't even gotten to Sanctuary.

"I wanted to say… thank you." Fallon whispered behind me while I was deep in thought. "You know… for yesterday morning? I'm not sure what got into me. I've never done anything like that before. I didn't mean to offend you. Thank you for being such a great friend."

A friend wasn't exactly how I wanted to be viewed. I rolled my eyes knowing she couldn't see me before setting my pen down on the table. "I am glad when you lost your mind it had been with me. Any other guy would have allowed it, no matter how much it would have hurt you in the end. I know you better than anyone. It wasn't what you wanted."

"Well, thanks again. I am off to check on the babies, Sarah is doing health checks." Fallon said softly before walking away.

I leaned back in my chair and ran a hand through the stubble on my face. I hadn't taken the time to shave in a while, not that I minded much. Maybe one day I would grow a full beard just to see if I could. Growing a beard wasn't exactly a talent of mine. To me, I just look silly trying to grow one. The girls in school never seemed to notice either. In fact, the only one who ever noticed had been Fallon, who would poke fun at me and follow it with a comment about how much she had loved my soft face and not the harsh hairy one. I smiled at the thought and glanced back at her as she walked away. When I turned back to the table with a smile, I felt as though I had been being watched.

I found Jared's eyes on me from across the room and smiled

at his playful grin and slowly shaking head. Even my father had watched the exchange between me and Fallon, though I guessed they had been too far away to hear the conversation. The two of them laughed as my dad gave Jared a playful punch in the arm. I couldn't imagine what life for them had been like at Haven. They were men at my age. They had been soldiers at my age. Making adult decisions about your future while still just a teenager seemed odd to me. Sure I felt like a man, but that didn't mean I had grown up enough to be one. My parents once told me that they had been given permission from the Haven Council to marry when they were just sixteen, but that they had chosen to wait until they felt ready. A second appeal had been made by the council granting them permission a year later. Apparently, growing up had been rather important to the council.

Standing from the table, I grabbed my flashlight and started toward the entrance to the cavern. When we had pulled in I had informed my father to stick to the left side and follow it through the split. To the right sat a cavern used as storage for the main living area. The items I had been instructed to locate hadn't been in the cavern meant for living. As I walked, I passed the area we had used to house the animals and caught sight of Dave and Chase standing in the pig pen. We had stacked crated to form small areas we filled with fresh straw in order to contain them. The cats and rabbits had been left in the transport truck for their safety. Chase looked up and quickly pointed at me, speaking in hushed tones to Dave before climbing over a crate and walking in my direction.

"Checking out the chamber tonight? Mind if I join you?" Chase asked as he kept pace with me.

"Why not, I might need the help." I replied.

We walked into the split and turned to head into the other cavern, flipping the switch to the flashlight as we went. The light from the main cavern didn't reach out this far and now we were heading into darkness. My first order of business would be to find a different light source as the batteries in my flashlight had been getting rather low. I made mental note to make the request at tonight's meeting for batteries to be added to our supplies. As the darkness grew ahead of us I scanned the walls for any sign of a switch or secondary generator that could supply power to the area, and saw nothing.

Chase stopped walking and stuffed both fists into his pockets,

"Look kid… I can't keep walking into the dark like this. Do you think you can find a switch while I stay here? I am already on edge about being underground." He said as he turned to look behind us. "My war days… I get nervous and edgy in these spaces."

"No problem." I stated as I continued on alone. In the time he had spent with us, I had noticed he had a real aversion to anything suggesting the need to go underground. Since the moment we entered the cave, he had become more nervous and quiet. On several occasions I had caught sight of him at a dead run for the entrance to the cave, seemingly escaping into the outdoors. "I got this."

The cavern opened up ahead of me as I stepped into further darkness. I scanned the walls with my flashlight and found a switch box. I followed the wiring from the box to the top of the rock over my head and noticed it ran back the way we had come. The system had to have been connected to the generator in the main chamber. Opening the panel box, I found several switches with small labels and flipped the one indicating the lighting. A low buzz moved across the room and the lights flickered before becoming stable. I flipped another one that claimed to turn on a secondary lighting system and a much louder hum moved off into the distance behind me.

I turned to find a chamber smaller than the one we had been staying in, but this one had much more storage then we had seen. Larger crates lined the walls on either side along with large metal grated lockers displaying firearms I couldn't identify. Fifty-five gallon plastic drums in blue and red sat against the far wall collecting layers of dust in groups of ten. The largest items had been placed down the center of the room, which included two military transport trucks larger than the one we had been using, and a military style jeep. My eyes scanned over the stockpile in wonder. Just the sight of it all confused my emotions with excitement and anxiety.

A loud and long whistle blared behind me as Chase walked in to see the stockpile. "Well I'll be damned kid… you've done hit the mother lode on this one. Those transports are five ton, the one you have is a deuce. Those over there… I bet those crates are packed with weapons. It is like Christmas in here!" He laughed as he rubbed his hands together. "Where to start?"

I smiled at his excitement and bolted for the closet crates

while Chase laughed behind me trying to keep pace. The first crate we came to was about the size of a twin sized bed and about as high. Using my pry bar and Chase's brute strength, we popped the nails on the lid and placed the lid on the floor. Inside sat the largest cash of grenades I had ever seen... thousands of them. Chase gave a mighty yelp of excitement reminding me of Matt at his seventh Christmas when he had been given his first wrist rocket and pellet gun. I laughed loudly and ran for another nearby crate, giving the lid everything I had. It cracked open with a loud squeak and the lid clattered to the floor. I stood stunned looking into a crate the size of a crib filled with nothing but loose ammunition.

"That is nothing but fifty caliber rounds... a whole crate full. Who are these friends of yours kid? These guys mean serious business." Chase said with one hand on his hip and the other smoothing the short whiskers on his chin. "I haven't seen anything like this since I left the Army."

I watched Chase walk over to the drums, still excited though now a little less so. He forced open one of the lids while I worked to open another crate. Inside sat row after row of M16 rifles, spare magazines and ammunition boxes. While I opened two more crates, Chase had moved out of sight behind the farthest five ton transport. The next crate had been the same as the last few: M16s, ammunition and magazines.

I stood counting to myself when Chase walked up slowly with a look of concern played out across his face and both hands stuffed into his pockets. "Listen kid...," He said as he glanced back in the direction he had come from. "These people had big plans for this stuff. I think we should leave. Are you sure we are allowed to take this stuff?"

"That is what I was told. Some of this is meant for us but the rest stays... why?" I asked in confusion.

"I haven't found much in the drums but one of them I opened is packed with caster beans." Chase stated in a low voice. "Fifty-five gallons of dried caster beans."

"Caster beans... What are those for?" I asked as I looked off in the direction he had pointed in.

"They are poisonous like you wouldn't believe! The only reason these guys would have them is to make Risen. Back in the day... we fought terrorists who used it. About twenty years ago it was a popular tool to kill many people at once. It doesn't take a lot to kill someone, but these guys have fifty-five gallons of the beans used to make the powder. Sure you could have someone eat them just the same, but inhaling the powder is much quicker and takes far less beans." Chase said as he shifted his weight from one foot to the other. "I don't think we should tell anyone about this discovery. Only Jared if possible. I can seal up the drum and probably stash it so that no one else happens across it... but I would rather haul it outside and bury it deep in the ground! No one needs that kind of weapon."

The idea that the Patriot forces had the means to create Risen bothered me greatly. I sat back on the edge of the crate I had just opened and crossed my arms in thought. Gordon and his brother had helped the Patriots create the stockpile; he had to have known about the beans. I had no intention of explaining this information to Chase but knew I would need to have a conversation with Jared. "I agree. Tell no one about the beans. Seal it up and set it aside. We keep this to ourselves. Be careful opening everything... there is no telling what we might stumble onto." I said to Chase who nodded and walked away.

For the next hour we opened crate after crate only to find tear gas canisters, rocket launchers, mines, riot gear, and even one crate packed full of flak jackets. I left Chase to open the last few crates while I hunted through some of the lockers. I managed to locate one of the items I had been entrusted to find for the greater good of Compound. A box no bigger than that of a toaster oven containing nothing but silver coins for trading or to make medicine. It had been heavier than I expected, but I had set it aside to be carried to Jared for delivery. Another small box of equal size had been filled with gold; this box as well had been designated to go to Compound. One large locker held hazardous material suits and gas masks. Chase had stumbled onto a crate filled with military issue side arms and promptly claimed one for him as a prize.

When we returned to the main cavern I cornered Jared and explained everything we had located. He listened intently and nodded knowingly when I informed him of the weapons we had stumbled on. His reaction to the caster beans had been the same as Chase, and he insisted on checking it out after dinner... alone. We spoke for several minutes in hushed tones while Angela set the table. It had been decided we would take one of the five ton transports and leave the smaller farm trucks behind. We would also take along a few of the rocket launchers, hazardous material suits, and a few items we needed to recoup what we had used. Jared had a list of items that Gordon had instructed him to grab and he had made up his mind not to leave the cave until after they had been acquired.

"We leave tomorrow afternoon for Sanctuary." Jared said later during our dinner meeting as he chewed a forkful of chicken smothered in gravy. "Jacob here located a five ton military transport truck that we will be using. We will leave a note in the kitchen explaining to anyone who comes through here that Gordon allowed us access and that he did not survive. He had connections here and they may not be aware of his death."

Fallon nodded as she frantically took notes beside me, shaking her hand on occasion to relieve the cramping. The meeting had been almost identical to the ones we normally had back at Compound. Everyone had been gathered over dinner, each with a list of things that they had been tasked to locate. Bentley squirmed in my arms as he drained the bottle, obviously needing to burp. I gently sat him upright on my lap, placing his chin in my hand and patting his back with the other until he burped several times and smiled.

"Chase and I will stay behind to shut this place down and follow in the truck I gave to Jacob. We will need to start loading everything we can tonight when we are done with the festivities. We have three lives to celebrate as well as a birthday." Jared smiled as his eyes met mine. "You missed out last night."

I sunk deeper into my chair though the effort I knew would be wasted. Angela and Fallon promptly explained they had located supplies in one of the cabinets and combined with the fresh eggs from the chickens had managed to make a cake though candles could not be located. My mother jumped from her chair and ran to the locker cabinet closet to her bunk bed; bring back with her a few small brown cardboard boxes she allowed the children to decorate with crayons. I hadn't been in the mood for a party but by the look of things I didn't have much choice in the matter. I sat silently watching everyone scramble while Jared and I stayed at the table watching the chaos. Bentley smiled up at me as his eyes closed, chewing on his fist.

"Open this one first." My mother said cheerfully as she

handed me one of the cardboard boxes.

I opened a series of boxes starting with the one my mother handed me. Inside them I found a new pocket knife, ammunition, a pair of new jeans in my size, a bottle of aftershave, a framed photograph of my family that we had taken before the blackout, a necklace made of noodles from the children, a belt made out of para cord and my father's copy of the complete works of William Shakespeare. I thanked everyone for the gifts and handed them to Matt who carried the load back to my locker for me. Dave and Chase poured everyone a small plastic cup of Brian's special brew and passed them around to make a toast.

"To the boy who is now a man... we celebrate. We also celebrate those we have loved and lost. Brian Simon, Megan Sanders, and Miranda Henley will be forever missed by their friends and family. Their deaths have opened a hole in our hearts that cannot be filled. They gave their lives for their family on a journey to safety... their sacrifice has not gone unnoticed. We thank them for helping to get us this far and we hold them in high esteem for their bravery and courage." My dad called out as he held his glass high in the air. "May we never forget how much they meant to us and keep their memories in our hearts forever... from one generation to the next."

The rest of the evening had been a mix of emotions. We enjoyed the excessively large birthday cake that Angela and Fallon had concocted and spoke in heartbroken tones about those who had given their lives. The party would be the last gathering the cave would likely see and Jared wanted to make the most of the time we had together. Come morning we would be pushing to leave the cave as one large group in an attempt to reach Sanctuary without further casualties or delay.

As I watched Fallon and Emily gather the children and rush them off to bed, I thought about what may be waiting for us at Sanctuary. According to the things we had been taught over the years, there were many family wings complete with shared living space and private quarters allowing for groups to stay together. Miranda had once explained the layout resembling that of a tree, with branches that connected family wings to other places within the complex. There would be a large mess hall for meals, and a medical facility, a library and a school just to name a few. The entire complex sat deep into the mountain on multiple levels. I had never been there and had hopes to never have to go as living there meant living with survivors from Haven as well. Though I had tried to place my mindset in that of a Haven Soldier, I had no plans to mix with them for an extended length of time. It would be good to see my friend Jasper again, providing he was still alive and would be heading to Sanctuary as well.

When everyone began to clean up and Jared had left to see about the beans, I hastily showered and retired to my bunk for the night. I curled into my bed and managed to fall asleep without even having to try. The sounds of Compound member murmurings bouncing off the walls lulled me into a swift and deep sleep.

The following morning had been a rush of activity as we packed up and loaded the vehicles for the trip. Since we would continue to use the military transport we had brought with us, the children would all ride with what had been my team. Dave cleaned out his truck with the help of Chase while the two mumbled curses and kicked the tires. Dave had argued with Jared about leaving the best trucks we had behind, but Jared wouldn't budge on the issue. The animals had been loaded into the five ton transport in what I could only describe as a clustered mess. It had taken us until nearly midafternoon to complete the preparations.

When we finally left the cave in the late afternoon hours, we set out to drive all night through the woods. We left behind the trailers, and all the trucks except for the one Jared drove. I even talked them into allowing me to take the jeep as my personal vehicle. My father insisted on driving the two and a half ton transport as usual though now my mother rode at his side. Dave took to driving the new five ton transport fully loaded with animals, save for the caged ones left in the other transport truck. It didn't matter who chose to ride in which truck as we just piled into them as quickly as possible. Fallon chose to ride in the jeep with me, leaving Bentley's care to my mother who insisted on spending time with him. Jared eventually found what he had been searching for, though he didn't let anyone else know what it had been. Only I knew and I wasn't going to spill the beans to anyone.

We pushed on through the woods and onto an old paved road as the sun set behind the ridge. Though the cave sat half way between Compound and Sanctuary, we knew we could make better time on the last half of the journey. Staying as far as possible from cities and small towns, we moved quickly through the evening and into nightfall. Jared had instructed me to drive ahead of the caravan while he pulled up the rear. The directions to Sanctuary had been fairly simple so long as I stuck to the map he had given me, I wouldn't have a problem finding the place. In order to avoid any hazards, I continually took back roads as often as possible, eventually bringing us back to Highway Ninety-Three.

Two hours into the trip we stumbled onto a couple of teenagers hunting for game in the woods, armed only with a couple of rifles and a game bag. They explained to us that they normally spent several days at a time hunting deer and other game, trading half of the spoils with a nearby town for supplies. We gave them enough food to last each of them for three days, and several boxes of ammunition for their rifles in a gesture of kindness before wishing them the best of luck. With excited waves and cheering, they thanked us and continued on into the woods.

On the outskirts of another town, we met a lone hiker on a mission to make it to Oregon to check on his little sister and her family. He had just come off the Appalachian Trail when the power had gone out and promptly set out on foot, passing through several states and towns along the way. Most of his life had been spent hiking across the country anyway, so the journey hadn't been a problem for him. He explained the condition of some of the cities and towns, telling us to avoid them all as illness had begun to spread in the more populated areas. Jared gave him several MREs and a large bag of candy which made the hiker overjoyed to have met us. We waved to him as we set off again, all of us hoping he would make it to Oregon alive and locate his sister.

Fallon eventually fell asleep at my side as I watched the road ahead for any sign of trouble. We hadn't truly spoken since we left the cave, though I suspected she had chosen to ride with me in order to talk. After the hunters and the hiker, the drive had been rather boring. I entertained myself with thoughts of Sanctuary and counted the miles off in my head as I drove. We had been on the road for several hours already, and I had nearly jumped for joy when we managed to avoid the last town completely and hit the open road.

Fallon shifted, "How long do we have left?" She asked as she rubbed the sleep from her eyes. "I can't take much more of this traveling it is killing my back."

"We passed the last town without an issue. You slept right through it! We have nothing but open deserted highway through the mountains from here on out. We have less than half an hour I would say." I excitedly replied. "Are you excited to get there?"

"Not really. I just want off the road." Fallon huffed as she stretched her legs out and sat up. "I half expected it to take twice as long as the last leg had. I am a little shocked no one has tried to rob or shoot us."

"I took every back road I could to avoid any possible issues. It is fairly easy to hide in these mountains if you know how to do it. As soon as we get there I am falling sleep, I am exhausted." I replied as I glanced at the map before pulling onto a dirt road. "Just down this dirt road a ways and then through a series of gates, we should be seeing something here soon I bet."

"Do you think anyone from Haven has arrived yet?" Fallon asked as she held her hair back from the wind with one hand.

I frowned to myself as I thought back to the day we had changed course on the highway in order to avoid a trap. Though it had seemed that day had been years ago, it had in reality been little less than a full week. "Not sure really, but I can't see how anyone could have beaten us here, not if they had to defend the community. They would have locked the area down and waited to send teams out until they knew it was safe. It could have taken days from what I can figure. Your dad said there is a small group that stays up here for part of the year in order to care for the place."

"Is that the gate?" Fallon interrupted excitedly as she pointed to a small gatehouse on the side of the road.

"It is the first gate. There are several layers of defense." I explained with a grin.

I scanned the large fences that spread out before us only to disappear into the trees on either side of the roadway. Metal signs indicating the area strictly for military personal hung as a stark reminder the facility had once been a military base. The road ahead of us sat blocked by a large gate and metal bars that stretched across the single lane road, preventing entrance. One armed guard stood by the gatehouse, M16 aimed at the jeep as I pulled to a stop.

"This facility is for military only. No one is allowed to enter." The guard said firmly as he positioned himself in front of the jeep, his weapon now pointed directly at me. "We are locked down. No one goes in and no one comes out."

"My name is Jacob Dunn. My caravan here is all that is left of Compound." I said loudly as I placed my hands in the air. "We are the survivors."

The guard's thick frame sagged slightly as his broad face fell into a look of sadness. "The survivors? You suffered a loss of life?" He asked as he lowered his weapon and came up alongside me. "I am sorry to hear that. How many vehicles are in your party?"

"This jeep, the two transport trucks behind me, and a pickup pulling up the rear. That is all." I replied as I watched the guard step back slowly and scan the road behind us.

"Do you have Jared and Miranda with you? Were you followed?" The guard asked as he pulled out his radio, waiting for an answer.

"Jared is in the pickup truck… Miranda did not survive the journey here. She was killed a few days ago." Fallon choked out as she leaned across my lap. "I am Fallon Henley, daughter of Jared and Miranda Henley."

The guard nodded sadly and stepped into the gatehouse, speaking into his radio slowly. I could hear the sadness in his voice as he explained to the person on the other end that Compound had arrived at the gate but that a loss of life had been suffered. He asked for a team to be sent to him in case we had been followed. The voice on the other end agreed to the demands and requested we be allowed in at once.

"You are all set." The guard called from the gate as he opened a lock and pushed the gate open. "There are three more gates up ahead. I am sorry for your loss. Welcome to Sanctuary."

CHAPTER EIGHTEEN

I watched Jacob smile sadly as we continued through the first security gate, pulling down a long road toward the second checkpoint. I blinked the tears from my eyes and continued to watch the road ahead of us, praying secretly that we wouldn't have to explain again who we were. The first guard must have called us in as the next two gates we had come to sat wide open, the guards saluting us with tears in their eyes as we passed. After everything we had been through, we had finally arrived at Sanctuary... most of us at least.

I wiped my eyes with the sleeve of my sweatshirt as we came to the last security gate. Three guards stood talking around a jeep parked in the middle of the street. As we slowed to a stop, one of them turned and walked toward us. This guard seemed to be much younger than the others we had seen so far, and his bright blond hair had been cut in a neater fashion. He looked more like a business man than a guard as he wore a freshly pressed dress uniform rather than the military combat gear the other guards wore.

"Good evening Ms. Henley and Mr. Dunn. Please let me welcome you to Sanctuary. My name is SAS Roscoe and I am your Sanctuary Arrival Specialist. I will be showing you to your quarters and helping you learns the ins and outs of the facility. We are all terribly saddened to hear about your losses but we are excited to see you. Haven has yet to arrive... you are the first." The young man said before smiling a sad smile. His dark blue eyes reminded me of the trim color of Angela's house back at Compound. "I will be driving the jeep ahead of you. Please follow me as I will be taking you to the facility. The main mess hall is closed, however your quarters contain a common kitchen. I have called ahead to have some food items delivered for you."

"Thank you Roscoe. We are excited to finally be here." Jacob replied as he reached across the seat and squeezed my hand.

The young guard nodded before walking back to his jeep and climbing in. My mother and father had been here several times in their lives, but this was my first experience with Sanctuary. The journey to get here had been an emotional one, and the days spent to get here had worn me down. I blinked several times in an attempt to clear my blurred vision as we followed the jeep deep into the grounds of the facility. Several small buildings in various states of disrepair sat on either side of the road, obviously original with the property and either abandoned or left to look so.

We slowed to a stop in front of a large set of metal doors thirty to forty feet high and nearly sixty feet wide. Both of the transport trucks and my father's pickup pulled to a stop behind us to wait for instruction. Another armed guard approached the jeep we had been following, then waved to another guard who quickly flipped a hidden switch. The massive doors slowly slip open exposing a room easily four times the size of the cavern we had left behind. The entire room seemed to resemble a large aircraft hangar turned garage, as military vehicles sat lined up in rows on one side of the space. Bright lights and grey paint gave the space the look I had expected to find. No longer a military facility, though still the place ran like one... a true talent of Haven and their society.

"Over glorified cave." Jacob laughed as we followed the jeep through before it stopped in front of us and turned off the engine. "Ms. Fallon Henley... you have arrived." Jacob played.

We slowly climbed out of the vehicles and stretched as the transport trucks pulled up behind us, everyone grateful to have the journey over once and for all. Dave and Chase laughed after they climbed out of the trucks and gave each other a pat on the back as we gathered together beside the jeep. The children stood in shock, eyes wide and whisperings as they looked at the lines of military vehicles parked on the other side of the space. My father walked up and exchanged a few words with Robert that I couldn't make out, though whatever the conversation they seemed excited to be here.

"Attention everyone... please can we quiet down a moment?" The young guard called out as he stood by his jeep with a clipboard in his hands. "Gather around please. As I said to Mr. Dunn and Ms. Henley at the last security gate, my name is SAS Roscoe and I am your Sanctuary Arrival Specialist. Welcome to Sanctuary. You are currently standing in the loading bay. There is no rush to unload your caravan at this time. Those items can be dealt with in the morning. Grab only the items you will need for the night. A team will be dispatched to take any livestock to the farming level. Cats, dogs, birds, and the like are allowed within your quarters so please remember to grab your pets before we leave."

"Excuse me, Roscoe?" Angela asked as she slowly raised her hand. "We have barn cats. They don't deal well with enclosed spaces or around people in general. Can they be sent to the farming level... maybe as rat catchers or something?"

Roscoe smiled, "By all means ma'am. We currently have only one barn cat on that level working pest control. I will alert the team of your wishes. Every animal brought into the facility will go through a full health inspection and be tagged with your group name. That process begins tomorrow. For now, let me show you to your quarters." He smiled again and turned on his heels, motioning for us to follow.

Jacob grabbed my hand, lacing his fingers through mine as we walked through the loading bay. Jessica cooed at Bentley behind us, baby talking to him about our arrival. *He is going to think you are nuts if you keep that up,* I thought to myself. Roscoe stopped at a large door and punched a code into a key pad. The door slid with ease opening into a long corridor with several doors and connecting hallways in every direction.

"First floor, ladies formal wear." Jacob whispered jokingly. I smiled and playfully punched him in the arm.

"This level is for the security forces. This is where most of us live and work. You are welcome to come and go from this floor as you like, however in a lock down situation this floor is sealed off for your protection. Leaving the facility will be restricted, I'll explain about that tomorrow." Roscoe informed as he lead our group down the hallway and to a series of staircases. "Normally the elevators are working and we wouldn't be using the stairs. They are being serviced at this time to prepare for the arrival of either you or Haven. We didn't expect you so soon... my apologies." He blinked at my father who simply nodded. Roscoe smiled before descending the staircase, "Every level has their own security team, though much smaller than the one that lives above you. Your floor has a team of twenty armed guards who are in place in the event someone breaks through our defenses. In the event of chemical ware fare or contamination the level above you holds the Isolation Department complete with Decontamination Facility. There is also an Isolation Department on the second level as well as a holding facility. We will go over all of that in the morning. Each level has a purpose which we will also go over tomorrow. For now, we will go directly to your living quarters."

"Great job, Roscoe!" My father smiled as we rounded a landing and began down another set of stairs. "Unlike Miranda and I, the rest of our community has never been here. You are doing a great job as the new SAS. Congratulations on your promotion by the way."

Roscoe smiled, his dark blue eyes lighting with excitement. "Thank you Sir. I couldn't have done it without you. I admit your referral helped seal the deal. I had tried for this post for years, as you well know. I feel overjoyed to be granted such a great position here within Sanctuary."

As we entered a brightly lit corridor that led to a set of double doors, Roscoe turned to the crowd. "Ladies and gentlemen, this is the third floor living quarters. You are about to enter into the main commons. There is a library to allow for you to check out books, a smaller medical facility to handle minor injuries, and a large meeting space. The main hospital, school, gym, and Marketplace are on the floor below you. You won't need a code like I use. These doors are password protected as they are in the stairwell. Elevators do not require them."

Roscoe tapped a code into the keypad seconds before the doors beeped and unlocked opening to revealing a large room filled with several sofas and tables spread about in various configurations and colors. Tan carpet covered the entire floor from grey wall to grey wall. Large potted trees sat around the room making the space look more like a garden tea party or a fancy doctor's office. I blinked against the exhaustion as my eyes moved from one end of the room to the other. A beautiful dark brown door sat on the left, the word Compound scrawled onto a brass plate in the middle.

"Alright Compound, listen up." My father said as we entered

the room. "I will explain what this is tomorrow. SAS Roscoe and I will take you on a tour in the morning. The door to the left is our new home. Once you enter you will find what Miranda and I have spent many years putting together for you. Find your living space by the labels on the doors once you enter. I am going to stay out here for a minute and go over who has arrived and who has not, as well as other intake procedures. For those of you who do not have a private quarters, please wait at one of the tables for me. We will find you a place to call home."

At six in the morning I awoke to the sound of a gentle jingle of soft bells coming over the loud speakers. The female voice that followed caressed my senses, gently waking me like a slow moving sunrise. When I had been told the night before that Sanctuary had a morning announcement every morning at six, I expected it to be rather annoying. Instead, I found her voice inviting and trusting as she explained what would be in store for the day.

"Good morning Sanctuary. Today is Saturday the sixteenth day of May, two thousand twenty." The soft and gentle voice spoke after the bells. "Welcome to another beautiful day. Today is a low Level One. Please remember to carry your mask with you at all times. The Glazier Grill will be serving breakfast from six to eight o'clock this morning. The breakfast special is French toast. There will be a council meeting at three in the second floor Grand Hall. The Marketplace Theater will be showing a classic comedy film tonight with the first showing at six o'clock and a second showing at eight o'clock. Have a wonderful day." She ended as a second set of bells followed.

I pulled myself into a sitting position on the edge of the bed and rubbed my eyes with the heels of my hands. Our arrival at Sanctuary still came to me in blurs of memory. My father had stayed behind to have a conversation with Roscoe, and I had fallen asleep without a word to anyone. Blinking the blur of memories from my mind, I stood and wrapped a bathrobe around me before padding across the tan rug that covered the cement floor of my bedroom to peer into Bentley's crib. I barely remembered my father requesting the crib be brought to my quarters from the nursery before I fell asleep. In fact, I hadn't remembered Jessica putting him to bed for me the night before. *Or was it in the early morning when we arrived*, I asked myself as I watched Bentley sleep.

My room had been decorated just the way I had asked for over the years. When my parents prepared to make their usual trips to Sanctuary, they always took the time to ask everyone if there was anything special they wanted them to bring or do. I had asked my parents on several occasions to make sure I had a queen sized bed and tan rug with chocolate colored linens throughout. As I looked around the room with a mind no longer clouded in exhaustion, I surveyed every detail. The room was a cozy fifteen foot by fifteen foot space decorated in several shades of brown and dark green; colors I requested in order to bring a warm and earthy feel to my private environment. My bed with three storage draws underneath, end table and wardrobe closet were a dark cherry wood with polished gold accents and handles. Nothing resembling what I had left behind in my tiny garden home had suggested my Sanctuary home would look like this. My private living quarters nearly doubled the size of my place at Compound, but my parents had insisted that living underground in a similar small space would drive me crazy after a while.

I turned the battery operated baby monitor on and slipped from my room as quietly as I could, being sure to grab the receiver before I went. I remembered being told the monitor would only work within the Compound unit as interior walls had been built with wood and not concrete or steal, and the radio range would be minor. Most of the facility had been built to allow for same floor communication, though no communication through radio could work from level to level.

My plan had been to enjoy every inch of my own private bathroom with flushing toilet, a shower, and roman style soaking tub recessing into the floor. My place at Compound had only offered a shower and I desperately craved a long soak with bubbles. Setting the monitor on the counter and filling the tub, I quickly undressed and located the small bottle of lavender scented bath oil that Jessica had insisted my mother stockpile for me. She had made large batches of it over the years and knew I adored the scent. Jessica had even gone so far as to make special lavender shampoos and soaps for me to use once she found out. I never missed a chance to use it as it had become my daily ritual of relaxation.

I poured the contents of the small decorative bottle into the tub and followed it with two capfuls of a thick lavender scented foaming bath bubble. As the bubbles gently grew I remembered my oatmeal body scrub and searched the dark cherry wood cabinets. Great pains had been taken to create the perfect bathroom space for me complete with every detail as elaborate as my bedroom. Upon finding the body scrub I closed my eyes and inhaled deeply, allowing the scent of oatmeal and lavender to fill my body like a calming wave on a gentle sea. Slowly, I slipped into the tub with a groan as my tight muscles began to relax for the first time in weeks.

Sanctuary had remained ever changing and growing after the property had been purchased by my grandmother. The nearly constant construction and renovations and been intentional, allowing for adequate space for growing families. My private quarters had been created when I had been only five years old. Not knowing if or when we would ever need to use it, my parents had designed it with the knowledge that I may be a grown woman and have a family of my own in the event of use. I had a bedroom for myself, a spare bedroom with two bunk beds, a bathroom and a large sitting area all to myself. My own apartment without a kitchen. Bentley was still much too young to be sleeping in the spare bedroom alone. For now he would share my bedroom.

Slipping under the water I blotted out the world around me, floating in the center of a warm water realm. I held my breath and moved slowly, feeling the water move around me. It is physically impossible to cry underwater. My mother had taught me that when I was young. Every time I felt like crying as a child I would remember my mother's words and wish for a tub or pool to sink into. I popped up out of the water and ran my hands over my wet hair, squeezing out the extra water before scrubbing myself down with the oatmeal scrub. Though the bathroom looked nothing like home to me, the beautiful bouquet of scents that filled the room reminded me of home. If I closed my eyes I could almost swear I was back at Compound. That realization both pained me as well as calmed me.

I made quick work of shaving before draining the tub and wrapping my body in a large chocolate colored bath towel. As I stood looking at myself in the mirror I almost didn't recognize myself anymore. My face had thinned slightly, giving more definition to my high Irish cheekbones. I didn't look as if I had been starving for the last two months; rather I had grown and become weathered and worn out. My lips seemed chapped and beaten by miles of dust and heat. Large green eyes stared back at me in dark sunken sockets. I hadn't packed my makeup to be brought to Sanctuary and I knew there probably wasn't a stockpile of it anywhere in my private quarters. I made a mental note to check the Marketplace on the lower level to see about some skincare products.

A gentle knock on the front door broke my eyes from my sad reflection. I left the bathroom and crossed my private sitting area to open the door. Jacob stood with a smile, now quickly fading into a look of shock as I watched his eyes take in the sight of me. "Yes Jacob... I am in a towel." I confirmed with a smile. "You look as though you have never seen me half naked before."

"I... I brought you breakfast." Jacob stammered as he lifted a small cardboard tray of food. "I hit the Glazier Grill this morning. It is nothing more than an over glorified mess hall really. Did you know they ration the food? I had to get special permission just to leave with two breakfast orders! Odd to me seeing as eating there is apparently free."

I giggled as I watched the look of confusion on his face, his eyes moving from me to the cardboard tray. He must have gotten up fairly early as he was clean shaven and wore a clean pair of blue jeans with a black tee shirt, the sleeves hugging his tightly muscled arms. His hair had been combed to the side and gently gelled into place, giving him the same look he had sported before the blackout. *Far too much aftershave*, I thought to myself as his scent overpowered the French toast he was offering.

"I'll just get dressed and meet you in a minute." I replied as I gently closed the door.

After quickly brushing my teeth, running a brush through my hair and dressing in my favorite pair of blue jeans and green top, I double checked Bentley. He still lay sleeping soundly in his crib. With the baby monitor in hand, I slipped out of my private quarters and into the Compound common area. The room was easily the size of the main deck we shared back at Compound if not larger, and consisted of a couple of large tables, some book shelves, a sitting area and a small kitchenette with maple cabinets and electric stove. Several doors led off the common area, each one with names on them indicating who occupied the space behind it.

My own door had been labeled with *Fallon Henley and Family* scrawled onto a large brass plate. Everyone seemed to have their own space. Even my sister Jade had a private quarters also built with the idea she would arrive one day with a family of her own.

"How do you like your new home?" I asked as I slid onto a chair across the table from Jacob. "Each of you has your own place like Jade and I do, right?"

Jacob nodded as he stuffed a forkful of French toast into his mouth. "Sure do. I have a two bedroom place a couple of doors down from you. Haven't seen much of it though, I took a shower and walked around for a while. I did get some sleep but it was out here on the sofa. Do you know how creepy this place is? It is like we stepped into some sort of freaky world where everyone pretends things are normal."

I stuffed a forkful of food into my mouth and chewed. "Why do you say that?"

Jacob leaned back in his chair and wiped his mouth with a napkin. "This level is huge. Across from us are apparently several doors saying the place belongs to Haven. That whole massive common area we share with them is weird all on its own. There is a massive kitchen too. I guess someone thought we would share meals with them or something. There are even doors labeled for other groups I have never even heard of before. Our group has got to be the smallest one here. The whole level is like a creepy dorm building."

"So what you are saying is that we have our own private space, everyone else has private spaces like we do, and then a shared space?" I asked as I cut another bite of French toast. It tasted heavenly, reminding me of the years we had spent back home.

"Did you seriously not notice a lick of it last night when we came in?" Jacob asked as he leaned back over his breakfast. "They are like big apartments but in a weird way. Two stories of them! Our level is actually two floors. There is a landing that goes all the way around and the ceiling is vaulted and wide open. I tried to guess how many people would live behind those doors, but there is no telling how big the units are. I found the quarters for the security team though, they are near the elevator. After we eat I can show you the weirdness first hand."

I had been about to ask him to explain all the places he had been when he should have been sleeping, but I changed my mind and stuffed another bite into my mouth. I hadn't paid much attention at all to the shared area outside our door when we arrived. I had to admit that our living space did resemble that of an apartment with doors that oddly enough, led into other apartments. The design had made sense to me though, as it allowed for family groups to shut themselves in and be together when they wanted to be, or join other family groups in the shared commons. Briefly I wondered if Jacob had managed to make it to other levels in his snooping.

Just then, the main door opened with laughter as our families walked into our common area, behind them Roscoe followed with several stacks of papers and books. Everyone looked cleaner than I had seen in little over a week, each with a smile as they chose their seats around the tables and on the sofas. I watched Jessica and Angela relax onto one of the sofas with the children, speaking in hushed tones about the Glazier Grill and French toast. They all must have been returning from breakfast and had run into Roscoe on their way back.

"Good morning Compound." Roscoe said. "Before we take a tour there are a few things I need to inform you of. First as a reminder, every morning there is an announcement over the PA system at exactly six. During that time you will be told what the day has in store for you and what security level has been assigned. It is important to listen carefully. A Level One means that the threat is low and you will only need to carry your mask. A Level Two means we are elevated and you are required to carry your CBR gear with you throughout the day. A Level Three means you need to wear your CBR at all times. If you do not know what these terms mean, I have included them in your handouts." Roscoe informed as he walked from person to person handing them a small stack of papers.

Jacob glanced up at me and made a mocking face, spinning his index finger around next to his head when Roscoe had turned his back. I promptly stuck my tongue out at him and giggled, shaking my head at his immaturity. I flipped through the pages in front of me explaining the terms normally used within the facility, making mental note to study it later in the day.

"We will tour the entire complex today before the council meeting at three. Today many of you will be assigned certain jobs around the complex. You will be required to arrive on time to work." Roscoe said as he set a stack of books onto the counter of the kitchenette.

"Wait a minute... we have jobs?" Matt probed as he leaned over the edge of the table he had been sitting at.

"Yes." Roscoe smiled before continuing, "With the help of your skill set and talents, you will be placed into a work group. This helps you earn your own money to be spent at the Marketplace and keeps you from going crazy. Living underground has its own downfalls, one of them being a sort of cabin fever. Don't worry the work you do will be for the greater good of everyone and help the entire complex run smoothly." He turned and opened a folder that had been sitting on the book. "Why don't we get to that now shall we?"

A low muffled groan rose up behind me as Chase and Dave slumped into their chairs in an attempt to hide. I smiled back at them and shrugged when Dave rolled his eyes, resembling more a rebellious teenager rather than a grumpy old man shirking his duties. Roscoe pulled several small slips of paper out and glanced up occasionally as he sorted them.

"Excuse me, Roscoe?" Angela spoke as she ran her hands through Cassandra's hair, the child squirming in her lap. "I know Haven hasn't arrived yet, so is the school set up at all or are we going to wait for them?"

"I am getting to that shortly." Roscoe answered as he held up the small pieces of paper before pulling the first slip from the stack. "Dave Ratcliff...," He said aloud as he read the name on the slip. "...your file indicated you have a talent for wood working, brewing alcohol, large and small equipment repair and safe fuel storage and handling. It also stated you know how to smoke and preserve meats. We have put together a short list of places we think you would best fit, however I would like to press upon you the need for your services in the generator and boiler level. A great mechanic is extremely hard to come by. We have three shifts that work around the clock to keep this place running. Pick a shift and let me know." He said as he walked over and handed Dave the slip of paper.

"What the hell?" Dave mumbled as his eyes scanned the paper. "What you be sayin' is I can be a pickin' a job, but I be a pickin' the job you want me to be a pickin?"

"Sounds like you have been volun-told." Chase whispered,

causing me to giggle to myself.

"Not exactly Mr. Ratcliff. You do have a choice. However, when Mr. Henley and I discussed your talents we both came to the conclusion you are best suited for the Power House." Roscoe assured before moving to another slip of paper. "Jessica Dunn. Your file indicates medical knowledge and skill in yarn craft, candle making, and soap craft. We have created a list for you as well. I would like to stress that the small medical facility on this floor is in need of someone. Two shifts run the medical department. Please pick a shift and let me know."

Jessica reached over, taking the paper from Roscoe with a frown. "Thank you Roscoe."

"Good." Roscoe smiled. "Travis Dunn. Your file indicated a great love for the medical profession. You have extensive knowledge and real world experience. We could use you in the main hospital. Several shifts run that department. You would do best with a morning shift as your classes will be afternoon and evening classes."

"Oh man! You mean I still have to go to school? You are kidding right?" Travis groaned as he snatched the slip of paper from Roscoe's outstretched hand. "What has to happen to get away from it?"

"A zombie apocalypse." Matt whispered from the side of his mouth causing the rest of us to giggle.

"Very funny." Roscoe smiled before crossing his arms over his chest and shaking his head. "Where is Sarah Simon?"

I glanced around the room realizing I hadn't noticed her, and found her sitting alone in the corner of the common space, petting one of her dogs as he stretched beside her on the chocolate colored sofa. She hadn't showered as far as I could tell, and looked as though she hadn't slept or eaten in days.

"There you are!" Roscoe said as he noticed her, "I am impressed with your experience. I don't have any choices for you… my apologies. Your presence has been requested in the hospital as well. With so many years of experience, you are the closest thing we have to a prenatal doctor right now."

Sarah reached up and accepted the slip of paper without speaking a word. I watched her as she glanced at it before setting it down on the end table, not a single emotion on her aging face. Brian's death had done more than take her best friend and husband from her, it had destroyed her completely. I wanted to run to her and wrap my arms around her, but something told me it wouldn't help her. She returned to her slow rubdown of the hound dog as if the conversation around her had never existed.

"Fallon Henley and Jacob Dunn," Roscoe called as he read our names on a slip of paper. "You two will be on the second level. Fallon, you are taking your mother's place on the council as well as being placed with the department that handles request forms. Jacob, we need you on the security team. Your experience in weapons has matched you perfectly for armory detail. You will also be on the council per the request of Mr. Henley and your father."

Roscoe reached over and handed me the slip of paper. There wasn't a list of jobs to choose from as many other members of Compound had. Just one job description neatly typed across the slip detailing which department I would be required to report to come Monday morning at eight o' clock. I read the slip of paper several times, ignoring Roscoe as he went from one person to the next explaining the duties they would be choosing from. My heart sank at the thought of having to replace my mother on the Sanctuary council. Standing from my chair, I slipped the paper into my pocket and walked toward my private quarters. I didn't need to hear another word about jobs and replacements. It seemed so pointless to live in such a manner as to suggest the world wasn't falling apart above us.

I closed my door and walked into my bedroom to check on Bentley. He slept just as peacefully as he had before I left. Pulling out the slip of paper from my pocket, I gave it one more scan before tossing it on the end table and flopping onto the bed. Sanctuary was nothing like Compound at all. The only place in the whole facility that was remotely like Compound was our private common area. The rest of the facility resembled more the makings of a nightmare. *The stuff nightmares are made of*, I thought to myself as I rolled onto my back and rubbed my eyes. In truth, none of us were Compound any more. We had become Sanctuary, an entirely new society with Compound and Haven influences. According to the papers I had flipped through at the table earlier, I wouldn't even be allowed to carry more than one firearm on my person outside of the family housing area unless I worked with the security forces.

"You totally missed everything!" Jacob whispered excitedly as he walked into my bedroom.

"Jacob... you didn't even knock." I complained as I sat up on the bed and shot him a dirty look.

Jacob frowned. "Sorry about that." He replied as he walked over to me and sat on the edge of the bed. "Matt was told he has night classes too and was asked to help clean up after the animals on the farming level. You should have seen his face it was priceless! Emily got the school house teaching preschool but that isn't the best part...," He smiled smugly before continuing, "... did you noticed your slip doesn't have your school hours on it? Anyone sixteen or older isn't required to attend classes. Emily asked about it when she noticed it. Travis and Matt almost died when they found out! So you, Emily and I don't even have to worry about it!"

"That is different." I said as I pulled the hair band off my wrist and used it to toss my hair into a ponytail.

"Yes and it gets better. Check this out..," Jacob laughed as he turned to face me, pulling one leg onto the bed. "...your dad works on the second floor with us as the OIC. Roscoe said it meant he was the officer in charge. Apparently he is going to be the big wig and run this place until Haven arrives. Jade is too young to have a job apparently but she does have to go to school with the other children. My dad is going to be working as security for the Intake and Processing Department on the first floor."

"What about Chase, Edward and Angela?" I asked as I turned to face Jacob.

"Angela is going to the Glazier Grill. Edward is in the hospital like Sarah. Chase...," He frowned before continuing, "...he was to head over to the library but caused such a fuss that Roscoe and your dad changed their minds. He said he refuses to live underground and that the time he has spent with us underground already has caused serious issues with his head. He lectured Roscoe about Operation Enduring Freedom and explained he wasn't some sort of sand dweller. It got pretty ugly out there. He has requested to live outside the complex either in one of the small buildings or in the trees."

"What?" I asked as a shocked laugh escaped my lips. "He can't be serious."

"He is more than serious. Roscoe is going to talk with the surface security force and see about finding him a job tailor made to his needs. It might end up being on one of the scout teams."

Jacob said as he stood up and stretched. "You ready for this tour yet or what? They are getting ready to take off here soon. Sarah said she is staying here and is willing to take care of Bentley for us."

"Yeah no problem just let me grab my notebook and pen. I want to take notes as we go." I said as I stood up and reached for my things. "I don't ever want to get lost in this place."

We began the tour on the top level near the loading bay. Roscoe had handed each of us a map which I quickly took notes on. The majority of the unmarried soldier security force for Sanctuary lived and worked on first level. They had their own offices and living spaces that took up much of the level. Roscoe also had been quick to point out the Intake and Processing Department where Robert would be working, the Quarantine and Decontamination Department, and the Isolation Medical Facility… which according to Sanctuary ran completely different then the Quarantine Department though I didn't understand the difference in the two.

The elevators had been finished from their servicing just before the morning announcements, allowing us to travel with ease between levels. Ten elevators in total made up the main transportation from level to level, each larger than any elevator I had seen in my life. Our entire tour group fit into one elevator with plenty of room to spare. Roscoe had explained the size had been to allow large amounts of supplies and people to travel between floors without having to fight for space.

The second level housed the entire office staff, council meeting room, small medical facility with a secondary Isolation Medical Facility, and the armory. It had been explained that the security teams on the first floor had plenty of weapons for themselves, and that the armory on the second floor supplied the entire underground security force. Special requests made from the surface forces could be granted if the armory could spare them. Roscoe took the time to explain to Jacob that the armory had multiple storage areas set aside for civilian weapons storage allowing for weapons to be stored by family groups that they may not want to store within their living space. We toured the council's Grand Hall meeting room, some of the offices, and even got the chance to see where I would be working though the office had been closed.

Skipping the third level living areas to save it for last, we were taken to the fourth level where the Marketplace was located. The main area stretched easily the size of three hundred yards wide and as far as I could tell, seven hundred yards or more long. Two floors made up the giant space with the center vaulting high above us. To the left of the elevators and recessed into the wall sat the Glazier Grill with its metal tables and chairs, clean white floors and cafeteria style buffet line. Jacob had been right when he described it as nothing more than an over glorified mess hall as nothing about the place suggested restaurant dinning like the name had suggested. On the right side of the elevators sat the hospital which unlike the Glazier Grill actually resembled a hospital facility. Roscoe made sure to explain that the center of the fourth level had been designed with the idea that family groups could set up stalls to sell or trade items they could make by hand. The theater resembled the one back home in Baker, Nevada as it was nothing more than a ticket booth and a room that held one large screen.

The school consisted of two large rooms with a child daycare facility to the right, connected by double doors. One room would be used for ages four through nine, the other room would be for ages ten through fifteen. To my surprise, the woman in charge of the daycare facility had Bentley's name written on her list of children who would need use of the facility and asked for Jacob and me to bring him by every morning by half passed seven. She took the time to hand me a small stack of intake papers I would need to fill out as well as a pricing sheet as I would be paying her to handle his care while at work. The thought of a complete stranger caring for Bentley had made me nervous as I scanned the papers and nodded without speaking.

After the daycare, Roscoe took the time to show us the banking office which shocked me. Each original member of Compound had a preset account with funds that had been deposited over the years. He even explained that Compound as a whole had a company account which could be used for repair or renovation costs of the private living spaces. The bank locked away all monies and issued what they called Sanctuary Notes as a form of currency, based on the current gold standard. Each note had the emblems of the communities that hoped to call Sanctuary home printed on them in green and blue ink. I passed the sample note that we had been allowed to inspect to Jacob, who shivered playfully as he mocked it.

The fifth level housed the Farming Facility as well as the entire collection of Sanctuary livestock. The level easily mirrored in size to the market complex. We had toured several wooden stalls with our group name on them, housing the animals we had brought with us. One large room that shot off the right side of the main floor held the Composting and Soil Division where all animal waste would be turned into usable compost for the indoor farming complex. Each family group had designated farming plots to be used how they saw fit, to grow special items they could sell or trade if they chose to. The level even housed their own veterinarian clinic in charge of keeping all livestock as health as possible.

When we came to the Power House level that housed the boilers and generators Dave groaned loudly, complaining about being stuffed away like a prisoner to work in the mines. There wasn't much to see as the place consisted of wall to wall machinery I couldn't identify. Roscoe showed us the expansive heating and cooling systems, the steam room, and even a Water and Waste Treatment Facility. Jacob made a disgusted face when the subject turned toward water recycling and reclaiming procedures. I fought to hide my laughter as the look on his face changed from disgust to pure horror when the handling of black waste had been explained. We were then informed that under us stood other levels that were used for storage, some strictly to be used in the event of large weapons attacks, saying that tunnels ran deep into the mountain to a secondary area we could escape to if bunker busters ever became a problem.

We returned to the third level living quarters that housed the units for each of the family groups. The large center commons held everything I had seen the night before with exhausted eyes, but also much more. A library and medical clinic sat tucked into small offices with glass doors. Two full stories littered with labeled doors surrounded the large common area. My eyes followed the upper walkways and staircases that came down into the shared space in several areas. Jacob jabbed me in the ribs with his elbow to get my attention and pointed to a large stack of boxes piled near the unit designated for Compound members.

"Wonderful!" Roscoe cheered as he caught sight of the boxes after watching Jacob. "Your belongings from your vehicles have been delivered. This is the end of our tour. There will be an announcement shortly explaining the afternoon plans as well as the meal. You are free to put your things away. Please remember to read through all the handouts I have given you and remember there is a post office system here to handle deliveries to other floors. This is where I leave you. Jared, Fallon, and Jacob… I will see you at three o'clock for the council meeting on the second level."

CHAPTER NINETEEN

I sat stunned, my pen no longer writing notes as I allowed my brain to process the information Roscoe and Officer Bowman had given us. Robert slowly rose from the large meeting room table and moved closer to the map on display, one hand on his hip and the other running slowly through his hair in frustration. Jacob had spent most of the meeting pacing the large room slowly, chewing his lip as he thought. My father hadn't moved from his seat. He sat with elbows resting on the polished oak finish of the meeting room table, hands pressed together with his fingers resting on his lips. I gently set my pen down on the table, trying desperately not to shake.

"Mr. Bowman, I'll need you to explain this one more time and please go slowly so that my daughter can catch up on the notes. We need to hear it again." My father finally spoke as his eyes watched Robert deep in thought at one of the maps.

The tall frame of Officer Bowman stood, the perfectly sculpted muscles of his massive chest pressed hard through his overstretched blue tee shirt, hiding nothing. Not a single grey hair could be seen in his military style hair shockingly darker than the color of pitch. He was strong and clean cut like the perfect warrior. Even in his mid to late forties he put the younger soldiers to shame when it came to athletics and strength. His black eyes scanned our faces before he met my shocked gaze, and nodded again.

"Yes, Sir." Bowman began as he spun on his heels in true military fashion and walked to one of the large maps which had been secured to the white board on the wall. "Our surface teams have been conducting missions within a fifty mile radius of the facility for the past sixty days. Our mission has been to locate, observe, and protect incoming civilians from each of the groups said to use this facility. Take out hostel forces. Clear a safe passage. Keep it clean." He explained as he traced the bold red circle shown on the map with his finger. "Though civilian hunters and refugees are left to complete their travel though the area, for the past twenty days we have disposed of several large groups of hostels within the target range. Two of these groups appeared to resemble United States military soldiers. Both teams had been observed targeting large groups of civilian refugees escaping the nearby cities… here and here." He said as he pointed out two cities on the map.

"Your surface force is the reason the drive here had been so uneventful." Jacob stated as he paced over to the map and ran his finger across the route we had taken from the cave to Sanctuary. "We only managed to run across a hunting party and a hiker."

"Yes, Sir." Bowman nodded. "Our job is to make sure each group has safe passage and are not followed. You managed to pick up a tail on your caravan just outside the city limits of Twin Falls; once we spotted them in range we handled the situation quietly." He said as he pointed to the area on the map. "We had your group surrounded and monitored your progress until you arrived safely inside the gates. Part of the reason you were not automatically quarantined upon arrival had been due to this. You did not pass through the identified infected zones."

I leaned back in my chair as I watched the exchange between Jacob and Bowman. For the past several hours we had been held up in the Grand Hall conducting the most important council meeting we had ever had, and the first of many to come here at Sanctuary. Both Roscoe and Bowman had explained not only the inner workings of the facility but also a detailed description of every mission being led on the surface. Roscoe now sat silently four chairs down from me, also watching the exchange though not nearly as shocked as I had been.

"And these identified infected zones… are pockets of illness." Robert said as he walked back to the table and pulled out a chair.

"Yes, Sir." Bowman confirmed as he spun on his heels to face Robert. "A strain of SARS has been identified in these areas," He began as he pointed at the map, "As of yet we haven't identified the specific strain, however it holds classic markers similar to the strain that emerged in two thousand eleven thought to have arrived from Africa or Asia. Studies conducted over the years had come to the conclusion that if left unchecked, the mutation would create a super flu, a global pandemic. These areas indicated show signs of what we believe to be this SARS virus. Symptoms include headache, joint pain, vomiting and high fever to name just a few. Trouble breathing, kidney failure, and unexplained bruising has also been identified. Your team did not pass though the identified areas."

"And you are saying that isn't the only problem we are facing?" I asked as I looked at the notes I had taken earlier in the meeting. "You stated earlier that you may have identified a clear contamination zone caused by the meltdown of nuclear power stations?"

"The nuclear reactor power plants, yes." Bowman said has he pointed to a second map, this one of the entire country. "As of now, the United States has one hundred ten nuclear power plants around the country. This facility is strategically placed so as to avoid contamination. The state of Montana and the surrounding states do not have nuclear power plants. The nearest one is here in the state of Washington."

"You said it is the same type of power plant as the one that went down years ago in Japan?" I asked as I looked up from my notes. "What did you mean by that?"

"Yes ma'am, The Fukushima disaster. Both that reactor and the one in Washington are Boiling Water Reactors. When the primary power source went down during the blackout, the secondary power backup systems also went down. Unable to stay cooled causes reactors to melt down. We are not close enough to that facility to have to worry about the instant effects of the melt down; however any radioactive particles that escaped in the steam explosion are a concern. We have been watching weather patterns and are prepared in the event of radioactive cloud as we do not know the strength of melt down or explosion. Reactor melt downs and fallout zones are unpredictable in nature. We have recently also identified two small groups of refugees from the radioactive area trying to escape. Our forces did what was necessary to protect this facility." Bowman informed as he straightened his posture and made eye contact with my father.

"You murdered them." I spat in anger.

"Ma'am, with all due respect," Bowman said as the stern look on his face began to soften, "The death caused by radioactive exposure is unlike anything you have ever seen. The lucky ones die at ground zero. Those who survive die slowly. The two small groups we came across showed serious signs of radiation toxicity. They were contaminated and the items they had brought with them were also contaminated. As much as it pains me to say Miss Fallon Henley… they were dead the moment the solar flare hit earth. We did what we had to do in order to keep the spread of radioactive material from coming anywhere near Sanctuary."

My father stood and walked slowly to the maps. "Two concerns… a super flu and radiation, one on either side of us." He said as he ran his fingers across his chin. "And you believe that these military units you disposed of had been targeting the city refugees in order to contain the virus?"

"We believe that had been their mission. Contain the virus before global spread. The problem had been the groups they had targeted had not been exposed to the virus. They were people fighting to escape before becoming exposed. The units we believe, had been order to quarantine the entire city… infected or not, and wipe out those who tried to leave." Roscoe said as he stood from his chair.

"What about Haven? What are their chances for making it to us with everything going on out there? Between the radiation, Patriot war, and the virus… how do we make sure they are safe?" I asked with concern.

"Once your team arrived, we sent two scout teams of volunteers to get to them. It is our hope they are already headed in this direction. Upon their arrival they will be quarantined, tested, and held before being released into the facility if the need is there for it." Roscoe answered.

"How can you be absolutely sure our group hasn't been infected with either radiation or the virus?" Jacob asked as he turned to face Roscoe.

"That is easy. Nevada does not have nuclear power plants. When you traveled here you came through Idaho where nuclear power plants also don't exist. Your arrival did not set off the alarms in place to test for radioactive materials. Your people, vehicles, and belongings came in clean. As far as the virus…," Roscoe said with a sad smile, "…you would have shown signs of the infection long before you arrived. Due to the fact the members in your team that died had died during battle we had been assured it hadn't been illness related. You didn't pass through the infected zones and have not shown a single sign of even a fever."

I rubbed my eyes with the heels of my hands. "What you are saying is… we got lucky."

"Maybe luck isn't the word for it, but yes." Bowman replied.

I quickly stuffed several bites of spinach lasagna into my mouth in rapid succession as the Glazier Grill began to clear out for the evening. The council meeting had run well into the dinner hours and being a weekend, the council assistant staff hadn't been around to bring us dinner. I had sat through the entire meeting listening to and feeling my stomach rumble and secretly prayed no one else could hear the horrible growls it had given me. Skipping lunch hadn't been the best of ideas, but I had been excited to have my things delivered to Compound's family unit. I had helped to sort everything into piles based on who the items belonged to, and had put all of my stuff away while the others had gone to lunch. Everyone that was, except for Jacob who had been more than willing to help, and Sarah who proceeded to lock herself in her private quarters to sort her husband's things.

Once the meeting had ended, I nearly ran to the elevators and arrived at the fourth level Glazier Grill in time to catch the last call for dinner. I had chosen a table against the far wall near a large painting of Glazier National Park, a place I had never been though always had dreams of seeing. Sanctuary wasn't far from the park, but going there would never be an option. My eyes slowly moved across the painting taking in every swirl and ridge of texture placed by skilled artistic hands. Pure talent. I had to stop myself several times from reaching up with my fingers and running them through the paths left behind by the brush that had painted it.

Tossing my cardboard tray into the recycle bin, I stepped out into the Marketplace square on my mission. I remembered seeing a few small shops on the tour though none of us had toured them individually. We simply walked by them making our way to the most important areas on the tour. Several people laughed and talked in small groups as they sat on benches or stood near potted trees. My first stop would be the bank to collect Sanctuary Notes from my account, and then I would find some sort of makeup if possible, and a nice outfit for work. I crossed the square and found the bank open even at such a late hour. After being identified as Fallon Henley, I was issued a plastic card that indicated my account and promptly told my current balance. My parents had deposited gold and silver coins on every visit for several years, as paper currency apparently did not count on the Sanctuary economic system. The woman behind the counter smiled brightly as she checked the books in front of her and upon learning this experience was my first time within the bank, made quick work of explaining the process.

    I walked out with what amounted to roughly four hundred fifty notes, and quickly dove into a tiny shop I thought might have what I had been searching for. The woman behind the counter had been more than happy to help me as she hadn't sold any cosmetics. She explained that when the soldiers received orders to be stationed at Sanctuary, the families moved as well, most of them asked to open businesses within the facility or take on jobs like teaching. Most of the wives simply traveled into the nearest cities to buy supplies so as not to take away from the stockpile meant for the arrival of our groups. After the blackout, the traveling to the cities had stopped but each family had their own stockpile in their units to rely on when needed. Compound had been the first of the groups to arrive at Sanctuary, making me the first woman to come into her shop to buy something rather than just to have a conversation. Together we went through the makeup counter and managed to locate a liquid foundation in my shade, several shades of eye shadow and lipstick, a powder box, two shades of eye liner and a tube of mascara. Her assortment of cosmetics spanned all colors of the cosmetic rainbow and seemed able to keep hundreds of women supplied for many years to come.

    I bought the makeup we had chosen together along with a fancy bottle of perfume called Vanilla Silk, which had soft tones of vanilla and lavender. The storekeeper found several sets of cheap jewelry she thought I might be interested in after I explained where I would be working, and after looking through the sets I settled on one of them. The silver chained necklace I had chosen held a single faux emerald stone pendant surrounded by small cubic zirconia with a pair of matching earrings and bracelet. While she bagged my purchased items she informed me of a woman who, before the blackout, had been a licensed Esthetician and ran a small spa in the Marketplace. Apparently she had cheap prices for nail work and the storekeeper thought it best I stop in there before Monday morning. I thanked her for being helpful as she slipped two bottles of nail polish, a file and nail buffer into my bag, free of charge.

I walked out of the tiny shop carrying a small neon pink paper bag and a pocket fifty notes lighter than before I had entered. Walking slowly and taking the time to scan every storefront, I caught sight of Travis and Emily leaving the theater hand in hand and laughing. I smiled as I thought about how they must have been on their first real date, and then panicked that my presence might spoil the mood. Not wanting them to see me in the Marketplace, I promptly dipped into what looked like a clothing store and hid behind some racks of dresses as they passed the storefront window.

Once I had been assured they hadn't noticed me, I began to flip through several racks. The woman behind the counter commented on my beautiful green eyes and long auburn hair, suggesting that a green skirt suit might be exactly what I had been looking for. The skirt suit fit amazingly well though we both had felt the skirt had been just a little too long for my frame. She promptly offered to shorten the skirt while I searched for a blouse and shoes. She explained to me that her and her sister ran the store and did tailoring on the side, handling the soldiers' uniforms when needed. I bought the green skirt suit, a black briefcase for work, a white blouse, a pair of black pumps with matching handbag, and two sets of nylon leggings in the color of nude. Before I left, the woman slipped a tan colored pocket book into my bag free of charge, explaining how excited she had been to see me shopping.

Noticing the late hour, I walked as quickly as I could to the spa and found it was also still open. I explained to the woman who it had been who had sent me and instantly gained a steep discount. Three other women lead me to a chair where I promptly received a pedicure and leg polish, hand massage, and a glass of champagne. I settled on a French manicure style in acrylic nails, cut short yet still elegant. As a special gift, small silver designs with tiny rhinestones had been decorated onto just my pinky nails as an accent. By the time I left, my eyebrows had been waxed into perfection, my nails looked professional, and I had even managed to get my first hair cut since the blackout. Though I had only had them removed the last three inches of my hair that had been damaged from travel, I had been talked into a deep conditioning treatment that made my hair feel like silk.

I smiled as I strolled down the Marketplace square with my bags, only to stop mid step as my eyes fell on Jacob leaning against a large potted tree, his arms crossed over his chest and an evil grin across his lips. "So you found the day spa did you?" He laughed as his gaze ran the length of my body. "Looks like you had some fun shopping."

"I needed stuff for work apparently. The description said office attire would be expected." I taunted as I walked passed him toward the elevators that would take me back to the third level. "Jeans and tee shirts are not allowed."

"Wait…," Jacob called as he ran to catch up to me. "Did you get everything you needed?"

"I believe I did. If I am missing something I wouldn't know it." I laughed as I raised my bags to show off my prize. "I think I bought the whole place in one night."

Jacob peered into each bag, "No, you definitely forgot something important. I can tell."

I stepped into the elevator and pushed the button for the third level as Jacob followed. "You have got to be kidding me, Jacob. I am serious when I say I literally bought a head to toe look back there."

Jacob laughed and handed me a small bag I hadn't noticed him carrying. "You forgot these." He said with a smile. "I was following you in my true stalker tendencies. You didn't buy anything for your hair and I figured it might have just slipped your mind. I also talked that beautiful woman in the makeup place to sell me a broach that matches the jewelry set you bought."

"You followed me?" I asked in shock. "You are such a turd! Why would you do that you creeper?"

"My mom wanted to take Bentley for the whole night. She said that since she is going to be working twelve hour shifts she won't see him as much. After I helped her move the crib to her place I had some free time. I came down to see about buying you something special and saw you come out of the bank. I went in and pulled some notes of my own and figured I would watch you to see which stores you liked most. All I did was go into them after you left and talk to them about you and what you had bought. I knew right away what you had been doing. There is nothing like preparing for your first real job." He smiled as the elevator doors opened onto the third level.

"Thank you for the gifts." I thanked with a smile as I stepped from the elevator before crossing the commons toward our family unit. "It means a lot to me that you would stalk the hell out of me and spend your money on crap I probably didn't need." I playfully teased.

"You deserve much more than some hair junk and a broach... whatever the hell that is. Did you know the woman in that store had to explain it? I still didn't see the point of one or what it is used for." Jacob said as he opened the door for me. "I don't know much about women I guess."

"No, you know enough about women to get yourself into trouble." I laughed as I opened the door to my private quarters and stepping inside. "Good night Mr. Dunn. Thank you for escorting me home."

"Can I come in?" Jacob asked with an evil grin.

"It will take more than a hair decoration and a decorative broach to get into my private quarters." I smirked before shutting the door and crossing my sitting area with a giggle.

The gentle and beautiful sound of the bell chime filled the air as I stretched and groaned. The same soft female voice I had hear the day before quickly gave the date, day security level, meal times and the special of the day for the Glazier Grill. I would be looking forward to pancakes with eggs and sausage if I managed to make it to the breakfast service. I climbed out of bed and padded to the bathroom to begin my morning routine. I brushed my teeth and hair as quickly as I could and dressed in a pair of jeans and black tee shirt with my military boots. Today would be my last free day before I would be forced to report to work in the morning. *Maybe I can catch a movie or plant something in the family garden plot*, I thought to myself as I ran out the door of my private quarters, closing it behind me.

"Wow girl! Where are you off to in such a rush this morning?" Jacob asked as he stood at the kitchenette sink in the Compound common area. "Are you really in a hurry to eat breakfast?"

"I am starving. Want to go with me?" I asked as I opened the door to the family unit and stepped out. "You are welcome to shadow me to the Glazier Grill if you desire."

I couldn't be sure what Jacob had been doing, but he quickly ran from our unit trying to catch up to me by the time I pushed the button on the elevator. As we moved down to the fourth level he explained that my father had a special request to speak with me about something as soon as possible and that everyone had already left for breakfast. My father had hopes to catch me during breakfast and insisted the conversation take place immediately. When the elevator doors opened I stepped out into the Marketplace with Jacob at my side. The sound of laughing filtered out of the Glazier Grill and echoed off the steel and concrete walls that helped to lock our world away underground.

My father stood by the elevator doors, arms crossed and leaning against the wall. The moment he saw me his eyes lit up. "Hey kiddo, glad you could join us. Jacob, can I speak with my daughter privately for a moment?"

Jacob nodded and with a smile, kept walking toward the source of the laughter and smell of pancakes. My stomach rolled and growled forcing me to place one hand on my stomach in an attempt to keep it quiet. Jacob would likely fill a plate for me as well, seeing as I would be detained. I closed my eyes and inhaled with a groan. "Alright dad, what is more important than sausage?" I asked playfully.

"It is Emily. She is a Perez; we did not put anything in place here at Sanctuary to handle Papa or Emily. With Papa gone she has nothing left and barely brought anything here with her. She has been staying in Megan's private quarters with the children because she has nowhere to go." My father spoke softly. "I spoke with her last night and she has requested to take over Megan's private quarters for the time we are here. If you don't mind her doing so, I would like her to keep the place and help with the children. They love and trust her."

I sagged slightly as I realized the conversation really was more important than sausage. "By all means." I said as I leaned against the wall beside him.

"Also, Sarah has elected to give Chase the personal funds from Brian's account as he arrived here as Emily had, with nothing. Haven set up an account for Edward before he came to stay with us. This leaves Emily. She doesn't have any money to help get her started and she starts work tomorrow the same as you." My father said as he ran a hand through his hair. "Look, I know losing Mom has been hard on you... but I would like to know if you mind allowing me to take a portion of your mother's account to give it to Emily to help get her going."

"Whatever you feel best; Mom would have wanted to help her out. I don't have a problem with that at all." I said sadly as I thought about how I had forgotten Emily hadn't been a member of Compound my entire life. "Do it. Give her the money... hell give her all of the money from Mom's account."

"I thought you would say that," My father smiled as he wrapped his arms around me. "Jade said the exact same thing this morning. I can't even begin to tell you how proud I am of you girls."

When we let go we walked together arm in arm into the Glazier Grill. It didn't take me long to find Jacob sitting at a table alone in front of two overflowing plates. He sat devouring a short stack of pancakes heavily drown in maple syrup and butter. It was easy to see how someone living this way could forget that just above them the world was crumbling to the ground. I sank into the chair across from Jacob as my stomach growled. I would have some serious catching up to do if I planned to finish my plate before Jacob.

As I dipped my sausage links into my syrup, I thought about the council meeting and the information Roscoe and Bowman had disclosed. I could shop in every store on the fourth level, have a hot rock treatment with full body massage, and go to work like everyone else; it still wouldn't change the facts. The world above us was coming apart violently. Sanctuary had been designed to pretend. Designed to fool you into forgetting the hells of the world above. You could live your entire existence in the facility and if done right, never know the despair of a collapsing society.

The blackout had been just the beginning for all of us. Power would the least of our worries. Compound had continued on as if the blackout had been insignificant. While we had enjoyed our lives, a turf and water war had broken out in our town. People had been killed or died fighting for basic needs. None of us had noticed. Fleeing our home had been our first taste of the down fall and only then did we truly suffer. Now we were tucked away in an underground world thriving yet again, ignoring the death and destruction ripping our country apart.

I desperately wanted to help people. The guilt of being raised in my world fought to flood my eyes with hot tears and my heart with sadness. Somewhere out there on the surface a mother was holding her sick child tight, watching them die and completely lost as to how to save them. People unaware of how to prepare had inadvertently caused the deaths of their family and friends. Instead of taking the time to grow a garden or stash a few supplies, the people who hadn't prepared now jockeyed between burying loved one and killing people over rice or beans.

A tear escaped my eye as I tried to hide it by sipping my coffee, wiping my eye with the edge of my hand. For the briefest of moment the day before, I had actually managed to have some fun. I forgot about the surface… and laughed. How can that happen? Even with the bad news the council meeting had brought, just hours later I was sitting in a comfortable chair receiving a manicure and a pedicure with a glass of champagne. I closed my eyes and inhaled sharply, privately vowing that if the chance ever came my way to help someone I would do whatever it takes to help them. Survival groups like my own shouldn't hold all the cards and privilege. If surviving meant ignoring it all and watching people die, then I wanting no part of it.

Jacob looked up from his pancakes, his dark eyes watching me intently. He sat back and wiped his lips with a napkin. "Listen Fallon, there is no need to feel guilty or start having thoughts of hero grandeur. You are not responsible for what people did or didn't do before the blackout. For almost ten years the media and scientific communities gave warning after warning, flooding books and television with them. Those that didn't listen are now paying the price. I agree it is horrible and heartbreaking to think about… but it isn't your fault." He said as he leaned across the table and took one of my hands in his own.

"You don't know what I think about, Jacob. What makes you think…," I mumbled as I broke my own sentence off with a sip from my coffee cup, unable to determine how to end my thought properly.

"So you mean to tell me that you weren't just sitting there thinking about the council meeting and your little shopping spree where for the first time in two months you actually had fun?" Jacob teased as he pointed his fork at me with his free hand. "I can read it all over your face. You have nothing to feel guilty about. You are a survivor. You are not a hero. You can't save them all, Fallon. One of these days you will be faced with a serious choice. I am convinced that in the long run, you will do what is right for yourself and for your family. Risking your own life to save strangers will only kill you. Those on the surface will either die or find a way. The strongest and smartest will always find a way."

The sudden urge to change the subject and bury the pain had brought a thought to my mind and I smiled. "I saw a tavern last night when I walked the Marketplace looking for stuff. I would like to swing in there and see about a gift for Chase. Even on the surface he needs a delivery service. Since he refuses to reenter the facility... how about we stop in for something special and go for a visit today?" I asked before stuffing a bite of pancakes into my mouth.

Jacob simply nodded with a smile as he let go of my hand and continued to finish his plate. We hadn't seen Chase since he had apparently argued with Roscoe and stormed out of the facility. I wanted to warn him about the virus and the radiation as I knew he probably hadn't been informed of either. The gift from the tavern might be just the excuse we need to locate him and give him the information he needed. Jacob stood, now finished, and held his hand out to me. I quickly stuffed the last several bites into my mouth and chugged what had been left of my now lukewarm coffee.

We crossed the Marketplace and walked nearly the entire length of the open square before locating the tavern. I had yet to investigate the place as in the back of my mind, I was still only sixteen years old. Thought Haven and Sanctuary had a different view of adulthood and age, I hadn't been able to test the concept. Unlike other shops along the square, the tavern had been built to resemble a rustic old world pub, with knotty oak paneling, wooden benches, and large wooden barrels stacked up along two walls. My eyes brightened when we walked through the open door and caught sight of a large map of Ireland along the wall behind the bar.

"You both are rather early... don't you think?" The female bartender laughed as she stood wiping off a wooden barstool with a damp towel. "If you plan to be boozing up for breakfast, am I not even close to being ready for you."

"I'm sorry ma'am, we aren't here for breakfast. We actually

wanted to ask you a favor." Jacob said as he sat in a stool at the bar. "A member of our group refuses to live inside the facility. He has a deep love for alcohol. We came to see if we can bring him a gift."

The bartender rubbed her chin with her thin fingers and walked behind the wooden bar. She stood tall and thin, her long chestnut hair pulled up into a pile atop her head. She looked to me as though she couldn't have been more than forty years old. "Are you talking about Chase? I had the pleasure of meeting a member of your party last night. He kept going on and on about his crazy friend Chase. He called the guy a total boozer and told me wild stories about grenade chucking."

I smiled with a laugh, "You must have met Dave then. Yes, Chase is the guy we are here about. Before the blackout he was a desert hermit. He had this kid he knew make deliveries to him once a month."

"Well I guess I could help you out. The name is Rissa by the way," She said as she tossed the damp towel she had been holding into the sink. "I might have something but it isn't very cheap. I'll have to check to see how much of it I have. Tell you what... I'll give you a discount if you can get Dave to come back in tonight. He is adorable and I enjoy his company." She smirked as she placed both hands on her hips, her brown eyes moving from me to Jacob.

"I am Jacob and this is Fallon." Jacob pointed, "We will have a talk with Dave and send him back in as soon as possible."

With a playful nod, Rissa turned on her heels and walked through a door behind the bar, disappearing for several minutes. When she returned she carried an old plastic milk jug in each hand. Placing them onto the bar with a thud, sliding them toward us with a smile. "Because you don't know how I run the place, let me fill you in. This is my bar, not a Sanctuary bar. I didn't come here with family, I was contracted. I have my rules and own way of doing things. No violence, no rough housing and no fights. I made every scrap of furniture in this place and if I ever have to bust one of my stools over you... I won't be happy. I also allow patrons to run an open tab, so long as they pay it off on time by the end of the week. If he wants deliveries than I need him to talk with the council and allow me access to his bank account to pay for it... since he won't come down here and pull his own money. He does have money right?"

I nodded, "Yes he has an account. He inherited Brian's account. Sarah signed it over and donated the funds to him. I am on the council and so is Jacob. We can probably work out a weekly system of transfer for you. I'll talk to the bank as well."

Rissa smiled brightly, "Good. Then I won't charge you for these today. I'll set him a tab. You can tell him the total cost for these will be charged as thirty notes each, however if Dave shows up tonight as you have promised... I'll drop the price to ten notes each. You can let Chase know that I made this stuff myself. It is extremely strong so he needs to go easy on it or he will be face down in the dirt and gurgling on his own vomit. If he can put requests through the head office, I can allow my mop boy to make one delivery a week to the processing station to be delivered to him. There is no way I am sending that poor kid out into the open unless the guards instate their usual mandatory sun time."

"Thank you, Rissa." I said as I grabbed the jugs and made my way to the door, Rissa waving at us behind me.

After we thanked Rissa again and carrying the two jugs of mystery liquor, we nearly ran to the elevators. When we found Dave on the third level we informed him of Rissa's wishes. He promptly dropped what he was doing and thanked us for the message before catching an elevator down to the fourth level. We rode up, arriving on the first level with jugs in hand. Jacob explained to the Intake and Processing Department that we had a delivery for Chase. The man behind the counter informed us that access to the surface is normally restricted, but that at this time clearance would be granted as the risk levels were low.

Laughing as the guard opened the door, we ran through the loading bay and into the morning light, stopping briefly to close our eyes and smell the millions of scents that made up the great outdoors. A silent conversation between Jacob and I began the moment our eyes met. We would make the most of our first trip out of the facility since we had arrived. Jacob grinned before grabbing my hand and leading me further out into the day toward where we had been told Chase was living... not to return until nightfall.

CHAPTER TWENTY

"Oh hello Mrs. Henley," The short heavy set woman in a blue pants suit said cheerfully as I stepped through the door. "It is so good to finally meet you. My name is Rebecca and I am your assistant." She informed as she crossed the room and stuck her hand out.

"Please, call me Miss Henley. Mrs. Henley was my mother." I smiled as I reached out to shake her hand.

She smiled brightly, her brown eyes shining as she turned and motioned to a door on the other side of the room. "Of course, Miss Henley, as you wish. This is your office. Should you need anything at all please ask. If you choose to work through your lunch hour I need advanced notice in order to have your meal delivered to you. Every department has submitted their requests and the storage department just delivered their inventory lists."

"I am not exactly sure what I am to do here," I said as I followed Rebecca into the office that I had been assigned. "Am I the only person here?"

"Oh yes…," Rebecca said excitedly as she laced her fingers together in front of her. "…this department consists of only the two of us. I handled all I could before you arrived, but you have more power than I do. It was like pulling teeth just to have forms approved as you need council approval for many of them. Let me fetch you a pot of coffee. I was told you drink it with half of one sugar and two creams?" She asked as she walked back through the door and stopped on the other side. I nodded before she disappeared from sight.

My eyes panned over the room as I stood frozen in shock. The reception area of the department had been deceiving with its small space, single desk and water cooler. It had looked like a doctor's office to me, complete with padded chairs arranged into a seating nook and the stack of magazines on the short table. My office was nothing like the reception area had been. Unlike the light blue rug outside my door, my office had chocolate colored carpet covering the massive floor space from wall to wall. A massive oak wall unit bookshelf stained a dark burgundy, stretched the entire length of the wall behind my matching desk. There was a small wooden bar to one side with several decorative glass jars partially filled with brown, yellow and clear liquid. I opened the cabinet under the jars and found a small refrigerator and a shelf of drinking glasses. *Why do I need my own bar?* I thought to myself as I turned to investigate other areas of the six hundred square foot marvel. The entire left wall contained curtains that stretched from the floor clear to the much too high ceiling.

Rebecca walked in with a wooden tray containing a French press, small cream and sugar containers and a decorative coffee mug, placing the tray on the edge of the desk. "You'll want to know about the windows I am sure. Do you like cityscapes, ocean views, or the rainforest?"

"Uh... I like the rainforest I guess." I stammered in confusion.

"Wonderful! I do as well." Rebecca said, as she clapped her hands together and turned to the wall of curtains.

Grabbing one end of the brown curtains that were several shade lighter than the carpet, she pulled them open as she walked the length of the massive wall. My mouth fell open when I saw what the curtains had been hiding. The wall itself was glass, framed in as a window would be with wide wooden frames, resembling the massive windows a person might see in a high rise office complex. Recessed a few inches behind the glass sat what looked like a gigantic movie screen.

"They designed it with the idea that spending so much time in here would make a person crazy after a while. No one wants to be cooped up underground for long periods of time, right?" Rebecca explained as she walked over to me and stood at my side. "This is the remote to control the system. It uses very little power so don't be afraid the turn it on everyday if that is what makes you comfortable." She explained as she held up a small black pad with screen. "The time is automatically set so the scene you choose will darken or lighten over time, almost as if you are truly there!"

Rebecca tapped on the remote and the screen lit up with the image of the rainforest. Instantly I felt as though my entire office had been transported to the middle of the Amazon. Birds flapped from one tree to another as they went about their day. Rain water dripped down leaves to pool on the forest floor. Slowly I walked toward the window completely captured by the scene as it played out before me. This wasn't a picture, rather a video of a rainforest habitat.

"This is incredible." I laughed as I turned to Rebecca. "Are you serious?"

"Yes ma'am." Rebecca answered as she held up the remote. "All you have to do is pick which scene you like and then chose which view options you would like. If you want a cityscape, you can select which city. Some of the cities have ocean views. The video is roughly twenty-four hours long but they restart automatically. There is even sound and you can adjust the sound level for a more fulfilling experience." She explained as she placed the remote onto the desk.

"I could play with this system all day. How am I to work when I have a system like this?" I teased as I walked behind the desk and set my briefcase on the floor.

"Trust me, after a few months you will be begging the Technical Department for new scenes." Rebecca laughed as I sat in the large black leather chair. "You will love working here. The job is fairly cut and dry, but what you do here can make or break businesses and departments." She explained as she sat in a black leather chair across the desk from me. "Every department submits a form daily. Some departments request extra supplies, renovations, repairs or even declare extra supplies that hadn't been used. Your job is the read the requests, locate which department has the items requested and reassign the items or decline the request with explanation. You then write up a delivery notice to be delivered to the department explaining the supplies you are reassigning. Those are picked up at the end of the day by the mail service and delivered by the following morning."

"That is a lot of paper." I mumbled as I looked at the three piles of paper at the edge of my desk.

"It can be. They eventually go to the Composting Department." Rebecca nodded before standing and walking toward the door. "The binders on the shelf behind you are the inventory charts." She called over her shoulder as she opened the door. "Call me on the intercom if you need anything."

I watched as she left the office and closed the door behind her. Alone in my office I could hear the gentle sound of birds singing in the rainforest scene that played in my window wall. I removed my green blazer, tossing it on top of my briefcase at my feet, unwilling to walk across the room to the coatrack by the door. Grabbing a small stack of request forms from the pile, I placed them in front of me to be reviewed.

Special Access Request Form
Rissa O'Malley
Emerald Tavern
I request special permission to make weekly deliveries to the Intake and Processing Department every Friday to be accepted by Chase McGee. I would also like to request special permission to be granted invoicing privileges with automatic payment from his bank account as he refuses to enter the facility due to mental health reasons. I need a member of the council to approve banking action.

I smiled to myself as my eyes scanned the paper. Chase had been overjoyed at the message from Rissa and agreed excitedly after tasting her mystery liquor with us the day before. In the time he had spent with us, I hadn't seen him happier. He had chosen an abandoned watch tower as his new residence which still needed some renovations to create a living space. Although he had been excited to see us and the delivery, he was quick to inform us that he had found a job with the security teams that patrolled the radius around the facility.

I quickly picked up a pen and put a check mark in the box on the paper that indicated my approval to the request from Rissa, scrawling a short note in the space provided and signing my name on the line. A quick intercom call to Rebecca helped me to locate what she had called the Department Fulfillment Forms, which were nothing more than a memo that would need to be filled and delivered to the bank as well as the Intake and Processing

Department, informing them of the granted request.

The next request had been from the main office of the surface security forces, requesting two hundred hand grenades to supply the patrols, a uniform and flak jacket for a civilian volunteer who had joined the patrols, and two five gallon buckets of ground coffee. I slid from my chair and pulled down the binders from the shelves that contained the inventory for the armory and the Food Storage Department. Inside the armory binder sat the most up to date list of items being stored, dated for the night before. My eyes ran down the lists until I found the area that detailed the private storage for family groups. I knew we had brought grenades of our own when we had arrived and not wanting to have them go to waste, I had made the decision to share some of them. If we ever had the chance to leave Sanctuary, there would be no use for such a large stockpile to be taken with us.

The system of requests didn't make much sense to me as I felt it would be much easier for departments to submit requests directly to the other departments instead of placing me as the middle man. I flipped open the binder for the Food Storage Department and scanned down the list until I saw the supply of coffee. Four hundred fifty-five gallon drums of ground coffee sat as a backup in a level of Sanctuary that hadn't been on the tour when we arrived. I remembered Roscoe explaining at the time that the levels below housed massive amounts of storage. This seemed like a request I could grant.

The other items on the request had been in the armory in good supply. I checked the box indicating the request had been granted, and in the space provided wrote a short note explaining the order would be fulfilled as soon as possible, signing my name on the line when I had finished. I knew only members of Compound and those who worked in the Armory Department would have access to our personal storage room, so I wanted to make note that Jacob would need to be the one to fill the order. I filled out a Department Fulfillment Form, addressing it to the armory and listed the requested items to be prepared and delivered to the surface forces. In the area indicating special requests, I made note to have Jacob Dunn retrieve the grenades from the Compound storage room instead of the main supply warehouse. I filled out an identical form for the Food Supply Department, listing the items requested and asked the order prepared and delivered to

Darkness Falls

the surface forces.

For the next hour I read, replied, and filled out forms until my hand began to cramp. Rebecca had stepped into my office just as I had reached the middle of the stack of papers to ask about lunch. I knew my work would last long into the afternoon and asked to have it brought up to me. I wouldn't be out of here for hours yet. What remained of my morning coffee grew cold on my desk as I moved about the office checking inventory binders, work orders, special requests and supply charts. The storage capabilities for Sanctuary had been far more expansive than I had originally thought. This was more than a bunker; it was an entire underground city.

The Glazier Grill wanted fresh eggs from the Farming Department to the count of two hundred, two fifty-five gallon drums of flour from the Food Storage Department, and five gallons of butter powder. The movie theater requested to have a repair made to the drywall, saying the owner tripped over his own feet and made the hole in the wall with his head. I granted the request though I had suspected the hole had been placed there a number of ways and not as the form had stated.

As I nibbled my lunch a few hours later, the intercom unit beeped, followed by Rebecca's voice, "Ms. Henley? Jared Henley is here to see you." She informed quickly.

"Send him in." I replied as I quickly smoothed my white blouse and stacked papers and binders into piles as neatly as I could.

"Look at you, so grown up." My father smiled as he entered the office and crossed the room, taking a seat at a chair across the desk from me. "How is it going in here?"

I plopped down into my chair. "Do you want me to be honest?" I asked with a giggle, "This job stinks! There is no efficiency here. I want to change how this system is done, revamp all of it. I calculated the numbers and if I am allowed to change it, we can save paper too."

My father smirked as he leaned back in his chair, resting the ankle of one leg onto the knee of the other. "Why Miss Fallon... what did you have in mind?"

"Alright, Let us begin with the daily inventory reports. I have checked through multiple weeks' worth for each department and very little ever changes. It makes more sense to me to have each department submit a once a week report." I said as my father knowingly nodded, still with a smirk. "If the whole purpose of this department is to keep accurate records of who wants what, then I need a copier machine. Requests could then be approved or denied and copies of that request can then be delivered to the departments in question and the original can be filed. We wouldn't even have a use for envelopes if the papers were then folded into thirds, stapled and addressed on the outside."

"So you want to rework the system." My father laughed, "The woman who created the system had a very confusing way of doing things. You were placed in this department to overhaul it. I wanted to give you a day to do the work and get a feel for it, to really understand how to up the efficiency level and cut need for supplies by half. It sounds to me as though you have figured it out before noon all on your own."

"Is that my job, to overhaul the system?" I asked as I leaned over my desk.

"Eventually you will be in charge of overhauling every department in the facility. The amount of waste in this place is astounding. I'll have a copier brought up from the storage warehouse on the bottom level. I helped put it there last year so I know it is in good shape. I'll have paper and ink delivered as well as a couple of filing cabinets." My father said as he stood from his chair. "Is tomorrow morning alright with you?"

Before I could answer, the sound of an alarm came over the loud speaker system followed by a panicked voice requesting all council members to report to the Intake and Processing Department as soon as possible. I jumped from my chair and followed my father as he ran from the door, through the waiting area and into the corridor.

"What the hell is going on?" Jacob yelled as he dove through the door of the armory and into the hallway ahead of us.

There wasn't time to wait for an answer, I simply shrugged in confusion at Jacob as I ran passed him and up the stairs behind my father to the first floor, the door unlocked and open. I could hear the sound of Jacob's boots clang up each of the metal steps behind me as I tried to catch up to my father. By the time we barreled through the door and into the first level corridor, teams of armed soldiers were running and screaming orders as they moved toward the loading bay. Robert stood just outside the door to his office, ushering soldiers into the loading bay and barking orders.

"Robert! What is going on?" My father yelled as we managed to reach him through the crowd.

"Civilians from the infected area," Robert yelled back, "They attacked Gate One and broke down the security gate."

I watched Robert turn and run out the door and through the loading bay out into the afternoon sun. Blood pumped into my ears, my heart racing with such speed I could feel the thumping against my chest. Soldiers ran on foot, some jumping into ready jeeps and scattered out into the distance as I watched in horror. For the first time since my arrival at Sanctuary I managed to see the extent of the forces available to protect the facility.

"I need clearance!" Roscoe yelled as he bolted into the hallway from the Intake and Processing Department. "Surface forces are requesting to fire. I need council approval because they are unarmed civilians looking for help. They have several virus infected members in their party. I'll explain everything later but they are violent and breaking through defenses!"

"No!" I screamed as I pushed to run through the door to the loading bay.

"Do it! You have clearance! Call it in!" Jacob yelled as he wrapped his arms around me, fighting to keep me in the facility.

"Clearance granted!" My father yelled behind me.

Roscoe yelled into his radio, "Fire at will!"

Outnumbered in votes, I sank to the floor as I heard gunfire erupt in the distance followed by screaming. Jacob still held me, unwilling to let me get any closer to the door. Blinking back the tears I fought against Jacob, punching him with everything I had in me.

"We are locking down the facility!" Bowman yelled as he came through the door from the loading bay. "All civilian and council members need to retreat to the third level or lower. We need to sanitize this floor and protect the population. You need to move, NOW!"

The alarm sounded again, this time the same soft female voice followed, "Security forces to standby. Civilian and council staff members please evacuate the first and second floor levels. All shift staff for first floor Decontamination and Containment are to report immediately." The alarm sounded a second time before the message repeated.

Jacob yanked on my arm, pulling me to my feet as the door to the loading bay slid closed with a loud clang just feet in front of me. I scrambled, tripping and trying to find footing as we ran to the stairwell, Bowman yelling for us to pick up the pace. The elevators at the other end opened, spilling people half dressed in white body suits and masks into the corridor. They fought to finish dressing in their emergency gear as they flooded our direction waving at us to move to the stairs and evacuate the level. We were a hive of activity.

We hit the stairs and ran as quickly as we could, passing the door for the second level. My father ran behind me, catching me twice when I had nearly tumbled. Jacob blew through the doorway to the third level, stopping only to hold it open as my father helped me move through it and into the massive common area. The same message and alarm sound played on, announcing the evacuation of the first and second floor levels. The security forces for our floor had divided into two groups to man both the elevators and the stairwell, armed with M16s.

"SAS Roscoe and I are returning to the second level to aid the security forces. We will let you know when it is clear. Elevators will still run but the first two levels will be locked until the all clear signal." Bowman yelled before turning on his heels and running back up the stairs.

I stood, stunned and confused as I watched people move about the large common area living space. *How did they get so close to the complex?* I thought to myself. Everything had happened so quickly I hadn't had the chance to ponder the situation. I walked over and plopped into a large burgundy recliner and placed my face into my hands. Trying to remember the information in the Emergency Procedures Manual that Roscoe had given to us when we arrived, I ran through multiple security measures in my mind. When I looked up, Jacob was gone.

Four hours went by before the first announcements began to come over the loud speakers by way of soft bells and a female voice announcing the second level had been sanitized and deemed accessible, Council members were to report to the Grand Hall for a briefing as soon as possible. The armed security guard by the elevator informed me that he had seen Jacob get into the elevator with other people headed to the fourth level Marketplace. He had obviously left to check on Bentley and Michael at the daycare center as apparently the people in his group had been discussing the children in the school.

When I finally reached the Grand Hall I sank into the same leather chair I had taken during the first council meeting. The room sat empty and sterile, smelling heavily of disinfectant. I had taken the time to swing by my office and retrieve my briefcase. The same overpowering smell of disinfectant nearly ran me out of my own office. Pulling out a small notebook and pen from my briefcase, I placed them in front of me on the table. The first person to enter the room had been Jacob as he nodded with a concerned look on his face and sat across from me at the table.

"The children alright?" I asked in a whisper.

"They are fine. They hadn't noticed anything going on. The entire fourth level didn't seem to care and continued on as usual. I went to each level and checked on everyone." Jacob explained sadly. "The hospital staff told me Sarah had left work at noon and didn't come back. I couldn't find her but then again, this place is huge and I didn't go off storming into bathrooms are dressing rooms."

Just then, my father, Roscoe, and Bowman walked into the room and closed the door behind them. My father smiled sadly, placing a hand on my shoulder and giving it a squeeze before taking his seat at the head of the table. Roscoe set to work organizing his papers while Bowman stood looking at the maps and marking new areas with a thick red marker.

"Before we begin, I need to inform you that Robert Dunn will not be joining us during this meeting. He has been held up in the Isolation Department. He has been decontaminated, however he is under observation. We do not believe him to be infected but we are taking extra steps to keep this situation under control." Bowman said as he finished marking with his marker and placed the cap back on. "The first level is under lockdown until all exposed or possibly exposed persons are cleared and the floor is sanitized again."

"How long until my dad is cleared?" Jacob asked with concern.

"We cannot be sure, my apologies Mr. Dunn. As soon as I get the information I will let you know." Bowman informed as he moved to the table and took a seat. "Roscoe, please begin."

Roscoe stood, his hands shaking slightly as he cleared his throat and placed his hands onto the edge of the table in order to steady them. "Today, our patrols allowed a small group of people to migrate into the perimeter, not realizing they had been infected. Normally small groups of survivors are allowed to move through the area freely and quietly so long as they stay a certain distance from the facility. If a group does manage to get too close, we send a nonthreatening team out to pose as a group of heavily armed survivors. Their mission is to guide them off the mountain, making sure they move away from the facility and have no knowledge of what we do here. That did not happen today. The team that normally handles that mission was never dispatched." Roscoe explained as he straightened and moved to the map on the wall.

"You see," Bowman began as he turned in his chair and pointed at the map, "This particular group arrived within the patrolled perimeter in the same place your group had. We watched them carefully. We did not make any moves on them as they had been accompanied by a Haven transport."

"What?" I yelled as I jumped in my chair, startled. "These people were Haven people?"

"No ma'am, they were only in possession of the Haven transport. We believed them to be Haven in the beginning... we allowed them to come far too close to the facility before we realized our mistake." Bowman said sadly. "The teams we dispatched to locate Haven have yet to report to us. We are completely in the dark as to their whereabouts. Seeing as these people possessed a transport belonging to Haven, we can only assume that the Haven teams are somewhere on the road and heading this way... but may have been met with trouble. One team at least as they only had one truck. Most of the group of infected people had been on foot."

My father rubbed his chin and he leaned back into his chair. "Tell me something, do you believe this group had been in possession of information that led them here?"

"The path they had taken had been one of the exact paths marked out on Haven maps. The transport was thoroughly searched before being disposed of. They were in possession of a map belonging to Haven. They fully intended to come here for help, probably thinking we would have the antiviral medications needed to treat the dying." Roscoe picked up his pen, "In truth, the

Darkness Falls

scientific community never released an antiviral. They were still working on creating one when the blackout struck. No one can fight this thing… not even us."

"How many people came looking for help?" I asked in almost a whisper.

Bowman and Roscoe exchanged a look before Bowman turned to me, "The group was made up of roughly fifty people. While cleaning the scene our teams could not identify any of the dead as being a member of Haven. We have teams combing the entire area within the perimeter to search for anyone who may have taken off on foot, or used the group as a diversion to distract us from a larger group. So far, everything seems clear. Haven is out there somewhere just outside the area. We will find them."

I placed my face into my hands as my eyes began to sting with tears. Somewhere just beyond the fifty mile radius, a Haven team had come into contact with an infected group of refugees. There was no way of telling if they had survived the encounter only that they had lost one of their trucks. Desperate people traveled here expecting help for themselves and loved ones, only to be gunned down at the gates. My heart felt as though it had been shattered into a million shards like broken glass.

"Where is Chase, is he going to be isolated as well?" My father asked slowly. "He lives on the surface."

"Chase is not under isolation at this time. He elected to go on patrol and assured us that if it turns out he has been infected, he will not be returning to the facility in order to protect the population. There is something else however…," Roscoe began as he walked back to the edge of the table, "…Sarah Simon."

"What about her?" Jacob choked as he slowly rose from his chair.

"The Intake and Processing Department has informed us that she left the facility under the guise of hunting wild herbs for the hospital about a half hour before the attack." Roscoe said as he lifted his gaze from the table to my father. "She slipped out the first gate in the confusion, and hid until the second gate had been opened to begin cleaning the bodies. They tried to catch her when she slipped through. One of our soldiers saw her run out through the third gate and into the woods."

"What the hell?" My father asked as shock washed across his face. "Why they hell would she do that? Do we have a tail on her?

Can someone bring her back?"

Bowman slowly shook his head, "Mr. Henley... we tried that. The team we sent to follow her had intended to bring her back and isolate her as she had walked straight through the bodies of the infected when she escaped. When they found her standing on a rock ledge at the ravine, they tried to convince her to return but she refused... instead she jumped to her death."

"What?" My father screamed as he jumped from his chair, "What? That doesn't make sense!"

"How can that be?" Jacob choked out through a flood of tears. "She jumped? Why would she do that?"

"I am sorry for your loss. Due to the fact she was possibly infected and the depth of the ravine... we are currently unable to retrieve her body. It will take some time to come up with a logical solution." Bowman informed slowly. "I am deeply sorry we were unable to stop her in time."

A hot flood of tears broke through, pouring down my cheeks uncontrolled. I wanted to curl into a ball and scream. I wanted to run from the room and go somewhere... anywhere other than here. The farming level, my office, anywhere that would allow me to completely lose my mind would be better than here. Jacob sobbed heavily as he fell into his chair, placing his elbows onto the table and both hands into his hair. Sarah was gone, Robert had been placed in isolation, and Chase may or may not have been infected and had taken off to patrol. Chase may not ever return to us if he had been infected. I burst into a violent fit of tears and crumpled into my chair, my father crying beside me.

CHAPTER TWENTY-ONE

I tried. I tried to pretend I could cope, but the fact is I am lost. I am lost without him. Most nights I cry myself to sleep. There is no happiness here for me. I died right along with him that day. I am not sure what to say. I love each of you, but being without him has made my life not worth living. I can't go on without him. I do not want to be in a world without him. Why fight to survive what is out there if there will be no joy on the other side? We could come through this and survive to watch the nation rebuild, but it wouldn't be the same without my husband. I stopped by the farming level this morning and signed the dogs in as farm dogs. They will be great helping hands to the nice people down there. I signed over my entire bank account, dividing the money equally between the children of Compound. It is the least I can do. I just cannot see a future for me in this world. Bless you all.
Sarah Simon

  My eyes burned with the pain of her words as I gently lowered Sarah's suicide note onto the table in Compound's common area. I had read the note three times to myself when it had been passed to me by Matt, who broke down into tears next to me at the table. I sat silently, my eyes felt as though they were on fire though not a single tear fell. I had gone dry with the tears that had fallen for the last two hours. Travis reached across the table, his face puffy from crying, and slid the note to Edward who refused to read it. I had never seen such a large man break down until the moment I watched Edward fall to his knees in sobs when we broke the news to everyone. My father had called an emergency meeting for all members of Compound, requesting they return to the family unit as soon as possible. Sarah's note had been placed on the table in the common area after we found it in her quarters.

Roscoe had helped deliver dinner service from the Glazier Grill, taking it upon himself to see to it that we would have one less thing to worry about. No one managed to eat. Instead we had picked at the food with little to no appetite. Angela and Emily had explained to the children that Sarah wouldn't be returning to the facility, but that they could always go down to the farming level and visit the dogs whenever they wanted. Jade spent most of the time sitting in the chair Sarah loved to use when petting her dogs, and cried to herself. Since the day the world went dark, we had lost several members of our community. Sarah's death had been by choice, something we had never faced before.

"I'm going to take Bentley to bed." Jacob whispered as he took Bentley's sleeping body from Jessica's arms before walking into my private quarters.

As I stood from the table, my body sagged with the exhaustion of the day. I slipped through the door of my private quarters without speaking a word to anyone. As I closed my door behind me I could hear Jacob crying again, the sound coming through my closed bedroom door. Tossing my briefcase and blazer onto the small sofa, I made the decision to let him be. No one had managed to gain a private moment to mourn and I didn't mind allowing him to break down somewhere he felt comfortable. I walked into my bathroom, closing the door behind me. Flopping down onto the toilet lid I let go. I cried for Sarah. I cried for my mother. I cried for everyone we had lost in the last several months.

When I had finally finished, I no longer heard the sounds of Jacob sobbing. I washed my face, stripped my clothing and wrapped myself in my bathrobe before heading for my bedroom. Jacob sat at the edge of my bed, his gaze fixed on my tan rug and both hands resting on his knees. I gently closed the door and crossed the room, taking a seat on the edge of the bed by his side. He slowly reached over and laced his fingers through mine.

"Fallon...," Jacob whispered, "...I would never leave Bentley. You know... if something happened to you? I would never do what she did and leave loved ones behind."

"I know." I whispered back and I squeezed his hand. "We may never understand the choice she made, but it was her choice

Darkness Falls

to make."

"That is where you are wrong." Jacob said as he turned, pulling one leg onto the bed as he faced me. "I understand completely why she did what she did. She loved her husband and was lost without him. She wasn't thinking clearly, only with her heart."

I read the pain that played out across his face as our eyes met. "Jacob."

"Tell me you love me." Jacob said louder than a whisper, as a single tear ran down his face. "Tell me you see me as more than just a brother. Promise me that if something ever happens to me, you will continue on and raise our son. Tell me." He choked as he let go of my hand, placing his hands on either side of my head. "Tell me you want to spend the rest of your life with me."

I sat silent for several moments, unsure as to what to say to him. I loved him. I wasn't ready to admit it, but I love him. "I... I need time." I whispered as tears ran down my face.

"Time?" Jacob exploded as he bolted off the bed. "Time? Why would you need time?"

"Keep it down or you will wake the baby." I whispered loudly as I climbed off the bed to stand in front of him. "Yes, I need time. I have to sort myself out. Is that too much to ask?"

Jacob ran both hands through his hair as he paced back and forth between the wall and the bed. Without warning he stopped, his back to me, and dropped his hands to his sides. "Fallon, I love you. I will always love you. Do I have to beg for you to love me?" He spun, nearly running to me and wrapped his arm around my waist, lifting me from the floor and pressing me against him. His free hand instantly tangled into the hair at the base of my head the moment his lips found mine.

I had meant to fight him. I had meant to push him away from me and yell at him for his actions. Instead, I wrapped both my arms around his neck and pulled him closer to me. Every confusing and painful emotion exploded into that kiss and I gave into it. One moment without thinking. I didn't want to think anymore and I didn't want to hurt. I didn't want to remember the blackout, the virus or the radiation that was leaking from power plants miles from us. I just wanted to be in this one moment.

Jacob pulled away from me, looking into my eyes with a smirk on his face. "So you do love me... you just won't say it." He said as a small laugh escaped his lips. "Is that what you need time for?"

"I... I want to be with you. I do. I just need to understand how I feel." I stammered as I pushed myself away from him. "I should be in high school and... and be a teenager, not just skip to being an adult doing adult things."

"You'll have to let that go, Fallon. That world is the old world." Jacob whispered as he touched his lips with the tip of his fingers.

"I have to adjust." I whispered as I took a step back. "That is all."

"Tell me you love me." Jacob insisted as he stepped closer to me. "Tell me you love me and just need some time for yourself. I can accept that... just as long as I know."

I swallowed hard and took a step back. "I don't see you as a brother."

"I am not your brother." Jacob smiled and took another step toward me. "How do you see me Fallon?" I stepped back, my legs hitting the edge of the bed behind me. Stepping closer, Jacob pinned me with his body against the edge of the bed, his lips gently grazing my own. "Tell me you love me," He whispered before lightly kissing me.

"I love you." I spoke in barely a whisper against his lips before closing my eyes, fighting to hold back the tears.

Jacob slowly moved both of his hands into my hair, his lips gently kissing my own. Then he smiled and stepped back, dropping his arms to his side. "Thank you. Have a good night Miss Henley."

I watched in silent shock as he slipped out of my bedroom and closed the door behind him. I closed my eyes, inhaling sharply as I heard the front door open and close gently. Alone in my room, I fought to control the swimming of my head. I had admitted my love for Jacob, something I thought I would never do.

After three days of trying, the surface forces had come to the conclusion that Sarah's remains could not be retrieved from the ravine without putting other lives in jeopardy. It had been too steep and far deeper than the project safety team felt comfortable allowing. The Compound Council had given permission to have Sarah's death announced over the PA system as was customary within Sanctuary society, and had held a public service in her honor in the Marketplace. Many shopkeepers closed their doors for the day in order to attend. Though they did not get the chance to get to know her on a personal level, Sarah had been the first person to die at Sanctuary. Robert hadn't been allowed to leave Isolation in order to attend, though he did manage to watch the entire recorder service later via a small camcorder on loan from a nurse in one of the clinics.

Edward had been granted the ability to take over the Simon private quarters as his own, moving out of the quarters he had been sharing with Matt. We cleaned most of her and Brian's belongings out of the unit and sorted them into two piles, though each of us had been allowed to keep a few things in memory. One pile had been boxed up and placed within our storage facility, the other we delivered to the crematorium. With no physical remains to be cremated and placed within the Sanctuary columbarium, we had elected to cremate items belonging to Sarah and Brian, having both of their names placed on the wall marker. As each niche had sat empty, my father had the chance to choose a spot rather than having it assigned. Together, we chose one nearest to the elevator about halfway up the wall, low enough for the children to reach it to place flowers if they wished. The children we agreed, would never be told her remains had never been recovered.

No word had arrived from the scout teams sent to find Haven, and the teams sent to patrol had yet to report as well. Chase had not returned, as was to be expected as the incubation period for the virus hadn't passed. The two members of the surface team who had been exposed to the virus without protection had been placed within quarantine, including the guard who had fled from his post when the infected group had broken down his gate. The first level of the facility still sat in lockdown for the week, and only allowed for items or certain people to move through the second level quarantine under strict regulations.

My father had done as promised and delivered the copier machine and needed supplies to my office. After I had explained to my assistant Rebecca the plan I had to overhaul the entire request system, she had nearly broken my ribs with hugging me. She had been waiting for someone to listen to her complaints and until I had come along, no one had bothered to overhaul it. Together we created a memo and had a copy delivered to every shop and department within the facility explaining how the new system would be run. The next day, not a single complaint had come in.

Instead, we sifted through notes approving my plan and explaining how excited people were that we could save resources and cut the stressful way of handling requests. The new system also allowed for requests to be processed much more quickly, allowing for very little wait time.

Jade spent most of her time either in class or down on the farming level. She wanted to spend as much time as possible with the hound dogs. After begging our father to allow her to break into our Compound seed vaults, she had taken to planting a large variety of tomato plants in the Compound planting plot, many of which Sanctuary hadn't been growing. Maintaining the garden plot after school every day had given her the freedom she needed to pet the dogs and mourn without having someone around to bug her. Originally my father had worried that Jade may have been depressed, but after speaking with her about it she informed us that she hadn't felt that way at all. She just wanted to grow and sell tomatoes to help cover the extremely high cost of the fresh flowers she would be delivering to the niche marker as often as she could. The fresher the flowers she explained, would prove to everyone how much Sarah had been loved. Being only eight years old, we no longer worried about her state of mind after that.

Even with very little training in a facility setting, the experience Travis had in prenatal care had temporarily promoted him into Sarah's role as the prenatal doctor of the Sanctuary hospital division. It had been explained that he would stay on in his current title until a more skilled doctor arrived from Haven, though no one knew how long that would take. When he had arrived to dinner in a white lab coat and explained his promotion, Dave had nearly laughed himself out of his chair while comparing Travis to a character from a classic television show from way back in the nineteen eighties. None of us had known what he was talking about though my father and Jessica had laughed.

In the week since Sarah's suicide, life had continued on as usual with the exception of a few bouts of tears. Everyone returned to work and school after being given a day or two to handle the shock and the arrangements. On a trip to the Marketplace to buy a second outfit in order to rotate my work clothing, I had run into Emily and we had made a day of it. It had been the first time in over a month that we had managed to spend some quality time together without the children in tow. We even managed to catch a movie together, watching an old romantic comedy that had apparently been a huge hit in the nineteen nineties.

"So how is everything going in your department with the new overhaul?" Emily asked the next morning while I stood in the bathroom preparing myself for work. "Your dad said you are doing amazing up there."

I set down the hair brush and picked up the rhinestone hair pin that Jacob had bought me the night before my first day on the job. "I am really enjoying it. We have saved so much paper already. We completely did away with half the forms we had originally." I replied as I pulled the front and sides of my hair back leaving only one curl on either side of my face, pinning the locks at the back of my head. I would leave my hair down today rather than my usual bun or up-do. "You know… it is kind of nice to be doing something that in the long run will help everyone out around here."

Emily smiled before returning to the mirror beside me and applying her mascara. While we had been in the Marketplace I had taken her cosmetics shopping. "I love teaching the children. I managed to find a collection of children's books in that little bookstore above the day spa. Jade and I came up with a fun way to use them to teach the younger children how to read." She said as she closed her tube of mascara and placed it back into her makeup bag. "Oh! I almost forgot… Do you want me to take Bentley to the daycare with me in the mornings? I work right next door and have to be there early every day. I actually got my hands on a double stroller so it won't be any trouble to take Benny with me when I drop off little Mike in the mornings. I could even bring him back in the evenings."

"That would help me out more than you know." I laughed as I applied my own mascara. "Jacob has been heading up to the Isolation Department to see about his dad nearly every morning before work. I have been late for work twice now and had to skip breakfast just to make it on time. Thank you for the offer."

"No worries at all." Emily grinned as she zipped her makeup bag closed and stepped from the bathroom to place it in her purse on the sofa. "By the way…," She called behind her, "…when Travis took me on that picnic a few days back to the farm level, he told me a little secret that he made me swear never to tell you."

"Which obviously means you are going to tell me the moment

you catch me alone?" I winked with a grin as I turned off the bathroom light and crossed the room to grab my green blazer off the sofa. The new tan suit I had bought wouldn't be done at the tailor's for a few more days.

"Apparently Jacob is planning something big for your birthday." Emily giggled before picking up her coffee cup from the small end table. "I can't be sure exactly, but it sounds like he has a private party planned because he asked Travis and I to babysit."

Instantly my mind flooded with memories of the cavern where we had spent Jacob's last birthday, and my embarrassing actions that morning. I turned away from Emily so that she couldn't see the look of shock washing across my face. "Really?" I choked out through quaking lips. "What sort of plans?"

"No idea... but I did manage to overhear the two of them chatting the other day while Travis was packing up his private quarters. I was packing up his bathroom and I guess they couldn't tell I could hear them." Emily said after she sipped the last of her coffee and set the cup onto the table. "Travis is moving in with me. I need the extra help with the children and he lives alone. We figured it for the best. Anyway, from what I heard... I bet you would be shocked to know that your dad has given his blessings to Jacob?"

"What?" I asked as I spun to see the growing smile on Emily's face. She nodded frantically like an excited child. "Emily, don't toy with me."

Emily closed her eyes and held up both hands, "Serious as a heart attack I am. Jacob had a talk with your dad at the cave and your dad gave his blessing for Jacob to ask for your hand. That is all I know. I don't know if that is what he has planned for your birthday or not, but whatever the plan is it is big. Travis and I are babysitting all night for you."

I swallowed hard, "Tell no one Emily. Not a soul."

"If he does ask you, what will you say?" Emily giggled before stepping through my open bedroom door and pulling Bentley from his crib. "I mean... will you deck him in the face or say yes?" She called playfully from my room as Bentley squealed in delight.

"I don't know." I said sharply as I quickly grabbed my briefcase and nearly ran for my front door. "Thanks for taking Bentley... I have to go." I said as I ran out the door bumping into Travis as he waiting with Michael in the double stroller.

"Sorry. Gotta go." I said quickly before running through the Compound common area and out the door. I didn't wait to see if Travis acknowledged my apology or to see Emily exit my private quarters. I simply bolted for the elevators in an attempt to make it to my office as quickly as possible.

When I opened the door to my department, Rebecca was waiting for me with a smile and a small pot of coffee. The waiting area which normally sat filled with empty chairs and ugly blue carpet now sat covered in plastic. Rebecca had taken my advice and decided to renovate the waiting area in order to make the space more inviting. I smiled to myself as I quickly made my way to my office and opened the door.

"You have a meeting with your father at nine o'clock to go over the requests that have been submitted to the council for review. One of the requests is for a marriage license. That wonderfully cute guard on the surface with the tattoo of the dragon on his arm... you remember him right? He is requesting permission to marry that adorable young lady Georgia who runs the library." Rebecca gushed as she placed the coffee tray onto the edge of my desk. "They have been dating forever; I am very excited to see them finally taking the jump."

"Aren't they my age?" I asked in horror as I set my window scene to a cityscape with ocean view. For several seconds I watched random people walk the streets from a high-rise view point, absentmindedly wondering if those same people were still alive after the collapse.

"Oh yes!" Rebecca giggled. "He has a great paying job and she loves the library but it doesn't pay much. They will have a beautiful life together. Don't you think?"

"I guess so." I answered as I set down the wall remote and stepped behind my desk. The pile of requests wouldn't take nearly as long as it had before the overhaul.

"Well, I would love to stay and help you out but I have a team coming to finish the job on the waiting area. We still agree on the paint color right? The deep cherry with the pop pillows and sofa?" Rebecca asked as she crossed the room and opened the door to my office.

"Yes ma'am." I called out playfully with a smile.

I watched as she nodded and closed the door behind her before I pulled the first page from the stack on the edge of my desk. The new system allowed for far less stress and a more enjoyable work day for both Rebecca and me. Instead of working ourselves into the ground trying to remember how many of each form we needed, we had managed to spend some time together during working lunches that had been nothing more than enjoying a meal together in my office and laughing. Together we processed twice as many requests daily, pushing to have general orders fulfilled before the end of the day. Our mail carrier had promptly agreed to do a twice a day pick up of outgoing mail, allowing in many cases for emergency requests to be fulfilled before noon on the same day the request had been submitted.

The ten year old son of a clinic nurse had taken great care in submitting his request as his wording and penmanship had impressed me. He wished to be granted a permit to set up a booth he could run after school in the Marketplace Square. His request listed several items he had hoped to sell, including handmade candles his mother makes in her spare time, some Native American styled dream catchers he makes with things he finds on the surface, and some sketches he makes in pencil he had called art. I checked the box indicating his permit had been granted and wrote a short note to congratulate him on his new business. The copier allowed me to make a copy of his request and of his permit and file the originals before stapling his new permit to his request and dropping it in the outgoing mail stack. He would have his approval before noon under the new system I had created.

By the time I had finished the pile of request forms and alerted Rebecca to prepare them for mailing, she had finished sorting a second pile for me to handle after my meeting with my father. I only had a few minutes to spare before he would likely arrive. I spun my leather chair around to face the tall shelving unit behind my desk, my eyes scanning the many binders and books that detailed the different departments within the facility. Eventually I would overhaul each and every one of them with the help of my trusted assistant.

"Miss Henley, your nine o'clock has arrived early. Would you like me to send them in?" Rebecca called out over the intercom on my desk.

I turned back to my desk and pushed the button, partially confused as I had only expected my father to arrive. "Yes Rebecca, thank you."

When my office door opened, Rebecca escorted both my father and Bowman into the room. I quickly stood, running my hands down my hips to smooth my skirt. "Officer Bowman, what a nice surprise! Please, take a seat." I said while motioning to the two leather chairs in front of my desk. I continued to stand until both had settled into the chairs. "I had expected my father as my nine o'clock appointment. I hadn't expected you, my apologies. Please, let me have Rebecca fetch you some refreshments?"

"No thank you, Miss Henley." Bowman interrupted with a motion of his hand. "We are fine. I won't be long."

I nodded to Rebecca as I sat in my chair before watching her leave the room and close the door behind her. "So gentlemen, how may I be of service today?"

Bowman smiled brightly, "I wanted to let you know that contact has been made with the scout team at the furthest edge of the patrol zone. They have spotted a single Haven transport being led by a Sanctuary escort headed in this direction. It has been confirmed as Haven, and they will be monitored and protected clear to the gates. Obviously we will be taking extra precautions due to recent events, and they will be quarantined and evaluated before allowed access to the facility. I wanted to be the one to inform you personally."

"That is wonderful news!" I said excitedly as I clapped my hands together. "Officer Bowman, you are amazing. Let no one tell you otherwise. What you do here is top notch. If I could award you some sort of title or award to reflect it, I would."

Bowman's face quickly flushed, "Thank you Miss Henley. It means a lot to me." He said before standing. "I need to get back to work. Happy birthday by the way, Miss Henley."

"Thank you, Officer Bowman. Have a great day." I replied before watching him cross the room and leave my office. I turned to my father then, waiting to see his reaction.

"You have the authority to bestow metals and awards on the forces, you know." My father laughed. "You have more pull around here than anyone else. You served on the Compound Council which granted you access to a spot on the Sanctuary Council. Combine that with being the next in line for leadership of Compound... you are a Goddess here."

"Give me a break." I replied sharply as I leaned back in my chair. "Why did you give your blessing to Jacob for us to get married?"

"Sheesh cut right to the heart of the matter why don't ya?" My father said shocked as he leaned back in his chair. "I have my reasons."

"Explain them." I snapped.

I watched my father's gaze as it left mine, his eyes now fixed on the window scene. "I grew up in Haven. Your mother grew up in Haven. I know how they work. I will forever be a member of them because that was where I was born and raised. I served in their forces, I married your mother. But you... you are Compound. Let no one ever take that from you. While we are here we are Sanctuary, and that is true. But on the inside... you will always be Compound. I want you to hold onto that and never let it go."

"You never would have approved a young marriage in Compound." I growled, more to myself than to my father though I knew he heard me.

"Fallon," My father whispered as he leaned over my desk toward me. "This facility is a Haven facility. We have rights to this place only because of your mother. She went rounds with your grandmother just to get us one little family unit to call our own. You don't know how the Haven society works. I am trying to save you all."

"You want Jacob and me to get married and fit into their society?" I asked sarcastically as I leaned over my desk closer to my father being sure he caught the intensity I shot at him with my gaze.

"Your mother is gone, Fallon." My father replied sadly. "I am all that is left of the original leadership. If something happens to me they will absorb Compound. Make no mistake about it. Robert and Jessica are from Haven, if they try to take our places and run Compound the Haven Council will consider Compound an extension of their society and gain control slowly over time."

I leaned back in my chair. "So you want me to marry Jacob and become the new leadership? Dad, nothing will happen to you. You can't think like that."

"Do you want to lose Bentley?" My father asked in a serious tone. "You have no idea what these people are capable of, but I do. If something happens to me they will take that baby away from you because you will be unmarried and unworthy. They will raise him in their world and absorb all of you. That is, if they don't try to force you into an unwanted marriage with one of their own in order to gain control of Compound. Mark my words, with me out of the picture they will gain control of Compound by forced marriage… and every one of you kids will have no choice but to become Haven."

"What are you saying?" I asked in shock.

"If you don't marry Jacob now, even if you treat it as only being on paper…," My father whispered, "…and become the new council of Compound… they will take it in whatever way they see fit. I know you love him Fallon, I am not stupid. I can promote Robert to be your military advisor. He will still hold a seat at your side. We can help you do this. I know you don't want to see those little kids serve in Haven armies. I know you don't want your son to either. If you want to keep them safe… you have to marry Jacob."

"Or they will force me into a marriage with one of them and take it all away." I said flatly more as a statement then as a question.

My father rubbed his eyes in defeat, "All I am asking is for you to put the ring on and pretend for now if that makes you comfortable. While we are here, I want you two to be considered a family. File a record of marriage. Hold a ceremony and make people believe it. Move in together. They can't marry you off if you are already married. They can't gain control of the Compound Council if a married couple is running it. We all knew you two would get married eventually and yes, I gave my blessing for it. I know it is a lot to ask, but you know I wouldn't do this if it wasn't important. You are a grown woman now in their eyes. You have to let go of what you had and start protecting what is left."

"Are you stepping down from leadership, Dad?" I asked as I reached across my desk and grabbed one of his hands.

"I have to. If I don't, they will find a way to take Compound. I didn't want to come here to Sanctuary but we didn't have a choice in the matter. It was come here or die out there. I knew you were strong enough to fight them. You may not agree with the choices I have made, but I made them with every member of our community in mind." My father said as I single tear escaped his eyes.

"What the hell did you get us into here, Dad?" I whispered as I watched my father close his eyes.

My father squeezed my hands tightly, "I gave Jacob my

blessing with the intent that one day in the future you two would work it out. Now everything is different. I didn't think they would arrive. They are coming… I am sorry for this entire situation sweetheart, but they are coming. Once they get here everything will change. You have to take control of Compound with Jacob and hang onto it with everything you have. The first chance you get and the surface is safe, I want you to run. Pack everyone up and run from here as fast as possible. If for whatever reason I am lost or can't go… I want you to leave me here and run with the children. Take them to the cave we used before. Until then, put on one hell of a show. Watch them carefully and be mindful of how they run society. Don't stay here too long."

"I'll do it. I'll marry Jacob. I'll play the part and make it look good, you know I will. I am not ready for this at all but if it means I can save the children… I'll do it." I cried softly. "How long do we have?"

My father smiled sadly, "Until the end of today."

CHAPTER TWENTY-TWO

For the first time since I had landed my own office, I took full advantage of the small bar unit on the side of the room. When I had awakened this morning I had wished myself a happy birthday and made a wish as I had done every year. My wish had not been for this. My wish had been for peace. Peace in the hearts of those I loved most as they struggled to cope with the many deaths we had faced since the blackout. I had wished for Robert to be released from the Isolation Department and return to us. I had wished to be home again.

I poured myself a small glass of an unknown brown liquid that smelled as horrible as a bag of rotten potatoes that had been sprayed with disinfectant, and crossed the room to sit at my desk. My father had left my office and informed my assistant that I had wanted to be alone. He had spoken to Jacob the night before and had planned to return to him to finalize the details. We would have to make it look real to those within Compound as well as the facility. If the members of Compound questioned the nature of our rushed marriage, Haven could be tipped off and call our bluff.

The liquid tasted horrible, burning my lips and tongue and stinging my throat like an acid. I coughed and choked against the burn as it moved lower in my body leaving only a trail of pain followed by watering eyes and nausea. Jacob would be joining me in my office for lunch per request of my father, and I would need the liquid courage. An announcement would be made over the Sanctuary PA system, inviting everyone to attend our wedding in order for as many people as possible to witness the event. The more people believed we truly wanted this, the more believable the marriage would be.

I thought back to the day of the blackout and of Jacob, Emily, and me sitting in our math class watching the film on benefits of math in the real world. The moment we had realized everything had changed and we would have to make it home, I had been scared. When we had to leave Compound and travel to Sanctuary, I had been scared. Nothing had prepared me for the fear I felt now. For the first time since arriving at Sanctuary, I truly feared the arrival of Haven. I hadn't had a reason to fear them before now. In fact, I had never put much thought into how things would change once they arrived. Now I feared them. I feared being trapped within their world, unable to leave and go back to what felt right to me. I feared growing up and accepting the responsibility of marriage. *Would they really try to force me to marry some kid?* I asked myself as I turned my chair to face the shelves. *Would they really take Bentley from me for being unmarried?*

The conversation with my father had revealed a side of Haven I hadn't before put much thought into. I didn't want to become a member of Haven. I didn't even want to be a member of Sanctuary yet here I was, trapped underground and made to play it out in order to gain safety. This wasn't the Sanctuary my mother had painstakingly described to us our entire childhood. She had made it sound like a wondrous place we could rely on if we had ever been faced with a complete societal collapse. We hadn't been warned about the politics, probably because she never saw the need to scare us.

The cave would save us if I could only manage to get us there. We would have to wait for the outside world to calm down and for the virus to pass before we could attempt such a feat. That wasn't bound to happen anytime soon. The thought made shivers run down my spine. In order to keep a tight hold onto Compound, I would have to wait for the right moment no matter how long it took. I closed my eyes and braved a second sip from the glass, praying I wouldn't instantly vomit as it burned my throat. Today I turned seventeen years old. Today I would marry Jacob Dunn in order to hold onto Compound.

"Miss Henley, Jacob Dunn is here to see you. He is rather early I know, but he is insistent." Rebecca called over the intercom.

Before I had time to reply, Jacob stepped through the door and into my office closing it behind him. He hadn't been wearing his usual uniform required for his job in the armory. I watched him cross the room in a black pair of jeans and blue flannel shirt like the ones Brian and Dave used to wear back home in Compound. His dark eyes fell onto the glass I held in my hand as a wicked grin played out across his thick lips. He pointed quickly to the bar, almost in such a way as to ask if he could have some as well. I nodded with a smile before watching him pour himself a glass. By the end of the day, he would be my husband; he might as well have a drink.

"This wasn't how this was to happen. Not like this." Jacob said sadly as he crossed the room and sat in one of the leather chairs across from me. "My big plan today was to take you to the surface to show you something special, not marry you in a rushed ceremony. I was going to wait a year or so before I tried to ask you. When your dad came to see me last night he had explained that in the event Haven arrives, what would happen. Bowman told me this morning about the contact and from that point... I knew your dad would come to see me again. I am finding out the same as you. I always thought that when I gained the courage to ask you, it wouldn't be like this at all."

"So we truly don't have a choice in growing up." I stated as I braved another sip, pretending it didn't burn as badly as it felt. "This isn't what I want, but it is what I will do for Compound."

Jacob swigged the small amount of liquid from his glass and set it on the table. "You don't want to marry me?" he asked as he reached into his pocket and pulled out a small box.

"I am too young to marry you." I said flatly.

"I know you love me... and I love you. This isn't ideal and we both know it." He said as he rounded the edge of my desk and fell to his knees in front of me. "This is for now. This is for Compound. Someday it will be for us. When we marry for real, I want you to be the one who makes that choice. I want you to want to be my wife. This is why today I will not be asking you to be my wife. I know the choice isn't your own and I want you to say yes to me one day and mean it completely. Instead, I am simply asking you to help me save Compound. Yes, there are probably other ways to save it... but this is the best way to help insure we all make it out of here as a family."

"Jacob, are you marrying me to save Compound or are you marrying me for love?" I whispered as he placed both hands onto my knees.

Jacob dropped his head into my lap as tears fell from his eyes. "You don't have to marry me for both Fallon; I know you are only doing this because we have to." He lifted his gaze, searching my face. "I am marrying you for both… but you need your time and I understand that. Just please make this relationship believable even if there are times you hate me." He begged as he opened the small box in his hand and held it up for me to see. "Fallon Henley, will you do me the honor of helping me save our families against your will?"

"Just give me the ring already and shut up." I laughed half-heartedly as I took my mother's engagement ring from the box and placed it on my finger. The thin gold band fit almost perfectly as it wrapped my finger. It felt cold and hard against my skin as I turned my hand over and over in front of me. I would do it for Compound. "Jacob, I will marry you. As far as being your wife… you know how I feel. This is why I will not agree to marry you for both Compound and for love. I will not commit to that. We will make this seem so real no one will question our choice. But you better believe that behind closed doors… you are not sharing my bed."

Jacob tossed his head back as he exploded in laughter, "I will take the spare bedroom I promise."

After Jacob and I quickly pushed through the last of the request forms, I informed Rebecca I would be leaving for the day with Jacob and would not be returning. As we stood there speaking to her, our wedding announcement played over the loud speakers. Her eyes grew wide as she listened to the announcement, searching our faces with a look of shock. When it was over she nearly broke my ribs in one of her bear hugs, explaining how excited she was for us and that she would be there to watch the event. My heart thumped in my chest as it slowly hit me that the public event would be the most public lie in history.

Together, Jacob and I rode the elevator to the Marketplace to see about a dress. After all, I had to show myself as the happiest bride in all of Sanctuary. When we had stepped out of the elevator it had become instantly apparent that the announcement had been facility wide, as people had clapped and cheered as we quickly walked down the square toward the only bridal shop in Sanctuary. Jacob had wrapped his arm around my waist and as I watched his happiness, I briefly wondered if he had been playing the part like a professional actor or if he had meant it.

The owner of the bridal shop explained that most dresses were custom made for the bride, but with so little time to prepare I would need to choose from the few racks she kept in the back. As soon as the announcement had been made she had checked her log book to see if I had been to any appointments with her. The moment she realized I had not previously registered with her, she knew we would be on our way. When we had arrived there were several items on the counters she felt we might be interested in seeing. The shopkeeper was frantic, complaining about our rushed wedding and how I hadn't given her the time she usually uses to plan weddings. At one point, she pulled me aside and asked if the wedding had been rushed due to unplanned pregnancy. I promptly informed her I wasn't pregnant, but all it had done was confuse her even more.

I browsed the racks of dresses while Jacob spoke softly with the nervous shopkeeper, trying to put her mind at rest by explaining we had just been working far too hard to set an appointment. Every gown seemed to be white or off-white, making me cringe in disgust at the sight of them. If my sham wedding was going to happen, I needed to make it bold enough to be remembered. I rolled my eyes as I listened to Jacob whisper behind me, making our wedding seem more and more believable to the now less panicked shopkeeper. I had nearly given up when I turned around and saw it. Displayed on the wall by the dressing rooms far in the back of the shop, hung the gown I knew I would wear.

Dark silver layers of satin hung from the drop style waist like waves in a calm ocean cove. Black bridal tulle peaked out from between the flowing layers of satin adding multiple facets of dimension and beauty. My gaze slowly lifted, running across the small flowers and swirls embroidered in black across the bodice that flowed from the thin rhinestone encrusted straps and down the left side to end at the hip. Oddly enough, it looked to me to be a beautiful blend of a wedding dress and a prom dress all in one. It was bold enough to not go unnoticed, but it also wasn't a typical white wedding dress. My wedding wouldn't be a typical one and my dress would reflect that even if no one else caught it. It would be my own inside joke. My own rebellion brought to the surface just enough to show I would be an individual no matter what Sanctuary or Haven had in store for me.

I glanced behind me to make sure Jacob and the female shopkeeper were both occupied before strolling over to the gown and pulled it off the wall as carefully as possible, darting into the dressing room. As I slipped the gown on, I suddenly felt as though I was a princess, feeling the fabric brush against my body. I didn't bother to look at the price tag. The cost would be worth the effect it would have on everyone within Sanctuary. I stood, staring at my reflection in the mirror as a slow smile moved across my face. The dress fit nearly perfectly on my frame and as long as I wore heels, the gown would barely brush the floor. I stepped from the dressing room and was promptly met by two shocked faces as the shopkeeper and Jacob gazed at me wide-eyed.

"You look... amazing in that dress." Jacob whispered as he slowly crossed the room. "I couldn't have chosen a better dress myself. It is stunning and one hundred percent... you."

I giggled as I spun in order to give him the full effect. "You really think so?" I played, knowing the shopkeeper would need to see an excited bride.

"Whatever the woman wants...," Jacob poke playfully at the shopkeeper, "...she gets. What can I say?"

"Are you sure about this dress ma'am? It is rather dashing... but I had made that dress as an example. It comes with a complete wedding package that is the most dazzling I have ever created, but also the most expensive." The shopkeeper informed as she stared at me in shock. "In all honestly ma'am, the price is astounding and I don't even think I could afford it!"

"I want it all." Jacob smiled as he wrapped his arms around my waist. "She deserves only the best."

The dress came with silver and rhinestone encrusted hair clip, and black vale made of bridal tulle that stretched from the back of my head clear to the floor. A black and silver corset with black thigh-high stockings and garter belt had to be shown to me alone as the shopkeeper refused to allow Jacob to view what she called the most intimate part of the complete package. The shoes had been taller than I had expected, and matched the dress perfectly in silver with the same black swirls and flowers. I had refused the black elbow length gloves as I had thought they would take away from the elegance of the gown, which the shopkeeper had agreed to once she saw how they had looked on me. Even the jewelry had matched with black jewels and rhinestones that hugged the neck and dripped down the collar bone, completing the entire look from head to toe.

Once we had the minor alterations completed with the gown, and the entire head to toe look boxed up, the shopkeeper assured me they would be delivered for me to the bridal suite in the chapel on the second floor of the Marketplace. Together, Jacob and I viewed the entire collection in one of the large fold out albums the shopkeeper placed in front of us. We listened to her rambled on as she darted from one end of the shop to the other, gathering pieces we had agreed on. Before we knew it, black champagne glasses with silver and rhinestone encrusted bows had been placed into a box alongside a deep silver colored guestbook with black swirls down the binding. I flipped the pages in the book and called out the items to the shopkeeper as Jacob and I agreed on them. The silver and black bouquet with the long black bow tails that hung nearly to the floor made of the same matching tulle. The silver and black cake serving set. Not every piece of the premade set would be used as we didn't see a need for them.

"Oh my God! I don't have a bridesmaid!" I yelled when we flipped to a section of the album that displayed beautiful models in black gowns holding silver bouquets of flowers.

"Oh dear," the shopkeeper said as she stopped, holding a collection of cake tops in her arms. "This is why I have couples make appointments. If you have someone in mind I do have one dress from that collection made. I never made any more. It was only a display."

"Travis and Emily." Jacob shot as his eyes met mine. "I'll be right back!"

I nodded frantically before watching him dart out of the shop and into the Marketplace. The thought hadn't hit me until that moment that our family and friends had learned about the wedding over the loud speaker the same as everyone else at Sanctuary. A slow wave of guilt welled up inside me as I thought about how hurt Emily must have been to feel completely left out and in the dark about the coming wedding. In truth, no one had been told of the pending ceremony as it had been a last minute event. I flipped to another page in the album while I waited. Life was about to get even more interesting around here.

"Fallon! You are such a turd!" Emily laughed as she barreled through the door into the bridal shop with Travis and Jacob close behind her. "Talk about keeping things top secret, I only just found out when the announcement came through! No wonder you acted so weird this morning when we were talking, you had already said yes!"

I couldn't tell her the entire wedding was a rushed sham and that we were only going through with it in order to protect the sanctity of Compound. I couldn't tell her that though I loved Jacob, I wasn't nearly ready to be his bride. Swallowing hard, I looked to Jacob for an answer. His eyes held a look of knowing as he nodded with a smile. We both knew that the announcement had come to our family and friends as a shock, though not entirely unexpected… in due time.

"We had been planning for a while now but wanted to keep things quiet until the right moment. We are sorry for not saying anything and we hope you can understand. With Sarah's death and everything, we couldn't tell anyone. With all the sadness we have all been through lately, we thought it best to bring some excitement and joy back in." Jacob smiled as he winked in my direction.

"Hell Jacob, fine way to do it!" Emily laughed. "Alright, show me this ring and after that, we have serious work to do!"

I knew the shopkeeper had overheard the conversation and I desperately hoped that Jacob's explanation had been enough to lay any doubt she had left to rest. She would likely gossip with the other shopkeepers later, and I wanted her to relay the tale of a couple madly in love and desperate to get married after a painful loss. We had to appear as though this decision had been a long one coming, and though the timing hadn't been perfect we had to appear as though we had planned it that way. Using Sarah's death as a reason to wait to inform family had been brilliant. No one would ever question a choice to allow for grieving before the announcement of a wedding.

I quickly flipped the page of the book back to the bridesmaid dress and showed it to Emily before the shopkeeper whisked her away to try on the only one she had ever made. Travis and Jacob busied themselves with black tuxedos with silver vests made of satin. With very little time left to cover even the smallest detail, we had to work as quickly as possible. I promptly chose a cake topper from the collection the shopkeeper had placed onto the counter, and moved it to the swiftly growing pile of junk we had chosen for the wedding.

For over an hour I watched Emily, Travis, and Jacob try on and alter the outfits they would wear during the wedding. Twice Angela had poked her head into the bridal shop to view the theme before scurrying off to spend the afternoon building the wedding cake. Eventually the shopkeeper agreed to lend her the album to view as she made the cake, in order to keep us from being disturbed. Jessica had even come by to share in our excitement and assure us that Robert hadn't been upset that we had chosen to get married while he was stuck in isolation. He would watch the video as he had done with Sarah's service.

"Alright everyone, you are done here. There is a small pre-wedding reception for the bride and her bridesmaid at the day spa where you will be pampered. I am closing the shop for the day to go handle the rest of the details. Who do I address the bill to?" The shopkeeper asked excitedly.

"The reception is being paid for by my husband and me, every detail of it. The bill needs to go to Robert and Jessica Dunn in the Compound unit." Jessica gushed as she wrapped an arm around me. Then with a wicked grin she continued, "Send the rest of the bill to Jared Henley, also in the Compound unit. The happy couple won't be spending a single note of their own money."

"Alright." The shopkeeper smiled, "Also I am not sure if you are aware, but Sanctuary has a honeymoon location. It isn't much but it is a private unit specifically set aside for the happy couples to escape for a couple of days to a week away. Food is delivered and everything, you'll love it! I will send my wedding gift there for the two of you to enjoy. You two will be the first to use it, since the only other weddings here are still in the planning stages. You guys have a reputation for plenty of firsts around here."

The thought of a honeymoon ripped through me as Jacob thanked the shopkeeper for all of her help. My father hadn't said anything about a honeymoon experience and I briefly hoped the unit had two bedrooms so that we wouldn't have to share a bed. Maybe Jacob would be willing to sleep on the floor if he had too. As our group stepped into the Marketplace my stomach did an instant tumble, flipping end over end as Jessica tugged on my arm leading me toward the day spa.

"Listen," Jessica whispered from the side of her mouth, "Don't worry about Bentley. The clinic gave me a whole week off because Jacob is my son and I would be needed to babysit. No one here knows the boy isn't biologically yours, so they are overly excited to see Bentley's parents make the relationship solid." She stopped and turned me to face her, wrapping me into her arms before whispering into my ear. "I know what this is about and I have no way to properly thank you. Growing up this fast isn't easy. Use every moment you have in that Honeymoon Unit to get your ducks in a row. Dealing with Haven isn't a picnic. I know you love my son so pulling this off won't take a lot of effort. Do this right… and we can all get out of here as a family when the coast is clear."

I squeezed Jessica tightly, "I'll do what I can."

Jessica pulled away, breaking the embrace and nodded before motioning to the day spa. "Ladies… your pampering begins now. See you later in the bridal suite."

I gently set my glass of champagne down onto the small end table between Emily and me. For the last few hours we had been made victim to various forms of torture in the name of wedding preparedness. Body waxing and polishing, deep tissue massages, creams that would take the redness away from our skin so that the tortures wouldn't show. Our hair had been styled up with loose curls that hung down sporadically to give it the look of elegance as well as a messy rush job. I never could understand the style, though now I would be sporting it at my wedding… and my birthday. The entire afternoon had exhausted me and several times I had to fight to keep my eyes open.

Emily had taken the experience to full advantage, enjoying every moment of it with a smile. She rarely had the opportunity to get time away from the children at home or in the classroom. As I watched her slowly sip her champagne I couldn't help but think that she seemed to be enjoying this more than me. *Would someone notice?* I thought to myself as I reminded myself to smile in case someone had. Our belongings had been placed into small bags and set next to our lounge chairs to be brought with us to the bridal suite. Apparently we would be walking there in our bathrobes so that we wouldn't mess up the perfect hair and makeup job that had taken nearly an hour to complete. There had been parts of me that

Darkness Falls

had been waxed that I never knew could be waxed, and I shivered at the horrifying memory of trying to recover from the burn while my hair had been done.

"I should have let you suffer through that waxing thing alone. It feels like someone hit me with a baseball bat between the legs." Emily laughed as though she had read my mind. "Tonight will be ruined for you if you hurt nearly as bad as I do right now."

"Ruined?" I asked before sipping my champagne and placing it back on the end table. "Why on earth would it be ruined?"

Emily sat up, removing the cooling pads from her eyes and set me with a curious stare. "Please tell me you didn't just say that?"

For a moment I had been about to question her, until the realization hit me. "Oh yeah, that." I blushed as I leaned back into my lounge chair. "I hadn't put that much thought into it I guess. You could be right about the waxing, I am still burning."

Emily laughed loudly, "Not much thought into it huh? If I were you I would be scared out of my mind! Something tells me that tonight will be a night you will never forget."

I swallowed hard as I closed my eyes. I couldn't tell her the truth. "Yeah maybe. I guess I wait and see. We need to get going now… finish your glass. I have a wedding to catch."

Ten minutes later we left the day spa and made our way toward the chapel, the whole time I felt naked and exposed as we walked through small crowds of people shopping and talking. I tried to look overly excited and not like someone who was scared to death of her own wedding. Emily giggled as she pulled me through the crowds and through the door of the chapel. A tall woman in a white suit promptly ushered us off to the bridal suite. I managed to catch sight of the shopkeeper from the bridal shop directing people with large black vases of flowers as we passed by. She smiled brightly and motioned for us to hurry and get ready.

When we walked through the large double doors and entered the Bridal Suite, my breath caught in my throat as I froze. The walls were shockingly white and sterile with four matching white sofas arranged in the center in a square. Four large white vases filled with deep red roses sat two by the doors and two by the large vanity the stretched the length of the far wall. In the corner of the room sat an alcove surrounded by white lace curtains that had been gathered back to reveal a white lounger. A large silver box wrapped in black ribbon had been placed on the lounger with my name written on the box, and my wedding dress had been hung just behind the edge of the curtain.

"This place is every woman's dream. Oh look... more champagne! Don't mind if I do." Emily laughed before heading for the table in the center of the sofas. "There is a note here for you Fallon. I think it is from Jacob."

I snatched the note from her outstretched hand and walked to the alcove, plopping down next to the silver box. I didn't need Emily anywhere near me when I opened the envelope in case the message had anything to do with the sham wedding. When I had been sure Emily had been occupied with pouring her champagne, I ripped the small envelope open.

My dearest Fallon,
You have no idea how radiant you look in that dress, you will make a beautiful bride. Don't think for a moment that your color choice has gone unnoticed with me. Sometimes you forget how well I know you. Please try not to stress yourself out and just enjoy the process. I only hope I can be everything you need me to be. Together we can face the world and every challenge that comes our way. We are Compound after all. Thank you for choosing me as the man you want to spend the rest of your life with, even if you aren't ready for forever. I can wait as long as you can for a proper marriage. You mean that much to me. For Compound – and for love.
Yours forever,
Jacob Dunn

I folded the paper up and placed it back into the envelope. His wording had obviously been coded in a safe manner. Together we could indeed face the challenges ahead of us. We would need to stick together if we had any hope of holding onto Compound. I tossed the note onto the small end table by the lounger and opened the silver box with the black ribbons, finding all of my under garments neatly packed inside silver tissue paper.

"Here, have more champagne." Emily giggled as she walked up and handed me a glass. "Wowsers... that is what you are planning to wear under your dress? That will take forever to get into! Okay, you might as well start getting ready."

I couldn't be sure if the swimming in my head had been caused by the flurry of activity or the champagne I had been drinking throughout the afternoon. I closed my eyes and leaned back waiting for the feeling of nausea to slip away from me. Emily grabbed one of my legs and sat on a small stool in front of me. I could hear her humming away as she slid the first stocking onto my foot. "Emily?" I asked as I opened my eyes and watched her reach for the other stocking, "Have you ever been faced with something so scary and life changing that you weren't sure you were doing the right thing no matter which option you pick?"

Emily slipped the other stocking onto my bare foot and pulled me up off the lounger. "You are nervous is all… you and Jacob are perfect for each other." She said as she dropped to her knees on the floor and stretched the stockings up to my thighs. "This is the biggest decision of your lives. From this day onward you will be Mrs. Dunn… and that isn't such a bad thing. He adores the ground you walk on. Here, change into this poor excuse for underwear so that we can get the rest of this on you."

I slipped into the panties that resembled a strand of ribbon more than underwear, and dropped my robe onto the floor. Emily promptly wrapped me in the garter belt and pinned my stocking up before helping me into the corset. I felt as though I couldn't breathe when she finally finished the laces and I tried to sit back down. Sitting proved to be more difficult than it looked as I couldn't bend, or stretch in and sort of comfortable fashion. I quickly gave up on sitting until after the ceremony ends. Emily rushed off to the door after a soft knock sounded. I heard her whispering to someone while I tried to step into the skirt made entirely of tulle and fluff that would cause my dress to look as though it had been inflated.

"We have less than an hour before the ceremony!" Jessica called out as Emily let her in and closed the door behind her. She looked stunning draped in a thin strapped burgundy dress with matching heels. Her hair had been left down and curled into perfection. "Oh dear, you still have a long way to go I see." She turned to Emily and clapped her hands, "Emily, go get ready I can take care of Fallon. Thank you for helping her until I could arrive. If you don't get dressed too we are all doomed."

I watched Emily nod before spinning and taking off to the other side of the room to retrieve her own dress. Jessica smiled brightly as she walked around behind me and pulled my overly fluffy skirt up, tying the ribbons into place at my waist. While she checked my corset laces I couldn't help but think about my mother. She should be the one helping me into my gown today. If she were here however, I wouldn't be getting married on my seventeenth birthday. I fought to hold in the tears so as not to mess up the makeup and wiped my nose with the back of my hand. I missed her terribly.

"Fallon, it is time for the… hey are you alright?" Jessica asked as she stepped in front of me. "Oh honey, let me get you a tissue." She said before reaching over to the table and handing me one from a small decorative box. "You gonna be alright?"

"Yeah, it is just my mom." I choked as I closed my eyes and dabbed the tears that fought to spill onto my cheeks.

"I know sweetie. She would be proud of what you are doing for us. She would be proud to see you marry my son." Jessica whispered. "We have to hurry though and get you into this dress. Your father and Dave are handling the children and that can't be good."

I laughed with a nod as we moved closer to the alcove and the dress that I would wear to marry Jacob Dunn. I couldn't deny I loved him any longer, but the ceremony would be beneficial to our entire community. Sham wedding or not, I couldn't help but feel like this wedding would be one of the most important events of my entire life. Our marriage would have an impact that would affect us all. Maybe even more of an impact on my life than I had previously thought.

CHAPTER TWENTY-THREE

I swallowed hard as I stood staring at the large set of double doors that led into the chapel. My nervous hand held my black and silver bouquet in a white knuckled grip. I hadn't taken a proper breath since the moment the gown had been carefully lowered over my head. My whole body shook hard as I fought to control the urge to run screaming out into the Marketplace and to the elevators. My father stood silently at my side, my free arm tucked into his as we waited. The only sound in the hallway had been my own ragged breath. Emily stood waiting patiently at the front of the line tapping her foot as Travis rounded the corner adjusting his collar. He shot her a sheepish grin and promptly took her arm.

While in the bridal suite, Jessica had given me a garter as my something new item to wear down the aisle. My mother's engagement ring helped to serve as my something old and had been moved to my other hand to make room for my wedding band. Emily had given me a small rhinestone clover pin to pin into my bouquet as my something barrowed. I thumbed that pin now as I stood looking at the doors. No one had managed to give me something blue. It hadn't mattered to any of us.

I sucked in a breath when I heard the music begin and I gripped my father's arm tightly to me. The doors slowly opened and Emily and Travis were quickly rushed in before the doors closed again. My heart pounded in my chest so loudly I swore I could hear it thumping against the fabric of my corset. These would be the last steps I would ever take as a Henley. By the time I returned to this hallway I would be a Dunn for the betterment of Compound.

"Here we go sweetheart." My father whispered as the doors opened again and he led me forward.

The room began to move as people began to stand and turn to have a look. Gasps broke out randomly around the room as the many faces of strangers caught their first glimpse of how Compound handles weddings. The aisle was far longer than I expected, making the journey slightly more embarrassing. The decorations had matched the entire theme perfectly, though I hadn't been exactly sure what the theme had been, only that the colors had all been the same. Large vases sat on pedestals around the room packed full of silver and black flowers. The end of every pew we passed had been decorated in small bouquets that matched the one Emily had carried before me.

Remembering that I am to be an excited bride, I smiled brightly and tried to meet the gaze of those who currently stared at me as if I were a princess being led to take the thrown. People cried and wiped their eyes as we walked by. People I had seen around Sanctuary or hadn't even met smiled and wished me luck in my future. I couldn't believe how many people they could fit into the chapel. The place had been deceiving from the outside, suggesting a small place that couldn't possibly be big enough for a large wedding. I had been wrong as our wedding had drawn a crowd far larger than I had expected, and they had room to spare.

Emily stood smiling at me as I neared. In that moment I couldn't have been more proud to call her my best friend. Through the recovery of her parents' death, her transition into living with Papa, and the blackout with everything that followed… she remained. I couldn't have chosen a better bridesmaid even if it was a sham wedding. I turned my head and saw Travis looking dapper in his black tuxedo with silver vest, a grin from ear to ear. He showed his thumb on the sly and winked at me which forced me to giggle.

When my eyes fell on Jacob, my heart instantaneously flipped end over end. My stomach spun in one direction before flipping in reverse. He stood proudly by his brother's side in a matching black tuxedo, though his silver vest had the same black embroidery as my gown. I smiled brightly at him as I nearly giggled with nervousness. A single tear rolled down his cheek and he quickly wiped it away.

Nice show you are putting on, I thought. For a brief moment, I thought about how he might not be acting at all. He had said numerous times in the past few months that he wanted to marry me.

I bit my lip as we came to a stop, the crowd settling into their seats. The elderly man before us began to speak, though I hadn't heard a word of what he had said. I felt as though I had left my body and was floating somewhere in the room far enough away to only hear low murmurs.

"Her mother and I do... as well as the entire Compound community." My father replied, followed by an uproar of cheers behind me.

I hadn't heard what question my father had answered, all I had managed to catch was the mention of my mother. I desperately wished my mother could have joined me. To have seen me standing in front of all these people and pledge my love for Jacob. *But this is a sham wedding right? Only on paper, this was on paper right?* I asked myself as my father turned and hugged me tightly. *This is just a formality. Just a public display that gains us witnesses we can use to prove the marriage is real.*

"Take care of my girl." My father whispered as he shook Jacob's hand.

Remembering what the shopkeeper at the bridal shop had told me, I quickly passed my bouquet to Emily before Jacob gently grabbed both of my hands and led me up a small step to stand at his side. The man before us rambled on as my mind wondered in a completely different direction. I thought about the children of Compound. I thought about the possibility Haven could claim them. I thought about how I would manage to return everyone to Compound one day when the surface becomes safe.

"I do." Jacob whispered as his dark eyes found mine.

I hadn't heard the question at all. Shocked, I turned to the elderly man and listened carefully to what he was asking of me. The man smiled and slowly asked me if I would take Jacob Dunn to be my husband through this life and into the next. I swallowed hard as I thought about the implications. *Surely the question was a formality meant to convince the crowd right?* I asked myself. Then a thought hit me that I hadn't expected. Jacob hadn't been acting... and neither had I. This ceremony may not be a sham though the marriage might be. I looked to Jacob, seeing tears running down his cheeks.

"I do." I whispered before I realized the words had escaped

my lips.

Jacob ran his thumb slowly over the back of my hand several times as if to calm me down. It felt soothing and I couldn't help focusing on the rhythm and closing my eyes against the world around me. When he let go of my hands I instinctively reached for him before opening my eyes. Travis was handing him a ring. The exchange between them had only taken a moment though it had felt like an eternity. When Jacob grabbed my hand and began to slip the ring onto my finger, I immediately recognized it as my mother's wedding band. *The one she had been wearing when she died*, I thought to myself as tears began to fall from my eyes uncontrolled. Robert had taken it from her finger and had returned it to my father.

Jacob began to speak though my thoughts had been on my mother and the ring I now wore on my finger. Though someone had taken the time to clean the years of grime from the thin gold band covered in diamonds, it still once belonged to my mother. Wearing something so special and important to my mother tugged at my fragile heart and I closed my eyes, silently thanking my mother for being so strong and giving so much for her children.

Emily stepped to my side and tapped me gently on the shoulder. When I looked to her, she handed me the matching ring to the set... my father's wedding ring. Shocked, I spun searching for my father and found him sitting in a chair holding up his bare hand and crying with a smile. In a chair beside him sat a decorative frame displaying the smiling face of my mother. Holding the ring in my hand, I stepped down off the step and nearly ran to him. He hugged me tightly and for a moment we cried, the world around us melting away. He quickly kissed me on the forehead and motioned for me to return.

Jacob was laughing to himself as I returned to face him. He ran his thumb down the side of my face, wiping the tears from my cheek as he playfully shook his head at me. I couldn't help the opportunity to stick my tongue out at him as my normal response. The tension and sadness from the crowd after watching the exchange with my father completely evaporated, and the room roared in laughter. Jacob playfully gave me a look of mocked horror before both of us nearly doubled over in hysterical laughter. The crowd clapped and cheered loudly around us as we fought to regain control of ourselves. I wasn't nervous anymore.

"Do you see what I have to put up with?" Jacob laughed to the crowd prompting several shouts of playful agreement and laughter.

The elderly man before us tried to stifle his laughter as he motioned for me to place the ring onto Jacob's finger. I quickly slid the diamond covered band onto Jacob's finger, sliding it on with ease. The ring was only slightly too big for him but he didn't seem to mind. I managed to catch the elderly man asking me to repeat his words, which I did in robotic response. The second the words left my lips the memory of what I had just said vanished like a vapor into the room. My heart thumped harder in my chest resembling the beat of wild jungle drums.

"You may now kiss the bride." The elderly man giggled.

In that moment I realized what I had just done. I had just married Jacob Dunn in front of a chapel packed with people, and used my parents' wedding rings to do it. Jacob stepped forward, wrapping one arm around my waist and placing one hand on the side of my face. Instantly I found myself lost in his eyes as he searched my face. There in that moment I couldn't help but smile. I loved this man and he loved me. Sham marriage or no, I had married Jacob not just for the betterment of Compound. A part of me had married him for love. A part of me desperately wanted to be his wife. I smiled up at him, sliding my arms around his neck and pulling him to me. When our lips met the world evaporated leaving only the two of us holding each other tight.

The room exploded in cheers as people jumped to their feet and clapped wildly. I paid no attention to the crowd as Jacob laughed and kissed me again, wrapping both arms around my waist and lifting me from the floor. I laughed against his lips; breaking down into a fit of giggles I could no longer control. The tears had stopped falling. Jacob gently set me back onto my feet and stepped back, looking at me through new eyes. He looked as though he had aged several years in a matter of minutes, and for once he looked truly happy.

"I present to you… Mr. and Mrs. Jacob Dunn." The elderly man said nearly yelling over the roar of the crowd.

I was no longer Fallon Henley. From this moment onward I was now Fallon LeAnn Dunn, wife of Jacob Dunn. Jacob quickly grabbed my hand and gave me the same look he had shown me numerous times in our lives. His mischievous grin grew from the corner of his mouth as he motioned with a tilt of his head down the aisle. Together we bolted as we laughed, running down the aisle and through the double doors out into the hallway. As the doors closed behind us the crowd roared on, the atmosphere crackling with excitement.

I couldn't be sure of where we were headed, but my feet kept moving. We tore down a hallway in the opposite direction of the bridal suite and through a set of double doors, closing them behind us. We placed our backs against the inside of the doors and erupted in laughter. From the other side of the door we could hear people laughing and speaking in excited tones as they passed by the doors.

"Where are we?" I asked as I wiped my eyes with my hands, still laughing.

"The groom's room, it was the only place I could think of to escape for a moment or two before we go to the reception." Jacob said as he turned to look out the small peep hole in the door. "They are on the move."

"I can't believe we just did that." I whispered as I rested my head against the door.

Jacob turned to me, his dark eyes scanning my face as he smiled slowly. Placing one hand on the door beside my head and wrapping his free arm around my waist, he moved to stand in front of me. "Fallon Dunn... I know you love me. I can feel it in your kiss. I said before that I understand you are not ready to be a wife. I'll give you all the time you need to adjust to this. But right now I am going to kiss you and if you could just forget about the ceremony and the crowd of people that are looking for us...," He whispered as his lips brushed mine, "...I would love to be lost in it for a moment."

No words escaped me as his lips gently claimed my own. Alone in the room and listening to the fading sound of the crowd, I let go and slipping into his kiss... lost in him.

Being the first couple to marry within Sanctuary afforded us certain luxuries other couples wouldn't be given. For one, reception catering had been planned to fall on the families of the happy couple. Wedding cakes could be ordered from the private sector or from the talented back room of the Glazier Grill. As our wedding hadn't been announced until noon on the day of the ceremony, and being the first wedding, the Glazier Grill catered the entire event. Most of the people living in the facility couldn't help showing up to the biggest event to take place since the blackout. The Glazier Grill simply packed up the food and followed the crowd.

Though Angela had designed and made our wedding cake herself, she worked within the Glazier Grill and should have charged us for the order. I found out as I arrived to the reception that Angela and her co-workers had all pitched in and gifted the wedding cake to us free of charge. Rissa had personally donated several bottles of her private reserve champagne to supply at least the toast as her wedding gift to us. The most surprising move had come from my father, who instructed the reception music to be played over the PA system for all of Sanctuary to hear. Just knowing that Robert could hear the party while within the Isolation Department had sent Jacob into frenzied hugs and thanks to all of those who had made it possible.

After we had managed to stuff our faces with enough pot roast and wine to feed an army, Travis stood and captured everyone's attention by announcing he would like to toast the happy couple. Matt quickly joined at his side, and together the two of them embarrassed us repeatedly with wild tales from our childhood as the room came alive with laughter. Jacob held my hand in his under the table, his thumb slowly running along the back of my hand but his attention on his brothers. I watched Jacob's face as smiles of recognition came and went from his lips. Once, I hid my face behind his shoulder when Matt had taken it upon himself to explain Jacob's moonshine induced marriage proposal at Compound. Jacob simply shrugged to the crowd playfully as they erupted again in a wave of laughter.

Not a single member of Compound talked about Bentley being an orphan as one by one they stood on a small stage telling tales of our relationship. It had been fairly common knowledge within our group to allow Sanctuary to believe the child had been ours from the start. When a woman from the day spa asked about Bentley while Emily gave her speech, Emily had wasted no time changing gears and telling the tale of Megan's frantic birth claiming the experience had been mine. No one in Compound corrected her as they listened, half smiling and half saddened remembering Megan. It had been predetermined that in the event someone asked, Megan's tale would be given.

When the speeches had drawn to a close, Jacob grabbed my hand and led me to the cake table for our cutting. I barely remembered what the shopkeeper in the bridal shop had said about the process, so I was excited to see her standing there whispering instructions to us. The cake was massive, towering six tiers high and silver with the same swirl patterns and flowers from the design on my gown done in black frosting. The inside of the cake shocked me the most as the cake had been dyed black with a cream filling lightly tinted to a shade of grey. Jacob played as though he would smash his piece into my face, then shrugged and placed a bite between his teeth and kissing me. As the crowd thundered in excitement I made metal note to punch him later for such a public embarrassment.

When it came to tossing my bouquet I stood for several minutes waiting for the single women within the reception hall to calm down as they playfully elbowed each other and shoved themselves into better positions. I turned back to the wall and hurled it over my head as hard as I could muster while the crowd erupted in screams of laughter. I spun in time to see Rissa vault over a woman I didn't know and catch it while it spun wildly toward one of young women who worked in the Library. Dave instantly ducked into his chair playfully as Rissa held her prize out at him and laughed.

Jacob whispered for me to just go with it and not to fight his plan when it came to my garter toss, as he sat me in a chair in the center of the dance floor. He turned to the crowd, moving his arms up and down in an attempt to raise the energy of the crowd and get them on their feet. I placed my face in my hands trying desperately to hide as the crowd cheered wildly. When I gained enough bravery to peek through my fingers, Jacob winked at me with an evil grin before diving completely under my dress only to return holding a large plastic mixing spoon. I looked at him in shock, trying to figure out where he had managed to hide it as he held it high above his head with pride. As if he had just realized the item had been a spoon, he pretended to be shocked and slowly turned his gaze at me as though I had tried to trick him. The crowd came alive. On his second attempt he retrieved a rolling pin, giving me the same shocked look as before.

He removed his tuxedo jacket and rolled up his sleeves before going in for a third attempt. For a moment, I expected him to come back out with another item taken from the kitchens; instead I felt his teeth graze my thigh. Instantly I froze in horror, feeling him catch the garter in his teeth and slide it down my leg. I closed my eyes tightly and covered my face with my hands to keep the terror on my face from the crowd. When he returned with the garter in his teeth, the crowd of single men had grown behind him. As if it had been a rubber band, Jacob shot the garter into the crowd which now resembled a shark tank during feeding time. Men moved in every direction climbing over each other for the chance to catch it. I hadn't seen him in the crowd at the time, but Matt had moved with speed, catching the garter as it bounced off another man's head.

When the Father and Daughter dance had been announced I wasted no time running to the center of the dance floor. My father emerged from the crowd, his eyes puffy from crying and scooped me into his arms with a smile. We danced circles around the room in silence while tearful eyes watched. Jade danced wildly with Bobby at the edge of the crowd, giggling to themselves as they tried to twirl and spin.

"Dad… is it working? Do they believe?" I whispered up to my father.

"The only one in this room who doesn't believe is you." My father smiled as our eyes met. "He is a good man and the love you have for each other is rare and real."

"I'm not ready to be a wife, Dad." I whispered as I searched his eyes for answers. "I can pretend until the cows come home… but I can't be a wife yet."

My father smiled sadly, "Do you love him?"

"Yes." I admitted in embarrassment as I shifted my gaze to the floor.

"Then the two of you will find a way. If it is time you need, that boy will bend over backward to make sure you get it. It is easier to pretend to be a happy couple when you are a happy couple. The love is there, Fallon. When you let your guard down, this whole place can feel it." My father whispered before spinning me out toward the crowd and bringing me back into his arms. "The Haven team arrived before the wedding and is being held. Use the time you have in the Honeymoon Unit and have a talk with Jacob when you get the chance. By the time you both come back, the members of Haven will still be isolated."

"Thanks for the information Dad, I'll be sure to talk with him." I said with a smile. "By the way, why did you give Jacob your ring?"

"Matching set sweetheart." My father said proudly, "You two remind me of your mother and me when we were your age. I am convinced your love can weather the storms coming your way. The set stays together as a united force."

When the song ended I hugged my father tightly and watched as he walked off into the crowd. My next few dances had been booked up solid in advance. I danced with Jacob and then with Dave. I danced with Matt and Travis before being passed off to the man who runs the movie theater because no one could find Edward. About the time I had thought me sore feet would fall off my ankles, I had saved the last dance of the night for the entire collection of Compound kids. Cassidy, Cassandra, Becky and Bobby danced like chickens around me in a large circle while I tried to dance just as silly as they were. Before I knew it, the crowd had joined in the fun and filled the dance floor.

As the music paused to change songs I plopped into the nearest chair completely exhausted as my feet throbbed inside my shoes. I scanned the room desperate to locate Jacob and escape the party to remove my shoes. I caught sight of Dave and Rissa sitting in the far corner on the other side of the dance floor, his arms around her and whispering in her ear. It had been the first time I had seen him interact with a woman and the display slightly embarrassed me. I turned my gaze from them and watched the crowd moving on the dance floor to the loudly thumping beat of the music.

"You ready to get out of here, Mrs. Dunn?" Jacob's teasing voice whispered into my ear from behind me.

"My feet are going to protest if we stay any longer. Did you get the chance to say goodbye to Bentley before he left? Your mom just took him back to the unit to put him to bed." I asked with a smile as I stood from my chair.

"Yes. I ran into her after talking with one of the guards in charge of the Honeymoon Unit. I got the key." Jacob said as he shot me a wicked grin and grabbed my hand.

The last thing I wanted was to be alone with Jacob in a strange Honeymoon Unit where we couldn't be disturbed, but the thought of being able to take my shoes off had been the deciding factor in allowed Jacob to sneak us from the reception and out through the doors that would lead us into the Marketplace. The party would likely last well into the early morning hours with the exhausted filtering out two or three at a time. The energy level in the reception hadn't dissipated much since the moment the party had started. We rode in silent exhaustion until the elevator stopped.

"The unit is on the second floor of the Living Level. Think you can climb some stairs?" Jacob asked as we exited the elevator and stepped into the common area. "I don't want to trip while trying to carry you up those blasted things."

"Not only will I be able to climb them, I'll beat you to the second floor!" I shouted before hiking up my dress and sprinting in my heels to the first staircase I could see. My feet screamed at me with each step I took though I continued to laugh as I heard Jacob scramble up the stairs behind me.

When I landed both feet on the second floor I clapped playfully as I watched Jacob shake his head in defeat. "Alright woman, we are this way." Jacob laughed as he pointed to the far end of the landing. "What am I going to do with you anyway?"

I walked slowly in the direction Jacob had pointed. "Don't confuse the stairs as an indication of energy; I am so beat right now I could pass out in this dress if I am not careful."

"Tell me about it. I am might just fall asleep standing up." Jacob laughed as he laced his fingers into mine. "I forgot to tell you, they had a team up here earlier dusting the place and getting it ready for us. I have no idea what is waiting in there, but I think we can guess."

"Do you think there is food? I think I danced off the pot roast somewhere around the second hour." I giggled as we reached the door and Jacob pushed the key into the lock. "Do you know what I could go for right now?"

"A cheeseburger?" Jacob laughed as he turned the key and opened the door.

"Yes, a fat one with bacon and two patties of meat." I played as I stepped toward the door.

"Wait! Don't go in yet!" Jacob whispered loudly as he grabbed my arm to stop me. "I have to carry you in."

"No you don't!" I protested loudly seconds before Jacob grabbed me low around the waist and tossed me over his shoulder. I closed my eyes and placed both fists on Jacob's waist trying to push off as I hung upside down. "Put me down you turd! All the blood is rushing to my head! I swear if I vomit it is going straight down the back of your pants!"

Jacob kicked the door closed behind him and moved swiftly into the room before muttering quietly to himself and setting me back onto my feet. "Let me lock the door. Don't move!" He yelled as he spun on his heels.

I turned to catch a peek of the room behind me, my mouth falling open at the sight. The room easily spanned the size of my office if not slightly larger with tan area rugs across dark hardwood flooring. A large bed that resembled two queen sized mattresses pushed together had obviously been made the center of focus as it sat upon a slightly raised platform directly across from me. The decorative four post bed frame was surrounded in white lace curtains. It was promptly obvious to me what the intent of this room had been.

A gas burning fireplace with sunken seating area filled with pillows of all sizes sat to the left of me, a fire flickering inside. As I scanned the room I noticed something that made my heart skip a beat. Floor to ceiling curtains stretched nearly the entire length of the walls to each side of the large space. I knew instantly what these curtains would reveal. Moving quickly, I grabbed the edge of one and slid it down the wall to rest in a wall nook near the bed. I spun, finding the remote on the foot of the bed and picked it up. As I moved to the other side of the room and pulled the curtain back, I smiled.

"Those can't be what I think they are, right?" Jacob asked in shock as he stood in the center of the large room.

I scrolled down the list of scenes, "Sure is! These aren't the same as mine though, this list in entirely different. You have your choice of the Ireland Coast, Hawaii, Bahamas, Spain... the list just keeps going." As I scrolled I found a scene labeled *Waterfall in Rainforest* and couldn't help myself. I made the selection and watched the screens behind the glass morph on either side of me. The sound of rushing water surrounded us as I turned to watch the nearest screen.

Looking to Jacob for agreement I watched him nod playfully before walking toward a small stainless steel kitchenette near the door. He stopped at the small dining table to examine the large vase filled with red roses, an equally large basket of eatables, an ice bucket with a few chilled bottles of champagne and two tall champagne flutes.

"Mrs. Dunn... would you care to join me in a glass of champagne and some chocolate covered fruit or cookies?" Jacob played as he motioned to the table, "You might want to chug a glass before you try to take a bath or shower at any point this week." He smirked with an eyebrow raised as he slowly pointed to a side of the room I had yet to inspect.

I turned in confusion, nearly dropping the remote to the floor. A toilet sat in a small pocket of space with sliding door for privacy; however the shower sat open to the room. No doors, curtains, or walls sheltered the multi-head shower nook. Equally as distressing to me had been the large sunken soaking tub that could easily fit several people that sat near the shower and just as terrifyingly exposed.

"You have got to be kidding me." I said as I walked toward the small table to retrieve my glass from Jacob's outstretched hand. "Why would they leave it all open like that?"

"Did you seriously just ask that?" Jacob laughed. "This room has one purpose... you know that."

I choked on the sip of champagne I had been attempting to swallow and plopped into a chair at the table. "I'm just exhausted."

Jacob smiled as he set his glass down on the table and dropped down onto the floor in front of me. "Here, we can start with getting those horribly high shoes off of your feet." He spoke softly as he gently placed my feet into his lap and began to undo the tiny silver buckles. "I can't believe you wore these things all night. Your feet must be completely swollen."

I leaned back in the chair and closed my eyes. "They made me tall enough to look into your eyes didn't they?"

"Tell you what," Jacob smiled as he set the heels under the edge of the table, my feet now bare. "As soon as we get you out of that dress and into something comfortable, I'll rub your sore feet if you like."

"You are not helping me change Jacob!" I nearly shouted as I sat upright in my chair.

Jacob rolled his eyes and stood, "Give me a break my love, I am not trying to trick you into anything. It took what... two or three people to get into that gown? How do you suppose you will be able to unzip and unbutton the back of it by yourself?"

I blushed with the realization that he had been right. There would be no way for me to peal out of the wedding gown without some help. "Sorry. I didn't mean to come off like that."

Jacob took hold of my hand and led me up onto the platform by the bed. "I need you to turn around and hold onto the post. Can you do that for me? Try to stay still." He whispered softly.

I nodded slowly as I wrapped my arms around the bedpost, resting my face against the coolness of the dark colored wood. Jacob walked to the chair next to the bed and removed his tuxedo jacket and vest tossing them into the chair before rolling up his sleeves. His intense eyes never left mine though as I watched, sadness and understanding replaced the fire behind his gaze.

As I closed my eyes I felt him slip passed me seconds before I felt a small tug at the back of my gown as buttons came undone. One by one I felt them spring open as his hands slowly moved down my back. I held my breath and fought to steady myself as my body erupted in uncontrolled trembles.

"Fallon, you act as though I am about to attack you. Calm down, alright?" Jacob whispered before dragging the zipper down my back. "I promise you I am not into any funny business. Sex is the farthest thing from my mind. My biggest concern is getting you comfortable. You are sort of freaking me out right now."

I relaxed slightly as I sagged against the bedpost. "I'm just not ready for any of this."

"Let go of the bedpost now, we are going to pull this off." Jacob whispered.

I dropped my arms to my sides as Jacob slid my straps down over my shoulders, pushing the dress to the floor. "See, I didn't eat you for Pete's sake. We do have a problem though. We need to untie this weird looking skirt because you won't be able to step out of this like that."

Before I could protest I felt the ties on the skirt come loose. Jacob wrapped one arm around my waist and the other under my knees, lifting me out of the pile of fabric before setting me on the bed. "You know... this thing you are wearing now is amazingly hot! It is a shame we will have to take it off." Jacob played.

It was in that moment as the fog of exhaustion began to fade with his words that I remembered what I had been wearing under my gown. "Jacob!" I screeched.

Jacob laughed loudly, "You can't untie it yourself and you

know it. I saw the lace job and it is double knotted. Let me untie it and then you can finish the job from there. I won't even look if that makes you happy. Just remember to set it all aside so that when you decide to be a wife I can give it to myself for Christmas."

"You are such a pervert." I stated as I stood to face him. "Just get the back. Where are the bags by the way? I have to change into something. I can't run around naked."

"Honey, I am a guy. A guy who is standing in the middle of a room helping his hot new wife out of her pretty little underclothes... and not touching her." Jacob whispered playfully, "How many guys do you know who have that sort of composure? I couldn't let you get away without a single comment about it." Jacob spun me around and worked the laces quickly while he continued, "There is a large silver box on the pillow at the far end. Did you happen to see it?"

"I'll open it tomorrow. Are you sleeping on the floor?" I asked softly as I slowly felt the corset begin to loosen, finally allowing me to take a full breath.

"In a bed that size? Not on your life! You should be able to get this torture device off now. I'll find the bags. Then I think you can take one side of the bed and I'll take the other." Jacob said as he spun to search the unit for the bags.

"You better not look while I change!" I called out as I laughed.

"Is it fair to remind you that you broke into my shower the morning after the moonshine and saw me naked?" Jacob laughed as he ducked into the closet by the door.

"No!" I yelled back, still holding my corset to cover my chest.

"You are right. I'll hold that card for another day." Jacob smirked as he returned to the room.

My new husband... is a pervert, I thought to myself.

CHAPTER TWENTY-FOUR

I hadn't slept well since the moment we had arrived at Sanctuary. Something about this place rubbed me the wrong way. I didn't blame Jared for making the decision to come here. It wasn't like we had had much choice in the matter. I stretched my legs as I rolled onto my back, pulling my arms up over my head and feeling the stiffness begin to release. Stretching hadn't done much for the body aches I still felt from my head to my toes. After trying to put Fallon's fears to rest last night, I had talked her into sharing the bed. I didn't push her for anything else. I knew better. She would have killed me in my sleep if I had. Besides, I had wanted nothing more than to sleep and sleep I got. A lot of it. I couldn't be sure as to the current time, but for the first time in months I felt fully rested.

I rolled to face Fallon and found her softly snoring on the far side of the massive bed. I hadn't realized how paranoid she had been that I would touch her until the moment she climbed in at the edge and refused to come any closer to my side. *Silly girl*, I thought to myself, *When I make a promise I tend to keep it*. She never feared me before the wedding and deep down I wondered what had changed that. It wasn't like I instantly had rights to take advantage of her and Lord knows I wouldn't dream of it in the first place. When the time is right and she is ready, then we will see what happens. Until then I would give her all the space she needs.

I sat up and swung my feet onto the floor as my eyes caught sight of the stockings, garter belt, and corset tossed over the arm of the chair. She had made the most beautiful bride I had ever seen. She had also made the most alluring bride in the sultry outfit she had hidden under that massive gown. I hadn't lied when I had told her to set them aside. I did fully intend to hang onto them to give them to myself for Christmas… by giving them back to her. I stifled a laugh as I tossed the edge of the bedding back onto the bed and stood for one final full body stretch that could loosen my back.

I thought about the hours leading up to the wedding and how in the beginning I could have sworn she had been acting the part. But in that moment with her father during the ceremony, something changed in her. I had cried during our vows as did she. Though I couldn't be sure why her tears had fallen, my tears had fallen at the realization her vows had been spoken from the heart. It was as if her father's ring on my finger had been the switch. One moment she was nervous and skittish, the next moment she had been transformed into the most amazingly beautiful woman I had ever seen, spilling her love onto the floor for the entire world to see.

I padded over to the kitchen as quietly as I could in my desperate search for coffee and found a small coffee maker and two mugs. *My wife likes her coffee with half a sugar and two creams*, I thought to myself as a smile touched my lips. Fallon LeAnn Dunn… I definitely liked the sound of that. I was pretty sure that if someone had come to me before the blackout and informed me that one day I would marry Fallon, I might have laughed as I hadn't seen myself as ever having a chance with her. Sure, there were boys who tried to ask her on dates but she had either hit them or ignored them completely. Staying in the brother figure zone had afforded me the luxury of never having to ask her on dates. We went shopping together in the city on the rare chance we had gone, went to the river for swimming, and hung out in town. I never needed a date to get to know her better or spend quality time with her; I was at her hip my entire life.

While I waited for the coffee pot to brew, I slipped off to the small closet by the door and pulled out a couple of empty hangers I had managed to find the night before while searching for our bags. Both of us had been unwilling to hang anything, instead electing to toss our clothing into the chair and fall asleep, leaving an open bottle of champagne and two half full glasses on the table. *A small price to pay to finally catch up on some sleep*, I thought to myself as I made my way back toward the bed.

I wrestled Fallon's wedding gown onto a hanger and gently laid it across the bed before fighting my tuxedo onto one. I couldn't be sure if Fallon had planned to keep her dress but my mother had assured me that women usually did that sort of thing. I made a mental note to myself to have it cleaned for her and preserved as my mother had told me is usually the norm. I gathered both the tuxedo and the gown and padded off across the room to hang them up in the closet where they would be safe.

I managed to find a plastic bag hanging from an empty hanger and used it to bag up the stockings, garter belt and corset for safe keeping before stashing it in the closet near the gown. A quick glance at Fallon confirmed she would remain sleeping at least until I had managed to get dressed. I hoped she would stay asleep until after I had left to check on my father in isolation, as had become my normal morning ritual. My absence would allow her to shower in peace as the room gave little in the way of privacy. Besides, I was currently running around the Honeymoon Suite in my underwear and if she had caught me, she would likely yell at me for being indecent.

There hadn't been many items in the bags Compound had packed for our honeymoon and I wondered briefly if they had realized our honeymoon wouldn't be a typical one. I did manage to find some clean underwear and a pair of jeans which I promptly put on before chancing another glance at my sleeping wife. I slipped a brown tee shirt over my head as I padded back to the kitchen, finally smelling the strong scent of coffee in the air. Moving as quietly as I could, I poured myself a cup of coffee before taking the mug to the table. I quickly put on a pair of clean socks and my boots before strapping my gun belt around my waist.

If I played my cards right, I could slip from the room completely undetected allowing Fallon to wake up on her own and prepare for the day in my absence. After searching the kitchen counter for a paper and pen to leave a note, I quickly scribbled a note telling her to shower and that I would be back shortly. I made sure to tell her how much I loved her before I signed the note and placing it near the coffee maker. *She would check here first*, I thought to myself with a smile, *that woman loves her coffee.*

I picked up my coffee cup and slipped from the room, being

sure to close the door behind me as quietly as I could. When I turned to begin walking toward the stairs I was met with the shocked face of a middle aged woman pushing a cart filled with food in my direction. "She is still sleeping, is that for us?" I asked with a smile and watched the shocked woman nod. "I can let you in for a moment to leave it by the table. She will be up shortly. I just have a few things to do while she sleeps."

The woman smiled as I slowly opened the door and watched her disappear with the cart into the room. If the smell of coffee didn't wake Fallon, than surely the smell of hot food would. When the woman stepped back out she nodded with a smile and walked quickly back down the hallway in the direction she had come. I slid the door closed and followed her down the hallway, making mental note to return to the room before the food managed to go cold.

The common area sat empty save for a woman in a white uniform vacuuming the sofas. With the arrival of Haven, the people who worked within the Cleaning Department would be putting in extra hours to prepare for Haven's release from isolation. I smiled giving her a small wave and descended the stairs strolling to the elevator. She promptly smiled back and congratulated me on my new marriage as I stepped into the elevator and pushed the button for the First Level.

Maybe if I could make the trip a quick one, I could go to the surface and find Fallon something special as a gift. I had heard it was customary for the married couple to give each other gifts though I had no idea why. Fallon was the only gift I would ever need. Women were a different sort of creature however, and she may be expecting something special from me. I thought I had remembered seeing something the last time I had visited the surface and reminded myself to check it out.

When the elevator doors opened onto the First Level, I moved quickly down the corridor toward the Isolation Department. My first stop would be my father as I wanted to make sure he had heard the reception over the loud speakers the night before. My mother likely hadn't had the time as of yet to bring him the video tapes she had made of the event so I knew he would want the highlights straight from the horse's mouth. Knowing him, he had been awake for a while already as he seemed to be eternally set on a pre-dawn schedule.

"Here again I see... and on your honeymoon?" The young

man behind the counter laughed as I entered. "Killer wedding you had. That wife of yours looked stunning! I have never seen a dress like that before. I was telling my wife this morning that I am pretty sure every person here had gone, most are probably hung over as all get out."

"Thanks Kurt." I said as I walked to the counter and gave him a fist bump. "She is a one-of-a-kind woman that is for sure. Is my dad up and moving yet? I need to see him."

Kurt Banning had become a friend of mine during the time my father had spent within isolation. He wasn't much older than me yet had a pregnant wife and two small children. Originally from Haven, he had been assigned to Sanctuary as a form of punishment for getting drunk at the pub on Haven land and causing a bar fight. Normally Haven soldiers fought to get orders to the facility. Kurt had wanted to stay in Utah to be closer to his brothers and being sent here seemed to have been the punishment the council had deemed fit. Some days I would return to the counter and have a cup of coffee with him after visits with my father. That wouldn't be the plan today.

Kurt leaned across his desk behind the counter and pulled the signing notebook toward him. Though he wore his work uniform neatly pressed as usual, his blond hair looked as though he had simply rolled out of bed to report to work. I suspected he was likely hung over as were many people. "You bet your ass he is up and moving!" Kurt laughed deeply as he flipped the notebook open, "He keeps telling everyone that his son got married last night, like none of us knew. I am not sure he slept at all. Your mom hasn't brought the tape in yet this morning so he is on pins and needles waiting for the blow by blow of the entire thing. When I spoke with him earlier he nearly begged me to spill the beans." He smiled as his blue eyes met mine.

"I bet." I laughed as I signed the sheet and spun the notebook back to Kurt to be signed by him as well. "I won't be long today. I am hoping to hit the surface before returning to my wife. She loves lavender and I remember seeing some out there when I took her up there last time."

"I know right where you are talking about!" Kurt smiled in excitement, "I noticed it too... over there by the busted up house right?" He asked as he signed his name on the line and closed the notebook. "That is a killer gift man. Good on you. Hey, when you

Darkness Falls

guys finally emerge from the Honeymoon Suite, come on by and bring the family. My wife makes mighty fine lasagna that will make you weak in the knees. We can let the women get to know each other."

"Sounds like a plan." I smiled as I reached for the identification badge Kurt held out to me. "I'm set right?"

"You are ready to go man. You can leave your cup here on the counter if you like." Kurt said as he gave me a knuckle bump. "Have an awesome visit."

I set my coffee cup on the counter and turned for the glass door that would be the first of the checkpoints I would need to clear before being allowed to see my father. The woman behind the desk on the other side of the door smiled brightly as I lifted my pass to show it to her. She nodded and pushed a button causing the glass door to buzz loudly and unlock. As I pushed the door open and crossed through the room I thought about Kurt's dinner offer and smiled. The guy had begged me several times to come over for a visit and I wondered if maybe he just wanted Fallon to distract his pregnant wife for a while to give him some peace.

Fallon had been slow to make friends within the facility, spending most of her time in her office or hiding in her private quarters. There were times I worried she had been working herself too hard just to keep her mind busy. Once the overhaul had been completed in her department I had expected her to take shorter work days. Instead she chose to stay in her office up until her assistant begged her to go home for the night. It hadn't been like she had ignored everyone; rather she dove into her job feet first and refused to do anything until the job was done.

I hit the buzzer on the second glass door to alert the elderly man behind the counter to my presence. He glanced up with a smile and pushed the button to unlock the door. "Hey man, beautiful wedding you had last night. Congratulations." He said before motioning to the door on the other side of the room. "You know the rules; I don't have to say them. Have fun."

"Thanks, Jim." I said as I crossed the room and walked through the door.

The corridor stood empty as usual with its white walls and tiled floor reflecting the lights from the ceiling almost painfully at my eyes. Maybe I too had managed to drink a few too many glasses of champagne last night. I passed several closed doors along the way while I briefly wondered which rooms those from Haven had occupied overnight. I stopped in front of a large white door with my father's name written on the clipboard hanging in the center. According to the paperwork he hadn't shown a single sign of infection and could be released as soon as the incubation period passes completely. I tugged at the clip for my badge, yanking it off my shirt and slid it into the reader by the door. The red and green lights flashed on the reader several times before the green light stayed on and the door unlocked.

As I walked in, I could see my father sitting in a chair reading a book on the other side of the glass wall that separated us from each other. The same white walls and tiled floor from the corridor also covered the isolation rooms, making me wish briefly I had brought a pair of sunglasses to shield my eyes from the reflected light. I crossed the bare room and slipped into the chair at the small table against the glass. My father's side of the glass room seemed to me to be the most boring place in the entire facility. All that my father had to keep him company had been a small bed, table with chair, and a few items we had managed to pass him once we had gained clearance. The place seemed more like a medical prison than an isolation ward.

I pushed the buzzer to alert my father that I had arrived and the moment he heard the sound, his eyes shot up from the page he had been reading. I laughed at his shock as I frantically pointed at the phone that hung on the glass. He instantly jumped to his feet and crossed the room, dropping his book on the floor.

"You are on your honeymoon boy! Why the heck are you visiting me? I am waiting on your mom to show up." My father spoke into the phone after pulling it from the cradle that rested on his side of the glass room. "Shouldn't you be sleeping in or… something?" He laughed with a raised brow.

"She is passed out so I snuck away for a few minutes. I'm heading to the surface to pick her some lavender but wanted to see you first." I smiled as I spoke into the phone in my hand. "I can't wait for you to see the video. I'm sure we are the talk of the facility now."

"Son, you better hope she isn't angry at you for leaving the Honeymoon Suite alone. You'll learn soon enough that women are not to be trifled with." My father smiled, "I bet your night was eventful. She didn't kick your ass last night I am betting since you aren't sporting a black eye."

I shook my head as I grinned, "Nah, we were exhausted and fell asleep. Trust me Dad; I am giving her all the space she needs right now to figure herself out. The last thing she needs is her new husband getting all perverted and creepy. Say, do you know who came in yesterday from Haven?" I asked in an attempt to change the subject.

My father leaned back in his chair, "You better keep the lack of sex thing between the two of you. You don't want Haven catching wind that you have yet to consummate your marriage. They are sticklers for that crap. It might come off as being a marriage of convenience. That reminds me, tell Fallon to stay away from any wellness appointments in the clinics if she can help it. If they figure out she is a virgin they will question not only your marriage but also the birth of your son. Keep that to yourself too." My father informed. "As far as who arrived I don't have much of a clue. I thought I heard one of the nurses say that Jasper might have been with them but don't quote me on that."

"Your chart says you don't have much longer in here. Maybe when you get out we can stop in to see Rissa and have a beer?" I suggested as I ran a hand through my hair. "She fancies Dave I think. They were all over each other last night… it was gross."

My father boomed with laughter, nearly dropping the phone into his lap. "That old fart has some skills to land himself a woman half his age. I'm not sure how he managed that."

"I hate to cut this short Dad but I am seriously on a time crunch. My breakfast is getting cold back in the room." I said quickly. "Knowing Mom she will want to visit you alone anyway."

"Sure thing," My father said cheerfully, "See you in a few days. Take care of Fallon and make sure you two have a chance to talk about this Haven thing. I had a long conversation with Jared yesterday and we are both more than a little worried about who might have shown up in that transport. Be careful."

"I will. I love you Dad, see you soon." I said before placing the phone back into the cradle and waving.

I watched him place his phone back in the cradle and wave as I stepped through the door and into the corridor. Once the door had closed I nearly ran down the corridor and through the first checkpoint, stopping only a moment to thank Jim and wish him a good day. By the time I made it back to Kurt I tossed my badge onto the counter as I breezed by his station, promising to swing in and collect my coffee cup on my way back in from the surface. If I wanted to pick that lavender I had to be quick about it.

The morning announcement chimes began as I ran through the door to the Processing and Intake Department. I had planned to be back from the surface before the six o'clock announcement had begun as I was sure it would wake Fallon if she wasn't awake already. The plan had been to give her just enough time after the last chime to ensure she could take a proper shower, then surprise her with the largest bunch of lavender I could pick. Finding the desks in the office empty I peeked down the short hallway and found no one in sight. I spun the sign out sheet across the counter, deciding to sign myself out of the facility as there was no one around to check me out.

As I quickly signed my name and nature of my visit onto the sheet I noticed I would be the only one on the surface this morning outside of the guards. This would be perfect. I slid the forms back to where they had been before making my way through the corridor and out into the loading bay. The large doors to the outside sat open, filling the space with crisp morning air. I smiled as I jogged through the loading bay toward the doors. For a moment I had wondered where everyone had gone, as not a single soldier stood post at the doors. *They must be patrolling the area to make sure Haven hadn't been followed*, I told myself as my feet hit the dirt on the other side of the large doors.

I knew exactly where to find the lavender and quickly shot off in the direction of the abandoned house I had seen it near. My heart raced nearly as quickly as the pumping of my feet as I ran across the grounds and up the small dirt trail. The house sat in ruins with broken and boarded windows and crumbling walls. I jumped the small fence that surrounded the yard and ran around to the back of the house where the lavender had been when last I saw it. Fallon and I had done a little adventuring when we had delivered the jugs to Chase. We had found all sorts of neat places around the grounds that we had promised to investigate the next time we came out of the facility. She hadn't noticed the wild lavender behind the house. Once I had seen it I insisted on taking her in a different direction in order to keep the secret.

I fell to my knees in the center of the large patch of wild lavender and began picking as much of it as possible, placing the flowers in a pile at my side. Remembering the string I kept in my survival pouch on my gun belt, I pulled a spool and used it to tie several bunches of flowers together. I had no idea what Fallon would use the lavender for, but it reminded me of her scent and made me smile. Her favorite wild flowers seemed a better fitting gift than anything I might find in the Marketplace. It had been my plan to bring her here for her birthday, before the rushed wedding had been put into place. When I felt I had gathered enough flower bundles to make a mighty impression, I filled my arms with them and smiled at my prize as I rounded the ruined home.

The smile instantly faded as I caught sight of soldiers scurrying in every direction at the bottom of the hill. "What the hell?" I said aloud to myself as I slowly stepped backward a few steps. A loud alarm began to blare across the grounds as soldiers and guards screamed orders to each other as they moved. The scene erupted into a storm of activity right before my eyes. I slowly moved another step back, my mind running down the list of possible places to hide or run to. Before I could move, my eyes caught sight of Jared in the distance as he darted out of the facility and ran for a jeep. He wore a flak jacket with full battle gear... in his hands an M16.

I stepped back again, intending to drop the armload of flowers and take shelter inside the ruins of the abandoned house. Instead I froze at the sound of a click coming from behind me. My heart stopped beating as I closed my eyes. *Fallon I am sorry*, I whispered in my mind as I slowly turned to face the gunman. I opened my eyes and swallowed hard. He wasn't a soldier of Haven or Sanctuary. "No." I whispered seconds before he pulled his trigger. I stepped backward, the flowers falling to the ground around me as I fought to stay standing. I hadn't felt it. There wasn't any pain. As I fell to my knees in the dirt a large stain began to form on my shirt. *Fallon I love you. I am sorry*, I screamed in my head as I fought to catch my breath only to fall face down into the dirt.

I watched the gunman begin to move toward me. I closed my eyes tightly as I fought to gain some control of my body. A second shot rang out and my eyes darted open in time to see my would-be killer fall into the dirt fifteen feet from me, a single shot to the head. Not far from my hand sat one of the bundles of wild lavender flowers, now dirty and covered in my blood. *I can't give her dirty flowers*, I thought as I fought to reach for them. The effort had been too much for me to muster as I laid there bleeding and limp. I closed my eyes as exhaustion washed through me, all the while knowing in my heart, I would never open them again.

I slowly opened my eyes seeing only darkness around me. I felt weak, completely drained of all energy as I rolled my head toward the ruins of what once had been a window. The stars shined brightly in the night sky as I blinked at them in confusion. As the fog in my mind began to lift slightly I began to feel the mattress beneath me as well as the blankets that had been pulled up to my neck. Pain shot through me as I tried to take a deep breath, halting my movements with a groan.

"No moving, stupid boy." A young female voice with a heavy Russian accent spoke in the darkness. "Flowers… you must be crazy."

"Where am I?" I asked as my throat began to burn with the words.

"No more than fifty feet from where you fell. You are lucky that bastard hadn't used the right bullets… you would be dead if he had any brains." The female voice spoke.

I turned my head in the direction I thought the voice had been coming from and saw the hint of a shadow in the corner. "Who… why?" I coughed before the pain in my throat made it hard to speak.

"You'll live, stupid boy." She spoke before lighting a match and holding it to her face. In the firelight I could just make out her dark eyes as they stared me down with anger. She lit a cigarette that hung from her teeth at the side of her mouth before setting the match to a lantern. The room slowly filled with light. "Stupid boy." She repeated from her crouched perch on top of a stack of wooden crates in the corner, shaking out the match flame as she spoke.

"What… time?" I tried to ask as I lifted a hand to my head, my eyes on her.

She flashed me a wicked smile. Her long black hair hung on either side of her head from overly tightened hair bands making her look far younger than I had originally thought. She couldn't have been much younger than me, but definitely more dangerous. I watched as she inhaled smoke and blew it out without moving, her eyes watching me with intensity. She wore a tight fitted version of

Darkness Falls

the uniform normally wore by the Haven Guard, though with some obvious differences meant to make her stand out among the other soldiers. *Haven elite*, I thought to myself as I recognized the patch that sat on her chest. She wasn't a common soldier of Haven, she was a trained assassin.

"I know many things." She spoke, the cigarette still between her teeth. She jumped down off of the crates using only her legs and slowly began to cross the room. "You are not Haven and you are not Sanctuary. It tells me you are Compound eh? The wayward child of Haven." She laughed as she reached the edge of the bed. "You are not Henley. Not a drop of Irish blood in you." She spoke in her mixed accent as she sat at the edge of the bed. "That must make you a Dunn. The ring you wear tells me you are married; though only recently as it hasn't had time to leave an indentation." She smiled as she lifted my hand off the bed to inspect it. "I've seen this band before during trading missions between the villages... through my scope of course, on Mr. Henley's hand. You must have married the daughter, no? The pretty thing you brought out here last time?"

I nodded slowly as I fought against the exhaustion, desperate to stay awake. "Time?"

She pulled the cigarette from her lips and frowned as she blew smoke out through her nose. "Not long after nightfall." She said as she spit a piece of tobacco onto the floor. "You lost much blood, stupid boy. Lucky you to have stumbled into my domain eh? I have universal blood... you are now Russian, at least some of you anyway." She laughed before sucking on the end of her cigarette and tossing it onto the floor, grinding it out with her boot. "My name is Regina. Sleep now. We talk in the morning."

"Take me in... the facility." I tried though the words escaped in barely a whisper.

"Sanctuary is locked down, though for how long I am unsure. Sleep now, stupid boy. Come morning we speak again." She said as she crossed the room and turned off the lamp, thrusting us back into the darkness.

When the morning rays moved through the window and warmed my face, I slowly blinked as I fought the fog of confusion. My head didn't hurt nearly as bad as it had when I had awakened the night before in the darkness. Come to think of it, even my throat felt better. I attempted to swallow though my mouth felt as dry as the desert back in Baker, Nevada. I slowly lifted onto my elbow and looked around the room I had been staying in. The room consisted of nothing more except for a bed, some crates and a chair. There wasn't much of a ceiling left as it had at one point caved in and had been cleaned up.

"You are awake I see." Regina said as she shuffled into the room through the open hole in the wall that used to be a door. "No moving, stupid boy."

"My name is Jacob. Jacob Dunn." I said as I sat up slowly, my head spinning slightly with the movement.

"I knew you were a Dunn." Regina smiled as she crossed the room and knelt in front of me on the floor. "If you bust those stitches I spent so much time on, I will kill you myself." She teased as she pulled back the covers to exam the bandages on my stomach. "Single shot straight through... nice and clean. Not a major organ nicked one, which is rare. No bleed through on bandages. You move slow then."

"I have to make it to the facility. My wife must be worried sick." I said as I tried to stand, only to fall back onto the bed in a wave of pain.

"I left message with guard." Regina smiled as she tossed a few items into a bag beside me. "I am sure by now he has called it in and your wife knows you are alive. Stupid guard nearly wet himself at sight of me. Sometimes they forget I am here, no?"

"I didn't even know you were here." I replied in shock as she tossed the bag onto the bed.

"I've been here on and off for two years. I move between here and Haven when my services are required. The guards know of me though only few have seen me. I am legend see... like Bigfoot monster. Some of the guards think I am a wild story. I like it that way." She laughed as she moved to the hole in the wall. "As soon as the lockdown is lifted, they will send a team for you."

"Aren't you coming in too?" I asked as I fought to put my boots on.

"No. The group that attacked yesterday shouldn't have gotten that close. There is a hole in the defenses and I intend to find it. I tracked the two who managed to escape while you were sleeping. I plan to follow them." Regina whispered as she stared out of the hole in the wall. "You will not have to be isolated or quarantined. I have been nowhere near the infected zones. My boots have been stuck here since blackout. The medical staff will want to know who patched you up... tell them nothing. The last thing I need is more stupid boys out here trying to find me."

"What about the council?" I asked as I slowly stood; only managing a half crouch.

"Council fine, others no... unless it is that cute boy with the scar. I watch him sometimes." Regina laughed as she walked over and picked up the bag off the bed. "I must go hunting. Be brave stupid boy."

I nodded before watching her slip off through the hole in the wall and disappear into the daylight. Waiting for a rescue team to be dispatched wouldn't be an option; I had to make my way back to Fallon as soon as possible. When I attempted the first step I nearly screamed in pain as I crumpled to the floor. Every move I made caused a shockwave of pain to rip through my body. I crawled instead as the pain hadn't been nearly as bad. There would no longer be a need for my ruined brown shirt so I made the decision to leave it behind.

As I made my way over the piles of rubble I realized I had been held up within the ruins of the house by the lavender patch. Regina must have been hiding inside when I had been shot. I briefly wondered if she had been watching me pick the flowers I had planned to give to Fallon. The gunman's body no longer rested in the dirt though the blood stain remained. I followed the drag marks in the dirt that had left a trail of blood between the abandoned house and where I had been shot.

There in the dirt in front of me sat a large blood stain surrounded by bundles of lavender flowers. I crawled to a few of the bundles just inches from the blood stain that didn't seem to have any blood on them. I gripped them tightly in my hands as I moved. *I came here for some damned flowers and I am not leaving here without them,* I thought to myself as I crawled on my hands and knees toward the trail. Tears fell from my eyes and landed into the dirt as I fought against the pain. Twice my body shook as if I had been blasted with a cold wind.

When I heard the sound of boots running across the dirt, I lifted my eyes to see a few of the guards running up the trail with a medical stretcher. I collapsed into the dirt as the pain became so unbearable I began to scream. Holding the flowers as tightly as I could I rolled onto my side and pressed them to my chest as I fought to breath. The aroma overwhelmed my senses with everything Fallon. *Hang in there Fallon my love*, I thought to myself, *I am coming home.*

CHAPTER TWENTY-FIVE

I slowly licked my dry lips in an attempt to wet them before opening my eyes. I found myself surrounded by machines that beeped in various tones with wires and tubes of all sizes and colors that seemed to be connected to me. I blinked as I scanned the room desperate to put the pieces together. The hospital. I was in the hospital in Sanctuary. I couldn't remember being brought in at all. The last thing I remembered involved the flowers I had been holding.

"Glad to see you are finally with us again, Jacob." Edward's deep voice spoke softly at my side. "This time of course, we won't need a whiteboard and marker to communicate like last time."

I hadn't realized he had been standing there until he had spoken to me. I rolled my head to face him, "Edward, where is Fallon?" I asked as I tried to remember if I had seen her when I was brought in.

"That woman is on a rampage, don't worry. As soon as she is done ordering people around, she will return to check on you." Edward smiled, "I have taken over all of your care for two reasons, one of them being that I have seen field trauma and seem to be the only one who had the talent to patch you up."

"And the other reason would be?" I asked as I tried to sit up.

Edward frowned as he leaned onto the edge of the bed, "I don't know who it was who saved you out there, but they did a fantastic job. I did have to open you back up due to infection and close up a few areas in your gut that had opened... but someone

339

knew what they were doing. I insisted on handling you once I got the bandage off and found a note tucked in the folds." He slipped me a piece of paper as he grabbed my hand and helped me up. "It is meant for you and sealed. I didn't open it but I wanted to make sure it made it to you without being intercepted."

I ran my thumb over the paper in my hand. Regina must have placed it there when she had saved my life. I watched as Edward nodded and walked around the edge of the bed and closed the curtains that ran down the glass wall, shielding me from the eyes of the reception desk. When he had finished he leaned against the edge of the door and waited as he watched out the small window in the center of the door. The note had been small, sealed into a square the size of a quarter with tape. The words Stupid Boy had been scrawled in tiny letters across it in black ink. I glanced at Edward who kept his eyes watching out the window.

Stupid Boy,
I did all I could with little I had. You are not like the others. Trust no one not from your village. You know where to find me when you are ready. For Stupid Boy who likes flowers, I work for free.

I quickly crumpled the note into a ball and shot a glance at Edward who promptly nodded and walked back to the edge of the bed. He reached into a cabinet and pulled out a small metal dish and a lighter. "We will put it in the safest place I know," he said with a smirk as he flicked the lighter.

"Sounds good to me." I smiled as I tossed the balled up note into the dish and watched as Edward lit the paper on fire. It burned quickly, smoldering into a tiny pile of ash as I watched. "Edward, how did you know... besides the name... that it was for my eyes only?" I asked as I watched him set the dish down on a small table.

"During the last big war, some of the wounded arrived with messages like those. Some were meant for the medical staff but most were meant to be read by the soldier if they had lived. The person who patched you up, I have seen work like that before, commonly seen within field surgeries." Edward said as he checked on a couple of the machines and scribbled on a clipboard. "Experienced hands handled you. I found evidence of a blood transfusion and IV fluids. That doesn't happen very often. You are lucky the person chose to save your life."

"I don't remember." I lied as I leaned back against the pile of pillows and rubbed my eyes. "How long have I been here?"

"I had to induce coma in order for you to heal up properly. With the massive amount of blood loss and internal injuries I didn't have much choice. I pumped you full of fluids for the dehydration and antibiotics for the infection caused by the field surgery, as well as fixed the nicks in your intestine. Bullet went clean through you so you have stitches front and back." Edward informed as he walked back to the edge of the bed and set the clipboard down. "You've been out for a week now."

"Fallon is going to kill me." I groaned as I smacked myself on the forehead. "I spent the entire honeymoon in a coma all because of some stupid flowers!"

"She didn't think they were stupid. You had some when you came in." Edward said with a smile, "After interrogating everyone from the Isolation Department, and the Intake and Processing Department, she went on a rampage and demanded the guards show her where they had found you. It didn't take her long to find the lavender patch."

"I meant it to be a surprise." I whispered as I felt the sting of tears begin to burn my eyes, "She saw where I fell?"

Edward grabbed my hand and squeezed it, "She insisted on seeing it. No one had the guts to stop her. You have no idea how furious she is. Between her husband being gunned down and her father going missing…"

"What? Jared is missing?" I yelled in shock as I sat bolt up in the bed. "I saw him leave the facility right before I was shot! He headed for the gates!"

"Calm down or you will hurt yourself." Edward shot back as he pushed me back onto the bed, "Yes, he is missing. We have teams trying to find him. You need to rest now. Don't worry about him, we will bring him back."

I nodded slowly and relaxed into the bed. Edward searched my eyes briefly before scribbling onto his clipboard and walking toward the door. He stopped and turned, signally for me to get some rest by placing his hands together under his tilted head. I laughed and waved him off as I shook my head at him. Though I had apparently rested for a week, I didn't feel the need to relax any more. Pretending to follow his orders, I closed my eyes and rolled my head to the side as the lights in the room went out.

Why would Regina tuck a note into my bandages? I thought to myself. Though she had told me I could inform the Compound Council of her, I was beginning to think I would keep her secret to myself for a while. Her note had said to trust no one that wasn't from our village. I folded my arms over my chest as I thought about what that statement could have meant. Running over the list of people I knew, I wondered if she meant for me not to trust Edward as well. He was a member of Compound but hadn't been for long, he had come from Haven. He did pass me the message privately to ensure I had gotten it, and from the look of the tape he hadn't read it.

What had baffled me the most was that Jared had not returned. I had seen him that day jump into a military jeep and take off in the direction of the gates. My mind raced over the many possibilities that could have kept him from returning to Sanctuary. Had he been killed out there somewhere? Kidnapped? I rubbed my eyes in the darkness of the room as I tried to put the pieces together. Nothing explained why he hadn't come back. Jared would have done anything he could to have returned, even if he had been shot.

I calculated that those who had arrived from Haven were still being held, but that my father was now out of isolation and probably working. He would likely be by at some point in the day to see how I was feeling and I couldn't wait to see him. My mother would likely be by to see me as well. Maybe even Travis and Matt would come for a visit if they could get out of their duties for the day, if I was lucky.

I smiled to myself as I thought about what Edward had said about Fallon and her rampaging. She must have been worried sick about me and went mad with anger once she found out I had been injured and likely left overnight to die. Briefly, I wondered if she had plans to overhaul the procedures of the security forces. Once Fallon set her mind to something, no one was able to stop her. It was one of the qualities that made her a strong member of the Compound Council. In many ways, she had taken after her parents when it came to her drive and determination. *Must be the Irish in her,* I thought as I rolled gently onto my side, *must be the Irish.*

As I had been about to fall asleep, muffled sounds erupted from the reception area on the other side of the glass wall. With the curtains closed, there was no way for me to tell what had caused

Darkness Falls

the uproar. Though I could not tell who the voices belonged to or what was being said, one voice stood out as that of authority by the firm and demanding tone being used. The doorknob turned slowly as I watched with a smile. There could be only one person I could think of that would command a room like a leader when needed.

The door slowly and quietly slid open, Fallon's eyes on the floor as she snuck into my room and closed the door. She wore the black high heels and stockings she normally wore to work that made her long legs look alluring. Her tight fitting green skirt hugged her hips as she moved to set something on the floor by a chair near the door. As she bent over I closed my eyes, not wanting her to catch my eyes running up her body. When she stood and crossed the room, I heard the soft tapping of her heels across the floor.

She grabbed my hand gently, giving it firm squeezes before she sat in a chair pulled up to the bed. "Baby," She whispered, "Are you awake yet? Come on love, you need to wake up for me."

I slowly opened my eyes as a smile stretched across my lips. Her green eyes flashed in surprise then in relief as she sank into the edge of the bed. I laughed gently as I gave her hand a squeeze. "I am awake; I have been for a while now. Edward had been here when I woke up." I whispered before kissing the back of her hand. "I'm not in the mood to sleep anymore. I think I have done enough sleeping."

"Someone is going to pay for what happened to you." Fallon whispered firmly. "As soon as I figure out who is responsible for locking down the facility and leaving you out there all night, they are going to be punished. They should never have locked us down knowing you were out there like that. It was the longest night of my life! I thought you were dead!"

"I am alright. I just had a bad day was all. Never would have thought I would be shot while picking flowers." I giggled as I leaned back against the pillows.

"I saw them you know, the flowers." Fallon smiled. "You came in with some and refused to let anyone take them from you. I insisted the guards take me to where they had found you and followed the trail of flowers. The patch is beautiful, Jacob."

"It was a surprise. I wanted to bring them back to the room for you." I smiled sadly as I rolled my head back to look at the ceiling. "That flower patch reminds me of you. I left the suite and went to see my dad, and then went to the surface to pick as much as I could. I shouldn't have gone alone."

"It is fine," Fallon whispered, "It wasn't your fault. You are lucky to be alive and I am thankful that you are. My father is still missing but I have teams out trying to find him. Chase came back last night; Dave and Rissa have been talking with him about what has been going on. Once you were out of surgery I spoke with the guards in charge of the Honeymoon Suite and demanded another week, they gave us two more weeks."

"Two more weeks?" I asked in shock.

Fallon smiled, "You can't very well properly enjoy your honeymoon when you are laid up in bed recovering from a bullet to the gut can you? They gave us two more weeks so that you could recover. I have already spoken to your parents and they insisted on keeping Bentley longer. I don't think your mom likes working in the clinic anyway, so watching him after daycare hours helps her cope."

I closed my eyes and smirked, "An extended honeymoon and bed rest. Whatever shall I do with all that time?"

"Pervert," Fallon whispered with a laugh, "I'll take care of you but not like that."

I wasn't nearly as exhausted two days later when I had finally been given the official release orders from the hospital. In the rare moments I had been left alone; I put much thought into what Regina had written in her note. I had become suspicious of everyone I had come in contact with that wasn't a member of Compound. My instincts had been prickling the hairs on the back of my neck since the moment we had arrived at Sanctuary. The longer we stayed in the facility, the more unease I felt about it.

Fallon's constant attempts to care for me had already become a problem as I had little time to be alone. The last thing I wanted to do was scare her, but I had the need to speak with Regina. Though I had wanted to keep her a secret in the event I would need her, I couldn't find a way to sneak off to the surface to contact Regina without Fallon being alerted. On two different attempts I had managed to make it out of the Honeymoon Suite and to the first level, only to be told to return to the suite to finish my recovery. If I had any hope of talking with Regina, I would have to tell Fallon.

A soft knock on the door pulled me from my thoughts as I sat in the overly large bed pretending to read a book that Fallon had checked out for me. Fallon rose slowly from her stack of papers and sauntered to the door. Now that I had been confined to the Honeymoon Suite to recover, Fallon had brought her work with her in order to stay at my side. She had even insisted on staying within the room while I showered, though she sat at the table with her back to me to give me privacy.

"You'll never guess who that was!" Fallon smiled brightly as she crossed the room pushing a fully loaded food cart. "The wonderful woman from the Glazier Grill delivered a special lunch for you today. It looks to me like your first solid food is an extra special treat."

I positioned myself as I watched Fallon begin to pull the dome lids off of the plates. The moment I saw the first lid lift, my skin began to prickle and my muscles froze tight. I held my breath as my eyes scanned the food cart in horror. The first reveal had been a plate piled high with scrambled eggs smelling heavily of garlic, mushrooms, and onions. I swallowed hard as I watched her pull another dome to reveal French toast with strawberries. *This is the meal I said I had wanted as my first solid food*, I thought to myself as a slow burn crept up my throat. It hadn't been a conversation I had had with Fallon or the Glazier Grill... it had come up in a private conversation with Travis the day before, in this very room. My scalp began to tingle as I watched Fallon's hand move across the cart. *If this next plate has bacon, sausage, and a small tub of maple syrup*, I thought to myself, *I will just die!*

"Oh look sweetie!" Fallon smiled brightly, "Bacon and sausage... your favorite."

"Who ordered this meal for me?" I asked slowly as I tried not to shake visibly. "Does the paper say?"

Fallon frowned slightly before nodding and looking for the order slip. Her face brightened as she read, "It says here that Officer Bowman ordered it." Her expression twisted only briefly before she waved the slip and tossed it onto the cart. "How sweet is he? That was nice of him."

My stomach turned over slowly as I fought to quell the rising fear in me. *How did Bowman know what I had wanted for my first real meal*, I asked myself as I glanced up at Fallon, *if Travis hadn't told him?* Travis had been quick to explain that the meal would be too difficult to digest right away and refused to inform anyone of my wishes. Travis wouldn't have said a word to anyone let alone to Bowman. I swallowed as I reached for the fork Fallon held out to me with a smile on her soft lips.

Fallon placed a plate onto my lap and walked back toward the table as I stuffed a forkful of eggs into my mouth. I chewed slowly as I pondered what the breakfast order could have meant. If Travis hadn't told anyone, it meant that someone was either watching or listening to our conversation. Since the conversation had taken place the day before while he sat on the bed with me, no one else would have known about it. Briefly I wondered if the room had been wired and I closed my eyes as though I was completely enjoying my eggs. *Was it video cameras hidden somewhere? Was the room bugged for sound?* I asked myself as I opened my eyes again and watched Fallon at the table. *I need to know for sure.*

For fear my discovery and reaction would be recorded, I pretended not to notice and continued to eat in silence. I needed to convince Fallon to take me to the surface without informing her of Regina while inside Sanctuary walls. The last thing I needed was someone finding out about my secret savior. According to Edward, the guards had assumed I had patched myself up before they had found me. Only Edward had known that someone on the surface had patched me up. As far as I knew, Edward planned to keep that information to himself. Regina would remain my secret.

"Fallon, do you think it is possible for us to go to the surface today? I need some fresh air and a walk might do me some good." I asked before stuffing another bite of eggs into my mouth.

Fallon lifted her head slowly as though deep in thought and stared off toward the fireplace in silence. Absently, she chewed the end of her pen before speaking. "I think we can do that. I want you in a flak jacket though and since I know you will refuse the wheeled chair, you will take a cane at least... just in case you need the stability."

I smiled to myself as the realization hit me that she hadn't put up much of a fight on the matter. Fallon couldn't have known about my growing fears over the meal, but she must have noticed my reaction. *Did she suspect too?* I asked myself as I set the empty plate back onto the food cart. Since the day I had woken up in the hospital, Fallon hadn't said a single sarcastic word. She hadn't even fought sleeping next to me in the bed. In fact, it had been as though she had been playing the role of the perfect wife taking care of her injured husband. The thought hit me in that moment that she had been calling me by pet names and stroking my hair in public. Twice in recent memory she told me she loved me in front of other people. All of which was out of character for her. Fallon must have suspected something wasn't right with Sanctuary.

It had seemed to me as though the arrival of Haven had placed fear into the hearts of the facility's residents. People had begun to tighten up regulations and pay more attention to perfection. Fallon had been working overtime trying to keep up with the amount of requests as departments fought to make sure everything would be in top shape. With my forced recovery, I had all the time I needed to watch the events play out before me.

I swung my feet onto the floor and stood slowly before testing a step and then another. Though I had been healing up nicely, I sometimes found walking to be painful in my abdomen. Small and steady steps seemed to work best for me as it made walking a pain free experience. Bending over however, seemed to be the most painful experience of all. Crossing the room, I briefly gave Fallon a shy smile as the look of discontent and irritation at my efforts couldn't be hidden from her eyes.

"Are you sure you want to go adventuring today?" Fallon asked as she crossed her arms over her chest. "Your parents wanted to spend some time with you again today. You haven't even finished your meal."

I pulled my shirt off the hanger in the closet and huffed. "It isn't like I will spend all day on the surface; I just want to go back out there." I said as I pulled my black tee shirt over my head. "It is like being thrown from a horse, you know? I was tossed and injured so my next step is to get back out there."

Fallon's gaze followed me as I moved to sit in the chair across the table from her. A sly smile slowly crossed her lips before she rolled her eyes at me and tossed her pen onto the table with a giggle. "You are headstrong." She declared as she moved from her chair to help tie my boots.

"Well you are dense, so we are even." I played as I watched her tie the first boot.

"Not as dense as you think, Mr. Dunn." Fallon whispered as she tightened the boot laces and looked up at me from the floor. I could tell from the way her green eyes searched mine that she was worrying about something and didn't want to talk about it. "Boots are done." She said more loudly as she stood. "You can go without the cane after all if you feel you can handle it. You are too stubborn to listen to me anyway. Let me change and we can go get back on that horse."

I watched Fallon smirk before turning on her heels and heading for the closet. I chewed my lip slowly as I thought about how I would manage to find Regina. Her note had said I would know how to find her, though I had no clue how I would pull it off. The ruins of the old house by the lavender patch had been the last location I had seen her. For security reasons I assumed she wouldn't return to that location again. I could easily explain why I wanted to go in that direction if I used the excuse that I wanted to see where I had been shot. Returning to that area would put me close enough to get a good look at the ruins to see if she had returned.

The facility had been placed on high alert during that small invasion and I was sure the surface forces had been combing the area trying to figure out how a group of hostiles managed to get through the fences and into the innermost grounds without being detected. Regina would have been on the move in order to keep her presence a secret. It was true some of the forces had seen her slinking in the shadows and told tall tales of her existence, though the stories were usually ignored and thought to be fueled by the effects of cabin fever.

I stood and checked my firearm before returning it to the holster and strapping my gun belt to my hip. *How am I going to find her if she is constantly moving?* I asked myself in confusion. Then it hit me, I wouldn't be looking for her… she would find me! I needed to wonder into an area that would be safe enough to allow her to show herself. She would likely be watching our every move from various locations as she moved. Regina was a hunter after all, as well as a trained assassin.

As I turned, I found Fallon dressed in a pair of blue jeans and sneakers standing by the door, tapping her foot at me with a smirk on her lips. I moved as quickly as the pain would allow as she opened the door into the corridor. Briefly, I wondered how we would make it to the surface without someone turning us around again. With Fallon with me however, she would likely give the Processing and Intake Department no other choice except to allow us through.

"Miss Olivia, please see to it that the food cart is removed from our room before we return. Oh, please give our thanks to the kitchen staff... the meal was delicious but Mr. Dunn couldn't finish it all." Fallon smiled brightly at the heavyset cleaning woman as we passed her on the staircase. "We will be gone for an hour or so."

The woman nodded and hurried off up the stairs toward the room. My mind spun as I thought about the room being bugged with listening devices and whether the cleaning staff had placed them or knew of their existence. I quickly laced my fingers with Fallon's as we made our way to the elevator. *Why would someone want to spy on us?* I asked myself. Of all rooms to bug, why would anyone bug the Honeymoon Suite? In my opinion, listening to newlyweds enjoying some private time is a complete invasion of privacy.

I watched the elevator doors open and stepped inside; my eyes quickly scanned the walls for the slightest hint of something out of place and saw nothing. The uneasy feeling Sanctuary had given me when we first arrived hadn't gone away. In fact, the longer we stayed here the more uneasy I became. Now with Regina's words repeating in my head and the thought someone within the facility had been eavesdropping on us, I felt vulnerable.

We walked slowly down the corridor after the elevator opened onto the First Level, making our way toward the loading bay. My eyes stayed glued to the tops of my boots as we moved. I thought back to our lives at Compound, of the stories we had been told of Haven and Sanctuary, and of the times we spent on trading missions with Haven. Nothing I could remember from those days had ever hinted at what we currently faced. Miranda and Jared hadn't told us anything that would have warned us of trouble.

"We are heading out today. Mr. Dunn is feeling strong enough to view the location of his incident. We also plan to see Chase and maybe wonder around for a while to check security." Fallon stated to the guard as we neared the door to the loading bay. "Sign us out would you? We are in a hurry to see Chase."

The guard nodded quickly and opened the door before saluting Fallon. "Yes Ma'am."

I could tell by the exchange that at some point while I was in the hospital, the poor young guard had been the target of Fallon's rage. The guard stiffened as we walked passed him and out into the bay, his eyes trained onto the tiles on the floor. I smirked to myself as I heard the guard exhale behind us as we made our way toward the large doors that opened onto the surface. *Sorry sap must have wet his uniform when Fallon let him have it*, I thought with a giggle.

The moment my boots hit the dirt I stopped and closed my eyes, inhaling the smell that surrounded me. The light breeze whispered into my hair and across my cheeks as I stood with my face turned toward the sky. Fallon tightened her grip on my hand forcing my eyes open with curiosity. I glanced at her to see she had been doing the same as me, her face turned toward the sky. A slow smile began at the corner of her mouth as she lowered her head and turned to face me before opening her eyes. We were too close to the large doors for me to tell her the real reason I wanted to come to the surface. I would need to move quickly.

I walked slowly toward the trail, pulling Fallon by the hand as I went. I didn't want the guards to see me walking with a purpose and decide to keep their eyes on us. I gave a brief nod to the closer of the two guards that stood outside the doors as I wrapped my arm around Fallon's waist. He smiled with a nod of his own before returning his gaze to the pages of the book he had been reading. As we neared the trail I glanced back to make sure the guard hadn't been watching us. Satisfied with the sight of the guard nose deep in the text, I quickened my pace.

"Here is where the guards said they found you after you fell into the dirt. They said you were crawling?" Fallon asked as she pointed to the ground in front of us. "I followed crawl marks and found the area you had been shot in. It hadn't taken me long to find it."

I continued on without stopping for a look at where I had been found. "I crawled... from up here." I whispered as my eyes found the darkened stain in the dirt surrounded by dead lavender flowers. My eyes followed the blood trail and drag marks that led into the ruins of the house where I had met Regina. "I need you to follow me to the lavender patch." I spoke loudly as I stepped over the fallen fence. I wasn't speaking to Fallon, but she wouldn't have known that.

"Anything you want, Jacob. You just lead the way." Fallon said as she glanced behind us down the trail.

Stopping only briefly to allow Fallon to catch up to me, I glanced at the hole in the ruins where I had crawled through the debris. At one time there had been a door where the hole now existed. Fallon stopped at my side and watched me intently as the look of confusion crawled across her face. Her eyes darted between mine and the ruins as I continued to look for any sign of Regina's return.

I moved around the house to the lavender patch and stopped short. Fallon nearly ran into my back as her concern had been on the ruins. The patch looked exactly as it had the day I had been shot, except... something was different. My eyes panned the area desperate to figure out what had changed. "The lavender patch is where I had been. I was picking flowers." I stated loudly, hoping Regina would hear me.

"Yes, you were picking flowers." Fallon mumbled in confusion as her eyes began to trail the tree line around the ruins of the house. "Are you trying to remember what you have forgotten?"

I pursed my lips in frustration and shook my head. Then I saw it, the smashed down area in the flower patch where I had been sitting when I had picked the flowers. I had gone out in the same way I had come in, leaving only one trail to the center of the patch. As my eyes searched the area I noticed there was a second disturbed trail leading in from the tree line to the area I had been picking in. The trail had been subtle enough it had taken my eyes some time to find it; then again I had been looking for a sign from Regina when no one else would have been.

"The center of the flower patch...," I whispered as I walked down the same smashed trail I had left behind that day. "...It has to be!"

"What has to be?" Fallon asked quickly as she followed me. "What are you talking about?"

I fell to my knees being sure they sank into the original impressions left when I had picked the flowers, and placed my hands onto the ground beside them. Regina obviously had only one way to speak with me and that was by leaving clues only I would know how to find. My eyes quickly scanned the ground in front of me as my heart thudded in my chest. A small brown scrap of cloth the size of a quart lay no more than three feet from where I had been kneeling. Immediately I knew it to be a piece of the shirt I had been wearing when I had been shot. The shirt had been left on the floor of the ruined house when I had left. *So she had returned*, I thought to myself as I slowly crawled to the scrap and picked it up. As I turned it over in my hand I noticed an ink mark resembling an arrow and lifted my eyes to see it had been pointing in the direction of the second trail leading to the tree line.

"Jacob, what the hell are you doing?" Fallon asked with annoyance as she crossed her arms and rolled her eyes. "Please tell me you aren't losing your mind."

I stood, my eyes following the trail to the tree line. "I am not losing my mind. I am looking for something I lost when I came out here."

"Oh," Fallon brightened, "Did you lose it in the flowers? I could help you look if you like?"

"It isn't in the flowers...," I whispered as I walked in the direction the arrow had pointed. "...it is this way."

Regina had chosen to use the shirt in order to guide me to where I would meet her. *That must have been what she meant on the note when she said I would know where to find her,* I though as I stopped at the tree line and searched for a second scrap of my brown shirt. She wouldn't leave the scrap of cloth in an obvious location out of fear someone would notice it and follow her clues. I scanned the ground in front of me carefully before my eyes moved slowly up the trunk of the nearest tree. There tucked into the bark of the branch above me, was another scrap of cloth with an arrow on the back.

"Fallon listen...," I whispered as I stuffed the fabric into my pocket. "...there is someone I want you to meet, the one who helped save my life that day. We are following clues to the meeting location so keep your eyes open for small scraps of my brown tee shirt. She is using them to guide us to a safer location. I'll explain everything later."

Fallon's mouth fell open in shock. Though she remained silent, I suspected she had plenty to say as the look on her face changed slowly from shock to betrayal and then to anger. She nodded quickly before glancing in the direction I had been looking. "Where to?" She asked as her eyes again found mine.

"This way." I said as I pushed through the tree line, Fallon close behind me.

My eyes found a small trail and instinctively, I followed it. Twice we had to duck under limbs which caused a shooting pain in my abdomen and I recoiled, inhaling sharply. We moved swiftly and quietly as the trail twisted over rocks and down steep grades. I stopped when the trail disappeared momentarily and searched for

Darkness Falls

another scrap of my brown tee shirt. Fallon managed to find a small chunk of the cloth tied to a bush, the arrow indicating we would have to turn left and continue down the hill. Twenty minutes later we found an old chain linked fence nearly destroyed and claimed by nature. I climbed over the broken section with the help of Fallon and soon heard the sound of rushing water.

"Do you hear that?" Fallon asked as she fought to catch her breath. "There is water somewhere!"

"We have to be far enough away now." I said as I helped Fallon climb over the fence and down the hill. "We must be meeting at the river. We have to keep going. Quick!"

As we stumbled farther down the hill the sound of the river grew louder. I could just make out the sight of the river as we climbed down a pile of rocks and around a line of trees. Fallon jumped through the last of the trees ahead of me, passing me with speed and nearly fell three feet when the path dropped off onto a sandy flat at the river's edge. I climbed down the drop as carefully as I could and stood near Fallon, my eyes searching the river.

"There...," I said as I pointed up the river to a pool at the bottom of a small waterfall. "That is where she wants us to go."

I quickly grabbed Fallon's hand and pulled her behind me as I crossed over rocks and up onto the ledge of the pool. I expected to see Regina sitting at the water's edge with a rifle trained on us and a smirk across her face. Instead, I found the uniform she had been wearing when I met her laying across a large rock. It was wet and dripping into a small puddle next to her boots.

"Laundry day?" I asked loudly with a laugh as I turned slowly, my eyes searching for Regina.

Fallon inhaled sharply, "That is an Elite uniform!" She hissed in nearly a whisper. "Your contact is an assassin!"

I spun to face Fallon. "She can get us out of here, I know she can. She also has information we need. Do not underestimate her and do not piss her off." I warned.

When I turned back to the rocks I spotted Regina standing naked and covered from head to toe in a thick layer of mud, her rifle pointed to the sky with the stock resting on her kicked out hip. She stood without modesty with a look of confusion that quickly turned to playful annoyance, her lips curled into a smirk as she spoke. "Stupid Boy...," She laughed, "...so you come at last."

"Sanctuary... is it bugged?" I asked without hesitation.

"Good to see you again too, my friend." Regina toyed as she jumped off the rock and landed in front of me. "Yes, the facility is bugged. Just noticed, no? It means they have turned them on now. The people of your village are in danger here."

"I knew it!" Fallon nearly yelled as she stood next to me. "I knew it was bugged! Who came in on the Haven transport? Do they have anything to do with it?"

Regina curled her lips in irritation, "You brought wife." She snarled before turning to sit on the rock her uniform had been drying on. After briefly digging between some rocks, she pulled a cigarette and placed it between her teeth. "The transport did not bring right people here." She spoke before lighting the cigarette and inhaling. "They are out of quarantine later today, no?" Regina spoke through heavy grey smoke. "Haven as it had been, no longer exists. What you have in transport group is war. You will not be able to escape it... at least not right now."

"What do you mean they aren't the right people? Are they council members?" I asked as I stepped closer to Regina. "Are there any more transport trucks coming?"

"No transports left to come." Regina smiled sadly as she exhaled smoke. "Haven was lost from inside out."

"Inside... out?" Fallon whispered before chewing on her lip and crossing her arms over her chest. "Do you mean there was a revolt of some kind?"

"Greed brought death to Haven. Brother turned on brother." Regina informed as she stood and closed the distance between us. "Those left want control of the facility. They did not expect you to be here but it will only slow them down. They will take your village too. Trust no one not of your village." She smiled before continuing, "Welcome to war."

I slowly sank against a rock and crossed my arms over my chest. Between the raid on Haven and an internal collapse, there wasn't much hope of survivors left behind. If Regina was right about the group that arrived, we were in big trouble. Leaving the facility now would be disastrous as we would surely be followed. The threat from the virus still reigned as well as the radiation. Compound would surely die if we packed up and left now. There wasn't a choice – we would have to stay and fight.

"Play game and wait." Regina said as she inhaled from her cigarette. "Do not speak of leaving even when in your private quarters. Tell no one of plan. Too close to winter and too dangerous at time. You can wait seven months or so, no?"

"Regina... I need your help." I said as I stood again and faced her. "I need to save my people. I trust you, I know this. You can help us find a way out of this place as soon as the coast is clear. Will you help me?"

"When the snow melts, you will leave this place. Until then you fight. I have information to help you keep things in your favor." Regina winked with a grin. "I said before... for stupid boy who likes flowers, I work for free."

ABOUT THE AUTHOR

D M Hersey is a thirty-three year old artist and fiction writer from northern California. Together with her husband, she raises four children on a small homestead in the Sierra Nevada mountains.

Darkness Falls

PREVIEW OF
FEARS OF THE LOST
BOOK 2

"I don't care what excuse you plan to use Mr. Grant. My only concern is the safety of these pumps and the residents. Seeing as you failed last week's required inspection, I want these repaired immediately!" I steamed as I stared down the heavyset man with the shocked look on his face. "It is your job to make sure this facility can handle the community. All I have heard all morning are complaints about water backing up into sinks and tubs. If you cannot handle the responsibility, then maybe you need moved to another department!"

"No ma'am, please?" Mr. Grant begged as he wiped the sweat from his forehead with a greasy handkerchief. "I'll get the system back up Mrs. Dunn... I swear!"

"See to it then!" I blared before spinning on my heels and stomping back toward the elevator.

As the elevator doors closed me in and began to move, I exhaled with a loud groan. I couldn't recall ever having a friendly encounter with Mr. Grant. It wasn't as though the damaged pumps fell completely on his shoulders; the responsibility was that of the entire department, Mr. Grant just so happened to be my whipping boy. Turning the elderly man into an example put enough fear into the other workers to get the job done. Though it normally made me feel like the devil for doing it, the strategy worked more often than not.

I closed my eyes and leaned back against the back wall of the elevator as I thought about the rest of my day. I could blow off the last three meetings with the excuse I had an urgent matter to attend to on the surface. It would be the only way I could escape to meet with Regina now that I was running behind schedule. Our secret meetings were fewer and farther apart than they had been in the beginning – seven months ago when I had met her.

That day, I had no idea what to expect when my husband Jacob led me through a lavender patch and into the woods to meet his secret contact. It was during that meeting that I learned the insight I needed in order to deal with Haven. Since that first meeting, I made it a habit to keep her informed and she took to feeding me the information I would need to use against them, should they continue to fight for control of Sanctuary.

The elevator stopped at the level of the facility that housed the families who lived within Sanctuary. I smiled briefly before stepping aside to allow four armed guards to enter with several bags of gear. The four guards made up the team I had created to handle outside trading missions with the surviving locals outside of the Sanctuary Boundary. Today they would be heading out for a full one week shift.

"Good morning, Madam President." The taller of the guards greeted with a smile as he pushed his bag of gear against the back wall of the elevator. "It is a beautiful day for a mission, if I do say so myself."

I wrinkled my nose in irritation before forcing a smile. "Yes it is. Radiation levels are low today and from what I understand, the vaccine for the virus is working nearly half the time." I replied softly as I looked from the smiling guard to the other members of his team. "Just be sure to return on time or you won't make it out of quarantine in time for the Christmas festival."

"Yes, ma'am." The guard smiled before turning to his team with whispers of excitement.

When the elevator stopped at my floor I waved goodbye to the team and made my way toward my office. My first order of business would be to change into my ski pants and winter coat before hitting my minibar where I would stock the pockets with small bottles of liquor. I couldn't very well go to a secret meeting without a gift to share. It had been customary in the last few months to bring Regina alcohol in exchange for her services.

"Madam President, how did it go with the pumps?" My assistant Rebecca asked with a smile.

"Mr. Grant will have them repaired by the end of the day." I winked as I replied. "Poor guy must think I hate him after everything I have put him through."

Rebecca cocked her head to the side and raised an eyebrow, "It isn't every day the Sanctuary President comes down to yell at you. He should think it an honor you spend so much time with his department."

"Seriously Rebecca!" I laughed as I rolled my eyes. "Oh before I forget, I need the rest of the day cleared. I have an emergency on the surface I need to see to. Can you cancel my meetings?"

Rebecca frowned, "I have already canceled your meetings for the rest of the day. Councilman Reinhart stormed into your office half an hour ago and refuses to leave until he speaks with you. I called your husband and he is in there with him now."

I had been about to mutter a curse under my breath when the muffled sounds of an argument filtered through my office door and into the reception area. Jacob's voice boomed loudly from beyond the door as I shrugged at Rebecca and flung the door open. The last thing I needed was yet another encounter with Reinhart and his Haven Rebels.

"May I remind you Mr. Reinhart, that until you can magically produce Fallon's grandmother Ginny, my wife is the only surviving descendant of the Haven High Council?" Jacob boomed in a rage as he stood with his fists clenched at his sides. The muscles of his arms twitched wildly under his white dress shirt as he stood no more than three feet from the source of his rage. "When you arrived here without a signal member of the Haven High Council, there was a vote in which the residents of this facility agreed to place her in charge until a member of that council arrives! It has been seven months Mr. Reinhart... my wife will continue to lead this facility."

"Your wife is nothing more than a damned product of Compound, same as you! The residents of Sanctuary had no right to place any of you in charge. This facility is Haven owned and operated! I will no longer stand for your bullshit leadership!" Councilman Reinhart thundered back, his eyes filled with furry.

I couldn't blame Reinhart for his anger, after all he was right. The residents of Sanctuary hadn't had the right to hand over full leadership of the facility to me. They had only done so after the Haven members had been released from quarantine and informed everyone that the entire Haven High Council had been murdered, lost, infected with the virus, or died on the journey to the facility.

There had been rumors of another transport arriving that was said to have at least one member of the High Council, but it never arrived. The members of the Sanctuary Council remained the only leadership people could rely on.

"You watch your mouth, Reinhart." Jacob said firmly as he noticed my presence by the door.

The large man turned, his dark eyes finding mine as he stood firm. He was a massive man standing nearly six and a half feet tall with the chest width resembling that of a brick wall. His brown hair had been slicked back and cut tight to his head. I stiffened my stance as I watched his dry lips twist into a knowing sneer. "Speak of the traitor and the bitch arrives."

"Reinhart," I stated matter-of-factly as I set my briefcase down beside the coatrack. "If you ever speak about me like that again I will have your Commanding Officer demote you to scrubbing toilets."

"You scammed your way into your power and I intend to prove it." Reinhart boomed as he crossed the room toward me, stopping short. "I'm the one who should have control over this facility."

"Scammed my way in?" I nearly shrieked as I took a step. "I didn't kill my grandmother and I obviously didn't kill my own parents! You have clearly forgotten that the only reason I am in charge here is because you yourself told us the High Council is dead." I crossed my arms over my chest defiantly, "You put me in power Reinhart... it would be in your best interest to remember that."

"I refuse to answer to the likes of you." Reinhart whispered angrily as he stood inches from me, his face leaning down into mine. "You have the right to manage your own people; I will continue to manage mine. Keep your filthy Compound hands off my men. You would be wise to remember a woman's place. Haven will take this facility back as it doesn't belong to you or your traitorous family. When Haven does... you will hang, mark my words."

"Get out of my face, Reinhart." I whispered with a grin as I lifted on my toes to get closer to him, our lips nearly touching. "You and your Loyalists are one vote away from exile. Keep this fight going... and I will have no problem giving the order."

Made in the USA
Charleston, SC
16 December 2013